Stargazing with You

Jacquelynn Harbell

Cover art by Mary Ann Smith

Ebook ISBN 979-8-9916869-0-7

Paperback #1 ISBN 979-8-9916869-2-1

Paperback #2 ISBN 979-8-9916869-3-8

 Formatted with Vellum

To my husband and best friend, because supporting someone through medical school and residency is no joke, and you make it look easy.

Prologue

The entire auditorium was captivated by him, hanging onto his every word.

I couldn't blame them.

With the spotlight illuminating him on the dark stage, he emanated quiet confidence and charisma, from his dark hair down to his brown leather shoes. While every face in the many rows of seats was fixated on him, I looked around and watched their expressions, awed by the effect he had on them. My medical school classmates, seated on either side of me, leaned in to hear him speak, notebooks and pens or iPads on idle sitting abandoned in their laps. Every one of them, especially my female counterparts, had a small smile tugging at the corner of their lips, as if they couldn't help themselves from smiling in the presence of someone who seemed to radiate with sunshine, created entirely from within.

The speaker's voice grew soft, and a little coy smile played on his lips like he had a secret he was considering sharing with each of us.

"Looking at all of you today, I feel *so* incredibly lucky. I couldn't quite believe it when the committee asked me to speak," he said, gesturing with his arms open to the audience. "Seven years ago, when I first came up with the idea for the Artemis, when I was just a college kid with a lot of big dreams, I never could have imagined this day."

He took a deep breath, surveying the crowd from one edge of filled seats to the next, drinking in the sight.

"Of course, I couldn't have gone from that kid full of dreams to the man I am today alone. Not even a little bit. I have the most supportive family, who not only inspired the Artemis, but encouraged me every step of the way. I had the most amazing mentors who helped me turn my dream into a real, physical, tangible thing, that's out in the world helping people today. And I..."

He paused, looking down, considering. After just a moment of hesitation, he scanned the crowd again, this time with purpose. Looking for something. Looking for some*one*. Until his eyes locked onto mine and stayed there, unwavering. I could feel my classmates shuffling with interest beside me, turning to look at me, turning to see who had suddenly caught his undivided attention among the sea of faces.

"And I have someone very special in my life, who has always believed in me. From that very first moment. My muse. My greatest friend. Whose presence in my life has molded me into the man I am today. Who I would be completely lost without."

I swallowed hard against a lump in my throat that had appeared suddenly with a rush of overwhelming emotion. I gripped the armrests of my seat until my knuckles turned white. And in the silence that followed his declaration, every face who wasn't already looking turned to stare at me, to follow his gaze. To see the "muse" that had inspired Javier Valenzuela, brilliant inventor and savior of countless lives.

Chapter 1

Columbia University

First Year

The moment I met Javi Valenzuela, I was naked, and I was crying.

An hour before, I lay in my twin bed in my one-hundred square foot dorm room on the seventh floor of John Jay, listening to my neighbor Omar loudly have sex through the thin wall separating our rooms. Omar was an international student—Turkish, I think. He was very attractive and incredibly wealthy but forced to live in the squalor of a tiny single dorm room, as all first years were.

We had only been at Columbia University for just under a month, and he had already paraded an impressive number of glamorous women through our dingy halls. I couldn't imagine that these women were very impressed with our shared living space, but Omar's dad owned half of Gucci, or something like that. I imagined that was enough to make any woman overlook peeling white wallpaper and a bathroom shared by forty co-eds. Every time he brought a new girl to his room, I was subjected to approximately thirty minutes of heavily accented exclamations of ecstasy through our shared wall. But tonight was different.

Normally, I would put my noise-cancelling headphones in and tuck my nose back into my textbook. But on this night, my nerves felt like they were frayed and raw. It was 9:30 pm, and I was trying and failing to settle in for sleep. My tiny room felt stiflingly hot and muggy. The dorms had no AC. My window only opened about six inches—a grim preventative measure put in place by the institution to prevent me and my fellow Ivy Leaguers from offing ourselves in the event of a bad exam grade. Even with the window open those full six inches, the air was entirely stagnant, refusing to grace my tiny living space with even the smallest breeze.

Even before I heard Omar's door slam, and he and his companion giggle and stumble into his bedroom, I felt like the walls were caving in on me. A dull ache was growing in my chest just beneath my sternum. With every breath, my ribs seemed to grow a little tighter, the muscles of my chest wall a little more reluctant to expand. I felt like I was suffocating.

And when Omar's deep grunts started, it felt like the sounds were echoing around me. While my room was filled (as much as you could fill a one-hundred square foot space) in soft, cozy things that my mom had handpicked from Pottery Barn Teen, making a true echo in my room improbable, the sounds seemed to bounce against the walls of my skull, rattling around from one temple to the other.

I yanked my noise-cancelling headphones off my nightstand and shoved them over my head. But even as I turned the noise-cancelling feature on and the pressure weighed against my eardrums, I could *still* hear them. I wanted to crawl to the end of my twin bed and bang my fists against the wall to startle them. Maybe they would fall out of bed—God knows, there wasn't room enough for two grown adults in these things. Maybe it would spook them to the point where they would lose the mood for one evening.

Just one evening of peace—this evening, specifically—is all I really wanted. I wouldn't complain or make a fuss normally. I would find something to do elsewhere on campus, on any other night. But tonight was the night before my first General Chemistry exam, my first exam as a Columbia pre-med. I already wanted to vomit just thinking about it. And that was *before* I could hear the wet slapping of human skin on human skin, just feet away from my pillow.

I launched myself suddenly from my bed, tumbling down from the sheets ungracefully. Getting out of my bed was almost never graceful, as it was lifted on high risers to use the space beneath for extra storage. With only the dim light filtering through my window to guide me, I stripped off my sweat-soaked pajamas and threw them onto the floor. I grabbed my discarded towel off the floor from where I had thrown it this morning and wrapped it around myself. I grabbed my room key and shower caddy and slipped on my flip flops. I decided to take a long, cool shower, and hopefully my skin wouldn't feel so uncomfortably hot and itchy after I finished. And maybe, if I was lucky, Omar and his friend would be asleep or will have parted ways by the time I came back.

I half walked, half ran down the hallway in my towel toward the communal bathroom. I vaguely registered a couple of girls from my floor sitting at the end of the hallway, giggling in response to the noises coming from behind Omar's wooden door. The faster I walked, the quieter the grunts and giggles became. A wave of relief hit me when shutting the heavy bathroom door behind me was finally enough to drown out the noise and the pounding in my head. The bathroom was mercifully nearly empty—no sounds of partiers vomiting sour beer into the toilet. That was usually the Friday or Saturday night special, but Thursday nights like these were not always exempt.

I finally felt some of the tension in my shoulders release as soon as the water hit my skin. It was still early, I kept telling myself. If I spent thirty minutes in the bathroom and slowly made my way back to my room, it would only be just after ten o'clock. Still, plenty of time to get a good night's sleep before my exam at 8:40 the next morning. I would get up early, have breakfast and coffee in the dining hall on the first floor, and review a couple last-minute notes. Start the year off right.

I repeated this last phrase in my head like a mantra as I massaged shampoo into my scalp. I really didn't need to wash my hair for the second time in one day. I usually didn't wash my hair more than a few times a week on principle, but I needed to do something to pass the time. I washed and conditioned my hair, shaved my armpits and legs. Scrubbed my face with soothing exfoliating scrub. Covered myself head to toe in suds, twice.

I wrapped my fluffy towel around my wet body, gathered my shower supplies back into my caddy, and left the shower stall. I stood before the mirror and meticulously went through my hair and skin care regimen. I sprayed my long, brown hair with detangling spray and ran a brush through it. I massaged several products and moisturizers into my freckle-covered cheeks and beneath my blue eyes. Finally, when there wasn't anything else I could possibly do to delay, I walked slowly, hesitantly back toward my room at the end of the long hall of identical wooden doors with golden numbers. The giggling girls had dispersed. I stopped at my door, Room 736, delighted at the absence of distant grunts or moans. I fished out my ID card, which also acted as the key to my dorm room, from the pocket of my shower caddy and slid it into the key slot in my door.

The light flashed red.

I looked down at the card in my hand and felt my stomach sink into my ankles.

In my hasty departure, I hadn't picked up my room key. I had picked up my New York Public Library card.

Though I had unlimited access to Columbia's Butler Library (or as the students here affectionately called it, *The Butt*), I had found myself wandering the public library the previous weekend. Butler was the enormous, beautiful, historic structure, with a sturdy rectangular frame and tall sand-colored pillars, topped with the names of long-dead philosophers. But God help me if I knew how to check out a single book from its maze of wooden bookcases and ancient leather texts. Nor did I know if there was a single normal, non-ancient text to check out among its many rooms and hidden nooks and crannies.

With my pre-med course load steadily ramping up, I knew my free time was going to grow more limited. But if that free time ever came, I would like nothing better than to spend it curled up somewhere cozy with a steamy romance novel. But to achieve that end, I was not willing to walk up to the desk of Butler Library, the cornerstone of this over 260-year-old university, and ask someone where I could find books about women who fall in love with time-traveling Scotsmen or Fae High lords.

Even though those *were* my exact preference in reading material.

So, when I passed the local public library on my way back from the grocery store the previous Saturday, I had picked up the most heart-pounding love story I could get my hands on as a reward for when I aced this chemistry exam this week.

Except here I stood, 10:15 pm the night before my exam, holding out a library card in front of me as if it would magically transform into what I needed it to be before my eyes. My hair was dripping cold droplets onto the blue carpeted floor. I had no way to get back into my room, no way to crawl into my bed, to fall asleep and get a good night's rest before my exam.

And that moment, of course, is when Omar's "friend" emerged from his room. She jumped in surprise when she saw me, clearly not expecting another nearly naked woman to be standing a foot away from Omar's door, then smirked. She was beautiful, of course, if not a little mussed. Her lips full and swollen, with evidence of a red lip stain that had faded with the evening's activities. Her thick, black hair somehow looked purposefully disheveled. She was wearing a strappy black slip dress and combat boots. She had to be another international student. Effortlessly cool. She looked me up and down from my wet, dripping hair to my plastic shower shoes, then brushed past me with a laugh.

When she was out of earshot, I heard a noise, like a small and very pathetic dying animal. I realized only after it emerged that it was a sob escaping my throat.

I knew it wasn't the end of the world to get locked out of your dorm. Nearly everyone on the floor so far had gotten locked out, at one point or another. I was one of the luckier ones; it hadn't happened to me yet. This was just the most inopportune possible moment. Wearing only a towel, dripping wet, being laughed at by Omar's dazzling bed partner, the night before my first pre-med exam.

The only thing that could make the situation worse would be to have more of an audience to laugh at me, which—of course—was what happened the very next second. Behind me, the heavy wooden door to 735 opened and two boys emerged. They were mid conversation, but their sentences abruptly halted, I imagined, when they realized a wet, crying, nearly-naked girl was blocking their exit. I couldn't turn around to meet their eyes, but I also had nowhere to which I could escape. Nowhere to hide.

"You do know you're holding a library card, right?" said a nasally voice, high-pitched for a boy, as if he hadn't quite settled into his adult vocal cords yet. I recognized the voice immediately—Harrison, the occupant of Room 735.

"No shit, Sherlock," the other voice said, one which I did not recognize. "Why do you think she's standing here in the hallway?"

I turned my head ever so slightly at this voice, appreciating how quickly the owner of the second voice had understood my dire situation. I sniffled.

"Hey, are you okay?" the second voice asked, his worry sounding genuine.

I sniffled again, and nodded too emphatically, hoping they would accept the lie and move on with their evening. I knew if I voiced out loud any bit of my current situation, I would break down in uncontrollable sobs.

"Hey, what—" the nasally voice said again, but his voice was muffled by the sound of the wooden door closing in front of them. I guessed by the speed at which they retreated that they were uncomfortable by the sight of a crying girl. I hoped they were going to stay in there, leaving me alone to cry in the hallway while I figured out what to do next. But it didn't take me long to realize my hopes were fruitless. I could hear the two boys arguing softly inside the door, not loud enough to make out the words, just enough to know that they were indeed arguing.

A few moments later, the door opened again.

"Hey," the second, deeper voice said. And as the nasally voice did not respond, I knew it was directed at me, even though I still couldn't bring myself to turn to face them. I craned my neck until I could see them over my right shoulder. I had my shower caddy and library card clutched in one hand, my other arm held tight over my chest, convinced that, with my luck, some stray draft would rush through the hall at any second and loosen the towel, leaving me *completely* naked in this hallway.

The two boys standing in the doorway were polar opposites in appearance. The first, the familiar one, was my neighbor Harrison, who I had, for obvious reasons, seen many times before. He had curly, dark blond hair and very pale skin, with a scattering of freckles and pockmarks from a harsh puberty plagued by cystic acne. He was very tall, probably 6'4 at least, but so lanky he looked like he had been stretched in a taffy puller. His counterpart on the other hand, was average height, maybe 5'10 or 5'11. He was all warm, dark features—caramel brown skin and dark wavy hair and warm, chocolatey brown eyes. Incredibly kind eyes, that were smiling at me.

I finally turned to see what the second boy held out to me. It was a stack of black clothing.

"Here," he said, still smiling. "Put these on. I'll bring you to get a spare key."

I hesitantly reached out for the clothes.

Harrison scowled. "And they're *my* clothes, so I expect them back."

The second boy shot my neighbor a pointed glare. "Don't be a dick, Harrison. She's not going to steal your Star Wars t-shirt. And if she does, you know where she sleeps."

The smallest smile tugged at my lips at the instant support I had somehow won from this stranger. He turned back to me, his smile reappearing on his face as fast as it had disappeared while looking at Harrison. "Here. You can change in dickhead's room. We'll wait out here."

I did what he told me to do without argument. I pushed into the room between them and let the door slam loudly shut behind me. I found myself in a mirror image of my dorm room, if my dorm walls were decorated with movie posters and an impressive number of mounted light sabers of various colors. I quickly discarded my towel and pulled on the black athletic shorts and black t-shirt. I worried for a moment that Harrison's clothes, as lanky as he was, wouldn't fit me, especially in the hips. My saving grace was that he wore his clothes baggy, as one does when one's height is so grossly disproportionate to one's width. The shorts were only slightly snug in the hips, but both items hung well below my knees. I wrung the liquid from my hair into my towel and reemerged into the hallway.

I met Harrison's eyes first, muttering, "Thanks."

"It's whatever. Just bring them back when you're done." He shrugged, pushing past me into his room, leaving me in the hallway alone with his counterpart.

He offered his hand, introducing himself now that we were both wearing clothes.

"Javi. Javier Valenzuela, but my friends call me Javi."

I shook his hand. "Diana."

"Diana...?"

"Richards."

"Diana Richards," he said, smiling again. "Nice to meet you. I'm sorry you got locked out of your room."

"Me too," I agreed, a little pitifully. At least changing had given me a few moments to stop crying. "I have an exam in the morning. Gen Chem."

He winced on my behalf. "Pre-Med?"

I nodded. It was an easy guess—no one who actually

liked chemistry took Gen Chem. The class was made almost entirely of hungry, hopeful future doctors trying to fulfill the long list of prerequisites for medical school. It was too basic a science class for real scientists, but too boring and difficult for the casual intellectual.

"Let me walk you down to Hartley Help desk to get your key replaced. I have a buddy who's there right now for work study."

I nodded. I might have protested, if I had any idea where to find Hartley Help desk on my own. I dropped my shower caddy and towel in front of my door and let him lead me away.

Within five steps down the hallway together, he was making conversation. He was the *small talk* type, apparently. I had never been the type myself.

"Have you always wanted to be a doctor?" he asked.

"Always." I nodded. It was an easy question, at least. "Dad named me Diana Richards. *D.R.* Couldn't really be anything else after that."

Javi laughed. "Wow. I would bet your dad is a super low-key, down-to-earth kind of parent. Really laid-back type."

I only guffawed in response.

"I'm guessing your dad is a doctor?"

I nodded. "Cardiothoracic Surgeon."

We got into the elevator and pressed the button for the lobby.

"Ah yes, the most laid-back of the medical specialties." He chuckled. "I'm in the engineering school."

"Cool," I said, even though I didn't personally find engineering very interesting. "Do you know what kind of engineering you want to do?"

"No," he said. "I'm waiting for the right thing to speak

to me. My parents considered calling me 'Chem-E,' but they couldn't agree on it, so they settled for Javier."

I met his eyes and saw the laughter there, and a laugh stuttered out of me in surprise. His face broke into a brilliant smile, his whole face alight; like he couldn't find anything more satisfying than getting me to laugh.

We walked through the lobby doors and out into the breezeway, the gravel kicking up with the flapping of my plastic flip flops. We crossed the fifty feet to the adjacent dorm Hartley and walked through their front doors. I had never been in any of the other dorms before, even though the first-year dorms were all in very close proximity.

The guy at the help desk was playing something on an old Gameboy SP that sounded vaguely like a Pokémon game. He didn't raise his eyes from the screen until Javi held his fist out toward him.

"What's up, Jeff?" Javi said.

Jeff returned the greeting and glanced briefly at me. He didn't seem at all confused by my appearance, with wet hair and clearly borrowed clothes. In fact, I was certain by his ambivalence to my appearance that he had seen many a towel-clad or even fully naked college student grace his help desk before. The thought made me feel better, somehow.

"Nothing much. How are you fine folks, this evening?"

"Great," Javi said, though he probably knew I would not have agreed. "I was hoping you could get my friend Diana here a replacement key to her room."

Jeff nodded knowingly, handing me a clipboard before Javi could finish the sentence. "Fill this out with your name, ID number and room number. I can get you a temporary replacement, but you have to get it back to me soon or they'll put a hold on your record. Not important now, but you won't get your final grades at the end of the semester unless the hold is gone."

I nodded in understanding and started filling in my information. Jeff looked at my room number and went to a back room behind his desk, and I could see him flipping through envelopes in a card-catalog style system. Leave it to a university as old as this one to have such an archaic looking backup system for our room keys. He handed me an envelope with JJ-736 written on the front.

When we were outside in the commons once more, I turned to Javier.

"Thank you for your help," I told him. "Not many people would have walked me all the way down here."

"It's nothing," he said.

We made our way back toward the front doors of John Jay. I showed the security guard at the front desk my temporary key and started to explain why I didn't have my school ID , but he waved me through knowingly. When we got back into the elevator, I could feel my nerves start to creep back and settle into my chest. I tapped my temporary key against my palm. The ache in my ribs was starting to burn again.

I made the trip back down the hall of John Jay quickly and without chatting, my anxiety distracting me from acknowledging Javi, who was still at my side. I picked up my shower caddy and towel from beside my door and opened the door with the temporary key. I had one foot in the door as I turned to bid Javier thank you and goodnight, but he spoke before I had the chance.

"Hey," he said. "What would you say if I told you that you look like a girl who needs a milkshake right now."

My eyes went wide, looking at him incredulously.

"I would say that I should get to bed." I sounded a little more exasperated than I intended, especially toward someone who had gone out of his way to help me. I added, trying to soften the edge to my voice, "Exam in the morning."

I didn't think, when I had enrolled in an Ivy League school, that these things would require this much explanation.

"I know," he said. "Gen Chem. But can you tell me honestly that if you lay down right now that you're going to be able to sleep?"

I peered at him, unnerved. How could he possibly know how very unready for sleep I felt?

"My older sister Gaby has a PhD in clinical psychology. She has taught me a thing or two about anxiety. And you look anxious as hell." His observation made me realize suddenly that I had been picking at my nails, and I tucked my hands behind my back, feeling self-conscious.

"A milkshake?" I asked, skeptically. "How is sugar going to help me sleep?"

He grinned. "Milkshakes fix everything."

"Except lactose intolerance," I supplied, dryly.

"Except that," he relented, wavering slightly. "Are you—?"

"No," I said.

"Oh good, we're back on track." His grin returned. "Milkshakes, then?"

I hesitated.

"Miiiiilkshaaaaaakes?" This time he said it in a sing-song way, like trying to tempt a child. "My treat."

I realized suddenly that during this short conversation with Javier, standing in the doorway of my dorm room, that the burning in my chest had ebbed. But I could feel it there, sitting in wait somewhere around my diaphragm. It felt like the sea at low tide. I knew it was only a matter of time before it crashed against me again like waves on a shore. I did not want to feel that way again, and I felt like I would do anything to delay the rising of the tide.

"Milkshakes," I said, this time like an affirmation. He beamed at me. "But please, give me two seconds to get out of Harrison's Star Wars t-shirt and my shower shoes."

"Of course, take as long as you need." He turned around to face the other direction, as if closing the door between us was not enough privacy.

I threw on the closest shorts and t-shirt from each of my dresser drawers and slipped on socks and sneakers. I grabbed my wallet and my *actual* ID card this time— turning on my desk lamp and scrutinizing the plastic card to double check. I returned my shower caddy and towel to their hooks on my closet door. I carefully folded the borrowed clothing and emerged into the hallway.

He turned at the sound of my door and smiled at me, clearly pleased that I had reemerged. He was probably worried that I would change my mind and stay shut in my room once he gave me the opportunity to escape. I would be lying if I said I didn't consider it, once I could see my waiting bed and my gen chem textbook, still lying open on my desk from earlier in the evening. But the sight of the textbook made my breath hitch in my throat and that burning start to flare once more in my chest, so I made my way resolutely back out into the hallway.

I dropped the neatly folded pile of clothes in front of Harrison's door, and let Javi once again lead me out of John Jay, back to Hartley Help desk so we could return the borrowed key to Jeff. We walked out of the south gates to the sidewalk on Broadway, where the streets were still bustling with people coming and going and a mix of yellow and green cabs driving past us looking for fares.

"So, Diana Richards," Javi said, as we walked south- ward, the destination unknown. "Where are you from?"

"The upper east side," I replied. "Well, I'm originally from Westchester, but we moved to the city when I was in high school."

He laughed. "Wow. So, you're rich-rich."

I didn't respond immediately. How does one reply to being called "rich-rich?"

Before I could form an answer, he continued, "I mean, I knew this already, with the whole cardiothoracic surgeon for a father thing. But now you've confirmed it."

That wasn't even the beginning of it. My dad's personal wealth was impressive, but both my mom and dad had inherited generous amounts of money from their own parents as well. But that was not something I discussed with... well, *anyone*, much less someone I had just met.

"And what do your parents do?" I asked, posing it like a challenge. It's not like having a renowned surgeon for a father was a big deal, not at this school. Columbia's student body regularly hosted distant royalty, heirs to vast fortunes, and celebrities on hiatuses from their movie and TV careers.

"My parents did not go to college," he said. "They have a restaurant in Corpus Christi. That's where I'm from. My mom manages the business side of things, and my dad is the chef."

"That's really cool," I said, meaning it. Honestly, the truth was far more interesting to me than if he had told me he hailed from royalty or celebrity. "Are you first generation to go to college?"

He let out a nervous laugh. "First gen, yes. Definitely *not* first. My sisters would beat me if they heard me implying such a thing. They all have at least bachelor's degrees; the two older ones have graduate degrees."

"What do your sisters do? You said one of them has a PhD in psych."

"Yeah, my oldest sister Gaby. She did her thesis on kids in the foster care system, and does a lot of work with kids still. My middle sister, Manuela, is a paralegal. And my youngest sister works in HR at an oil company in Houston. Makes more money than the rest of us combined, I think. Certainly, more than me, since I make negative money."

I imagined what Javi's parents must be like, to go from having no college degree themselves to having four incredibly high-achieving children.

"What kind of restaurant do your parents own?" I asked.

He raised an eyebrow at me, grinning wickedly. He gestured to himself, as if his appearance should have been more than enough to tip me off. "Come on, do you even have to guess? Classic Tex-Mex."

"I wouldn't want to assume," I said with a laugh.

"They actually started franchising a couple years ago," he went on. "Now there are *Tia Alba's* all over Texas and Oklahoma. It's still weird to me. I basically grew up in the restaurant, and now it's a household name back in Texas."

"I'd love to try it some time," I said earnestly.

"But the chains are nothing compared to the OG," he insisted. "You really gotta come out to Corpus, to the original location. Nobody can cook like my dad."

"I would love that," I said, half because I wanted to try the food, half because I wanted to meet the combination of people who could have raised someone like Javi Valenzuela. He abruptly stopped in the street.

"Here we are," he said, pausing before the flashing neon sign. "Tom's Diner."

I looked at the place skeptically. I had seen this place about a hundred times and never once bothered to stop in. Even now that I lived a couple blocks away, the urge had never struck me to stop inside its doors. There was a "Highlights of NYC TV" tour that stopped on this corner several times a week, the crowds of tourists frequently blocking the entire sidewalk on my way home from the grocery store. "Tom's? Isn't this a tourist trap for Seinfeld fans?"

"Yes, it is," he conceded. "But it is so much more. It is my opinion that the option to dine in at Tom's should be almost exclusively reserved for the drunk, and you will see that the vast majority of their clientele agree with me. We can save that for another day. But take out, on the other hand, is for everyone, at any level of sobriety."

The bell over the door rang as we walked in. Javi went immediately to the counter, which was only occupied by a man with a cup of coffee and a half-eaten slice of pie. A waiter behind the old-fashioned cash register peered at us, cleaning a set of silver milkshake glasses with a white dish rag.

"Can I help you?" he asked.

"Two milkshakes to-go, please," Javi said to the man. "Cookies and cream for me, and, for my friend,—?"

"Do you have pistachio?" I asked.

"We do," the waiter said. "Cookies and cream and pistachio, coming right up."

"Interesting choice," Javi said.

"I know it's weird," I said, trying not to sound embarrassed. "But it's my favorite."

"Not weird," he said quickly, reassuringly. "Just different."

The waiter put down his dish rag and started shoveling out scoop after scoop of ice cream into two large silver cups. He topped them with milk before putting them beneath the classic silver milkshake spinners. He poured them out into two paper cups, the milkshakes so thick they poured out in big *glops*, before he handed them to us. That'll be $7.50."

Javi fished a $10 bill out of his wallet. "Keep the change."

We headed back out onto Broadway, milkshakes in hand. I attempted to drink from my cup, only to find the milkshake so thick that my cheeks hurt trying to use the straw. I laughed.

"This is impossible!" I exclaimed.

He laughed. "You gotta give it a minute. Let it settle."

We walked down Broadway together, holding our milk-shakes in both hands, letting the warmth of our skin radiate into the cups. Maybe, by the time we graduated, they would be thin enough to drink.

Without discussing the matter, neither of us made the turn down 114th street to head back to John Jay. We ambled toward college walk, through the wrought iron gates, through the branching trees swaying softly, and to the sundial at the very heart of campus. We stood atop it, him looking toward Butler library and me looking the other direction, toward the rotunda of Low Library, two proud facades peering down at us. There was barely a soul in sight, and it felt for a moment like we were the only ones in the whole school. In the whole world.

He sighed. "Do you ever look at this place and think we're the luckiest people in the whole world, because we get to live here?"

I had lived in or near New York City my entire life. I had been walking the lawns of Columbia's campus since I took my first steps and yet somehow, I had never noticed quite how beautiful it looked until I saw it through Javi's perspective. I took a deep breath, and it felt like the easiest breath I had taken in a long time. I smiled, turning around to look at him. He had turned to look back at me too.

"Yeah. Yeah, I do," I responded.

He lifted his paper cup to me to cheers.

"To the two luckiest people in the whole world."

I tapped my milkshake against his, and lifted the straw to my lips, delighted when the rich pistachio milkshake hit my tongue. We both started giggling in delight like children.

We sat down on the sundial drinking our milkshakes, talking about our classes for the semester. When the cups were empty, we tossed them in the nearest trash and started making our way back to John Jay. He walked me once more to my room.

I had been expecting, once we made the trip back to my room, that I would feel that wave of dread washing over me once more. I imagined that the closer I got to my bed and therefore to sleep, the closer I got to waking in the morning to take this exam, the more intense my anxiety would become. But I was pleased to find that, instead of those feelings waiting to sweep over me like the tide, I could sense the anxiety in a much more distant way, like the view of the horizon from the shore.

"Hey, Diana?" he said, and I turned, my hand braced on the handle of my door.

"Yes?" I asked.

"You're gonna kill it tomorrow."

I smiled. "Thanks, Javi."

Chapter 2

Columbia University

First Year

I did not, in fact, "kill it."

I woke up a full hour after I intended, missing my alarm. The leisurely morning I had planned, with a full breakfast, a hot cup of coffee, and some light note-reading, turned into a panicked rampage. I threw on the same clothes I had worn to Tom's the night before, gathered my backpack, a canned Starbucks espresso from my mini fridge, and a silver package of brown sugar cinnamon pop tarts. It would take me about ten minutes to walk across the campus, and with every quick step I made, inhaling my makeshift breakfast along the way, I felt like I forgot another important fact about chemistry that I had once known. My heart was racing by the time I made it to my assigned seat in the multi-tiered lecture hall, and it did not stop racing until well after I completed the exam.

A few days later, I walked down the stone steps in front of the white rotunda of Low Library, when I heard a voice call out to me, "Why, hello there, Dr. Richards."

I spun toward the voice, a smile lighting my face instantly when I saw Javi sitting at the foot of the bronze statue of *Alma Mater.* He had a half-eaten hero sitting in his lap.

"Please," I said, teasing. "Dr. Richards is my father."

He laughed, patting the cement next to him. "Are you in a hurry? Come join me."

I dropped my bag down on the steps and settled in beside him. I leaned back against my hands and closed my eyes, enjoying the warm sunshine on my face and shoulders. When I finally opened them, Javi was staring at me.

I raised an eyebrow at him. "What is it?"

He looked away quickly. "Nothing. You look really happy."

"I am," I replied. The weather was phenomenal today —a perfect 75 degrees, not a cloud in the sky. I heard the *ding* of my email notification sound from my phone and looked down at the screen. "Or at least, I *was*. Exam scores just got posted."

My hands shook as I frantically clicked through the online portal to find my score. And when I saw the black numbers against the white backdrop, my heart sank.

"76," I said, in shock. "I got a 76 on my exam."

Javi looked over at my screen, appraising it closely. He chewed on his sandwich in silence for a few moments.

"Hey!" he enthused. "Good job!"

I looked at him, aghast. How could any Columbia University student look at a 76 on an exam and say, *good job?* He must have had a *very* different high school experience than the one I had lived.

"Are you insane?" I asked him. "That is *not* a good score."

Javi snatched my phone from my hands, scrolling over on the screen before I could protest.

"Diana, look at this with me." He pointed to the header above the score. "What does this say."

"Raw score," I read aloud.

He scrolled over to the far right of the score report. "And what about this?"

"Final adjusted score…" I read slowly. "94? It was curved?"

"It was curved," he repeated, grinning widely. "You got an A on your very first exam. My buddy Clara is the TA for Gen Chem. She told me on Friday that the average on that exam was a fifty-something."

I was quickly learning that Javi Valenzuela "had a friend" or "knew a guy" for every facet of life, from every corner of this university. And he had only been here as long as I had been here, only a few weeks. I would consider myself lucky if I could name more than ten people living on my floor.

"You know what this means?" he asked. "We have to celebrate."

I shook my head at his declaration. He said it as if he had known me for years, not just a few days. "Celebrate how?"

"Dinner? Dessert? A Broadway Show?" he mused aloud. "All of the above."

I laughed. "It's a Tuesday, Javi. I have forty pages of *Lysistrata* to read by tomorrow."

"Oh, that's easy!" he exclaimed. "A bunch of Greek women tell the men they won't have sex with them until they stop going to war. Conclusion: women are the superior species. Reading done! Let's go to Broadway."

I shook my head. "You're ridiculous. Broadway shows are like $150 a ticket, minimum."

"*Not* if you know how to work the system," he said in a conspiratorial tone. "Come with me, and I'll show you."

I hesitated. There was a part of me—the good little high school student who would study every night from the time I got home until I went to sleep at an early, respectable hour—that protested, saying, *it's a school night.* But that part of me was smothered by the girl who had stood on the sundial at midnight the night before an exam and finally felt alive.

I sighed in mock exasperation. "What time?"

He did a little victory dance. "I'll pick you up at your room at five."

We parted ways soon after to attend our afternoon classes. On my way back to my dorm that afternoon, I texted my mom to tell her the good news about my first exam. The name *Helen Richards* flashed across my notifications seconds later.

HR: Great job, honey! Never doubted you.

A few seconds later, another text followed.

HR: Making friends too?

A soft smile pulled at my lips. My mom *would* be more concerned about me making friends than making good grades. Someone had to balance out my father, after all—he probably didn't care if I spent the next four years alone, so long as the end result was medical school.

DR: Yeah I actually did meet someone...
We're going out to celebrate?

HR: Going out, like a date????

DR: I don't think so?? But it is unclear.

HR: LOL, update me when you find out.
Wear something cute, just in case.

Jacquelynn Harbell

I looked in my closet skeptically, surveying my options. I had seen a few shows with my parents over the years, and they usually dressed up for the occasion. But my dad refused to step foot in a theater unless he had box seats, so I didn't know if the same protocol applied here.

I pulled up Javi's number, which he had freshly saved in my phone this afternoon.

> DR: Hey. What are you wearing?

A few seconds later, the "..." appeared as he was typing his reply.

> JV: Why, Dr. Richards. How forward. We only just met.

I blushed furiously, realizing only in hindsight how my original text sounded. I sent a face palm emoji back.

> DR: Not like that. I mean what are you wearing to the "Broadway show."

> JV: I take the quotations to mean you doubt me and my abilities to get us in.

> DR: I'm only wondering if I need to wear a black cat suit. How clandestine is this operation? Are we rappelling in from the rafters?

> JV: No rappelling necessary. But please, feel free to wear the cat suit anyway. I would enjoy that.

> DR: Seriously though, what's the vibe here?

JV: I'm going with "poor college student dressy casual," aka jeans that I haven't gotten chemical stains on and a shirt that hasn't been sitting at the bottom of my hamper.

DR: I can work with that.

When Javi knocked on my door at five o clock, I wore a black flowing jumpsuit—not quite a black cat suit, but hopefully Javi appreciated the effort. He, as advertised, wore dark blue jeans and a fitted blue button-down. We walked the few blocks to the subway station and caught the south-bound train to a stop just north of Times Square.

Javi led me toward the red-and-yellow umbrella over the Halal Guys cart on the street corner, with a line of at least twenty people waiting beside it. We ordered big silver platters filled with lamb and rice and loaded with a white, garlicky sauce. He carried the food as we walked toward the glaring, flashing lights of Times Square in the distance. I cringed a little at the sight. I avoided Times Square like the plague—fighting to get through the crowds of tourists did not appeal to me.

He wound through the throng with purpose. After a troop of Sesame Street imitators nearly separated us, Javi hooked one elbow through mine. I looked down at our intertwined arms curiously.

"I almost lost you to crackhead Elmo," he said, by way of explanation. "Your parents would never forgive me if I let harm come to their dear little future surgeon."

I cackled with laughter and willingly let him lead me by the elbow. We ducked down a side street, seeing the marquis for the Eugene O'Neill theater ahead.

"*The Book of Mormon?*" I asked with delight.

"That's the plan," he said. "You're not Mormon, are you? Or easily offended?"

"No and no," I said, grinning. "I have always wanted to see it."

"Hopefully, today is our lucky day," he said, leading us to join a line of about ten people sitting or standing on the sidewalk beside the box office. He sat against the wall behind the last person in line, fishing out the silver trays and plastic utensils from the plastic bag. Though the idea of sitting on the dirty New York City street wasn't exactly appealing, I was starving. Javi tore the plastic bag in half and placed it on the ground beside him, gesturing for me to sit on it.

I shook my head at the casual chivalry. I was certain that if Javi had a jacket on, he would have sacrificed it for me. They just didn't make boys like Javier Valenzuela in New York, I decided.

I settled in beside him, happily eating my halal food as we waited outside the theater. Over the next thirty minutes, a steady crowd built up around us. Some joined the line behind us, some milled about in front of the theater. An hour before showtime, a woman in a black *Book of Mormon* t-shirt appeared with a fishbowl and slips of paper, announcing that entries for the lottery were open. His antics finally made sense—I vaguely recalled hearing friends before mention student rush or last-minute lottery tickets to Broadway shows, though I had never sought them out myself.

Javi wrote our names down and placed them in the bowl. After ten minutes of people walking up to enter their names, the woman called out that she had ten tickets for thirty dollars each available, and that each person called could have up to two tickets.

One by one, they called out names from the fishbowl,

and the winners went to the box office to receive their tickets. For some reason, I *knew* he was going to win. Javier Valenzuela radiated luck. He was the kind of person who turned everything he touched to gold. Blessed by the gods, some might say.

"And the last two tickets go to Javier Valenzuela!"

Javi beamed at me. "Told you I had my ways."

I shook my head. "And how could you have possibly known you would win? There are probably sixty people here."

"My family says I was born lucky," he said, shrugging. "But if we didn't win the lottery, they have standing room tickets. That's why we were sitting in line."

He really thought of everything. We got out of the standing room line and went straight to the box office. We received our tickets—third row, center orchestra. Probably worth $250 each, and we paid thirty dollars each for them. We were both buzzing with excitement by the time they opened the theater doors, and the crowds of theatergoers filed in beside us. I bought us sodas and peanut M&Ms from the bar as a token of gratitude to Javi and his dumb luck.

We took our seats at the very center of the beautiful, ornate theater. The stage was decorated with a depiction of the heavens, radiant beams of light filtering through fluffy clouds, with faux stained-glass windows surrounding it. We perused the playbill until the lights went dim and the first few notes rang out from the orchestra pit. We were so close to the musicians that I could feel the sound resonating in my chest. The curtain rose, and the actors were so near, I could see the lead's freckles speckling the bridge of his nose.

After two and a half hours, my abdominal muscles ached from laughing so uproariously with so little respite.

On the walk to the subway and on the uptown train back to campus, we recounted our favorite songs and jokes from the show. Conversation with Javi flowed so easily, it was almost unnerving. I would not call myself antisocial by any means, but I didn't make new friends often or easily. I had some close friends in high school, sure, but moving schools after freshman year when my dad got the Chief of Surgery position at Columbia hadn't helped. And no friendship had ever bloomed so easily and effortlessly as it had so far with Javi.

I suspected that this was in no way specific to me, though. This was just the way it was for Javi, which would explain how everyone on campus seemed to love him. He made people feel seen and heard and special, all at the same time. So even if I was one of many friends he planned to make, I was happy to be included.

When we were back on campus, we were walking past Butler library when Javi stopped in his tracks.

His eyes glinted with mischief. "Would you, perhaps, still be interested in any clandestine operations this evening?"

I looked down at my watch. "I would tell you that it is eleven o'clock on a school night, but I imagine it would only fall on deaf ears."

"It would," he said. "Come with me."

"And where are we going this time?" I asked.

"The Butt," he said.

I looked up at the enormous structure beside us and back to him. "The Butt? I thought the point of tonight was *not* studying indoors."

"You are correct," he said. "We will be neither studying, nor indoors."

I shot him a skeptical look. I was learning not to question his brand of madness. My life, at least the small part of it which intersected with his, had only been improved thus far by letting the insanity happen. Javi approached the world with an open mind, with spontaneity and joy—characteristics I felt lacking in myself, but that I desperately wanted to learn.

I gestured toward the door of the library, as if to say, *after you.*

He led the way through the front door, and we scanned our IDs at the security desk. We took the elevator to the top floor of the building and walked through the black-and-white tiled hallways. We passed room after room of study halls and bookcases, filled with students who appeared to be having much less fun than we were having. Javi ducked into an unmarked staircase. We walked up a final flight of stairs to another door, propped open with a tattered copy of *The Iliad* (required reading for all first-year students at Columbia, now turned door stop).

When Javi pushed against the heavy door, the cool evening air hit us. We walked out onto the roof of the library and ran to peer over the ledge. The entire campus sprawled before us in all its glory – the sparkling white roof of Low, the red brick academic buildings with their green copper roofs, the tailored green lawns, *Alma Mater* and the sun dial sitting at the center, looking as small as insects from here. A few stragglers walked the paths between the buildings or down college walk.

"This is amazing," I told him. "I can't imagine we're allowed to be up here?"

"Not even a little bit," he said. "Strictly forbidden."

I rested my chin on my hands, feeling like I could stay up here watching over the twinkling lights on the campus below for the rest of the night.

"What made you choose Columbia?" Javi asked quietly.

I laughed, a little bitterly. "It's not so much why did I choose Columbia, but why did Columbia choose me. My dad's Chief of Surgery at the medical school uptown. Kids of faculty get free tuition. I couldn't exactly pass up a free education at one of the best schools in the country."

Javi whistled low and slow, clearly impressed. "Free tuition. Wow."

"That's not to say I don't love this school," I said. "I really do. It has always been one of my favorite places in the city. But with my dad working here and being who he is... sometimes I wonder if they even looked at my application before accepting me. I know it's stupid and that I have no room to complain. I'm extremely fortunate to have the opportunities I have been given. But just once it would be great to know I earned something for *me*. Because of who I am and what I have done. Not because of who my father is."

"I don't think that's stupid at all," Javi replied.

"What made you choose Columbia?" I asked him, trying to divert his attention from the subject I was most sensitive about.

Javi got quiet for a while, and for a moment, I wondered if he hadn't heard my question. I looked over, seeing that he had lay down on the ledge, looking upward toward the stars with his hands behind his head.

Finally, he said, "I applied to a couple good schools. I really didn't think I would get in, to be honest. I mean, my grades and my SAT scores were good, of course. But kids in my school didn't really go to the Ivy League. No one had gotten into one in anyone's memory. But my parents and my sisters encouraged me to shoot for the stars, so I did. And I got in."

Javi's voice sounded wistful and sad, about what I thought would have been a happy topic. And something in the tone of his voice told me there was more to the story, so I waited for the rest without saying anything.

Eventually, he continued.

"I was dating someone for most of high school," he said finally. "Sofia. She had already decided to stay in town and attend Texas A&M Corpus Christi. My plan was to go to University of Texas in Austin. It was only a three-hour drive, so we were planning on trying to make the distance work. But then, when I got into school here, unexpectedly, everything kind of changed."

I lay down on the ledge beside him, end-to-end, until our heads nearly touched. The stars were faded against the black sky, mostly drowned by the lights of the city.

"Everyone said we were going to get married some-day," he mused. "I know we were really young for all that talk, but in my high school, people regularly got married or at least got knocked up at our age. Sofia didn't think we could make it work cross-country. She begged me to stay. And I considered it. But my family told me I couldn't pass up a shot like that. To go to a school like this. So, we broke up.

And man, did it suck. It kind of tore our whole friend group apart, everyone choosing a side in the 'divorce.' And with me leaving, most of our friends chose her. I don't really blame them, and I'm glad she still has them. But it put a damper on graduation. On the whole summer, really."

After an extended silence, I finally said, "I'm sorry, Javi."

"It's alright," he said. "But I decided that if I'm going to sacrifice everything for this school, if I'm going to lose the girl and all my friends to come here, I better damn well make it worth the sacrifice. Not only am I going to study my ass off and get the fancy degree, but I'm going to treat this city like my playground. I'm going to do every dumb tourist thing and see every show and take advantage of every opportunity that presents itself to me."

His declaration seemed to echo between us long after he finished.

"Javi?" I asked.

"Yeah?"

"Would it make you feel better if I told you my high school boyfriend broke up with me the night before the AP Biology exam, because I was the only person with a better grade than him in the class?" I offered.

His surprised laughter broke through the contemplative silence. I smiled in triumph at the sound. It felt good, being the one to make him laugh. I could see why Javi liked making people smile and laugh so much—it was addictive, being someone's source of joy in an otherwise joyless moment.

"Thank you for taking me with you tonight," I said.

"Of course," he said. "It was a lot of fun."

"I know it doesn't make up for everything you had to sacrifice to get here," I said carefully. "But for the record, I'm glad you came to this school. Because, if you hadn't come, I'd still be tucked away in my room in John Jay, studying every second of the day, never stepping foot off campus, never bothering to branch out, to make new friends. And I would very much like to be your friend, Javi."

"You already are my friend, Doc," he said. "I'm glad you're here, too."

We stayed up there for a while longer, lying on the cool tiles of the rooftop, talking about everything and nothing. The city buzzed below us, a constant hum of life and energy. From the few stars that he could make out, Javi pointed out constellations, telling me stories about each one, his tone so calming I nearly nodded off.

"We should probably head back," he said, glancing at his watch. "It's getting pretty late."

"I didn't think too late existed for Javier Valenzuela," I said, stifling a yawn.

"For a night owl like me, you are correct, too late does not exist," he agreed. "But too early does. And I've got lab in the morning. As much as it pains me for this night to end."

We made our way back to John Jay. As he had done before, Javi dropped me off at my door, even though he lived two floors above. When he dropped me off at my door, there was no awkwardness to our goodbye, no expectant pause between us. No indication that this was the end of a *date*. Part of me was grateful for that, but another part harbored just the smallest disappointment.

"Good night, Doc," he said.

"Good night, Javi," I replied.

He smiled, turning from me with his hands in his pockets, to walk back down the hall to the elevator.

When I was in my bed a few minutes later, I texted my mom, not really caring if she knew how late I was up on a school night. Knowing my mom, she'd probably be thrilled I had spent this many hours in a row socializing.

> DR: Not a date. I think he's still recovering from a bad breakup. But it was pretty much the best non-date I've ever been on.

Chapter 3

Columbia University

First Year

A paper bag plopped down in front of me on top of my statistics textbook. My belongings were haphazardly arranged on the table before me. I had been parked in this corner of the Butt for hours, only moving to get a refill of my coffee from the cafe or to pee. I reached for the bag, peering inside to see the largest, flakiest chocolate croissant I had ever laid eyes upon. It smelled heavenly. I lifted it to my lips and took a bite. An involuntary groan escaped my lips, loud enough that a few eyes from nearby tables darted over to me.

"You are a saint, Javier Valenzuela. A god among men," I gushed. "This is the best croissant I've ever had in my life. And I've been to France."

"I waited in line for two hours for that pastry. It's from the new bakery downtown that's getting all the buzz," he said.

"You are insane!" I took another two bites. "But your insanity is my gain. This is amazing."

I was halfway through the croissant when I added,

"How do you have time to wait in line downtown for two hours? Am I the only one who has midterms this week?"

I had delivered a midterm essay this morning to my professor for Contemporary Civilizations, sat for my French midterm the day prior, and I had a statistics exam the following day. And from my generally disheveled appearance, it was clear that I hadn't escaped from the library much in the last week. Javi, on the other hand, was clean and unruffled. He had joined me, here and there, for study sessions, usually bringing me a coffee or a food item when he did. But unlike me, Javi never spent more than an hour or two at a time trapped within the stone prison walls of the Butt.

I liked to think that in the six months since I met Javi, I had acted as a good influence on him. He, of course, was *quite* the influence on me.

Somehow, in just a short time, we had left our mark on every corner of this city, even to the outer boroughs. I showed him around the parts of the city I knew best—the upper east and west sides, Central Park, the east village, Brooklyn and Queens. And he made sure we saw every other inch of the city that I didn't know as well. We took the Staten Island Ferry and visited Ellis Island. We saw more museums than even I knew existed in New York City. We saw the classics—The Museum of Natural History, The Guggenheim, and MoMA, of course —but also the Frick, the Transit Museum, the Museum of Sex.

We waited in line for and tried whatever trendy food was making news that week. We got lottery tickets to three more Broadway shows after seeing *The Book of Mormon*. Every time I thought we had seen it all, Javi came up with a new list of things he wanted to do and places he wanted to see. And New York was happy to provide him fresh new distractions each time. Even though I had lived here for years, seeing Javi fall in love with my city made me fall in love with it all over again.

I, in turn, got Javi to sit down with a book once in a blue moon. I made him use his monthly stipend in the dining halls before the credit expired. I took him grocery shopping, so he wouldn't need to venture out for *every* snack and meal. I taught him the joys of an evening in, watching movies in our dorm rooms with a bowl of popcorn. I liked to think that we balanced each other well as friends.

Every time we had an exam, we got a milkshake from Tom's the night before. It was our tradition. And we frequently ended our evenings lying atop the roof of Butler, scanning the faded stars above, talking until we could barely keep our eyes open. We talked about our families. We recounted bad dates we went on with people we met from school. Javi would regale me with dozens of his brilliant ideas. He had a mind unlike anyone I had ever met. He was constantly thinking of inventions and experiments. I was convinced that he was Da Vinci reincarnated, and I never got sick of hearing his mind at work.

Javi fell into the armchair across from mine.

"I need to talk to you," he said.

I looked at him over my half croissant, concerned. Javi rarely sounded so serious.

"Okay," I said. "What's up?"

"What are your plans for spring break?" he asked.

I smirked, relieved that the topic of the discussion did not match the tone. "I can't even think about spring break until I get through midterms this week."

"You're not going anywhere with your parents?" he asked, and I feigned gagging on my bite of croissant.

"Actually, I planned on doing anything *but* spending time with my parents," I informed him. "They're going to Aruba that week."

"You're not going with them?" he asked.

"God, no," I retorted. "A week on a cruise ship with my parents? Stuck in forced proximity with my father, my only means of escape jumping into the sea? No, thank you."

He looked away from me. Javi was always direct, especially with me. Being evasive wasn't in his nature. I could tell he was nervous, uneasy.

"What's up, Javi? Why do you want to know what I'm doing for spring break? I have no plans other than becoming one with my bed and reading a couple romance novels."

"I'm going home for the break," he said.

"Great," I said. "I'm sure it will be nice to see your family."

"I was wondering if you might come with me?" he finally asked after a loaded pause.

I stopped everything that I was doing, putting my croissant down and shutting my textbook with a *slap* of the smooth pages.

"Go... with you? To Corpus Christi?" I asked.

"Yeah," he said, more assuredly. "Come with me to Corpus Christi."

I didn't know what to say to that. I looked at him, a little dumbfounded. Though I had long been curious about meeting the people who had raised Javi, I never thought in a million years that he might invite me home to Texas to do so.

"I know it's a lot to ask," he said. "But when I went back home for the winter break, I was miserable. I love my family more than anything, but being back home reminded me of everything that went down last summer. I felt trapped in the house, like I was going to run into my high school friends everywhere I went. So, I never went out. I was on edge the whole time, wondering if someone would bring up Sofia. Hoping half the time that someone *would* bring up Sofia so I could figure out what she was doing or if she was okay. I had to fight not to lose all willpower and call her, even though I knew it wouldn't be fair to either of us. I was a wreck. My whole family noticed. I made everyone else miserable. Not even my nieces or nephews could stand me. And I wondered, if you came… maybe things could be different."

I blinked at him for several long seconds. Of the two of us, Javi was generally the more composed one. He was the one who had, time and time again, pulled me up off the floor of my anxiety before tests. He was the one who knew exactly what to do and say when I needed him. And for once in our friendship, I felt as if he was the one who needed me.

"Of course," I said. "I'm there."

He breathed a huge sigh of relief.

One week later, we took a cab together to JFK and boarded a plane to his hometown. When I had asked my mom for the cost of the airfare, she had balked a little, not over the price but the destination—*Texas? For your first spring break? Are you sure you don't want me to get you guys a place in Cabo?* But I declined, asking only for the ticket to Corpus Christi.

As our plane descended over the glistening blue water, Javi fidgeted beside me. I couldn't tell if he was more excited or anxious, or an equal mix of both.

After we had collected our bags, we walked out the sliding glass doors, the warm, humid Texas air meeting us like a welcoming hug. It was wildly different than the crisp, cool air of NYC when we left. Winter had clung to the city well into March, the last snow shower falling only a week before.

Javi waved as an old black SUV approached. The

woman in the passenger seat launched herself from the car before it had even come to a full stop.

"*Mi hijo*! Welcome home!" Javi's mother swept him up in a bone-crushing hug—indeed, I thought I did hear bones in his back cracking beneath the pressure. But I soon found myself in those same strong arms as his mother drew me into the hug as well.

"And you must be Diana. We have heard so much about you!"

"It's so nice to meet you, Mrs. Valenzuela," I laughed in her soft, warm arms.

"Please, call me Alba," she insisted. Javi's father emerged from the driver's side. He was a man with kind eyes—Javi's eyes, I realized—and deep-set wrinkles in his tan face.

"Welcome to our home, Diana," he said. "We're so glad you're here."

Javi's father loaded our bags into the back of the car, and we made the drive back to Javi's childhood home. Screams of laughter and a wave of amazing smells greeted us as soon as we walked in the door. Three young girls and two boys, the youngest boy barely big enough to toddle clumsily after the others, were screaming and chasing each other through the house. Three women, who must be Javi's sisters, were drifting between the kitchen and living room. Their husbands were perched on the couch watching the TV, every now and then either verbally or physically intercepting a fight between the children.

Javi introduced me to the whole lot, and each one of them eagerly embraced me. They enveloped me in the chaos of their family as if I had always belonged there.

The next few days, we spent our mornings entertaining the nieces and nephews with games, a trip to the aquarium, and dips in the pool. Afternoons were spent helping at the restaurant, and evenings were spent sharing stories and laughter around the dinner table. The food was as amazing as I always dreamed it would be.

After dinner on the third night, Javi and I went to the beach alone, taking the opportunity for a few moments of quiet, away from the house and his bustling family. The setting sun reflected off the water with a kaleidoscope of gold and pink and orange as we walked barefoot along the shore, our shoes in hand.

"I'm glad you came," Javi said, breaking the comfortable silence that had settled between us.

"Me too," I replied, my voice soft. "Your family is amazing."

He smiled. "They really like you."

"I like them too. It's nice to be around a family that's so... normal," I said, then quickly added, "Not that my family isn't normal, but you know..."

Javi chuckled. "I get it. We're pretty close. Sometimes it can be overwhelming, but it's home."

The contrast between our families could not have been more glaring in my mind. Javi's parents were completely in love with each other and not afraid to show it—they constantly displayed their affection for each other in little glances and touches and whispered terms of endearment. My parents, at least from the outside, often looked like they could just as easily be business partners as husband and wife. My family home was always immaculately clean, as if a lifestyle magazine was about to stop by for a photo shoot at any time. Javi's family home was chaotic, in a warm, lived-in way that I adored. It was clear from Javi's interactions with his parents and siblings that there were no secrets, no tensions between them. I struggled to talk to my own father in the rare hours when he was home from the hospital. I was much closer to my mom, but even that felt strained whenever my father was around.

We walked in silence for a while, the waves gently lapping at our feet. I looked over at Javi, his profile silhouetted against the setting sun.

"Did I ever tell you the story of how my parents started the restaurant?" he asked.

"No, I don't think you did," I replied.

"Well, my mom and her brother, my Tio Arturo, crossed the border when they were barely teenagers. They had some family who lived here already. They got jobs in the original restaurant, as a waitress and a busboy. My dad was a line cook at the time. For my mom and dad, it was love at first sight. They got married the second they were both eighteen. My dad was born here, so my mom got citizenship after that."

I stayed quiet, sensing there was more to the story.

"My uncle, though. He never could find a way. He lived in fear every day of his life of getting deported, of being stolen away from his family here. And it was a problem, because he was sick. He had epilepsy, from childhood, but he would never see a doctor. Never get the medicines he needed."

Javi stopped and looked out at the water as the sun disappeared beyond the edge of the horizon.

"Years went by, and he still was too stubborn to get help. My parents had my sisters and me. My parents and my uncle took over ownership of the restaurant. One night, I was sick with the flu, and my uncle told my parents to head home early to take care of me. He offered to close the restaurant after everyone had left.

My parents got there the next day to open the restaurant and found my tio on the floor. He had seized, but they think he never came out of it. And no one was there to help."

My eyes went wide with shock. "Oh, Javi. That's terrible. I'm so sorry for your family's loss."

Javi shrugged sadly. "It was a long time ago. But I still think about it all the time. I know it's ridiculous to blame myself, but sometimes I think, if I hadn't had the flu, maybe he'd still be alive today."

I threw my arms around his shoulders, squeezing him tight to me. "You can't think like that. Of course, it isn't your fault."

"Deep down, I know that," he said. He smiled at me as I pulled away to look at him. "But I do think about him a lot. I want to create something— a device, like a little EEG to detect seizure activity. Something someone can wear, so no one has to go through what my family had to go through."

His voice took on that same, familiar wistful tone that it did whenever he was dreaming and inventing out loud. Javi's mind was a constant churning factory for new ideas, but this one felt different. This one felt exceedingly personal, and I knew somehow that he had been holding onto this idea in his heart, waiting for the right moment to share it with me. And this was that moment—on this beautiful beach, in his hometown, after I had been given the opportunity to meet the people that made him who he was. I felt honored that he had shared it with me. But I knew that, even though Javi constantly came up with new ideas, he rarely sat with one idea for long; rarely thought of a plan to see his ideas through. But this was the one he needed to see through.

"I think this is the one, Javi. I think this is the invention you should make. It's worth something. When we get back to school, I think you should start working on it for real." I squeezed his shoulders to emphasize my words.

He grinned. "Thanks, Doc. You know, I think I will."

We walked along the beach until long after the sun had set.

The rest of the week flew by in a blur of laughter and delicious food. For our last night, Javi's parents planned a huge barbecue in their backyard to send us off to NYC the next day.

Javi and I volunteered to do the last-minute grocery shopping. The local supermarket was bustling with people stocking up for the weekend, and we searched the aisles with our shopping list in hand. Javi was hefting a bag of charcoal onto his shoulder, when I heard a sound beside us.

There was a soft, "*Oh,*" accompanied by a gasp of surprise and a sudden crash. Seeing the girl beside us had dropped her basket of items, various groceries scattering in all directions away from her, Javi dropped the bag of charcoal into our basket and sprang to help her.

"Here, let me—" he began, but his words were suddenly cut off in his throat with an unnatural, strangled sound.

"Javi?" The girl asked, with a mix of surprise and warmth. She was breathtakingly beautiful. She had thick, long, dark hair; full lips; and a sweet, heart-shaped face. Her long, dark lashes were the stuff of mascara ads. And I knew who she was, beyond a shadow of a doubt, without him needing to say anything. His expression of surprise and hurt was more than enough confirmation.

"Sofia," Javi replied, his tone neutral and polite. Without saying anything more, Javi gathered her items and handed her shopping basket back to her. Almost imperceptibly, I noticed

Javi flinch, ever so slightly, when their hands touched. It was like she had electrocuted him with the brush of her skin. I felt like an intruder in a private moment. Sofia's gaze flicked to me, then immediately back to Javi, her eyes narrowing.

Javi glanced over at me, his eyes going wide in panic as he pieced together what Sofia must be thinking. "Sofia, this is Diana, she's—"

"Already?" she asked, her eyes going watery as she searched his face. "It hasn't even been a year, and you're already bringing someone home?"

Javi's head shook immediately, denying it. "It's not like that, Sofia, she's—"

"I know I shouldn't be surprised," she whispered, though I could still hear every word clearly, even from several feet away. I wished desperately that I couldn't, that I was anywhere else. I flattened my back to the shelves, averting my eyes from them. I wanted to walk away, to give them space, but knew it would be even more awkward if I moved and drew attention to myself.

"You were always so charming. *Everyone* loves Javier Valenzuela."

She said it so coldly, like it was a bad thing. I frowned. I supposed I could see how Javi's natural charm might cause some jealousy issues, but he was also the most fiercely loyal friend I had ever known.

"Sofi, I swear, she's just a friend—"

Though I knew the statement to be true, some unpleasant feeling coiled inside me at the sheer force of his denial that we were anything more than friends. As if the alternative, that we were dating, was somehow inconceivable. His protests did nothing to cushion my ego, and it stung more than I cared to admit.

"I should get going," she said quickly, starting to turn in the other direction. "It was good to see you, Javi."

He stood watching the spot from which she had retreated for a long time. He ran his fingers through his hair in frustration, sighing quietly. He turned back to me and grabbed the shopping cart. I trailed after him, unsure what I could say to make the situation better.

We continued our shopping in silence after that, a tension in Javi's shoulders in the wake of Sofia's abrupt appearance and just as abrupt disappearance. I cursed our dumb luck that we had run into her. I found myself angry at a girl I had never met for breaking my friend's heart, and, while it was incredibly selfish to even think, I was angry at her for tarnishing what had otherwise felt like a perfect week.

We didn't speak about her for the entire drive home, and we let the preparations for the party distract us from acknowledging it.

A few hours later, the Valenzuelas' backyard was filled with the mouth-watering smells of grilling meat, the sound of music, and the chatter of happy voices.

I sat at a picnic table with Gaby, Manuela, and Valeria, listening to them share embarrassing stories about Javi's childhood.

"He used to be such a bookworm," Gaby said, laughing. "He would spend hours reading and drawing in his room."

"Yeah, and now he's Mr. Social Butterfly," Manuela added, rolling her eyes. "Always out and about."

Valeria leaned in, her eyes twinkling with mischief. She nudged me. "Do you know he once built a robot out of our old vacuum cleaner? Mom was so mad when she found out."

I laughed along with them, picturing a young Javi tinkering with gadgets and making dangerous objects out of household appliances.

"He hasn't changed much, has he?" I added, smiling.

"Nope," Gaby said, shaking her head. "He has always been a little genius. And a pain in the butt."

Javi walked over, holding a plate filled with delicious-looking food. "Are you all talking about me again?"

"Always," Valeria said, sticking her tongue out at him.

He rolled his eyes and handed me the plate. "Here, I got you all the best stuff."

"Thanks," I said, taking a bite of chicken and savoring the smoky, tangy flavor. "This is amazing."

Javi's sisters watched him settle into place beside me, and I felt their eyes scrutinizing us, laser focused on our proximity.

"Come on, you two," Manuela said. "Be real with us. You mean to tell us you're really not dating?"

We had been staving off subtle hints and good-natured jibes from his family all week. I moved food around on my plate to avoid meeting his sisters' eyes, blushing furiously. I came here to make Javi feel more at ease. To take the pressure off him. And with the terribly awkward encounter with Sofia still weighing on the back of my mind, I knew the question would only make him feel more uncomfortable.

"We're just friends," I insisted.

"Best friends," he added, smiling gratefully at me.

We both chose to ignore his sisters' skeptical looks in response.

A few of the Valenzuelas' friends and extended family members took up instruments and started to play, filling the air with sweet music. Javi's father strummed a guitar. Valeria bounced up from the picnic table, settling in behind a microphone to sing a melody in beautiful, trilling Spanish.

Javi stood up and extended his hand to me. "Dance with me?"

I looked at him, surprised but delighted. "I'd love to."

He led me to the makeshift dance floor in the middle of the yard, where other couples were already swaying to the rhythm. Javi placed one hand on my waist and took my other hand in his, guiding me gracefully across the floor. The music was infectious, and soon we were both laughing and twirling, lost in the music.

"You're a pretty good dancer," I said, trying to catch my breath.

"So are you," he replied, spinning me around again.

We danced until the band played their final song—a slow, sad tune. I couldn't understand the lyrics but understood the meaning anyway. I had to fight the light sting of tears in my eyes. I blinked, trying to shake the feeling off. Javi pulled me in close. I leaned against his shoulder, swaying along with him to the music.

"I'm not ready to go back," I whispered. "I've had such a nice time this week. Your family is so wonderful, Javi. I'm going to miss everyone."

He squeezed me a little tighter to him. He whispered, "We'll be back. You may not realize it yet, but you've been adopted by the Valenzuelas now. You'll always be welcome here."

I felt a surge of warmth swelling through my chest at the idea. "Thank you, Javi. For everything. For inviting me here. For showing me your world. For telling me about your uncle."

"No, thank you," he said, his voice earnest. "For being here. For being you."

The last notes of the music drifted into silence, and the crowd began to cheer and clap for the musicians. Javi's arms remained around me, holding on a moment longer than necessary.

"Thank you for the dance," he whispered, his voice sounding suddenly thick with emotion. I searched his face, but he wouldn't meet my eyes.

"Anytime," I replied, forcing the words to sound casual. My heart thrummed a little uncomfortably in my chest.

After we helped clean up after the party and everyone went home, I lay awake on the Valenzuelas' couch. I could hear Javi's soft breathing from the couch across from mine. I could still feel light tingling on my skin where Javi had held me close on the dance floor. And for a moment, in the dark of the night and the safety of my thoughts, I pictured a world where this *was* my family. Where Javi and I were something more than what we were now. And riding the high of the week we had spent in his childhood home, I couldn't work out which feeling was stronger—wanting to be a part of this family or wanting to feel closer to Javi. Either way, the thought terrified me, for reasons I couldn't quite understand.

I remembered the look on Javi's face when he had seen Sofia earlier that day. He had looked so pained, staring at the girl he had once loved—probably still loved now. The girl he had assumed he would marry. I thought of how a girl who was once closer to Javi and his family than anyone now made him feel sad and uneasy. How he could barely stand the thought of coming home, knowing he might run into her.

And in that moment, I made a vow to myself in the quiet and the dark: no matter what happened, no matter what fleeting feelings might pass through my mind, I would never let anything get in the way of this friendship. Javi meant too much to me, and now his family meant too much to me. I drifted to sleep, feeling resolved.

The next morning, we packed our bags and said our goodbyes. As Javi's parents drove us to the airport, Javi and I sat in silence, lost in our thoughts. We hugged his parents goodbye, his mom teary as she squeezed us both tight.

"You come back soon, okay?" she said to me, holding my face in her soft hands. "And take good care of my boy."

"I will," I promised.

When we were settled in on the plane a couple of hours later, Javi reached over and squeezed my arm lightly.

"You okay?" he asked. We hadn't really spoken to each other since leaving the house, other than a few words while navigating through the airport.

"Yeah," I said, smiling sadly. "Sad to leave."

"Me too," he said. "But now that I can be here again and *survive* it, we can come back whenever you want. Thank you for making home a happy place for me again."

I linked my elbow in his and squeezed his arm back, "I'll hold you to that."

We started to watch a movie together on my iPad, splitting my ear buds so we each had one, but I fell asleep shortly after takeoff. I only woke up when the pilot announced our final descent into JFK. I still had one elbow linked through Javi's, my head had fallen against his shoulder in sleep. From his steady breathing and the weight of his cheek against the top of my head, I figured he was asleep as well. I closed my eyes again and didn't stir, letting the bump of the landing twenty minutes later wake him.

We caught a taxi back to school, watching the skyline approach ahead.

Javi said suddenly, "Diana, I've been thinking."

I stole my attention from the skyline and looked at him. "A dangerous pastime."

He grinned. "I know. But I have been thinking."

"About what?" I asked.

"About us," he said. "About our friendship."

My heart squeezed painfully. I thought back to the night of the barbecue, to dancing and laughing together. I thought of the confusing feelings I ruminated on in the living room of Javi's childhood home. The vow I made not to ruin what we had. I wondered if his mind had been racing with similar thoughts, after our trip together.

"What about it?" I asked, almost too worried to ask the question. This felt like a turning point for us—like his next words would decide the trajectory of our relationship.

He took a deep breath. "I've never had a friend like you, Diana. Someone who understands and supports me like you. Who makes me feel like I can do anything. I don't want to lose that."

"You won't," I said quickly, relieved. "You're my best friend, Javi."

He smiled, a hint of relief in his eyes. "And you're mine, Diana. I'm grateful for that. I just wanted you to know how much you mean to me."

I reached across the leather seat and squeezed his hand, letting it go shortly after. "You mean a lot to me too, Javi. More than you know."

We made the journey back to school and the adventures ahead in contented silence.

Chapter 4

Columbia University

Sophomore Year

I t wasn't often that I found myself wandering the halls of the engineering school. Even less often that I did so on a Saturday, when the place was nearly empty. But desperate times called for desperate measures.

I hadn't seen Javi in days, so it did not feel like an exaggeration to say that these were desperate times. We never went more than a day or two without seeing each other, at most. Not even the summer break had separated us, Javi staying in the city to continue his work in the lab developing his wearable EEG device. Though I had stayed busy too, taking up a scribe position in the ER at Mount Sinai West Hospital, we had been more inseparable than ever. We spent our free hours between shifts sunbathing on the grassy lawns, finding the restaurants and cafés on the upper west side with the best air conditioning, and pretending like we owned the campus in the absence of 90% of our fellow undergraduates.

Since the start of the academic year, however, things had been different. Our coursework this year, Javi's in biomedical engineering and mine in pre-med, had proven to be far more demanding compared to the previous year. Javi had always been a "show up and ace the test" kind of guy. I had always envied his innate and effortless genius. He absorbed knowledge like a sponge. He not only understood difficult scientific concepts incredibly fast, but he seemed to *enjoy* it too. I had seen the guy read a physics textbook as hungrily as I read a *Bridgerton* novel.

But Javi didn't seem to be floating through life as easily this year, not with his invention taking up so much of his time and mental energy. Now that classes had begun, Javi had to work his invention into the little free time provided by his packed course schedule. He had started dating a girl from the engineering school named Ava at the end of the summer, but she had called things off a month ago after feeling like he didn't have enough time for her.

Between the girlfriend and the invention, I had begrudgingly accepted that Javi had less time to spend with me this year. Our adventures in the city had come to a dramatic halt—but I didn't mind that part, really. I didn't care where we were in the world, as long as we got to spend time together. But that time had been dwindling steadily. Even when we did spend time together, Javi hadn't been himself lately. Gone was the carefree soul I knew and loved. In its place was left Javi: The Mad Scientist.

It took me some time to find Javi's lab—I had been there only a couple times before. When I found a door that looked vaguely familiar, I pushed against it, unsurprised when I saw his form across the room, hunched over a desk, illuminated by the harsh glow of his dual screen monitors. I moved quietly down the aisle created between the workbenches toward him. When I was within a few feet of him, I could hear him muttering quietly to himself, sounding frustrated with whatever he was working on. When I was right behind him, he still hadn't noticed me. I could see the tangled nest of wires and circuit boards between his hands.

He sighed and rubbed his eyes. I reached one hand out and rested it on his shoulder. He jumped nearly a foot out of his seat at the unexpected contact. He looked over his shoulder, his eyes narrowing until he realized who I was. His defensive posture—hands flat and raised as if he had been preparing to karate-chop the intruder—relaxed back into its previous hunched and tired form.

"Jesus, Doc," he breathed the words out with a shaky breath. "You scared the ever-loving shit out of me."

I fought a smirk. Though I was concerned about him and hadn't really intended to scare him, seeing him jump into full karate-stance had been hilarious.

"I'm sorry," I replied. "But I wouldn't have had to scare you if I hadn't had to track you down. When was the last time you left this lab?"

I handed him a cup of coffee, and he sipped at it gratefully. He looked at his desk thoughtfully, as if trying to decide when the last time was that he had seen anything else.

"I slept in my dorm last night. At least, I think I did. Maybe that was the night before..."

From the dark shadows beneath his eyes, I was skeptical.

"You need to leave this lab, Javi," I told him sternly. "There's a whole world out there that misses you. *I* miss you."

He smiled at me ruefully. "I'm sorry. I'm just stuck. I was making such good progress with the device these last few months, and I hit a rut this week. I can't seem to get past it."

I put a hand on his shoulder. "You know, sometimes it's

possible to be *too* close to a problem to fix it. You know what I mean?"

He shook his head, his brows furrowing in confusion.

"You know what the doctors I work with in the ER do when they can't figure out a problem? They take a step back, look at the whole picture. Talk it out with a colleague. Gain a new perspective," I explained. "I think that's what you need. You're getting lost in the weeds. Give yourself a little distance from the problem, and you may happen upon the solution."

"Any suggestions on how to do that?" he asked. He looked and sounded so tired, but willing to try.

"Come with me tonight," I suggested.

"Where?" he asked, and I had a suspicion he didn't remember what was happening tonight at all. He probably didn't even remember what day of the week it was.

"To the winter formal," I supplied with a grin.

He scoffed, running a hand through his greasy, disheveled hair as if to highlight the fact that he was not suitable for any formal occasions this evening.

"The winter formal? To do what, dance my problems away?" he asked skeptically.

"You never know where inspiration might strike," I coaxed. "But I *do* know that you need a break. You need to let off some of this steam. I can practically see it coming out of your ears…"

I feigned fanning off his head, and he batted my hands away with a laugh.

"Your brain is frying before my eyes. Give it a break, just for one night." I squeezed between Javi and his desk and leaned against it, forcing his rolling chair back a few inches. Maybe if I physically put myself between him and his invention, I could persuade him to spend one night away from it.

He sighed. "Aren't you going to the dance with that beef-head lacrosse player you've been dating? Brad, or whatever his name is?"

"Brooks," I corrected him, rolling my eyes. "And he's on the rowing team, not the lacrosse team."

"Same thing," he retorted.

"Not even close to the same thing," I countered with a laugh. "One is literally in water. One is on land."

He shrugged. "You're not going with Muscles McGee?"

I shoved him playfully. I *had* been planning on meeting up with Brooks, but I wouldn't say we were "going to the dance together." We had only been on a few dates so far, nothing serious. I would text him to tell him that my friend needed me tonight instead.

"Come with me," I insisted. "It'll be fun."

He sighed again, deeply, but I could tell I was winning the battle. Honestly, I couldn't remember a single instance since the day I met him that he had told me no.

"Fine," he relented, and I cheered. "But I'm not wearing a suit. I don't even think I own a suit."

"I don't care what you wear," I told him. I made a show of sniffing the air around him. "I do care that you shower though."

He laughed. "I can do that."

"If you go now, you could even take a nap," I suggested, still concerned by how much fatigue he held in his bloodshot eyes.

He nodded. "Not a bad idea."

"I'll meet you on the sundial at eight," I told him.

I watched him pack up his things and walked out of the lab with him at my side. We parted ways on Broadway to head back to our separate dorms.

A few hours later, I walked up the pathway leading

from Butler library to the sundial—a dangerous feat. The old cobblestones in front of the library were treacherous to tread upon on a good day, in sensible shoes. My shoes for the evening were not sensible—they were four-inch-tall gold heels with very thin straps.

I had decided last minute, after parting with Javi that afternoon, to make the trip to my parents' apartment to acquire a heavy garment bag from the back of my closet. My original plan had been to wear the same black cocktail dress that I had worn to a dozen other formal events before. That dress was flattering, but nothing special. The dress that I now wore instead was the one I had worn to my senior prom, and I had secretly been longing for any excuse to wear it again. The silhouette of the dress was rather simple—a satin sweetheart neckline, a tulle A-line skirt. But the structured corset, the high slit over my left thigh, and the bright, cherry-red color of the fabric made me feel like I was Aphrodite incarnate.

I lifted the skirts of the dress as I made my way a little clumsily down the path, watching my feet as I walked to make sure my heel didn't catch on any of the deep cracks in the pathway. I stopped suddenly when I saw an outstretched hand in front of me.

I looked up, knowing instantly who that hand belonged to. I beamed at Javi.

He grinned down at me, looking much happier than he had a few hours before. Of course it was dark out, but I couldn't see those large circles under his eyes anymore. I suspected he had taken that nap that I suggested. He looked clean and put together. He didn't wear a suit, as promised, but he looked nice in his black button-down and black slacks. He had on a long, gray coat that he had left open despite the chilly evening.

"You came," I remarked.

"I did," he replied, with a slightly guilty expression. "I considered staying in my bed and sleeping for the rest of the weekend, but I'm glad I came. Diana, you look..."

I raised an eyebrow when he went silent, waiting patiently for the adjective he was searching for.

"Like you're going to fall," he finally supplied, with a burst of laughter. "These pathways weren't built for heels. I think they were built before heels were invented, in fact."

I rolled my eyes at him. I don't know what I had been expecting, really—Javi didn't typically comment on how I looked. But considering that most days I spent with my hair in a ponytail, minimal makeup, sitting in the library wearing a t-shirt and jeans, you would think he would at least take notice.

I took his offered hand. He threaded his arm through mine, lending me a stable support as I crossed the commons. We made our way up the many steps of Low Library, past the statue of *Alma Mater*.

The music reached us well before we made it into the building. We checked our coats and made our way into the center of the building, the grand rotunda. Though the building was called "Low Library," it hardly contained any books. It had been the university's main library over a hundred years ago, before Butler was built. Now, it served as mostly administrative offices, doubling as an event center for nights such as these.

The theme of the evening was "A Night Under the Stars," and the space had been decorated accordingly. The room was lined with enormous marble pillars, and between each pillar hung heavy curtains of midnight blue. A celestial scene was projected upward onto the domed ceiling above.

After we had both taken a moment to stop and admire the beautiful venue, we started searching the crowds for familiar faces. Javi found several quickly, as he always did —some friends from the engineering school, some former floormates from John Jay. After that, I started to lose track of how he knew the people we spoke with, since it seemed like he knew just about everyone. But I didn't mind stopping each time to converse with people who loved Javi, because each time, his face lit up in a way that it hadn't in weeks. This is what I had been hoping for.

Javi was a social creature. He thrived on the energy of people around him. He loved being around friends, and they loved being near him. He didn't do well in isolation, and he had been isolating himself to an extreme. So, even though I was never particularly extroverted myself, I didn't mind pretending—I knew this was what he needed. So I chatted and socialized and danced at his side.

A slow song started to play, and our group dispersed, either to couple up or retreat to the periphery. Before I could turn to hide in the margins of the room, Javi held a hand out to me.

"Dance with me?" he asked.

I smiled, putting my hand in his and letting him pull me in for a dance. We started to sway to the steady rhythm of the song.

"Thanks for getting me out of the lab," he said against my hair.

"Thanks for *letting* me get you out of the lab," I responded. As we turned, I looked up at the flashing of faux starlight against the inside of the domed ceiling. I thought it bore some resemblance to the flashing of neurons inside the brain.

I stopped admiring the ceiling to meet Javi's gaze. "Has anything inspired you yet?"

He pushed me away gently into a spin. My red skirt fanned out around me, and I laughed in delight.

"Yeah, I'd say I've been pretty inspired," he said warmly, grinning at me as he drew me back in.

After a pause, he added, "Did I tell you yet that you look amazing tonight?"

A flush heated my cheeks at the compliment. "No, you didn't. You told me I looked like I didn't know how to walk."

He laughed at the reminder. "Oh yeah. I guess I did."

The laughter in his eyes settled into something different —something pointed and piercing. My skin tingled in a not unpleasant way in response.

When the song ended, I pulled away from him, avoiding meeting his eyes. I still felt very flushed and hoped he wouldn't notice.

"Thirsty?" he asked, his voice sounding a little hoarse. He cleared it before asking, "Want a drink?"

I nodded, grateful for the opportunity to collect myself in his absence, and I watched him retreat in the direction of the refreshments. I tried in vain to convince myself that the fluttering sensation of my heart was from dancing. But that little voice in the back of my mind—the one that had to be stifled every now and then—said traitorously, *friends don't look at friends the way he just looked at you.*

Stop it, I admonished that voice.

Breaking me out of my internal debate, I heard a deep voice behind me say, "Punch?"

I turned in surprise, seeing Brooks. He was wearing a blue suit with a Columbia blue shirt and tie, his blond hair swept up in a purposefully messy kind of way. He held a cup toward me with red liquid inside. I knew Javi would be back any second now with another drink, but I didn't want to offend Brooks more than I already had after blowing him off tonight. I took the offered drink.

"Thanks," I told him. "It's good to see you."

"Yeah. How's your friend?" he asked.

"He's good. Feeling a lot better," I replied. "He was going through a hard time."

He stayed quiet, sipping his glass of punch without meeting my eyes.

"Are you having a nice time?" I asked, trying to fill the heavy silence.

His broad shoulders lifted in a shrug. "Could be better."

I started to lift the cup to my lips as I thought of how to respond, wondering if I should apologize for my role in his less-than-perfect night.

It was then that Javi returned to my side, handing me another glass of punch that I awkwardly accepted.

"Dude, what's your problem?" Brooks asked Javi, and his angry tone immediately set warning bells off in my mind.

Javi peered up at Brooks, looking only vaguely concerned by his threatening tone. "What do you mean?"

"Can't you see we were talking?" Brooks demanded, his eyes narrowing. He inched closer to Javi, his chest seeming to inflate as his shoulders squared. Despite their obvious physical differences, Javi didn't seem at all intimidated by him. He held his ground firmly as Brooks approached.

"I was just bringing her some punch," Javi responded, his tone neutral.

"Are you blind?" Brooks asked. "She's got a glass right there."

My eyes darted between the two of them as they spoke. My mind reeled, trying to figure out how to dispel the tension before things progressed any further.

Javi shrugged. "Look, dude, it's no big deal—"

"No big deal that you're all over my girlfriend?" Brooks seethed.

What had before sounded like quiet warning bells in my mind now sounded like blaring sirens. Anger surged through me, hot and boiling and unexpected in its immediate intensity. For one, I wasn't Brooks' *girlfriend*—we had been on a few dates. We had no conversations about the exclusivity of this relationship, nor had he given me any signs that he wanted something serious with me. And Javi had not been *all over me*.

I shook my head in protest. "Brooks, we're friends."

"*Friends* my ass," he responded, never taking his eyes off Javi.

Javi crossed his arms over his chest, his voice still unnervingly calm despite the anger radiating from Brooks. "Seriously, bro, you've got the wrong idea."

Brooks looked from Javi back to me, his glare boring into my face. "Whatever. It's not worth the trouble for a dumb slut like you anyway."

The words pierced into my mind like daggers. The next few seconds seemed to pass in slow motion. I *knew* with every fiber of my being that Javi was not going to stand for this. He was not going to let Brooks get away with calling me such an ugly name. But I also knew that Brooks had six inches of height and fifty pounds of muscle on Javi and could put him in the hospital, if he so desired.

Before either of them could move an inch, I stepped between them, my back to Javi and my hands held out toward Brooks, though I still held both glasses of punch. Javi's chest pressed briefly against my back as I halted his approach, and I stumbled forward a bit with the impact, sloshing some punch on the floor in front of me. I could practically feel both their anger as a physical heat radiating between them.

"Walk away, Brooks. Just go," I instructed him calmly, despite my heart pounding violently against my ribs, my blood pulsing through my veins.

He sneered at me, turning to leave. But at the last second, he popped the cups out from my hands, the remaining liquid splashing upward onto my face and chest and the bodice of my dress. He strode away before I could react. I stood stunned for several long seconds before reaching up to wipe some of the dripping red liquid from beneath my eyes. My skin was already turning sticky with it. I felt my breath hitch in my throat and my chest grow tight.

I needed space. I needed to not be surrounded by people and sound and lights. I needed to get out of here.

I moved quickly to the back of the room, shoving through the heavy midnight blue curtains into the hallway. It was lined with administrative offices, with tall, official-looking wooden doors. The hallway was lined down the middle with marble busts atop pedestals. I braced myself against one of the statues. Now that I had a chance to register what happened over the last several minutes, my brain felt like it was on fire. My chest started to heave uncomfortably, my breaths becoming more ragged with each passing second.

Javi emerged into the hallway after less than a minute, his expression changing quickly from panic to relief when he found me.

"Diana," he said, approaching me slowly as if I were a skittish deer that might bolt at any moment. "Are you okay?"

I nodded, though I knew deep down it was a lie. My voice came out shakier than I wanted. "Yeah. Needed a second to breathe."

He looked conflicted—his face passing through a full

range of emotion. I couldn't process his emotions while I dealt with a full spectrum of my own—anger, embarrassment, panic. I slid to the ground, leaning against the statue behind me as my skirt billowed around me. I leaned forward and rested my face in my hands but was immediately grossed out by the sticky sensation.

"I've got so much punch on me," I complained.

"Here," Javi said, and he knelt on the ground in front of me. He held a damp cloth in his hands, and when I lifted my face to meet his eyes, he started to clean the sticky punch off my cheeks. I wondered vaguely where he got it, imagining him charming it off a waiter, but didn't care enough to ask. He lowered the cloth from my face as if to clean off my chest, but then stopped short. He handed it to me instead and stood once more, presumably to give me some space. I cleaned the sticky patches off my neck and chest, watching him pace in front of me.

I thought of how close Javi had been to being hurt, and I winced at the thought.

"What are you thinking right now?" I asked him quietly. His brows were furrowed, and there was a dark shadow in his eyes. I had never seen him look so agitated before. The question made him pause in his pacing briefly. He made an exasperated noise.

"I'm thinking you really know how to pick'em, Diana," he said, and his harsh words felt like they physically cut me as they left his lips. I flinched.

"You're blaming me for this?" I whispered feebly.

"*No!*" He ran his hands through his hair in frustration. "God, I'm sorry. That was the worst thing I could have possibly said. He's an asshole. He's not worth your time, anyway."

We stayed quiet for several minutes. He finally stopped pacing and sat on the floor at the foot of the adjacent statue six feet away. He stared into the distance, at the little marble statuette above my head.

Several minutes later, I heard him quietly chuckle. I looked at him curiously.

"What's so funny?" I asked him, my voice sounding as tired as I felt. All the adrenaline was starting to seep out of me, leaving a pit of exhaustion behind it.

"Of all the moments for inspiration to strike," he muttered, sounding almost annoyed at the idea. "I think I know how to fix my device."

"What was it that inspired you?" I asked, too tired to sound pleased, even if inspiring Javi had been the entire point of the evening.

He pointed to the figure above me. "The statue. It's Artemis."

I looked up at the little figure of a maiden in a toga with a bow and arrow, aimed at some unseen prey in the general direction of the dean's office. A tiny marble deer stood in wait near her hip. I didn't know if the curve of her bow had revealed some vector that he had been searching for to perfect his device, or if the sweep of her hair back from her marble head had shown him some perspective on the brain he hadn't yet thought of.

"The Greek goddess?" I asked. I looked around at the row of similar statues and busts. They all looked like gods or goddesses of some sort. I recognized them vaguely but wasn't particularly good with all that mythology stuff.

He stared at her intently, deep in thought. Even if he explained the logic behind what inspired him, I'm not sure that I would have understood it. But I was glad that he had found inspiration somewhere.

"Do I need to let you get back to your lab?" I asked him.

He shook his head, coming out of the spell he was

under suddenly. "No, the idea can wait until the morning. Let's get out of here?"

He posed it as a question, and I took him up on the offer gratefully. He lifted himself off the ground and lent me a hand, pulling me up off the marble floor. We followed the hallway all the way around the building, avoiding dipping back into the dance. We retrieved our coats and made our way out into the cold night.

We walked across the commons, directly toward Butler without discussing it. Rather than struggle to traverse the pathway again, I wrenched my heels off and held them in one hand as we walked. The security guard didn't even look up at us in our formal wear when we scanned our IDs to enter the library. The library was as empty as I had ever seen it, most of the usual occupants currently across the commons at the dance. Our path through the library was so familiar, I would have bet I could find my way in my sleep. Down the hallway on the top floor, through the gray door to the stairwell, up the stairs, past the tattered copy of *The Iliad.*

We had hidden a few blankets in the stairwell since the weather had turned cold, and we pulled them out now. When we were settled on one of the blankets on our familiar ledge, I linked my arm with his and leaned over to rest my head on his shoulder. Across the lawn, we could still hear the dull sound of dance music coming from the doors of Low.

"I'm sorry about tonight," I whispered.

He made an annoyed scoff. "Don't apologize for the actions of a dickhead like him."

I sighed. "I wanted this to be a fun, relaxing night for you. I wanted to give you a chance to be carefree, like the old days. Instead, you nearly got the shit beaten out of you, because of me."

"It wasn't your fault," he said. "But for the record, I think I could have taken him."

I chuckled, patting his knee in a consolatory way. "You keep thinking that."

He said, "Well, seeing you throw yourself in front of me like a fucking human shield scared the shit out of me, but it was also impressive as hell. So maybe I couldn't have taken him, but I think we could have fended him off together."

I squeezed his arm gently. "I was only able to be brave because I knew you had my back."

"It's you and me against the world, Doc," he said. "Always."

"Always," I agreed.

Chapter 5

Columbia University

Junior Year

I was on the floor of my dorm room, surrounded by a veritable pit of notebooks and textbooks—Physics, Organic Chemistry, French Literature, Immunology, Buddhism, and MCAT prep. The last was giving me the biggest aneurysm of all the subjects. The MCAT was about to drive me to the end of my already fraying rope.

I would be applying to medical school this summer, in just a few months. The deadline to get my MCAT score where I needed it to be in order to be competitive was a few weeks away. And that goal seemed insurmountable.

I had taken the test once already, back in the fall, and my score at that time was truly abysmal. I had my suspicions about why I had done so poorly, of course. I didn't have a PhD in clinical psychology like Javi's older sister, but I *had* taken a psychology class before. I was no expert, but I think it might have had something to do with the Earth-shattering, horrible new experience my brain decided to provide me with the night before my exam—a full-blown, heaving, crying fit of a panic attack.

I had always dealt with some test anxiety. But never

had my anxiety reared its head in such a physical, demanding, and all-consuming way as it had in that moment. The experience left me crumpled on the floor in the fetal position. I woke up for my exam the next morning, still on the floor, achy all over from sleeping on the uncomfortable surface, and I barely made it to my testing center in time. After the exam, I slept for two days straight, feeling like I had been chewed on at the edges by some invisible beast, leaving open wounds that only I could see.

Javi had been in Houston that weekend, visiting his sister Valeria in the hospital after the birth of her baby. He had wanted me to come too but knew I had the test scheduled. Obviously, I didn't blame him for being with his family for such a beautiful occasion, but I *knew* somehow that if Javi had been there to witness my attack, it wouldn't have hit me quite so hard. He might have even been able to prevent it from happening in the first place. He always pulled me out of my anxiety before tests, always knew exactly what to say or do. But he wasn't there to get me a milkshake or sit on the roof of Butler and talk my worries away.

And even though Javi was the person with whom I shared everything; I didn't have the heart to tell him about it when he came back from Texas. He was glowing with all his best uncle pride as he showed me pictures of the chubby-cheeked little princess with her full head of hair, ready for bows.

So when he asked me how the test went, I muttered a lame "oh, it went fine, I think" and moved on. I couldn't tell him about the panic attack, because I could barely voice it aloud myself.

I tried not to think about that day at all, if I could help it. I feared that acknowledging that that day existed might lower my brain's tolerance for stress to some point where it could happen again. I constantly sensed the possibility of another attack, lingering in the periphery like a predator lurking in the shadows, waiting to claim me again as its prey.

Javi didn't need to bear that weight too. He had enough going on, with his own classes and his invention, that took every moment of his time and energy when he wasn't in class or with me.

When Javi walked into my room on this sunny Sunday afternoon in March, I was sprawled across my soft rug, discarded coffee cups and snack packages strewn around me, in the middle of another one of my crisis moments. My hands covered my eyes to block out the room's harsh fluorescent lighting and avoid the headache starting to form after staring at lines of tiny text for hours. Javi stepped over me and simply said, "Hey, Doc."

My roommates must have let him in—they didn't really question his presence in our four person suite anymore. Luckily, they, like everyone who knew Javi, couldn't resist him, never complained about his frequent presence in our shared living space.

I peered between my fingers, watching him plop heavily down onto my bed, burying his head immediately into my pink pillow. I rose up onto my elbows, narrowing my eyes at his form with concern.

"Everything alright there, Jav?" I asked, though his posture was already answering my question for me, loudly.

He muttered something unintelligible into my pillow that sounded vaguely like, "*ama hofuffy*."

That couldn't be right.

"Come again?" I asked, a bit of amusement creeping into my voice. I crawled across the floor toward my bed and poked him in the side. He immediately rolled away from the contact as if I electrocuted him—note to self: Javi is *ticklish*. Just when you think you know everything about someone, they can surprise you.

With his face now out of my pillow, I could hear him clearly when he said, "I'm a nobody."

I frowned at his declaration, immediately hating hearing those words come from his mouth. Javier Valenzuela was not a *nobody*, not to anyone who met him. His professors adored him, other students worshipped him.

Columbia students normally hated people as brilliant as Javi—people who sailed through so easily without spending ungodly hours in the Butt. But once someone met Javi, they couldn't help but love him. Even if you envied him from afar, those feelings of resentment seemed to dissolve in his presence.

"Who told you that?" I muttered in a warning tone, clear that I had strong opinions on this person and plans to ensure their imminent demise.

"I did," he responded with a groan of frustration. "Because it's true."

I blinked in surprise. Well, there goes my grand plans for destroying the naysayer who bad-mouthed my best friend.

"Why do you say that?" I asked.

He sat up, sitting on the edge of the bed, looking down at me on the floor where I sat in front of his shoes. "My invention. The Artemis. It's right there, on the precipice of being something great. But I'm reaching the end of my and my mentor's abilities here. We need an expert to make sure we are fine-tuning it correctly before it's too late to go back."

"Okay?" I asked, still not quite sure how this led to Javi calling himself a *nobody*.

"And we're in the God damn greatest city on Earth," he exclaimed, and I smiled before I could help it. I loved how much he loved my city, and I loved the faintest hint of a southern drawl that always popped out when he cursed. Javi didn't have a strong accent, by any means, but you could hear the slightest twang in his deep voice when he got excited or cursed or got drunk. Sometimes I brought him extra drinks at parties just so I could talk to cowboy Javi for a little while (not that he had any idea that's what I called it).

"We are," I agreed.

"So *of course*," he continued, standing abruptly from my bed. He started to pace the tiny space in my room, weaving through my books and trash. "The exact person I need to make this device truly, decidedly *great*? Lives here, in the city. His name is Henrik Carlyle. He is the utmost expert on electroencephalography. He has a Nobel fuckin' prize for his work."

The name rang some vague bell in the back of my mind—where had I heard that name before? Had I watched his Nobel acceptance? Had my professors mentioned him during the neurology unit? The thought was itching my brain in some weird, inaccessible place.

"Great?" I asked, hesitantly.

"Not great," he replied brusquely.

"Not great," I echoed. "Why not great?"

"Because he won't give me the time of day," he finally said. "And that's putting it kindly. His assistant's secretary's *intern* won't give me the time of day. He is locked behind a brick wall of academic bureaucracy so thick not even my professors at the engineering school can get to him. I can't find a contact who knows him to save my life."

He stopped pacing to flop back onto my bed, screaming into my pink pillow for good measure, as if his frustration was not yet clear.

As he wallowed in self-pity, I thought again to that

name. *Henrik Carlyle. Henrik Carlyle.* By no means, a common name. It would stick with you, clearly, once you had heard it.

"And where in town did you say he works?" I asked, my mouth pursing as I mulled over where I could have heard that name.

He rose from the pillow to say, "The Med School. He's an MD, PhD here. The same *damn* institution, and nobody can get me an *in.*"

The realization sunk into my brain like the plop of a stone into the bottom of a river.

Oh. Dr. Carlyle.

His picture came into my mind more clearly than I would have thought—a short, somewhat portly, bespectacled, balding man with a vague trace of an eastern European accent. An accent that I had heard, multiple times: in my parents sitting room at cocktail parties, at reunions for my father's medical school class, chatting with my father at my mom's charity functions.

My mom's charity functions, I thought. I could almost see the light bulb flickering on above my head.

I opened my mouth to speak excitedly to Javi, and then stopped again abruptly, my mouth closing with a snap of my teeth. I swallowed hard, conflicted. I knew I could do it. I knew that *I* was Javi's in. Even more so, I knew that Javi had no idea that I was his in, even if he suspected that my father might know him.

And if he did suspect my father could put him in contact with Dr. Carlyle, I doubt he would ever ask me to do anything about it. He would never ask me to call in a favor with my father. He knew how much it would kill me to do it, to ask him for anything that he could then hold over me for the next ten years. And he would. I was certain of it.

But it was worth it, I thought, if it meant that Javi would get his invention into the world. That's what mattered.

I looked over at Javi's form, inspecting him. He was by no means a large person, at 5'11 and average build. But he looked very large and out of place on my pink and gold frilly comforter. I inspected his clothes—he wore faded blue jeans and a black henley, with a few red stains on the sleeves, likely from chemicals in his lab. Javi had told me multiple times before that he didn't own a suit. And even a suit wouldn't do, in this circumstance. I nodded, resolving finally that I knew what to do.

I stood, patting him impatiently on the shoulder.

"Come on. Get up." I kicked my bed post to make it shake a little. He glared up at me, gravely offended.

"Can't you just let me die here from self-pity?" he groaned.

I shook my head, saying firmly, "Sure can't. Let's go. We're going to midtown."

"Midtown?" he asked, confused. "What's in midtown?"

"No time," I said, gathering my wristlet and my phone from my nightstand. "I'll explain when we get there."

Javi followed me out of the dorms and down to the subway, peppering me with questions about our destination that I ignored. I called my mom as soon as we made it out onto the street.

"Hi, Sweetie," my mom's tender voice answered. "This is a nice surprise."

"Hey, Mom," I said. "I know you're busy this week, so I won't keep you too long. Any chance you have two extra tickets for Saturday? For Javi and me?"

"*Oh,*" my mom gushed. "Wouldn't that be lovely. You haven't been to one of my events in years, not since you started school. I would love that. I'm sure I can squeeze you in."

"Awesome," I said. "Do you think you could also call Pam and see if she could see us in like, thirty minutes? We both need something for the event."

My mom made another emphatic cooing noise, telling me how pleased she was with the idea. "Oh, if only I could meet you two! I have the final meeting with the florist, though. What a shame. But of course, I can get you in. I can't wait to see what you pick out!"

I smiled, a little feebly, though I knew she couldn't see it. Javi, however, was meticulously scrutinizing my face for some evidence of what I was talking about.

"Thanks, Mom," I replied. "Love you. See you Saturday."

Javi raised an eyebrow, expecting an explanation that I didn't give. I didn't think he would agree to it if I told him where we were going.

Half an hour later, we stepped off the elevator on the fifth floor of Saks Fifth Avenue into a room that smelled like Chanel No. 5. A familiar woman in a tailored, pink pant suit approached us as soon as we walked in. She smiled at us warmly, but I could feel Javi next to me recoiling at her approach. I peered over at him, watching his shoulders visibly begin to hunch and his strides grow shorter as if he was going to stop and turn back. He looked like he expected her to ask him to leave. I firmly linked my arm in his and led him forward.

"Miss Diana, how lovely to see you," the woman greeted me, with all the familiarity of someone who had watched me change about a hundred times. She leaned forward and kissed both my cheeks. "It has been *so* long."

I shrugged, a little awkwardly, but joked, "Only so

many dresses a girl needs to sit in a dusty library. That's all I seem to do these days."

She laughed at my joke like I was uproariously funny—I knew I wasn't. And though Javi also laughed at my jokes usually, when he wasn't petrified as he was now, he shot me a concerned look like he was worried about this woman's sanity when he heard that unnerving laugh.

I cleared my throat, which brought the laughter to an abrupt halt. "Pam, this is Javier Valenzuela, my best friend at Columbia. Javi, this is Pamela Jorgensen."

Javi offered his hand politely, but the small flicker of panic in his eyes made it look like he thought Pam might bite it like a rabid chihuahua. With her tiny frame, sandy blonde hair, and high-pitched, almost *yapping* laugh, it seemed like an apt comparison. I bit my lip to stifle laughter at his expression.

Pam took his hand and shook it vigorously. "So nice to meet you, Javier. I understand you'll be attending Mrs. Richards's charity gala this weekend as Miss Diana's date?"

Javi's eyes went wide, then flitted to me and back to Pam several times.

"I am?" he asked.

"He is," I confirmed, squeezing Javi's arm where it was linked in mine, trying to be reassuring.

"May I interest you both in a glass of champagne before we get started?" Pam asked, grabbing two glasses of golden liquid from the nearby desk that she handed to us. I took the glass from her and nudged Javi forward to take his when he didn't immediately accept it. He looked at the glass with all the confidence of someone who had only been of legal drinking age for a few months and was still worried about people calling him out for his fake ID. I had turned twenty-one more recently, but I had been drinking champagne in the Fifth

Avenue Club since I was probably fifteen or sixteen. It was my consolation prize for sitting in this room since I could remember, watching my mom shop for hours and hours on end.

I took a sip of the champagne, and the action apparently encouraged Javi enough to venture a sip of his own. I swore I heard the softest moan escape him at the taste. I felt the oddest little flutter in my gut at the sound but swallowed another large gulp of champagne to douse the sensation.

"Mr. Valenzuela, if you'll follow me," Pam requested, and she pulled his arm from mine to link it through her own. He looked back at me, still visibly terrified, as the tiny woman whisked him away. I gave him an encouraging smile and a thumbs up.

After a few minutes, Pam returned to me and took my empty glass. "Mr. Valenzuela is getting his measurements with our tailor now. Miss Diana, your mom gave me a short list of designers to choose from. If you'll come with me this way—I have some selections in your size that I think you'll find to your liking."

I spent an hour going through the dresses Pam had set aside for me, finally settling on a satin dress with a scooping, open back in a pale-yellow color that reminded me of sunshine. While I normally gravitated toward winter tones that complemented my creamy skin and blue eyes, I pictured the dress next to Javi's warm, summery features and thought it would complement him well. And this night was going to be all about Javi. I changed back into my normal jeans and Columbia t-shirt and ventured out to find Javi.

I looked around the room, seeing an unfamiliar figure next to the mirror in the distance. This was odd, I thought. Pamela usually held the room privately for my family when we came. They usually didn't bring up other clients at the same time, though maybe they would not extend the same courtesy to me without either of my parents here.

But then the figure turned.

It was him. Except it wasn't him.

I stopped in my tracks, my jaw falling slack.

He looked incredible. The black tuxedo on his form made his somewhat boxy figure, usually hidden beneath baggy, stained t-shirts, suddenly seem like the epitome of the perfect male form. His shoulders looked strong and broad, and he stood with impeccable posture, as if the clothing forced him to straighten his spine and puff out his chest impressively. It was a marked contrast to his usual posture, typically hunched over a lab desk or sprawled lazily across some piece of furniture. It was amazing what clothes could do to a person when they fit well.

He caught my eye as I approached and shot me a smile. His normal smile was already radiant. But right now, it was nearly blinding. I felt like I was looking straight into the sun. And it struck me suddenly that, while Javi was already charming, he had only ever reached a fraction of his potential. With the right clothes, he could be truly *heart-breaking*.

When I was a foot away from him, there was a sudden tightness beneath my sternum. My breath caught short.

I froze as he leaned forward. Pam had clearly spritzed him with some kind of cologne, because his usual scent was mixed with something else that I didn't recognize but smelled incredible. It made my mouth *water*.

I could feel his warm breath against my cheek as he whispered, "Di, this is really fun and all, but have you seen these price tags? I can't afford this stuff—"

"It's my treat," I insisted. I took a step back from him, feeling like my head was going fuzzy with the smell of Javi's scent and the cologne.

He shook his head rapidly. "I couldn't possibly accept—"

"You can and you will," I commanded. I crossed my arms over my chest. "My mom's annual charity gala is this Saturday. Dr. Carlyle never misses one of my mom's events. But you have to look the part if you're going to be my date."

Javi looked temporarily stunned by this information, before a slow, mischievous smile crept over his face. My heart gave another pang at the sight. And even though I had signed us up for an evening with my parents, my father in particular, I would have done it a thousand times over again if it meant I could make Javi smile like that.

Pam took our selections for alterations, promising she would have our outfits delivered to Columbia before the following weekend. As we stepped foot onto Fifth Avenue, Javi looked over at me, more than a little awe-struck.

"So..." he began, and I purposefully avoided his stare, somehow knowing what his next line of questioning would be about. "No offense, Doc, but you don't give off *personal-shopper-at-Saks* vibes. Or at least you didn't, until today."

I sighed. If there was anyone who I wanted not to see me that way, it was Javi.

"That's on purpose," I explained. "I've been shopping for my own clothes since I left for college. I brought some staples with me but left most of my designer stuff at home."

"But *why?*" he asked with an incredulous laugh.

I gestured up to the historic department store. "Because *this* is not who I am. At least, not who I feel like inside. I have felt like a doll being dressed up for my entire life. Only since I started at Columbia have I begun to feel like my own person. This place is another reflection of generations of family wealth and my dad's outrageously high-paying job. None of it has anything to do with me. None of that money is mine."

He laughed again. "But it will be yours *someday*, right?"

I frowned, shrugging. "I don't know. I imagine I'm one more mediocre MCAT score away from being stricken from the will entirely. Stay tuned."

His jaw dropped, and he looked panicked. "Fuck, Diana I completely forgot. I was so obsessed with my own shit. You've got the MCAT in a couple weeks. You're doing this all for me, and you've got the test coming up. I'm so sorry—"

"Don't worry about it." I gave him a reassuring smile, though my stomach lurched at the thought of the test. "It's a welcome distraction. Let's go get you your expert."

The following weekend, Javi and I ascended the steps of the Museum of Natural History to the gala, which this year was benefitting the ALS Association. The security guard found our names on a list, and we were ushered to a table with my parents and several of the highest-ranking doctors from the medical school. My parents greeted us— my mom with hugs, my father with handshakes. My mom looked lovely in a sparkling black one-shoulder dress. My dad wore his usual black tux, but even though he was an arguably impressive man, he didn't look nearly as spectac- ular in the suit as Javi did. The thought made me smile a little. We settled in beside them for dinner.

"So, Diana," Dr. Chaudry, Chief of Internal Medicine, asked me halfway through the salad course. "You'll be applying for medical school this year, will you not?"

I nodded, chewing slowly on a walnut. I swallowed. "Yes, sir. Applications are due this summer."

My father made a derisive sound in the back of his

throat, and I winced. "Not if her MCAT score has anything to say about it."

I flushed, looking down at my plate. My insides roiled with a hot whirlpool of embarrassment and shame. Out of the corner of my eye, I noticed Javi look from my father and then back to me. He was frowning deeply.

"Well, there's always Columbia," said Dr. Norwood, Chief Medical Officer of the hospital. "She could send in a blank MCAT exam and still get into Columbia."

A chorus of deep, hearty male laughter followed this sentiment. I clenched my fork so hard I could feel it leaving an impression in my skin. I stayed completely silent for the rest of the dinner and the speeches, waiting for the seated portion of the evening to conclude so I could leave this damn table. As soon as it was polite, I leaned over to congratulate my mom on another beautifully planned event and excused myself and Javi. I rose from the table, dragging Javi with me.

The gala attendees started to wander to the open bar or the dance floor, and I searched the crowd of faces, pulling Javi along with me all the while.

"Diana?" Javi asked. I didn't stop or turn around. "Diana, wait. Can you please stop for a second. Can we talk about—"

"There," I muttered to myself. "That's him."

I made a beeline for the man standing at the edge of the room.

I pulled Javi along, not acknowledging his protests as I did.

"Dr. Carlyle," I said formally as we stopped before him. "I don't know if you remember me—"

"Diana, is it not?" he asked kindly, extending a hand to me with a smile. "Hunt's daughter?"

I forced myself not to frown, nodding. "Yes, sir. Diana

Richards. I'd love to introduce you to my friend, Javier Valenzuela. He's top of his class at SEAS engineering school. He is developing a portable EEG device that you simply *must* hear about. I think, even as accomplished as you are, sir, that you will be impressed by his work."

Dr. Carlyle turned to Javi, his eyes going wide with obvious interest. Javi was still looking at me, concern evident on his face. I gave him an encouraging smile, nodding at him as if to say, *don't worry about me. Dazzle him.*

After a long moment, Javi turned away from me finally and began to speak.

An hour later, we walked down the steps of the museum, one famous EEG expert richer.

Javi stopped in front of the statue of Teddy Roosevelt on his horse, turning to me and scooping me up into a massive hug. He twirled me around and around as we laughed.

"You did it!" he cheered as he let me back down to Earth. "Diana, that was... this was... I can't believe you did this for me. Henrik Fucking Carlyle is going to help me with my device."

"I'm pretty sure that's not his legal middle name." I laughed. I straightened the straps of my dress, where they had fallen catawampus with his embrace. "But I didn't do anything. You did all the talking. I just introduced you."

He looked at me, amazed, and then gestured to himself, to his beautiful tuxedo. "I could never have done anything like this without you, Di."

I hoped the dark of the night covered my blush. I shrugged. "It was nothing."

"It was *everything*," he refuted immediately.

I looked up, and his gaze on me was so intense with the force of his adoration that it made my breath hitch in my throat. For a moment, we were locked there, staring at each other in wonder. My heart beat loudly in my ears. He was so close that his scent filled my nose, and I wondered if Pam had sent him home with a bottle of that cologne. I once again appreciated just how impressive he looked in that tux. *Heartbreaking* had been the description that had come to mind.

He's your friend, I admonished myself. *He's your best friend.*

I shook my head, trying to clear it, and stepped away from him. I averted my eyes, not wanting to get locked beneath his intense gaze once more.

"Shall we head back to school?" I asked him, my voice a tad high-pitched.

"Yeah... yeah, let's head back," he said, and I swore I heard the faintest hint of disappointment in his voice, beneath all that glee. "But I don't think I'll be able to sleep for hours."

"To the roof, then?" I asked.

"To the stars," he corrected with a brilliant smile.

Chapter 6

Columbia University

Senior Year

I was just another drop in a vast ocean of blue.

The steps of Low Library, all the way down to the sundial, were filled with row after row after row of bleachers, filled with graduates clad in Columbia-blue gowns and caps of different colors and shapes depending on the degree that the wearer was receiving that day. I sat in the middle of the section devoted to the graduates from Columbia College. I knew that somewhere to my left, Javi was there among the graduates from SEAS engineering school. The rest of the commons, turned over the last week into an enormous outdoor amphitheater, was occupied by graduates from the other schools: teaching, business, social work, international affairs, dentistry, medicine, law. The grassy lawns were filled from tailored hedge to tailored hedge with white folding chairs, occupied by the family members of every person graduating from Columbia University that day.

And I was one of them.

I couldn't believe that the most amazing four years was coming to an end. It had been grueling, but it had never felt as rewarding as it did today. The pre-med curriculum had been brutal, but I had made it through. And now here I was, getting ready to start medical school in August.

I, of course, was thrilled to be starting the next step toward my goal of becoming a doctor. But a part of me still felt a little discouraged, a little bitter, with the result of my application cycle. I had worked my butt off all these years, only for my lousy MCAT score to bridle me at the very end. After I had submitted my applications, I was distressed to find that most medical schools would not even give me the time of day. Most of them had a strict cut-off for MCAT scores beneath which they would not even look at the rest of your application. Despite my degree from Columbia, my tenure as editor-in-chief of the Journal of Global Health, my time volunteering at the women's shelter, and my work scribing in the ER at Mount Sinai, it felt like they had blacklisted me.

As I could have predicted, the only interview I received was here, at my home, Columbia. I was grateful for the interview offer. I was even *more* grateful when they accepted me for admission. But I suspected strongly that the only reason they accepted me was because of my last name. And it stung to know that I couldn't hack it on my own. Now I would be spending the next four years not only wondering if my father had something to do with my admission to medical school, but also working in the same hospital as him. Living in his shadow had always been figurative, but it was about to get real literal.

But I refused to dwell on that today. I would bask in what I had achieved: a diploma with my name on it. Written entirely in Latin, I might add, but at least it would look *very* fancy on the wall of my office someday.

After the commencement ceremony, the thousands of graduates dispersed in waves of blue, looking around to reconnect with friends and loved ones. I had arranged with my parents to meet afterward in the courtyard in front of John Jay. My mom drew me in for a hug when she found me, handing me an enormous bouquet of flowers.

"We're so proud of you, honey," she said.

My father patted my back a little awkwardly. "You did good, kid."

He was not particularly loquacious, especially when it came to praise.

My mom started taking an incessant number of pictures of me with my cap and diploma and flowers. I felt a pair of strong arms wrap around my shoulders, and I looked up to see Javi behind me. I grinned widely up at him over my shoulder, and my mom snapped the picture.

"Oh, that's such a good picture," my mom said, looking down at her phone. "You guys are adorable."

I turned in his arms until I could see his face. We beamed at each other in delight.

"We did it," I said.

"We did it!" he agreed and pulled me back into his chest for a huge hug.

He held me at arm's reach and said, "The whole gang is over in front of Hamilton. Meet us there when you're done?"

I nodded, promising him I would find them. He ran off in the direction of the statue of Alexander Hamilton in the distance. I looked forward to seeing the Valenzuelas again. I hadn't seen them since the previous winter break, and I missed them all dearly.

My parents got their fill of pictures and took my diploma and flowers from me.

"We'll meet you at the apartment for dinner at seven o'clock?" my mom asked, knowing I was anxious to find

Javi. I nodded, hugging her once more, before they turned to head home.

I weaved through the clusters of graduates and their families, toward the statue of the former treasury secretary ahead. I suddenly was tackled by a mob of giggling bodies. Javi's nieces and nephews called my name, grabbing at my robe as if they were trying to climb me like a tree. I looked over his oldest niece's head to see the entire Valenzuela clan: his mom, face smeared with streaks of mascara; his stoic but proud father; his three sisters. Valeria held the newest addition, a one-year-old little girl, on her hip.

The only person who appeared to be missing was Javi.

I hugged each of Javi's family members in turn, before turning to his mother.

"Where did Javi go?" I asked.

They turned westward in unison, where I spotted Javi standing in the distance, speaking to a tall, very tan man in a navy suit.

"Who is that?" I asked them.

"No idea," Gaby said. "This guy came up to him all of a sudden and asked to speak with him."

"Well, that's weird," I said.

I chatted with the group for another fifteen minutes before Javi joined us. I couldn't read the expression on his face, exactly, when he finally joined the circle of his family members. He looked excited, though I would expect as much on our graduation day. But there was a touch of something else on his face, maybe a hint of worry? The slightest crease between his eyebrows.

"Who was that, Javi?" Manuela asked. "That man who came up to you."

"That was..." he hesitated, sounding a little stunned. "An investor. Dr. Carlyle told him about me. He wants to fund the development of my device. He's going to pay for it—all of it. Everything I need to get The Artemis out there."

Javi's mother and sisters screamed and attacked him with hugs and kisses. I stared at him in wonder.

The Artemis. The device he had pitched to me on the beach in Corpus Christi during our first year of college; his passion project for the last three years. After years spent in the lab developing the prototype, it was going to be a reality. Something real and tangible that could help people.

When his mother and sisters finally released him, Javi's face was covered in kiss marks in different shades of red lipstick. His cap was knocked askew, his dark, wavy hair peeking out beneath it. He shook his head in wonder.

"Can you believe it?" he asked me.

I threw my arms around him, his cap flying off completely with the force of my embrace. "Of course I can believe it, Javi! You're brilliant! You're going to change lives!"

When I let go of him, he was blushing furiously, though he wasn't usually the type to get embarrassed. "Thanks, Doc. That means a lot."

Javi's family took about a hundred more photos—Javi with every combination of family members imaginable. I took a group shot of the whole crew, and then got dragged forward to join the shot, Valeria shoving her phone into the hands of a random stranger to take the picture. Javi's mom had us pose together in about a dozen different ways before she was finally satisfied.

"Hey, can I meet you guys later at the Airbnb?" Javi asked his family. "We've got a couple last minute things we have to do."

I looked at him, confused. We had made no plans together for after the ceremony. I assumed we would spend it together, as we spent most days together, but his tone made it seem like there were *plans*.

Javi's family hugged us goodbye and made their way toward the wrought iron gates.

When they were out of earshot, I finally asked, "A couple last minute things to do?"

He grinned conspiratorially at me, taking my right arm and linking it through his. He led us through the last of the dispersing graduates, down the walkway, to the side of Butler Library. He turned the handle on a nondescript door, looking unsure. But he looked satisfied when the handle gave, and the door opened to us. We ducked inside quickly, finding ourselves in the service stairway of the library.

"What are we doing?" I asked, whispering.

"Our badges are deactivated, as of today," he said. "I had to find another route."

"Loretta?" I asked. Loretta was the very kind, probably sixty-year-old librarian that Javi had sweet-talked out of reporting us two years ago, when she had found us sneaking out of the top floor stairwell, back from the roof during our second year. She had since become our friend and confidante, and the keeper of our greatest secret.

"Loretta," he confirmed. "I asked her to leave a door open for us."

We made our way up the stairs, one flight after the other, laughing as we grew out of breath with the climb. This was a lot easier when the elevator brought us to the top floor. When we finally made it to the top, the trusty, dusty copy of *The Iliad* still propped in the door, Javi grabbed a green grocery tote from beside the door.

"My home girl, Loretta, also hooked us up with a little graduation present." He pulled a bottle of champagne and two plastic flutes out of the bag. I grinned wildly. As I had many times in the last four years, I appreciated Javier's ability to befriend or charm just about *anyone*.

We settled on the roof in our usual spot on the ledge, blue graduation gowns now unzipped, caps discarded on the ground. Javi popped the bottle of champagne, a little splash of bubbles spilling onto the tiles beneath us. He poured each of us a glass, lifting his up to tap against mine.

"To the two luckiest people in the whole world," he said, and I repeated after him. We downed the first glass and poured another. We spent a long while peering out at the school we loved, watching the crowds disperse onto the streets below, parting ways after the ceremony. A team of workers was already disassembling the amphitheater from the steps of Low Library.

"Can you believe it's already over?" I asked. "It feels like just yesterday that we snuck up here during our first year."

"Time flies when you're having fun," he said, winking at me.

"Do you think we'll have access to Butler next year? When I'm at the med school and you're working here in the lab?" I asked hopefully.

Javi didn't answer me. I looked at him over my champagne glass and saw a contemplative look on his face. I would almost call it a pained look.

"Javi?" I asked. "Everything okay?"

He sighed. He put his glass of champagne down and ran a hand over his face. I was growing more and more wary as I took in his expression.

"Earlier, when I told you about the investor," he began, "I didn't exactly tell you the whole truth of it."

I waited for him to continue in worried silence.

"He is going to take the Artemis to the next level. He's going to connect me with all the right people. Write me a blank check to make it happen. But he wants me to move to California to do it."

California.

The word hung between us, laden with implications. It hit me like a punch to the gut, the air leaving my lungs with a great *whoosh*. We had been inseparable for the last four years. And while I struggled with the idea of being in such proximity to my father for the next four years of medical school, at least I had the consolation of being a few subway stops from Javi, here in his lab. Except he wouldn't be here at his lab, he would be a whole *country* away from me. And not a country like Belgium away, a country like the entire United States of America away.

"Wow," I said, my voice still stunned. "That's amazing, Javi. This is such a huge opportunity."

I met his eyes and was shocked to find them filled with tears when I did. My worry and fear dissipated like mist, and concern for him filled its place just as quickly. I threw my arms around him.

"Javi, what's wrong?" I asked. "Why are you crying?"

I held him at arm's length as he wiped his tears away, angrily.

"It's stupid," he said, admonishing himself. "I should be thrilled. I *am* thrilled. But this feels like high school all over again—like I have to choose between my dreams and the person who matters most to me in the entire world. I don't want to lose you, Di."

"Hey," I said, lifting his chin to force him to look directly into my eyes. "You're not going to lose me. You're never going to lose me. Especially not for this. This is too huge an opportunity to pass up. You cannot be considering turning this offer down."

"You say that now," he said. "But you'll be so busy with

school and me with the Artemis. I'm worried it will never be the same."

"It won't be exactly the same," I admitted, "but it doesn't mean you won't be my best friend in the world. We'll text and Facetime. I'll come visit you in California every break I get. And you have to promise to visit me whenever you get a chance."

"Of course I will," he said, sniffling a little pitifully.

"You cannot pass up this opportunity," I said, firmly. "You need this. The *world* needs this, Javi. The world needs you and your mind. I would never forgive you if you stayed in New York for me."

He downed his second glass of champagne and hiccuped.

"Thanks, Doc," he said. "I hope you know I feel the same way about you. The world needs your mind too. The med school here is lucky to have you. You're going to be an amazing doctor."

I leaned over and squeezed his hand in thanks. For a moment, we sat in silence, the weight of our impending separation pressing down on us. We sipped on champagne and watched the sky grow darker with the approaching dusk.

We had a lot to do in the coming weeks. I was moving to a little studio apartment a few blocks away, but all my worldly belongings were currently stacked in boxes in my bedroom at my parents' apartment on the upper east side. Orientation for medical school was scheduled for the first week of August.

Javi had been looking for an apartment, with plans to sleep on my couch until he could find something. He was also using my old bedroom as a storage facility in the meantime, though he had significantly fewer boxes than I did. Now, I supposed, he would be working on finding a place in California instead.

"Are we still going to visit with your family in Corpus this summer?" I asked him. "Do you think you'll have time, now that you're moving?"

"I'd like to," he replied. "I don't know how quickly they want me to be out there. I imagine as soon as possible. There is still a lot to figure out."

"I can come with you. Maybe we can go straight from Corpus to California together to look for places for you to live?" I offered. I had no plans for the summer—only to let my brain rot with as many books and Netflix series as possible before med school started.

"I would love that," he said. "We will figure all this out. I'm sad to even bring it up, but if we don't get off this roof soon, our families are going to send search parties for us."

I looked down at my watch and nodded in agreement. We packed up our discarded champagne and flutes and blue graduation caps and stuffed them into the grocery tote. Javi climbed down off the ledge, then reached his hand up to help me down after him. I took his hand and jumped down. I didn't attempt to stop the momentum of the descent and instead used it as an excuse to fall into Javi's chest. I wanted to blame the champagne for the "clumsiness," but I couldn't pretend it wasn't intentional or that I was anything less than sober. He wrapped his arms around me, holding me tight.

I hoped Javi couldn't feel my hot tears seeping through his dress shirt. His hand sketched soothing circles in the center of my back. I couldn't say anything, nor could I get myself to pull away from him and make the trek down the stairs back to our new reality. I wanted to stay here on this rooftop with him and pretend the rest of the world didn't exist, at least for a little while longer.

"Promise me," Javi said against the top of my head. "That no matter where we are in the world, no matter how busy we get, we'll always find time for each other."

"I promise," I whispered against his chest.

I squeezed him one last time and pulled away. We made our way back down the stairs, out of the library and onward to meet our families for the celebrations.

The following weeks were a whirlwind of packing, goodbyes and preparations for the future. Javi and I sat on the floor of my bedroom on the upper east side, sorting through our belongings, deciding what to bring with us to our next adventures and what to donate. Javi helped me load and unload the elevator in my new building with boxes and whatever furniture items we could squeeze into the tiny space.

My new apartment was a single small room, hardly bigger than my dorm room from John Jay, with a kitchenette and a tiny attached bathroom. We made the best possible use of the space that we could. We squeezed a full-size bed into the corner. We found a tiny, space-saving kitchen table with two barstools that stored neatly beneath it when it wasn't in use. We tucked a little desk into the corner opposite the bed.

My mom, the amateur interior designer that she was, managed to make the little space feel warm and homy with the wall art and soft, modern furniture she had chosen and gifted to me for my graduation.

My father's graduation gift to me was the first three months of rent, enough to last me comfortably until my loans for school kicked in. What he had *actually* proposed as his gift was four years of medical school tuition plus rent. And though I knew it made me certifiably, clinically insane, I had declined. I already struggled with going to the institution where my father worked. I already felt like I had earned almost nothing for myself, in my entire twenty-two years of life. The least I wanted to do was pay my own way, even if it meant taking the loans and paying them back slowly over my career.

My father had told me, in no uncertain terms, that I was making a mistake—that I would regret racking up years and years of interest on those loans. He had even offered to let me pay him pack directly for the total cost of tuition, sans interest. But I had inherited my stubbornness from my father, and I would not have the looming weight of owing him hundreds of thousands of dollars in the back of my mind for the next four years. I didn't know what I wanted to do with my life, what specialty would call to me, but I knew that if I chose anything other than cardiothoracic surgery, my father was going to have something to say about it. I didn't need the leverage of that debt making the decision for me.

It took us about a week to finish moving me into my new place, during which Javi would regularly step away to take phone calls from his mentors and his new investor, an insanely wealthy man named Nathaniel Caldwell, about the plans for the Artemis. They wanted him to be in California starting on the project by the end of the month, leaving us little remaining time to visit his family and move his belongings. We discovered, however, that finding a place was not going to be a problem, as he had an apartment in Palo Alto waiting for him, courtesy of his new investor—rent free.

When I heard this detail, it struck me suddenly how big of a deal this was. Obviously, I believed in Javi and his invention. I thought the Artemis was amazing, and I had known from the first week I met Javi that he was a genius. But here was clear as day proof that the world was going to know it too. While I couldn't be happier about Javi's success, it felt like I was losing a part of him that had always belonged to only me—that part of him that dreamed out loud of inventing things, lying next to me on the roof of Butler. Now that man was going to make things for the world instead of simply brainstorming them to me.

The day before we were set to fly to Corpus Christi, we did a highlight reel of our favorites around the city. We got pizza in the east village for lunch. We got lost in the Met, before diving straight into the park and wandering through it for hours. We went to Times Square, where I imagined we were going to attempt to drop in on whatever show had a lottery for that evening. But to my surprise, Javi walked right up to TKTS and bought two *full-priced* tickets to see *Hamilton.*

I raised my eyebrows when he did this, to which he replied, "Signing bonus from Caldwell. Hit the bank account this morning."

I shook my head at him as he grinned widely at me. He linked my elbow into his and led me to the Richard Rogers theater like we were the two richest people in the city.

After the show, we got milkshakes from Tom's and drank them (when they were sufficiently melted) on top of the sundial in the middle of Columbia's college walk.

When we could no longer ignore our exhaustion and the aching of our feet, we made the journey back to my new apartment. After we had settled in for the night, I lay awake in bed, looking up at the new, still unfamiliar ceiling.

"Javi?" I whispered into the dark. "Are you awake?"

"I'm awake," he replied.

"Tell me no if it's too weird," I said, nervously. "But I was wondering if you would come lay next to me. I'm having a hard time falling asleep."

He didn't say anything in response, but I heard him moving in the darkness.

"Scootch over, Doc," he said, lifting the sheets. I moved over until my back was against the wall, giving him enough room to slip in beside me, with a foot of space separating our bodies. In the dim moonlight through my window, I could barely make out the faint lines of his face, looking back at me. He reached his hand out and rested it on mine.

"I know laying in your bed is probably the wrong time to tell you this," he whispered with a soft chuckle, "but I don't think I've ever told you before, and I don't want to move across the country without saying it. I love you, Diana. I think life's too short not to tell the people you love that you love them."

"I love you, too," I said. "You mean so much to me. I am so grateful that you found me in that hallway of John Jay... even if I was naked."

He laughed so hard the bed shook beneath us. "I will never forget how cute and pitiful you looked, as long as I live. Crying in your little pink towel."

I shoved him in the dark but laughed with him at the memory.

"Good night, Javi," I said.

"Good night, Doc."

When I woke in the morning, I realized quickly that I was no longer pressed flat against the wall, an arm's reach away from Javi. I had drifted toward him in sleep until I was inches away. My hand was flat against his chest, and his arm was a comforting weight draped over my waist.

I surveyed his relaxed face in sleep, taking in every detail that I would soon be unable to see every day. I could see the smallest hint of the dimple that appeared on his left cheek when he smiled.

I found myself falling into a dangerous line of thinking. *What if? What if you woke up like this every morning?*

But I tucked the thought away into a distant corner of my mind as fast as it had appeared.

He's moving to California.

Chapter 7

Medical School

First Year

The first year of medical school felt like running a marathon at a dead sprint. Like taking a drink of water from a firehose. To survive each exam (and there were exams every two weeks), you had to consume information—every little possible detail about human anatomy, physiology, and pathology that a person could know—at a superhuman pace. I felt like I could never catch my breath.

It didn't help that whenever I introduced myself to my professors or classmates, the shadow of my father loomed heavy over me, like a thundercloud. *Oh, you're Dr. Hunt Richards' daughter? Your dad is the chief of surgery?* Was the typical chorus, tinged with a mix of awe and sometimes, I feared, skepticism. The disdain for children of nepotism was apparently a universal experience.

Making new friends, in general, had never come easy to me. But my lineage was making it nearly impossible, whether my acquaintances were intimidated or disgusted by me. I wanted to tell them there was nothing to be intimidated by, that I was struggling just as much if not more than anyone else, despite my father's legacy. But I also didn't want them to see how much I *was* struggling to keep up and take that as confirmation that I didn't deserve to be here.

Despite the difficulties, I had managed to find a few people who didn't seem to care who my father was and presumably liked me for me. My closest friend thus far was a girl named Blake Njoku, who I had met while sharing a cadaver in the anatomy lab. Dissecting a human body for hours a day, multiple days a week, in a cloud of formaldehyde, bonded you for life. At least, that is what Blake said to me when she declared that we would be best friends.

Blake was brilliant and blunt, with a dry wit that could slice through the tension of our toughest study sessions. She often said she 'hated people,' and was therefore going into anesthesiology, 'where she could keep her patients quiet and asleep.' But despite her big talk, she was one of the kindest, most genuine people I had met. She volunteered at the free clinic nearly every week. She befriended me despite the whispers she might have heard about me or my father and introduced me to her group of friends. If they had qualms about me joining their ranks, they didn't say as much. Soon enough, with Blake's fervent approval of me, they became my friends too.

In the spring, we survived what felt like the hardest exam of the entire year thus far. Ironically, the subject was cardiology, and I was quite sure Dad wouldn't be putting this test up on the fridge. When we stumbled out of the testing room, feeling like we had been personally violated by the exam, Blake insisted that we were going to be spending the entire evening at the local bar with our fellow classmates; to commiserate how terrible the exam had been and drink our sorrows away.

"You need to remember what the sunlight looks like,

Diana," Blake said to me while fixing her mascara in my mirror.

"It's dark outside," I replied.

"It's a figure of speech! I mean you need to get out more. The only thing we ever do together is study!" she yelled.

I looked through my closet for something to wear to the bar that could match Blake's level, not that that was possible. Blake was always impeccably dressed, even when she was sitting in a lecture hall.

Though Blake was from Pennsylvania, her parents were originally from Nigeria. Her dad, like mine, was a doctor—an ophthalmologist. Though, from everything I had gathered from her phone conversations with him, she seemed to have a much more amiable relationship with her father than the one I had with mine. Blake had continued her father's legacy out of respect and admiration, whereas I had continued my father's legacy because no other options had been presented to me.

Blake's mother was a designer of some of the most beautiful clothing I had ever laid eyes upon, and I had seen a lot of clothes in my day. Tonight, Blake was wearing a two-piece ensemble of her mother's design—a pair of fitted shorts and a structured peplum strapless top, in a bright fuchsia and purple pattern. Blake's clothes were always made with vivid colors and patterns that matched her bold personality. Only in the anatomy lab, when she was elbow-deep in body parts and fluids, had she deigned to wear the shabby scrubs provided by the medical school.

Tonight, her dark skin shimmered with glittery highlighter at her collar bones and cheekbones. Her natural hair in its tight coils made a halo around her face, with touches of copper highlights at the ends.

I settled on dark jeans and a strappy blue top—about

as daring as I was willing to go in front of my medical school classmates. It wasn't exactly clubbing attire, but it would have to do, as I was not willing to go to my parents' apartment to raid my closet for the more fashionable items in my wardrobe.

When we arrived at the bar, it was packed with our classmates in various states of inebriation in their attempts to bleach their brains of the terrible exam. The noise of the chatter and music was a physical thing, a wave of sound that assaulted you as soon as you walked in the door. I clung a little closer to Blake as we made our way to the bar to order drinks. Blake, true to form, ordered shots first.

"To survival!" she toasted, and we downed them quickly. The burn of the alcohol was painful but welcome as it scorched down my throat. We immediately ordered mixed drinks to follow.

As the evening wore on, I felt myself starting to relax. Spending hours upon hours each day studying, only for it to culminate in an exam every two weeks, was starting to wear on me. Prior to each exam, it felt like I was swimming from some deep depth to the surface, holding my breath until I could take one huge gulp of air when I reached the surface, only for someone to push my head back under again. But tonight, even though today's test was likely the worst exam of the year, I felt more at ease than I had in months. I cheered my classmates on as they took to the dance floor and even found myself being pulled into the fray, letting the music sway my body back and forth along with the current.

I was going back for my third—maybe fourth?—drink of the evening, when I ran into someone—*literally* ran into him, and the impact felt like hitting a brick wall. He was lean but muscular, and he loomed over me, much taller than my five feet two inches. He had cropped black hair with the sides closely shaved, just short of a military buzz cut. I apologized, and he reached out to steady me as I wobbled from the impact.

"I'm sorry!" he leaned down, yelling into my ear over the music. "I didn't mean to knock you over."

I waved him off, smiling sleepily up at him. "It's nothing!"

He didn't immediately move his hands from my arms after steadying me. "I think I've seen you around before! I'm Michael! Michael Deng!"

I giggled. "Michael Deng? Like M.D.?"

He laughed. "Exactly like M.D. Would you believe it if I told you my parents did it on purpose? Told me I wasn't allowed to be anything but a doctor."

"I would believe it!" I said, grinning. I shook his hand firmly. "Diana Richards. D.R."

We laughed at the irony. He bought two more shots and handed me one.

"To helicopter parents!" he said, and we downed the shots in unison.

I dragged Michael back to the dance floor with me. I felt completely unlike myself as I pulled against his shirt, dragging his chest into mine as we danced. His hands found their way to my belt loops, and he dragged my hips to meet his. We swayed together to the music. My brain was a blur of flashing lights and thumping music and body heat.

I don't really know when Michael started kissing me, but I returned the kiss— enthusiastically, if a little sloppily. We continued to dance for several more songs, until I felt a hand grab my elbow.

"I'm so sorry, Michael, but could I borrow Diana, please?" I turned to see Blake there beside me, reaching for me between the dancing bodies.

"Go for it!" Michael said merrily.

I followed Blake off the dance floor, grinning and laughing the whole way. Blake took my face in both her hands and stared at me.

"Diana," Blake said, far too seriously for the occasion. "I need you to look at me and answer a few questions, okay?"

"Okay!" I said enthusiastically, gearing myself up for the quiz.

"First question," she said, and she held up a peace sign in front of my face. "How many fingers am I holding up?"

"Two!" I said very confidently. "Next question."

"Next question," Blake said. "How many drinks have you had?"

"Two shots. Aaaand three drinks," I counted out on my fingers one by one.

"Okay," she said. "Do you want this? Do you want whatever is happening with Michael to be happening tonight?"

I nodded emphatically.

"Okay, good!" she said. "I'm happy for you! Do you need me to take you home right now and get you into bed?"

"No, actually I was hoping Michael would do that instead!" I yelled back, and immediately burst out into giggles. Blake grinned and shook her head at me.

"You're ridiculous!" Blake said, and she shoved a bottle of water in my hand. "I'm not letting you leave with him until you chug this though."

I complied with her instructions, chugging the water before handing her back the empty bottle.

"Thanks, Blake, love yooouu!" I sang to her.

"Love you too!" she crooned. "Have fun! Don't do anything I wouldn't do!"

I narrowed my eyes at her, confused. "But Blake, you don't sleep with men—"

"It is a *figure of speech*," she insisted, rolling her eyes at me. "Go! Have fun!"

I grinned at her before running back to the dance floor. I ran up to Michael and grabbed him by both hands. I leaned up on tiptoes to yell into his ear. "Blake said if I drank some water, I was allowed to take you back to my place!"

Michael looked a little dumbstruck, but pleased. He led me off the dance floor and out of the crowded bar. My ears rang with the absence of the pounding music when we made it out onto the street. He caught a cab, and I gave the driver my address. We kissed in the backseat the entire way home, the entire ride up the elevator to my studio, and stopped to kiss in the hallway every few steps. I fumbled with the keys to my apartment as he held onto me by my waist.

We pushed into the room, barely closing the doors before we started tearing clothes off each other. We left a trail of discarded items behind us like breadcrumbs as we tumbled toward my bed. I laughed with delight when he picked me up clean off the ground and threw me onto the mattress. I rolled over and opened my bedside drawer, grabbing a condom and throwing it to him. He joined me on the bed moments later.

He nudged my knees open, and I gasped as he plunged into me. I grasped at his shoulders, my nails digging into his skin. The tension growing in me as he moved inside me felt like a culmination of many things that I had been feeling for a long time: one was the pure, animalistic need of not having had sex in over a year; another, the building stress of medical school weighing down on me, needing any kind of release to make me feel like I wasn't being crushed beneath the pressure; and finally, the need for the intimacy of physical touch and being held by someone again.

He increased his pace, and I could feel the brink of the release I was looking for. I lifted my hips to meet his until he reached *just* the right spot. He shuddered his release, and I could feel him pulsing inside me with it. Just as he started to slow to a stop, my vision filled with stars, and I clenched around him with my own release.

He collapsed nearly on top of me, holding his weight off me with one elbow. He rolled onto his back. We both panted and laughed in the wake of it. It felt like only seconds later before I heard Michael's soft snores, and I didn't blame him. With the alcohol, the stress of the day we had, and the evening's activities, I was exhausted. I rested one hand against his bicep, closed my eyes, and let sleep consume me.

When the first rays of sun hit my face in the morning, the first thing I felt was the intense throbbing of my head. The second thing was the ache between my legs. The whole evening flooded back to me in hazy detail, and I fought the urge to groan at the memories. I didn't regret what happened, but I was surprised, nonetheless. I rolled to my back and opened my eyes completely, and I instantly felt like someone was hammering an ice pick into my parietal lobes when I did.

Michael was still asleep beside me, his back facing me, cradling one of my fluffy pillows in his arms. I had a floating shelf above my bed that acted as my nightstand, and I grabbed my phone off it, looking at the screen. It was just past seven in the morning. I realized I missed several texts from Javi and unlocked it. The first was a selfie in front of the white sails of the Sidney Opera House.

> JV: G'day from Australia!

> JV: Miss you. Wish you were here.

I hearted the picture, closed my phone, and threw it back on my nightstand. I rolled over back toward Michael, fully intending to go back to sleep for as long as my body would let me, when my phone rang loudly. I fumbled for it again, answering before I could even process who it was, just to make it shut up and avoid waking Michael. I looked at the phone in a panic, seeing a picture of Javi and me at our graduation as the caller ID.

"Hello?" I whispered, as I scrambled out of bed. I grabbed a throw blanket from my desk chair and clumsily wrapped it around myself.

"Diana?" Javi answered. "Diana, are you there? I can barely hear you."

I scrambled to open my window and climb out onto my fire escape. I closed the window nearly all the way.

"I'm here," I said a little louder than a whisper now that I was outside, though my voice was thick and hoarse with sleep and the hangover. I attempted to clear it. "How are you?"

"I'm great!" he said. "Things are going great with the project meeting here in Sydney. The group is really excited about the device. They're fighting to try to get it rolled out here before we even get it out in the States. And they're really wining and dining me trying to make it happen. It's crazy! I wish you could be here, Doc."

"That's so exciting, Javi," I said.

Javi paused on the other line. "Are you okay? Why are you whispering? And your voice sounds weird, are you sick?'

"No, I'm not sick," I said, hesitantly. I wasn't quite sure

why I hesitated. I had always told Javi about the men I had dated in the past, though things had never progressed quite so quickly as it had last night.

"I actually have someone over right now," I finally admitted. "He's asleep."

"Someone over? Isn't it super early there?" he asked. "*Oh... Someone over.*"

I cringed as he made the silent realization on the other line.

"Do I know this guy?" he asked, his voice losing all its enthusiasm.

"No, you wouldn't have met him before," I said. I didn't add, *because I just met him last night.* Javi had visited twice during the year so far, usually during purposefully extended layovers on his various trips around the world. He had met my core friend group and liked them all, especially Blake. They got on better than I could have ever hoped for.

"Oh," he said, as if he didn't know anything else to say about the matter. "I guess it's pretty serious though?"

"It's pretty new," I said through another cringe. It felt wrong not to be completely open with Javi, about anything in my life. But I didn't want to admit to him that I had drunkenly brought a guy home that I had just met. Javi wasn't the type, nor really was I until last night.

"Are you dating anyone?" I asked, hopefully, trying to redirect the topic.

"Nothing serious," he replied. "A few dates here and there. It's been hard with all the meetings and travel. I haven't seen my apartment in Palo Alto for more than two days in months. I basically live out of my suitcase. And I'm not really interested in a relationship that lasts the length of these business trips."

"That makes sense," I replied, peering into my window,

wondering if Michael was even still there or if he had noticed my absence and taken the opportunity to escape. But I could still see the outline of his form beneath my sheets.

"Well, I can't wait to meet him when I come visit in May," Javi said, and he seemed to have worked some enthusiasm back into his voice.

"Yeah," I said, noncommittally. "Can't wait."

"Are you sure you're alright, Doc?" Javi asked again.

"Yeah, I'm great," I said, trying to make my voice sound more cheerful and significantly less hungover.

"Okay..." he said, sounding very unconvinced. "Well, I'm going to get some sleep. My flight back to the states is tomorrow, and then I'm off to London in a few days."

"Send me pics from Big Ben," I said.

He laughed. "You know I will. Love you, Doc. Talk soon."

"Love you too," I said and heard the other line click.

I gathered my blanket tighter around me and turned to head back into my apartment. I fumbled with one hand to lift the window, the other holding up my blanket so I didn't flash the occupants of the building across from mine. As I was lifting the window up, though, it slipped from my hand and fell completely closed with gravity. I scrambled to try to force the window back open, trying to use the friction from my hands against the glass to work it back open, but it wouldn't budge. I sat, defeated, onto my fire escape. Here I was, once again, naked and locked out of my place.

It took me a long time to work up the courage to knock on the window. At first, I knocked quietly, but Michael was apparently a heavy sleeper. I knocked louder until he stirred. He looked around wildly, and I knocked again. He finally noticed me sitting outside the window and sprang into action. He grabbed his pants from somewhere around my kitchen table, halfway down the trail of discarded clothing we had left behind. He pulled them on and jogged to the window.

When he opened the window for me, he grinned. He squinted against the sunlight, his head probably aching as much as mine did.

"Well, good morning, D.R.," he said, merrily.

I smiled sheepishly. "Good morning, M.D."

"How did you wind up out here? Trying to escape?" He held out a hand to help me through the window, and I took it, using the other to keep the blanket wrapped around me.

"No, no escape," I said. "Just my dumb luck. I had to take a phone call and didn't want to wake you."

"That's considerate of you," he said. "Anything important?"

"No, nothing important," I said. "My best friend is in Australia at the moment, so we have to catch each other in the rare hours where one of us isn't asleep."

"I thought Blake was your best friend?" he asked. I started picking up my discarded clothing from the floor, throwing them into my hamper. I fished out fresh clothes from my drawers.

"My best friend from college," I amended, and quickly changed the subject. "You want coffee? Some breakfast? I think I have a couple bagels from the downstairs bakery."

"I'd love some," he said, and I was happy he didn't linger on the phone call for long.

I started the coffee pot before ducking into the bath-room to put on real clothes and freshen up. I served us coffee and bagels with cream cheese as we chatted about life and school. Michael was pursuing orthopedic surgery, which explained the muscles.

Ortho hopefuls had a distinct reputation for being the

frat bros of the medical world. They also tended to be the students with some of the best test scores. Michael met most of the bill for what I would expect of a future ortho bro—sarcastic, smart, competitive, hardworking, a little vain, in an athletic way. He made me laugh with stories about his helicopter parents that had pushed him—more like shoved him—down the path to medicine.

After breakfast, now dressed in the clothes he had worn the night before, Michael leaned against my door frame. He leaned down and kissed me once, very softly.

"I had a really nice time, Diana. Can I see you again?" he asked.

"I'd like that," I replied.

Chapter 8

Medical School

First Year

Over the next few months, Michael and I settled into a steady pattern. We mostly studied in the same room, occasionally stopping to get food or have sex. The relationship—though not all-consuming and fiery like in the novels I favored—worked for us. We lived the lives we had before, the intense study schedule we had grown accustomed to, now in the same room. We were exclusive—at least, I *believed* we were—without really discussing it, because who had time to go out and look for more people to date?

As the first year of school neared its end, I was eagerly looking forward to Javi's visit. I hadn't seen him in person in almost six months. Thirty minutes after he texted me that he had landed at JFK, I went outside to wait on the curb for his cab to pull up. When it did, the door was open before the cab had come to a full stop. He threw himself at me, picking me up and swinging me around in a half circle. I hugged him for what felt like a full minute, watching over his shoulder as the beleaguered-looking cab driver left Javi's suitcase and backpack on the curb beside us.

Javi extricated himself from my arms to hand the driver a single bill, and from the driver's improved mood, I would have bet it was a $100 note. I held Javi at arms' length when he returned to my side, taking him in. He had changed a lot in six months.

He had lost the softness from his cheeks that he had held onto for most of college, his jaw sharper at the angles and stubbled with a five o'clock shadow. His caramel skin was an even richer shade, presumably from all that sun in California. His hair was carefully coiffed with *hair gel*, something I was sure college Javi didn't know existed. He wore a *suit*—and not just a suit, a tailored blue suit that fit him like a glove. I had once theorized to myself that if Javi ever found himself the proper wardrobe, it would quickly take him from mildly attractive to devastating. And I had been *absolutely* correct. It was almost unfair how the person with the most brilliant mind and best personality of any human I had ever met was somehow also capable of looking this good.

My hands moved almost of their own accord, sliding up from his elbows to his deltoids, and every muscle between felt far more defined than I remembered.

"Wow, Javi," I said, my eyes wide. "You look... different."

The dimple in his left cheek appeared with his wide, genuine smile. My heart gave a small, painful flutter at the sight. That small detail was a reminder that, even though he otherwise looked very different than I remembered, he was the same boy I loved.

"Good different?" he asked.

I nodded emphatically but took my hands from his shoulders when I realized I was still squeezing them.

"Yes, good different," I told him. "You look great."

He shrugged. "A lot of hotel gyms during my downtime."

I had never once in our four years of college together seen Javi step foot in the multi-tiered gym at Columbia. I couldn't even convince him to go with me when I went. For Javi in college, there had always been things to do, places to see, and spending it in the dingy college gym had not appealed to him. At least, not to the Javi I had known.

"You look great too, Doc. But that's nothing new," he said, and he took my hand and twirled me so that my lacy white summer dress fanned out around me. I laughed.

I led Javi up to my apartment, taking his suitcase from him when we got to my studio.

"Where do you want your bag?" I asked him.

"You can leave it by the door," he replied, sitting on my couch. "I'll grab it later when I head to the hotel."

I wheeled around to look at him, stunned. "You're not staying here?"

He laughed at my reaction. "As much as I love your couch, you don't think Michael will mind some guy sleeping a few feet away from you?"

"Oh. Michael." I had not considered it as an issue. "I wouldn't call you *some guy*, though."

Javi said under his breath, "I fear Michael might not see it that way."

I shot him a glare.

"Don't worry about it," he added. "I have more hotel rewards than I know what to do with."

"How *is* the Artemis world tour going?" I asked. I settled in beside him on the couch, pulling my legs up beneath me.

"Pretty great, actually," he said, and he pulled a silver case the size of my fist out of his black leather backpack.

He opened it, taking the sleek black electronic out of the cushioning foam. It was a c-shaped device that clearly was meant to fit the back of someone's ear. The last time I had seen the Artemis, it had looked like a tangled mess of wires and 3D printed plastic. Javi took a few dime-sized pieces out of the case that looked like stickers.

"These are the electrodes. They work remotely, sending signals to the main device, which has several electrodes in it too. You only need one electrode on the opposite side as the device and one at the base of the skull for it to calibrate correctly. If it detects imminent seizure activity, it alerts the wearer to get to a safe location. If the alarm goes unacknowledged or the seizure activity lasts longer than a minute, it dials 911. It's ready for distribution as soon as the final FDA testing is finished."

I tenderly held the device. I couldn't believe how much he had accomplished in the last year. "This is incredible, Javi."

He beamed at me with pride. "I've been approached by no less than a dozen pharmaceutical and biotech companies trying to buy it off me. I'd never sell, though. I know that they'll ruin it. They're going to make it so no one can afford the device, unless they fit in the small intersection of people who have both epilepsy and endless disposable income. I don't want price to get in the way of people's safety. People's lives."

I shook my head, amazed.

He added with a grin, "*And* you can get it in multiple colors—black, silver, red, purple, blue, pink, green. Skin colors, if you want something more discreet, in 30 different shades, not just white."

I cackled. "You really have thought of everything."

"I try," he said with a shrug, and he tucked the Artemis

away, back into his bag. "What time are we meeting Blake and Michael for dinner?"

I looked at my watch. "Now is a perfect time to head out."

We headed toward the subway station and rode the train south for a few stops. When we arrived at the bistro, one of my favorites on the upper west side, Blake and Michael were already waiting with a table. Blake jumped up enthusiastically when Javi arrived and gave him a huge hug.

"Javi, it's so good to see you!" Blake squealed, and I was again reminded how much I loved that she loved him.

"You look stunning as ever, Blake," he said, and I grinned when he made Blake bat her eyelashes at him. He was, of course, correct—Blake had been wearing her hair in long braids recently, and she wore a bold summer dress that made her dark skin glow.

Javi then turned to Michael, who had stood from the table to meet us. Before acknowledging Javi, Michael turned to me. He grabbed me by the back of my neck and pulled me to him, dragging my lips to his in a kiss that lasted several seconds longer than I would have considered polite.

"Hey, D.R.," he said to me, before turning back to Javi once more. "You must be Javier. D.R. has told me so much about you."

Javi raised an eyebrow at me, and I read his mind as clearly as if he had screamed at me—*since when do you go by D.R.?* The look made me wriggle internally with embarrassment.

"And you must be Michael," Javi replied, and the two of them shook hands. When they let go, I noticed with some chagrin that both of their hands flexed uncomfortably, as if they had squeezed the other's hand as hard as they could. I rolled my eyes. I wanted to smack them both in the head. I had never known either man to be prone to displays of *machismo*. This felt like a poor omen of how the week was going to go.

Throughout the meal, I noticed the subtle ways Michael tried to one-up or undermine Javi, making it seem like his accomplishments and relationship with me were somehow better than Javi's. Neither was true. Michael was smart, and I was certain he was going to be a good orthopedic surgeon someday, but his mind didn't astound me the way Javi's did. And Michael didn't know me nearly as well as Javi did. While I would call Michael successful, considering he was at Columbia medical school, he was also just as riddled with debt as I was.

No one looking at Javi now could deny that he was successful. Javi didn't flaunt it in obvious ways. But I knew, my mom being the shopper that she was, that Javi's suit and watch were understated but incredibly expensive. More than that, he had the quiet self-assurance of someone who didn't need to prove himself and his worth to other men that questioned it, no matter how loudly. And Michael was *certainly* questioning it, in a way that made my stomach churn with discomfort and the need to defend Javi.

But Javi didn't need my help. His eyes frequently met mine across the table, and I could tell in the quiet mirth in his expression that he was terribly amused by Michael's attempts to get under his skin. Blake, usually one of the more talkative in a group, watched the two of them talk for most of the meal, her brows furrowing, her head shaking slightly at the silent battle ensuing. She looked embarrassed for Michael. I didn't know if I was more embarrassed or angry.

When dinner concluded, Michael kissed me again in a

way that made it clear he was flaunting it in front of Javi. The thought of needing to flaunt it was ridiculous, considering that Javi and I were friends, and he cared as much about who I kissed as Blake did. But Michael didn't seem to realize that. Michael only saw another *male* who was close to me, and apparently that was all that he needed to start pounding his chest like a gorilla.

"I'm meeting some of the guys at the gym," he told me, and I could have sworn he made the tone of his voice deeper as he said it. "I'll see you later?"

I crossed my arms over my chest, but didn't have it in me to call him out on his behavior.

"Yeah, see you later," was all I said.

When Michael had walked away from the three of us, Blake finally said, "Well, wasn't that special."

Javi exploded with laughter.

"I'm shocked he didn't whip his dick out and start comparing sizes right at the dinner table," Blake deadpanned, making Javi fall into another fit of giggles. I covered my face with both hands, too embarrassed to acknowledge them as they laughed endlessly at the situation.

"I promise, Javi, Michael usually doesn't act like that," I muttered through my fingers.

Javi shrugged. "I get it. New relationship. Male best friend. I'm sure I'd feel the same way, if I were in his shoes."

I uncovered my face, eyeing Javi skeptically. "No, you wouldn't."

"Yes," he said firmly, his eyes locking with mine resolutely. "I would."

His tone was so definitive that it washed all sarcastic retorts from my brain. I stared at him, curiously. What was he saying? Did he… did he *want* to be in Michael's shoes?

I was searching his face for a long moment when Blake cleared her throat, startling us both.

"I'm going to head back home," she said, her tone amused. "I'll see you guys later?"

She hugged us both and parted ways with us.

I pointedly moved past whatever had just happened between us, trying to settle back into our old routine.

Javi and I took advantage of the pleasant evening in New York and meandered through the city streets, enjoying the familiar cacophony of sounds that made up the melody of New York—honking cars, chatters of dozens of overlapping conversations, the distant cries of a street performer's violin. It felt good to be next to him again, a reminder of simpler times before medical school and the Artemis had pulled us into two separate orbits.

We wandered into our favorite little bookstore tucked away in the corner of a quiet street, the familiar scent of old pages and coffee as comforting as a warm hug. We browsed the shelves, occasionally pulling out a title to chuckle over or reminisce about. As I perused the new romance releases, Javi leaned against the bookshelf beside me.

"You've been really quiet about school," he commented, his voice tinged with concern. "How is everything going? You're handling the stress?"

I hesitated, biting my lip.

"It's been tough," I admitted, the weight of the last year settling on my shoulders. I was tempted to lie and tell him everything was great and that I was doing better than my wildest dreams. But lying to Javi felt like a completely foreign concept.

"If I'm being honest," I continued, "sometimes it feels like I'm barely keeping my head above water."

Javi's expression softened. "Di, why didn't you tell me things were this bad?"

I shrugged, avoiding his gaze. "I didn't want to worry you. You have enough on your plate."

He shook his head at my response. "I am *never* too busy for you, Diana. You know that, right? You can tell me anything."

I looked away from him, considering. "It's been relentless. Sometimes I'm so overwhelmed, I think about walking away from it all."

"Hey," he said, turning my face by the chin so I had no choice but to look into his eyes. The emotion burning there—the concern for me, the belief in me—made something icy cold and painful inside me melt into a warm puddle.

"You're one of the strongest, smartest people I know. You can do this," he encouraged.

I cleared my throat, which suddenly felt thick. I turned from him, freeing my chin from his grasp.

"Thanks, Javi," I said lamely. My heart thundered inside my chest.

As we drifted from the bookstore back out onto the streets, our conversation shifted to lighter topics. He walked me back to my apartment before heading to his hotel.

We spent every waking second of the long weekend together—finding good food to try, visiting our favorite museums, seeing a show on Broadway. It was just like the good old days.

But the weight of my academic struggles lingered in the back of my mind. While Javi always knew how to make me laugh and forget my stresses, the feelings I had in his presence were also confusing. Having him here, having him look into my eyes and identify my struggles with one glance, reminded me that no one saw me like he did. Blake was a wonderful friend. Michael was a good boyfriend. But no one could replace what Javi and I had in college. My chest hurt at the thought of what we had given up, even though I knew it was for the best for both our careers.

On our last morning together, a few hours before Javi would have to take a cab to the airport, we strolled through Riverside Park together, arm in arm like we used to. We had mostly walked in silence, but I could tell from his pensive expression that Javi had something weighing on his mind. Finally, the thought seemed like it could steep no longer.

"Do you really think Michael is the right guy for you?" Javi asked suddenly.

"What's that supposed to mean?" I demanded, immediately defensive. I pulled my arm out from his and looked at him straight on.

"Do you really see a future with him? Can you see yourself marrying this guy?" he asked.

I barked an incredulous laugh.

"Every guy I date does not have to be the one I marry, Javi," I shot back.

"Why would you date someone who you couldn't see yourself marrying? What's the point if there's no future with him?" His brows furrowed as he inspected me.

It wasn't often that Javi's southern upbringing was obvious. But his more traditional view on relationships was one area that had always seemed a little old-fashioned to me. He didn't date casually—he was an all or nothing kind of guy. It was one of the few subjects in which I was arguably the freer spirit of the two of us.

"I *can* see a future with Michael," I emphasized, though a part of my brain argued that I had never even *contemplated* what that future might look like. But what did that say about me? Didn't most women picture a future with their boyfriend? Was there something wrong with me, that I hadn't? But when I really thought about it, no one had ever inspired me to have visions of white gowns or babies before.

I shook my head, trying to clear these questions from my mind, but continued, "But even if I didn't, Javi, sometimes it's nice to feel *wanted*. And by someone who understands what I'm going through. I'm not thinking about marrying him right now, when all I can think about is surviving these four years."

"Are you saying I don't understand what you're going through?" he asked.

I blinked in surprise, unsure what he was implying. "That is... beside the point. But you *don't* understand, Javi. I am so proud of you and all your success, but you *don't* know what it's like, scraping by and struggling through your entire twenties to achieve your dreams. Those years that you're supposed to be *having fun* and traveling and meeting the person you're meant to spend the rest of your life with, wasted in textbooks and doing scutwork in hospitals. All in the hopes that someday you might make enough money to pay off your $300,000 in student loans. I know you try, but you can never know what it's like. You were rocket-launched to instantaneous success the second you graduated!"

He was quiet for a long moment, his mouth set in a grim line. "I know it may seem like that, Diana. But my job isn't easy, either. I know it seems like I'm just jet-setting and going to fancy dinners, but you *know* me, Diana."

He gestured to himself, to the gray suit he wore. "This isn't *me*. I'm not a fucking salesman. I'm an inventor. Yet, here I am, traveling all over the world, never staying in the same place, begging for people to give me their money so I can get my device off the ground. I've been so busy trying to suck up to the right people that I don't think I've used my engineering degree once since I graduated. While I may not know exactly what you're going through, Di, it doesn't mean my life is without struggles.

My expression softened. "I know it's not, Javi. I didn't mean it like that. I'm sorry."

He drew me in for a hug. "I just want you to be happy, Diana. Does Michael make you happy?"

My reply choked off in my throat. I wanted to defend my relationship, vehemently, but the words felt so hollow I couldn't even find it in me to speak them. I was afraid that if I tried, I would start crying, so I simply shrugged.

Javi sighed. "I think you deserve someone who understands you, who challenges you and supports you. Someone who sees how brilliant you are and cheers for you, not someone who sees you as the competition or who is just along for the ride."

I drew back from his arms, raising an eyebrow at his choice of wording.

He winced.

"I don't mean it like *that*," he corrected. "I'm saying that I think he takes you for granted."

I was thankful for his concern, but unsure what to do with his advice. Was I only with Michael because I was afraid of being alone, or because there was something real there? Asking myself the question seemed like answer enough in itself.

We walked until we had to go back to my apartment to get his things before heading to the airport.

He hugged me goodbye, whispering into my ear, "Please think about what I said, Di. I want you to be happy. I love you."

"Love you too," I said. I closed the cab door behind

him and watched his cab drive away, not knowing when I would see him again.

That night, as I lay in bed, the city's noises a soft murmur beyond my window, I allowed myself to really contemplate on what he had said. I wanted to be mad at Javi for questioning my relationship, but I couldn't find myself to be angry at him for voicing aloud the doubts that had been in my own mind as well.

But Michael *did* understand what I was going through. He was funny, smart, and pretty good in bed. He was worth giving a chance, I resolved. So, I would give it more time. Even if it didn't feel like a great romance from my novels, I had to be more realistic than that. Those were, after all, fairytales.

Chapter 9

Medical School

Second Year

During the weeks leading up to my Step 1 exam, the eight-hour long licensing exam that I had to pass to continue medical school, I felt like I was trapped in a small room with the walls steadily closing in on me. Each day added another layer of pressure, another whisper of doubt worming its way into my mind about my ability to go the distance. My panic attacks—once rare events that had only plagued me a few times before (the night before the MCAT, most notably)— seemed to occur with frightening regularity. Each time they happened, I felt like an animal was clawing at my chest, squeezing the air from my lungs, leaving me gasping on the floor of my apartment. I started to seriously wonder if I was cut out for this path.

The second year of medical school had ended a month prior. We were given extra, dedicated time to focus only on studying for the exam, the score of which would determine our entire future. A good score could open every door to every possible specialty. You could have your pick of programs in the specialty of your choosing if you succeeded. If you had a low score, or, God forbid failed the exam, you would be lucky to get a residency position *at all*. All those years, all that money, completely wasted.

Every time I sat to do practice questions or read my review materials, I could practically hear my father whispering in my ear that I would be expected to *continue the family legacy*. What if my score completely precluded me from *any* surgical specialty, much less cardiothoracic surgery? I remembered distinctly how horrible it had felt to have my MCAT score cripple me in my medical school applications, and I feared and dreaded the prospect of going through that again. To be ignored and ostracized from medical specialties, all because of one eight-hour period of my life.

The initial panic attack of the month came after my first practice exam, which I failed in spectacular fashion. I closed my laptop as my vision caved in, my breaths coming in short erratic gasps. Michael came over—we had made plans for dinner that evening–only to find me a gasping, sobbing mess in my bed. He seemed absolutely horrified by my state. I was certain only his sense of basic decency prevented him from leaving my apartment the second he realized what was happening to me. He stayed by my side, patting my back in a feeble attempt at comforting me as I spiraled into and eventually emerged out of the attack. But he didn't stay long once I had returned somewhat to a state of normalcy.

Since that day, I could tell that he was steadily distancing himself from me. If I was honest with myself, I would have to admit that we had been drifting apart for months, the strain of med school pulling at the seams of our relationship. We had become like two stars in orbit, seemingly close in proximity when you looked at them, but light-years apart in every way that really counted.

The moment he ended things with me, we were both stretched thin, our nerves frayed. It was a week before we were scheduled to sit for the exam. I wore clothes that I'd been wearing for three days straight. My hair was a mess, piled on top of my head in a disheveled bun. I hadn't worn makeup in weeks. He had asked me out for coffee, and I knew that this was going to be when he broke up with me. Coffee was short. Breaking up over dinner meant you would have to sit through the menu, the food, and the bill before you could physically part ways. Coffee was a cleaner break.

I hadn't even taken a sip of my cappuccino when he began.

"I can't do this anymore, Diana," he began.

I nodded in understanding, looking only at my coffee cup as he continued. I let him get it all out without interruption.

"This is a really hard time, I know. It has been hard for all of us. The stress has been getting to me too. But you know that I need a good score on this if I want to stand a chance at matching into Ortho. And I can't focus on my studies if I'm always worrying about you."

He said it as if he had rehearsed the words a hundred times. He barreled on, seemingly not caring that he was wrecking the last bits of my coping skills with each word.

I admired how clean a break he made it. I had noticed he had been subtly preparing to leave me for weeks. He had quietly taken everything out of my apartment he had ever left there – a spare toothbrush, a few pieces of clothing, some office supplies he preferred for study sessions. He hadn't packed them all at once, in an ostentatious way, but one at a time, over multiple visits. I had noticed, but never commented.

But even though I had felt it coming all this time, it

surprised me just how raw and broken it left me feeling. I really didn't think the loss of this relationship, mostly one of convenience, would affect me as much as it did. But the preparation for the exam had coiled me so tightly into such a fragile ball of anxiety, that the blow of the breakup simply broke me.

Not only am I failing at becoming a doctor, but I'm also going to be alone for the rest of my life.

After Michael had said his peace and left the coffee shop, I wandered back to my apartment in a daze. I crawled into my bed, pulling the blankets over my head as the heaving sobs began to ravage my insides. I wasn't sure how long the panic attack lasted this time, but it left me in a stupor for days to follow. I stayed in my bed, only leaving it to use the restroom. Even then this was rare, as I was not making any kind of point to feed or hydrate myself. I felt like I was withering away into nothing, and I was content to let it happen.

On the third day after the breakup, the third day in a row where I had not touched a book even though my exam was only four days away, I heard Blake knocking at my door.

"Diana? Honey, are you there?" she asked through the door. "I've been trying to call. I'm really worried about you."

My phone lay dead on my nightstand, untouched.

"Michael told me," Blake explained.

I winced.

"Please let me in, Diana. I'm here for you. Please just let me in."

She stayed outside my door for over half an hour; an admirable length of time, but it was like my brain and spine were no longer connected to the muscles of my legs. There was no communication telling my legs to move me to the door to let her in. I stared at the door in silent tears, finally turning away from it when there was nothing but silence waiting on the other side.

The next day, another knock came, this one firmer than Blake's had been. Blake had sounded so worried, her knocks so hesitant. This knock was loud, almost angry.

"Diana, let me in!" the voice resonated through my apartment, and my heart—which felt like it had sputtered out in my chest days ago –lurched painfully, as if the knock had been a defibrillator restarting it. My eyes shot open. The neural pathways from my spine down to my limbs felt like they were regrowing slowly at the sound of that voice.

I pivoted until my legs hit the floor and tested my weight on them, as if I was truly learning how to walk again. I pulled my blanket around me and stumbled to my door. I undid the lock and opened the door to find Javi standing there, his suitcase beside him like his eternal side-kick. He must have taken the red eye from California. His usual stubble was more of an early beard, his usual suits exchanged for a cream-colored fitted henley and brown joggers.

"Javi," I said, but the sound was less of a name and more of a strangled sob. I broke out into renewed sobs as he pulled me against his chest and held me there in my doorway for what felt like hours.

"Oh, Doc," he whispered sadly as I cried into his shirt, his hands rubbing up and down my back as it shook with my emotions.

It took me ages to stop crying enough to look at his face.

"What are you doing here?" I asked, blubbering and wiping at my face.

He brought me into my apartment, pulling his suitcase and a few reusable grocery bags I hadn't noticed before into the room before he shut the door. He guided me to the couch and settled my blanket around me, before sitting next to me.

"I would think the reason I am here would be obvious," he finally said.

"But how did you know?" I asked.

"Blake called me yesterday," he explained. "I came as soon as I heard."

I nodded, thinking that Blake was too good a friend to me for how I had treated her yesterday. I didn't deserve her. Didn't deserve either of them.

"Not to mention," he said, in a gentle but stern way that let me know that I was in trouble. "That you haven't answered *anyone's* texts or calls in days. Not Blake's, not mine, not your mother's. Everyone has been worried sick about you. Your mom's out of state visiting her sister, or she would have come. I had to talk her out of calling the police. But I thought you'd prefer me."

"I do," I said, sniffling.

"Good," he said, and he squared himself up like he was about to do important business. "Look, we've got a lot of work to do here, but let's tackle the most important tasks first. Give me your log-in for the Step 1 website."

"What?" I asked, feeling slow and dumb, completely unable to follow his line of thought.

"Give me your log-in," he insisted again. "Blake talked me through how to delay your exam. You *cannot* sit for this exam in three days in your current state. But you have to take it by the end of the month, or you delay the start of your third year, right?"

"Right," I confirmed.

"We're going to push your exam back a week," he said. He grabbed my laptop off my desk and brought it to me.

"But it costs $100 to change the exam date this—" I

argued, but he shot me a glare that shut me up halfway through my protest.

"Do I *look* like I care about the money? Log-in to the site, Diana," he commanded. I logged into the exam website without further argument.

After a few minutes, he shoved my laptop aside and turned back to me. "Okay, it's done. Your test is now ten days away. That gives us ten days to get you ready."

I shook my head, and if I had any fluids left in my body, I would have started to shed more tears. But every-thing about me felt dried up with dehydration. "There's no way, Javi. I can't do it."

"One thing at a time," he said to me, holding my shoulders in both hands. "We're not going to think about studying or taking the test right now. We're just going to control what we can control. And the first thing we can control is how you smell."

I sputtered out a sad little laugh. "I know I stink. I haven't showered in days."

"Now is the perfect time to change that," he said. He pulled me off the couch. He turned the shower on to let the water get hot. He went into my drawers and found a clean pair of soft pajamas and comfortable underwear. He handed me both, turned me around, and pushed me toward the bathroom.

"You shower," he instructed. "I will be out here when you're done. Take as long as you need."

I shuffled into the bathroom, placing my stack of clothes on the tiny counter. I shed my clothes and stepped into the shower, the warm water soaking into my skin and muscles, sore from lack of use after days spent in bed. I washed my hair and my body twice, convinced once wasn't enough to clear the grime.

When I finished, I toweled off and put on the fresh

clothes Javi had picked out for me. I wiped the oval mirror free of fog with my hand, and nearly jumped at the sight of my face. My eyes looked sunken, dark circles shadowed beneath them. My skin was paler than I remembered, even in the depth of summer. My freckles faded nearly to nothing. I looked like a ghost.

I emerged from the bathroom after I had brushed my hair and my teeth and looked, while not good, at least less like a zombie. In the time I had been gone, Javi had cleaned. The linens I had been stewing in for days were piled in the hamper, along with other clothes I had previously discarded on the floor. He had made my bed with fresh linens. He was straightening my desk, closing textbooks and organizing long abandoned study materials. He organized the space with such familiarity, you would have thought he saw it every day. A fresh pot of coffee was brewing in the kitchenette.

He looked up at me. "How do you feel?

"Better," I said. I didn't add that there had really been nowhere to go but up when he knocked on my door.

"Good," he said. He grabbed the blanket from my couch and wrapped it around me. He sat me at my kitchen table and brought me a cup of coffee. "Next item on the agenda is food. I apologize in advance for my cooking. Dad never taught me his ways."

I watched him silently as he moved about the tiny kitchen, taking items out of grocery bags and putting them away before making us cheese omelets and toast. He sat down across from me at my kitchen table. He didn't grab his fork until he watched me take the first bite, like he wasn't sure I was going to comply. I took a piece to get him to stop staring. He had warned me about his cooking, but it was actually pretty good. It was probably hard to gauge your skill when your parents were such excellent chefs. It might have been the whole not eating much for days thing too, but the omelet felt like the best thing I had tasted in a while.

After I was done eating, I told him, "Thank you, Javi. I can't believe you're here."

"There is no place else in the world I'd rather be," he said. It was saying something, considering it felt like he had been to just about every place in the world in the last two years.

"How long can you stay?" I asked, unable to keep the sad and desperate tone from my voice.

"I'll be here at least for these ten days," he said carefully, only indirectly alluding to my exam, careful to skirt around the subject. "Longer if I need to."

The answer surprised me. Javi had never stayed longer than a week before, always having some important meeting or destination to make.

"Are you really? You don't have anywhere you need to be?" I asked.

He shook his head resolutely. "No. Nowhere to be. Nothing that can't be rescheduled or handled by someone else on my team."

It was clear from his wording that he did, in fact, have other obligations. But I didn't argue with him. I was just so grateful he was here. I looked over and saw one of the grocery totes he had left on the ground. I leaned over and grabbed a box from the bag.

"*Ticket to Ride?*" I asked, inspecting the game.

"Yes. There are several games in there. You can choose which one and when you want to play, but rest assured, I will be kicking your ass at some board games this week."

I smiled, for what felt like the first time in a month. Leave it to Javi to always know exactly what to do to make me smile. I started unpacking the box and assembling the game between us. We settled into comfortable silence except for banter relevant to our match, and I was relieved when Javi didn't bring up the test or the breakup.

For a while, we were immersed in the strategy of the game, with Javi making exaggerated gestures of triumph whenever he claimed a crucial route on the board. The playful competition was a balm to the recent turmoil in my life, reminding me of simpler times. His presence had a way of grounding me, pulling me back from the edge of despair that had seemed so seductive only hours before.

The game ended—Javi winning, as predicted—but it hadn't been over for thirty seconds when he brought out Monopoly. I started setting up the new game while he went to the kitchen and made snacks. For the rest of the day, whenever we were between games or taking a necessary pause, it felt like Javi was shoving food at me.

I put a handful of popcorn into my mouth and said to him, "Why do I feel like you're trying to fatten me up like a lost child in a forest? Are you going to trick me into falling into the oven at the end of the evening?"

"You have foiled my evil plot." He cackled like a witch, making me grin. "But seriously, Di, you look like you've lost weight. I want to make sure you're taking care of yourself."

I was suddenly reminded that he was Alba and Juan Valenzuela's son, and the need to keep people happy and fed was deeply ingrained in his genes. The reminder of them made my heart ache with longing, wanting to see them again.

"I miss your family," I said wistfully.

He smiled. "They miss you. They ask about you every time I talk to them."

"Are they doing well?" I asked.

"They're okay," he said, and the sad edge to his tone set off alarm bells in my mind.

"Just okay?" I asked with concern.

He frowned. "My nephew Theo was diagnosed with epilepsy. Started having seizures a few months ago."

I gasped quietly. How was he just now sharing this information with me? Had I been so caught up in my own world, in studying for this infernal test, that he hadn't been able to share this pivotal news from his life? The thought made me feel sick.

"Oh my God," I breathed. "Is Gaby doing okay?"

He shrugged, nodding. "She's taking the news okay. She is worried, of course. But Theo had a custom-fitted, green Artemis sent straight from my lab before he could even get home from the neurologist's office. So that has brought her some comfort, I think. Theo, meanwhile, is doing experiments that I never even thought to run— namely, how many stickers can you fit on one device before it ceases to function all together."

I laughed at the idea, picturing the sweet, little boy in my mind.

Javi added, "In happier news, Manuela is pregnant again. Another little girl."

"Wow," I said in wonder. "Grandbaby number seven. Your mom must be thrilled."

"She is," he replied. "Really takes the pressure off me to provide grandkids when you have sisters as fertile as mine."

I laughed, and the sensation of laughing again felt good. His words brought the image to my mind of what Javi would be like as a father. I pictured him running after a toddler and picking her up in his arms, making her giggle as he tickled her sides. I pictured him teaching a child to ride a bike or helping a preteen through her math homework. He would be an amazing dad, I imagined. A part of my brain registered that in all my daydreaming, I had failed to include a woman who would be the mother to those children. My heart clenched painfully at the thought.

"Why are you looking at me like that?" he asked, making me realize I was staring rather intensely at him. "Do I have something on my face?"

"No," I replied, shaking my head. "I was just thinking that you'd be a great dad."

He blushed furiously. He wouldn't meet my eyes after the unprovoked compliment.

"Thanks, Di." After a long minute, he added, "For the record, I think you'd be a great mom, too. I mean, if that's something you wanted. I don't think I've ever heard you mention wanting kids. But I've seen you with my nieces and nephews. They love you."

I pondered the idea. "Clearly, now, I feel like I can barely take care of myself, much less another human being. But I think I'd probably want kids someday, yeah."

The thought hadn't truly crossed my mind until this moment, but they became true as I said them. We sat in thought for another minute, neither of us making a move to continue our game of *Scrabble*.

"Hey, there's still a little sunlight left in the day. What do you say we take a walk, get some fresh air? Maybe stop for some dinner on the way back?" he suggested.

"Well, considering you've been force feeding me snacks all day, I don't know how hungry I'll be for dinner. But I'm willing to give it a try," I said. I moved to get some real clothes out of my drawers to change into.

We walked the half mile to the Columbia undergraduate campus and wandered through it aimlessly, Javi pointing out places that had been important to one or both of us along the way. When we had walked long enough for me to find an appetite again, we grabbed burgers and fries at the nearby Shake Shack, shameless comfort food.

When we made it back to my apartment at the end of the night, I set to cleaning up our board games, and Javi started making a bed for himself on my couch.

"You're not staying at a hotel?" I asked him.

"No," he said. "I came here to be with you. I'm staying as close as you'll let me."

"Oh," I said, not knowing what else to say. We took turns in my tiny bathroom readying ourselves for sleep. When I had turned out the lights and climbed into bed, I stared up at the ceiling, knowing without asking that Javi was still awake.

"Javi?" I asked, my tone searching. He didn't respond or wait for me to ask this time. I heard him approaching in the dark.

"Scootch over, Doc," he said, and the familiarity of the circumstance was comforting. I scootched until my back was against the wall to give him space, but he held my hand between us as I fell asleep.

The next three days became a comforting routine of playing games and watching movies with Javi, who either made or picked up every meal and many snacks in between. He refilled my water bottle without asking me. He insisted we take walks at least once, sometimes twice a day around the neighborhood, insisting on fresh air and sunlight as part of my 'healing regimen.'

When the day came that I was originally scheduled to take the exam, I felt like a new person. Like the last month hardly existed anymore.

Over breakfast that day, as Javi handed me a plate of French toast, I said to him, "I think I'm ready to prepare for my exam again."

He looked pleased. "Great. How can I help?"

We found our new rhythm. Instead of finding ways to distract my brain from the situation, to keep me from spiraling into feelings of dread and self-doubt, we found ways to focus it. I sat down at my desk to open my review book, happy to find that the feelings of panic and terror did not flood my senses like it had so often this past month. We spent the week in a pattern of studying and taking breaks. Javi would sometimes read aloud to me from my textbooks, his warm, deep voice making the dry material seem interesting again. During our afternoon walks, he would quiz me from flash cards and celebrate me when I got most of them right.

The night before the exam, we walked in the direction of Tom's Diner without even discussing it. We got our milkshakes—cookies and cream and pistachio—and made our way to the sundial.

When we were settled in our old familiar spot, I said to him, "You didn't have to do all this, Javi. I don't know what I did in a past life to deserve you, but I will be eternally grateful for what you did for me this week."

"I know I didn't have to do it," he said earnestly. "But I wanted to. I wanted you to be able to focus on healing and studying, not on your next meal or running out of coffee or whatever happened last week."

"I'm still scared for tomorrow," I admitted after a while.

"I know it's scary," he told me. "But you're not alone in this. You've got me. Blake. Your parents. We are all cheering you on. Promise me you'll walk into this exam tomorrow knowing you're not only doing this for you but for all of us who believe in you."

I leaned my head against his shoulder, looking up at the twinkling lights of Butler Library with him. "I promise."

The morning of the exam arrived rainy and gray. Javi

rode with me on the subway to the testing center. He had packed me a lunch and snacks for the testing day, which he handed to me like a kid going off for their first day of school. He hugged me.

"Just do your best, Doc," he said in my ear. "That's all anyone can ask."

When I walked out of the exam eight hours later, my mind a blur of questions and answers I was already beginning to second-guess, he was there. The doubts and fears about the exam fled my mind the second he smiled at me.

On our walk from the subway back to the apartment, Chinese takeout in our hands for dinner, my phone rang in my pocket. The caller ID was a picture of Blake and me in ratty scrubs from our last day of Anatomy lab. I answered.

"Hi, Blake," I said, gearing myself for Blake to be angry with me.

"Diana!" She said, sounding relieved on the other line. "I'm so glad you answered. How was the exam?"

The lack of anger in her voice surprised me. "Uh, fine, I guess? Didn't feel particularly good, but how else can an eight-hour-long exam feel but terrible?"

"I feel the same way," she said. "Took mine on Monday. Felt awful, but it's done!"

"It's done," I agreed.

"Hey, is Javi still with you?" she asked. "Or did he try to make it to Zurich for the end of the Biotech conference?"

I peered over at Javi, with Blake still on the phone. "No, he's still here. Didn't say anything at all about Zurich, in fact. I'll talk to you later, okay?"

"Oh, okay, Di. Talk to you later."

When I hung up with Blake, I peered at Javi.

"Zurich?" I accused. "You missed a conference in Zurich for me?"

He shrugged. "It's fine. Someone from my team went in my place."

"It's not fine," I insisted. "That sounds like a big deal. You missed it for me."

"And I would do it again," he retorted. "Look, all these meetings and conferences to promote The Artemis are important to me. But they mean nothing to me without having people I love to share it with. You're as important to me as my family, Di. Would you expect me not to run back to Texas if they needed me?"

I said nothing. I knew beyond a shadow of a doubt that Javi would do the same thing for any member of his family. But even so, I couldn't help but feel that I had become a burden to him, as I had become a burden to Michael. To the point that he couldn't stand being around me anymore. Javi had handled it considerably better than Michael had, but it didn't change the fact that it was unfair of me to expect Javi to pick me up off the floor every time things got stressful in my life. I had signed up for a career that promised a considerable amount of stress. And I had to find ways to cope with that stress without it affecting and hurting the people I loved.

Two days later, when Javi hugged me goodbye and hopped in a taxi to the airport, I looked up the number for student mental health services at my school and called to make an appointment.

Chapter 10

Medical School

Third Year

A few months into my third year and the start of my clinical rotations, I felt a shift within myself. It was as though all the theoretical knowledge from my textbooks was finally breathing, living, in the flurry of hospital activity. Each day brought new challenges, new things to learn in exciting new ways. For the first time in my life, I was more than just a student, sitting behind a textbook and learning the theory behind a problem or a disease. I was part of a team, a part of something bigger than myself. I was helping *real* people. And for the first time since starting medical school, I felt like I truly belonged.

It also helped that I finally had my anxiety under control. I had started an anti-anxiety medication two weeks after my Step 1 exam, and when it started to take effect, my brain felt like an unfamiliar landscape, in the very best way. It was like all the cobwebs and unnecessary junk had been cleared from the corners of my mind, leaving me feeling clean and for the first time, not terrified on a daily basis. I was seeing a counselor every other week who helped me talk through everything—my fears, my self-doubt, my relationship with my father.

Instead of frantically treading water, I was walking on it.

When I started my neurology rotation in the fall, I felt like I might have finally found my place in the world. Maybe it was Javi's influence on me, but there was something about the complexity of the human brain that appealed to me and fascinated me. The neurology team, with its many residents and attendings, welcomed me with open arms, pleased by my obvious interest and quick learning.

Dr. Lena Karam, one of my preceptors for the rotation, noticed my enthusiasm immediately. She was a petite woman with sharp eyes and a sharp mind. Her passion for the field was evident in every patient interaction I witnessed, every discussion with residents that she led. At the end of my third week with her team, she pulled me aside after rounds, her expression serious but encouraging.

"Diana," she began. "Have you given serious thought to what specialty you would like to pursue?"

I hesitated, knowing that somewhere in this very hospital, my father was probably operating, thinking in the back of his mind that I would be following in his footsteps someday.

"I sort of always assumed I would go into cardiothoracic surgery," I replied, noncommittally.

She flashed me a knowing smile. "Is that truly what *you* want to do?"

"It's still early in the year," I hedged, "but these three weeks with your team have been amazing. I could seriously see myself going into neurology after this."

"That's what I was hoping you would say," she said, beaming at me with pride. "I'm currently spearheading a clinical trial for a new drug for Alzheimer's disease. How would you like to join our research team?"

The offer took me by surprise, and I instantly felt a mix of excitement and fear at the prospect. It was an honor to be recognized and sought out by someone as respected in her field as Dr. Karam, but I wondered if I was up to the task. Her faith in me, her belief that I could contribute something valuable, though, was incredibly affirming.

"I would love to, Dr. Karam," I replied, the words out before I could second-guess myself. Her smile, broad and genuine and proud, told me I had made the right decision.

In the weeks that followed, I met with Dr. Karam and her team of resident researchers several times, mapping out my involvement in the trial. I balanced my regular rotations with patient interviews, literature reviews, and data analysis. The work was demanding but rewarding. Instead of feeling pulled in multiple directions to the point of fraying, as I feared I would feel, I felt like I was juggling my responsibilities well.

Christmas break approached, and I felt nervous to spend it with my parents. Halfway through my third year and my clinical rotations, I imagined that the conversation with my father about my desired specialty was inevitable. No matter how little time I agreed to spend in my parents' home, it would be almost impossible to avoid the subject entirely. And I didn't feel mentally prepared to have that fight with him.

Javi called a few days before Christmas. As soon as I saw his picture light up my phone, my lips stretched instantly into an involuntary wide grin.

"From what corner of the globe do I owe the pleasure?" I asked when I answered the line. I walked home from the subway in my scrubs and parka. The first real snow of the year had fallen that morning, and I was pleased that the little fluffy piles on the corners were not yet black and gray with urban grime.

"Palo Alto, if you can believe it," he said on the other line. "But the Artemis hit US shelves today, figuratively speaking. I'm probably going to be stateside for a few months during the roll-out."

I shook my head, though he obviously couldn't see the gesture. "Can you believe it? It feels like just yesterday you were pitching me the idea on the beach."

"I know," he said. "I can't believe we made it this far."

"I can," I replied. "I knew you were going to see this through."

"Your belief in me has not gone unnoticed," he said. "And it is appreciated. How is everything going on your rotations?"

"Really well," I said. "Just finished up my Ob/Gyn rotation. Delivered a couple babies this month!"

"That's amazing! Reconsidering neurology at all?"

"No, still pretty sure about it..." I said, though the uncertainty in my voice contrasted my words.

"But?" he asked.

"But I'm terrified to tell my father," I finished. "I'm spending Christmas Eve at home, and I don't know how I'm going to avoid him bringing it up. I already hide in janitor's closets every time I see him coming down the hallway at work."

Javi laughed. "At some point, you're going to have to tell him. You can't hide in closets forever."

I laughed too. "I don't know, my parents' place has quite a few closets."

"You're ridiculous," he said.

"But you love me?" I asked, grinning.

"But I love you," he confirmed, with a tenderness in his voice that left me speechless for several long seconds. I shook my head at the sudden fluttering in my stomach. Maybe it was the Zoloft making my brain interpret everything in a more positive light, but it seemed like conversations between Javi and I lately had been different, somehow. Like there was an underlying current to our words, something demanding sitting just below the surface of our conversations.

"Will I see you soon?" I asked him, my tone sounding a tad more desperate than I wanted. It was rare that we didn't have a visit scheduled. I had seen him and his family for Thanksgiving break, but he had been so busy with the final preparations for the distribution of the Artemis that we had not planned anything since.

"Very soon," he promised. "I'll check my schedule."

"Wonderful," I replied. "I can't wait."

"Me neither," he said. "Talk to you soon, Doc."

"Talk soon."

A few days later, I was in my parents' living room for Christmas Eve. I wore a fitted sweater dress in a deep red color with thigh high suede boots for the occasion. My hair fell in soft brown ringlets to my shoulders. The Christmas lights twinkled through frosted windows and cast a warm glow across the polished floors. My mom had decorated beautifully for the holidays, with garlands draped along the staircase and a towering fir tree adorned with silver and gold ornaments dominating most of the entryway. The festive atmosphere, however, did little to calm the uncomfortable fluttering in my stomach as I awaited my father's arrival. He had been called in for an emergency procedure that morning, but he had texted us that he was on his way back.

The doorbell rang, and my heart skipped a beat before I remembered that my father would not be ringing the doorbell. I rushed to answer it, pulling the door open to find Javi standing in my parents' doorway. My breath caught at the sight of him.

"Surprise!" he exclaimed, unwinding his scarf as he moved forward to hug me. My heart lurched with relief at his appearance.

"Javi! I can't believe you're here!" I wrapped him in a tight hug, feeling the cold from his coat seeping through my dress. "How are you here?"

"A little Christmas magic," he joked, eyes twinkling with mischief. He handed me a bottle of wine. "For your parents."

My mom appeared then out of the kitchen, wearing an apron and oven mitts over her green velvet dress. Her face lit up at the sight of Javi.

"Javier, what a wonderful surprise!" She embraced him warmly.

"Mrs. Richards, so lovely to see you," he told her.

She chastised him, "Really, Javier, you can call me Helen."

It was then that my father arrived back home. He had already changed back from scrubs into his nice clothes for the holiday, and I marveled at how his salt-and-pepper hair always seemed to stay in the same perfect arrangement, even though I knew he had spent several hours in a scrub cap. When he saw Javi, he gave him a firm handshake.

"Good to see you, Javier," he said. "This is a surprise."

"And you, Dr. Richards," he said. "I thought it would be nice to surprise Diana for the holidays."

We settled in the dining room as mom served dinner. The evening began more pleasantly than I could have hoped for with the unexpected addition of Javi. He charmed my parents, as he did everyone, with tales of his adventures around the world and the progress on distribution of his device. My father seemed genuinely impressed with Javi's accomplishments. But as the plates were cleared and we settled around the fire in the living room with our desserts, I could feel the conversation shift to me, like a physical thing, a change of the wind.

"So how are the rotations going, kid?" my father inquired, settling into his favorite leather armchair. "All of your preceptors rave about you whenever they see me around. Surgery next, right?"

"Mm hmm," I mumbled, pushing chocolate pie around my plate. Without saying anything, Javi's knee moved almost imperceptibly until it was touching mine, providing quiet support.

"That's going to be the real test," he said enthusiastically. "Gotta bring your A-game! You're going to need those references for your residency applications next year."

I debated giving another non-committal response. But this was a conversation I needed to have with him, whether it was now or in six months when I began my applications. But it was rare to have my two biggest supporters in life in one room—Javi and my mom—to back me up. I had to take this opportunity to speak up for myself and my dreams.

"Actually, I've been thinking about it a lot." I looked across the living room at him. "I think I'd like to go into neurology."

My voice was steady despite the pounding in my chest, and I was proud of myself for that. Javi's knee gave mine another reassuring nudge.

"Neurology?" my father asked, his dessert fork clattering against his plate. "Why on Earth would you choose that? You have surgeon's hands, Diana. I know your Step 1 score was average, but you can't discount surgery already based on that alone."

My jaw clenched, my teeth grinding together at the

comment about my step score. To bring up that time of my life on Christmas, of all days, seemed like a low blow. But if I was being fair, he didn't know anything about how terrible my life had been back in June, when I had taken the exam. He didn't know how close I had come to quitting medical school all together. He only knew about the outcome: a mediocre score.

"It has nothing to do with my step score," I said, resolutely. "I want to do neurology because I love it. I've been working with Dr. Karam on this Alzheimer's clinical trial, and I love the work. I love the patients and the science behind it. This is what I want to do with my life, Dad."

"Neurology is a waste of your talents. I had high hopes of you following in my footsteps." The disappointment in his voice was a sharp, tangible thing, cutting deeper than I cared to admit. I put my plate down on the coffee table, my hands clenching into fists.

"This is what I'm passionate about. This is where I think I can make a real difference," I insisted.

"Bigger difference than you can make repairing hearts? You're being ridiculous, Diana. You'll see once you do your surgical rotation, I'm sure."

The room fell silent. My mom looked between us, worry creasing her brow, but said nothing. This is how it had always been with her. She was my biggest supporter when we were alone, and a silent bystander when we were with my father. I looked at my hands, my resolve crumbling. It was Javi who broke the hefty silence.

"Dr. Richards, with all due respect, isn't it more important for Diana to pursue something she's passionate about?" he asked, and I braced myself for my father's inevitable explosion. "I've seen Diana's dedication to neurology, her passion for this field, and it's inspiring. And I greatly respect what you do, Dr. Richards.

Undoubtedly, the heart is the most vital organ. But the brain?"

He paused for dramatic effect, and the flicker of a grin tugged at the corner of my mouth, knowing his penchant for a little drama.

"The brain orchestrates the symphony that is human experience. Comparing the two is like comparing the engine to the rocket scientist who figured out how to send a man into space. Both organs are complex, to be sure, but one of them pumps blood and the other encapsulates the entire cosmos of human experience and memory and emotion. She might not be doing what you do, sir, but I'd say she's diving into one of the ultimate frontiers. I can't imagine trying to minimize that."

I met Javi's gaze, glowing with the force of his pride in me.

Emboldened by his praise, I found my voice. "I couldn't have said it better. Dad, I'm going into this field because I believe in helping people live better, not just longer. It's where I can make a difference."

"And she will," Javi added, resolutely.

My father's brow furrowed, his mouth opening to retort, but I pressed on, "Just because I'm not following in your footsteps doesn't mean my path is any less valuable. I need you to try to understand that."

The room fell silent. My mom looked worried, her eyes darting between me and my father, while Javi was a steady and calming presence beside me. My father sat back in his chair. His expression was inscrutable for a long moment.

Finally, he nodded. "I see your point. Your passion for the field, *both* of your passion for it, is commendable. I suppose it'll take some time for me to come to terms with the idea of not sharing my world with you. But perhaps I need to look more into yours."

Relief washed over me. A huge weight seemed to float off my shoulders.

"Thank you, Dad," I managed, my voice thick with emotion.

Javi beamed at me. As the evening wore on, the tension dissolved, replaced with the cheer of the holiday and a cautious optimism between my father and me.

Javi and I bid my parents good night a little while later. When we were safely on the street and out of sight and earshot of my parents, I threw myself at Javi, squeezing him as tight as I could.

"That was amazing!" I exclaimed, the thrill of the moment making my voice breathier than I intended. "I can't believe you stood up to my dad like that."

"Me?" Javi chuckled, his eyes twinkling with a mix of adrenaline and amusement. "What about you? You were incredible!"

I released him from the hug, but reached up, cupping his face gently. As our laughter subsided, for just a moment, the space between us felt charged with an unspoken energy. The cold bit at our cheeks, which were flushed from our excitement. The snow fell gently in flurries around us. His skin was warm under my touch. He had me locked beneath his deep, inextricable gaze.

"You couldn't have given me a better Christmas present," I whispered, my thumbs brushing lightly against his cheeks.

The world around us seemed to pause in that moment —silent except for the distant hum of the city. The fog of our breath mingled in the crisp winter air between us. His eyes flickered down to my lips, and for a heartbeat, I could have sworn he was going to close the distance between us.

But then, as if snapping out of a spell, Javi's expression shifted from my face. He gave a slight, almost imperceptible shake of his head, as though to clear it. He stepped away from me, my hands drifting down from his face with the motion. He reached into his backpack with a rueful smile that didn't quite reach his eyes.

"Oh, I almost forgot," he said, his voice a touch too casual. He fished a little blue bag out and handed it to me. "Merry Christmas, Doc."

I didn't have time to consider what had just passed between us, but the air still seemed to hum with what might have been. My heart stuttered in my chest.

I looked at the bag with eyebrows raised. Tiffany blue.

"Javi," I said, my voice laced with fear. "There is literally nothing that could be in this bag that wouldn't be far too generous."

"Just open it," he pressed.

"Javi, a *thimble* from Tiffany's costs $300!" I insisted.

"Well, it's a good thing I didn't get you the thimble then," he said, laughing.

I shot him another disapproving glance, but I was far too curious not to open it. I unwrapped a white ribbon from around the little blue box, fished out a blue velvet bag, and poured its contents out into my hand. It was a silver bracelet, with a little charm dangling from the center link.

"It's a neuron," he said, clearly proud of his gift. And he had every right to be proud of it. It was an amazing, thoughtful, entirely too extravagant gift. I touched the little silver branches of the neuron pendant tenderly. The nucleus at the center was made of a single, small, glittering stone. I suspected, but was too afraid to ask, that it was a diamond. More than just a pretty piece of jewelry, this meant so much more. This meant that, even before he had seen me stand up to my father this evening, he had believed in me—believed that I was strong enough not to let my father's influence get in the way of pursuing my passion.

"Javi, this is way too much," I said softly. It was one thing to accept expensive gifts from my parents—it was another entirely to accept them from Javi, even if he did make good money now. Having him spend that money on me, and in such an incredibly thoughtful way, left me reeling.

"You can't take it back," he warned me sternly. "It's custom-made, and they were fresh out of other future neurologists to sell it to."

"I wouldn't dream of giving it back," I said, clutching the bracelet to my heart. The phrase *custom-made* did nothing to help the considerable guilt I felt. "It doesn't change the fact that it's entirely too much, though."

Javi shrugged but looked pleased by my reaction. "What good is having my device out in the world if I don't get to spend the money on people I love?"

"The thousands of lives you're going to save?" I asked him.

"Oh yeah," he answered, playfully nudging me with his shoulder. "I guess there's that too."

Javi called a cab to take us back to the apartment. When we were in my apartment again, stamping our boots free of snow and shedding parkas and scarves, I suddenly felt like being in such a small space with Javi was uncomfortable, in a way that it had never been before. He had literally slept in the same bed as me before, and yet I hadn't felt this flushed and nervous then.

I needed to distract myself from the uncomfortable feelings ruminating in my gut. I ran to my desk to fetch a framed picture I had left there.

"I, uh, also have something for you," I said, sounding shy as I showed him the gift. "I didn't have time to wrap it, since I didn't know when I would see you. I hope you like it."

Javi's face lit with excitement, and he inspected the picture carefully. It was a small painting, no bigger than a paperback novel.

"Diana, this is perfect. It's our view. Our exact view from the top of Butler. How did you manage it?" He touched the tiny paint strokes delicately with the tip of his finger.

"I know it's not Tiffany's," I joked, trying to ease the emotional weight of the moment. "But I figured we could both use a reminder of where we've come from, no matter where we go. I found an art student at Columbia who takes commissions. It only cost a *little* bit extra to get them to trespass onto the roof."

Javi laughed. His eyes softened as he looked from the picture to me, a mix of nostalgia and joy playing across his face.

"It's more precious than anything from Tiffany's. Thank you, Di," he murmured. "It's going right on my desk, and with me wherever I go."

He moved to tuck the picture away in the safety of his backpack, while I fled to the restroom to get ready for bed.

Javi and I spent the week catching up in warm coffee shops and bookstores. We took brief walks around the neighborhood before the chill brought us inside once more. We played board games and watched old movies, like we used to. I was happy that, even though Christmas had left me feeling confused and expectant, we settled into our usual routine easily.

When New Year's Eve arrived, the air was filled with a celebratory buzz in the city, and we finally decided to stop being hermits for the occasion. Blake invited us to join our other med school friends for a local party. I put my hair up into a high ponytail and wore a gold, sparkling mini dress for the occasion.

When I stepped out of the bathroom wearing it, I was gratified to find it had a dramatic effect on Javi. He did an actual double take at the dress. With my gold heels on, I was much closer to Javi's eye level than normal. I stepped close to him, brushing an invisible speck of dust off the glossy lapel of his black suit. I noted the bob of his Adam's apple in response to our proximity.

"Shall we?" I asked him, my red lips curving up into a coy smile.

He cleared his throat and stepped back to gesture to my door. "After you."

We arrived at the party to find Blake bedecked in sparkling emerald green and gold from head to toe. She wore a paper headband marking the year and put a matching one on my head as soon as I was in reach.

The party was lively, with music blaring and lights flashing as everyone danced and laughed, eager to ring in the new year. The glittering lights of the cityscape in the distance were mirrored by the sparkles of laughter and champagne that flowed freely throughout the night. As midnight approached, I positioned myself near Javi, our arms brushing as we stood watching the festivities. When the countdown began, a wave of excitement surged through the crowd. My heart leapt at the sound.

"Ten, nine, eight..." we joined in, our voices melding with the others.

"Three, two, one... Happy New Year!"

Cheers erupted and the air was filled with the festive sound of noisemakers. Tradition beckoned everyone to share a kiss with someone, and I glanced over to see Blake enthusiastically embracing a girl I remembered vaguely from my pediatrics rotation. Smiling at their antics, I turned to share a laugh about it with Javi. But instead of amusement, his expression appeared intense and a bit uncertain.

His eyes flickered down to my lips, and I took this as confirmation that he felt this too—this needy, heavy pull between us. I stepped forward until we were a breath away from each other. But I stopped short, my eyes searching his.

His hand wandered upward, bracing the side of my neck, and my whole world seemed to freeze as he drifted toward me. Finally, his lips brushed mine in a hesitant kiss —a fleeting connection that nonetheless sent a shockwave down my spine that rippled outward into my fingers and toes. I leaned in, diminishing the scant distance left between us. I placed one hand gently on his chest, where he felt like he was radiating heat, even through his black shirt and jacket. How could someone be so incredibly *warm* all the time? A little hum seemed to vibrate in his chest at the feeling of our lips together, and the sound and the feel of it against my palm made something inside me ache. I longed to pull him even closer, to deepen the kiss. To break whatever promises I had once made.

But he pulled away, and the world seemed to resume around us, the noise of the celebration crashing back into my awareness. The celebratory chaos seemed to swell back into focus. His eyes lingered on mine, flashing with a complex mix of emotions I couldn't interpret.

"Just a New Year's kiss," he murmured, his voice laden with silent questions, his eyes searching mine.

"Yeah," I whispered, my heart pounding even louder than the music. "Just New Year's."

Javi nodded slowly, a small smile playing at his lips as if to reassure both of us that our words were sincere. But there was a weight to the moment that lingered, like the final note of a song hanging in the air after the music had stopped. And I realized then that I didn't *want* it to stop.

As the party began to wind down, the guests trickling out into the early hours of the morning, Javi and I made our way out onto the street to head back to my apartment. The cold January air was sharp, but the tension between us felt sharper. We pulled our coats around ourselves, our breath visible in the frosty air.

"I'll be heading out tomorrow," he finally said, breaking the heavy silence that had settled between us. His voice was soft, almost hesitant. "Got an early flight back to California."

I nodded, not trusting myself to speak yet. I didn't want him to see the disappointment I felt at his departure, nor the tangled mess of feelings I couldn't quite understand myself.

"These visits are always too short," he remarked.

"They are," I agreed.

Javi seemed abnormally quiet on the subway ride home, on the walk back to my apartment, and while we readied ourselves for bed. After turning out the light, I stared up at my ceiling for a long time, knowing, as I always seemed to know, that Javi was not asleep. But this time my heart was pounding expectantly, so loudly in my ears I was afraid he could hear it in the tiny space. A part of me was tempted to call out to him, as I had done in the past. But this felt so different than those other times. Those times, I had been looking for comfort. This time, the memory of that kiss occupied the entire forefront of my thoughts. This time, if I called out, I wasn't sure if I was ready to handle the ramifications of what it would mean for us, for our friendship.

And I had to remind myself that he was leaving. He would be back in California before the day was done.

I stayed quiet until a fitful, restless sort of sleep finally overcame me.

I woke before the dawn, only a few hours later. I lay awake for those moments, listening to the rhythm of his breathing. When he finally stirred, I made us coffee and toast as Javi quietly packed up his things. I walked him out to the curb so he could catch a taxi to the airport. Javi pulled me into a hug.

"I'm so happy you came out this week, Javi." I pulled away from our hug to look up at him. Our eyes locked, and I could almost sense that same hesitation, the same unspoken words I wanted to say reflected at me in his eyes. But he shook his head and looked away, as he had before on Christmas.

My smile faded at his expression. "Is everything okay?"

"Yeah..." he replied, but his tone was hesitant. "It's just, I don't feel like I've been completely open with you this trip."

My heart thudded with concern. "Okay? What about?"

He seemed to collect his thoughts for a long moment before he would meet my eyes again. "I've started seeing someone. In California."

I stepped back from him as suddenly as if he had electrocuted me. A mix of emotions flooded through me, a complicated blend of jealousy, disappointment, and sadness, but I quickly covered it up with a too-bright smile that I forced my lips into with great difficulty.

"Oh, Javi, that's great!" I exclaimed, my voice a pitch too high. "I mean, that is so great. Just great. She must be great."

I shook my head, realizing just how many times I had said the word 'great' in one sentence.

"She is," he replied softly, sounding guilty at the admission. "It's pretty new. Her name is Alex. She works for a start-up in Palo Alto. We met at a tech conference a couple of months back. Only started dating a couple weeks ago. I didn't really plan for it to happen, especially not now, but—"

'But that's how the best things in life happen, right? Unplanned?" I cut in, my heart sinking a bit with each word. I felt like it was getting harder to breathe the more we spoke.

"Yeah, exactly," he agreed, a touch of sadness in his smile. He took a deep breath, seeming as unsettled as I felt. "I want to be honest with you, Di. You're my best friend. I should have told you when I first got here, I just... It just hadn't come up."

"Of course, no, I get it," I said, though I didn't really. Why *hadn't* he told me? We told each other everything— how could he leave out such a vital piece of information?

I took several small steps back until we were maybe six feet apart. It might as well have been an ocean apart. The silence stretched between us for an uncomfortably long time.

"Well, have a safe flight, Javi," I said quickly, a clear dismissal.

"Yeah, okay... Thanks, Di." He turned away from me, toward the street and the approaching taxis. "Take care of yourself."

I watched him go, my feigned happiness crumbling into the cold winter air.

My fingers lifted to my lips, brushing them gently. They were chapped with the frosty weather, but I could almost feel them still tingling from the kiss. They curved down into a grimace at the memory. I knew now that it had truly meant nothing to him, as he had said. *Just a New Year's thing.* And I felt a completely foreign emotion well up and boil in my gut at the thought—I was angry at Javi.

I couldn't remember ever really being angry at him before. But he had a *girlfriend*. He had kissed me, and *he had a girlfriend*. Of all the people I had ever known, I would never have dreamed him capable of toying with my emotions like this. Even though it was the briefest, most innocent kiss, I felt foolish and embarrassed that it had happened.

But if I was honest with myself, it wasn't his fault. It was mine. My mind had apparently been inventing things all week—furtive glances, soft touches, heavy pauses between us. I had given meaning to signs that had apparently never been there, that I had fabricated. That little part of my mind—the part that asked dangerous questions about what Javi and I were to each other—had reared its ugly head once more. I usually was better at keeping that part tucked away, stifled in the back corners of my mind.

But I had let it escape once again, in definitive and heartbreaking fashion.

Chapter 11

Medical School

Third Year

"How are we feeling about seeing Javi?" Blake asked. I avoided looking at her, instead staring past her out the airplane window at the California shore below.

"Great," I replied, my voice pitched a tad too high to be believable.

"Uh huh," Blake said, smirking. "And how are we feeling about meeting the girlfriend?"

"Better than great," I squeaked at an even higher decibel.

Blake laughed. "I would work on that voice before we see them."

After everything that happened over Christmas and New Year's, I tried to convince myself that it was just the heightened emotions around the holidays that had gotten to me. I had said as much to Blake, after I debriefed her on everything that had happened during that week. She had, unfortunately, disagreed with my conclusions. In fact, she was now completely convinced that we were both hopelessly smitten with each other, despite my adamant protestations.

Regardless, the last six months had proven that something had fundamentally changed between Javi and me that week. At least, it had changed for me. Since that day, we still talked and updated each other on our lives, but it felt cordial and forced, when conversation between us had always flowed so easily before. We didn't FaceTime every Friday or say 'I love you' at the end of conversations anymore. We had occasionally spoken in hypotheticals about future visits and when we would see each other next, but those plans had dissolved as quickly as we mentioned them each time.

When Blake suggested we take a trip together to commemorate the end of our third year—her only stipulation being that wine and sun had to be involved—Napa had seemed like the perfect location. She had laughed at me knowingly when I suggested it, but she was completely on board, even if she knew I had selfish intentions at heart. So we set our sights on an idyllic long weekend in Napa Valley, a much-needed respite from the demands of medical school. Meanwhile, I was determined to use this time with Javi to fix what we had broken; to not lose the greatest friend I had ever known.

The California sun greeted us as Blake and I walked out of San Francisco International Airport. Javi was there waiting for us, leaning against a sleek black Tesla, looking like he belonged on the cover of a magazine made to highlight the young (and in this case, heartbreakingly attractive) tech geniuses of California. He wore a black V-neck t-shirt and dark jeans. He had let his hair grow long, nearly to his jawline, and I had the sudden, horrifying desire to run my fingers through it.

There went any suspicions I might have harbored that my feelings in December were only a temporary moment of insanity.

My breath hitched painfully when he smiled at me, that dazzling smile that could outshine anything the California sun could offer. I hadn't realized quite how much I had missed that smile in the last six months. I left my suitcase ten feet short of the destination and ran for him. He lifted me off the ground as we embraced.

"Finally," he said as he set me down, his chocolatey brown eyes twinkling with delight. "You made it."

It was then that I realized that Alex was standing beside Javi, leaning against the hood of the car. She was striking in her effortless elegance, wearing a flowing white summer dress and a wide brimmed hat over thick, shiny blonde hair. Her smile to us was warm, with the faintest hint of caution in her eyes.

"Diana, this is Alex," Javi turned to her, still grinning widely at me. "And Alex, this is Diana. My best friend."

Alex stepped forward and shook my hand. "It's wonderful to meet you. Javier's stories don't do you justice."

I didn't really know what to say to that, so I just nodded and smiled feebly. "It's so great to meet you, Alex."

"Oh, and this is Blake Njoku, she's Diana's friend from medical school," he added, almost as if he had forgotten Blake was there for a moment. "Blake is going to be an anesthesiologist."

"Lovely," Alex said, shaking Blake's hand.

Blake smiled in a way, I knew from experience, meant trouble. "So great to meet you, Alex. Can't wait to spend the weekend getting to know you."

Alex nodded, looking a little unsure, as if she wasn't

certain whether Blake meant her words or not. I fought the urge to let out a groan. I could only imagine what Blake's words foretold for the weekend ahead.

Javi loaded our suitcases into the car and opened the doors for each of us. We made light conversation on the drive to Napa, getting to know each other as the city gave way to the rolling vineyards outside. Alex spoke about her work at GreenPulse, a startup focused on sustainable energy, with a passion that was both infectious and intimidating.

She was everything I could have feared she would be. She was smart and driven. From her account of her work and Javi's proud commentary, she played an integral role at her company. She was witty and well-spoken. Obviously beautiful. I was certain her features fit the golden ratio to a T. I wondered a little bitterly if she might be not-too-distantly related to Kate Upton. She was, it hurt to admit, a true bombshell.

If I had to choose someone to liken myself to, I would call myself more of a watered-down Lily Collins. I would never say I was ugly, but no one could ever mistake me for a bombshell. I was certain that having us side-by-side this weekend would make that abundantly clear to Javi, too, in case it wasn't already.

We decided to get straight to the vineyards without stopping at the Airbnb. Javi and Alex, who had been to the Valley a few times already, had chosen the vineyards we would be visiting this weekend. Javi pulled into a long driveway, and the first vineyard came fully into view out the window. It looked straight out of a postcard, with rows of lush green vines sprawling beneath the soft California sun.

When we met our guide, a man whose passion for winemaking was as vast as the vineyard itself, he led us through the sprawling fields. Javi and I naturally fell behind the tour group as we quietly began to catch up. But we hadn't been even relatively alone for more than a few minutes before Alex wandered over to take Javi by the hand, pulling him forward with her to speak to the tour guide about grapes.

I frowned, and Blake shot a withering look at Alex's back at the action.

After the tour, we settled on the vineyard's charming veranda, overlooking the expanse of green hills. A waiter set the table with a showcase for the local produce: artisanal cheeses, freshly baked bread, and a selection of wines chosen specifically to enhance the food selections and explained in eloquent detail.

We leaned back in our chairs with our glasses of wine in hand, cheeks flushed with the warmth of the afternoon. We discussed the food and the wine mostly, but eventually our discussion turned to our future aspirations.

"I think I'd like to go into a fellowship," Blake mused aloud. "Maybe cardiothoracic anesthesiology or critical care. What about you, Di? Do you think you'll stick to general neurology? Or are you thinking of doing a fellowship? How perfect would it be if you went into fellowship for epilepsy, after everything Javi has done with his device?"

"I haven't given it much thought," I said absentmindedly. The last thing on my mind today had been medicine, if I was being honest.

"Regardless of what she decides," Javi declared proudly, "she's going to make her mark on the field. But if she were to choose a fellowship in epilepsy, I am obviously partial to the idea of our career paths aligning someday."

He lifted his glass to me in cheers, and I felt Alex's stare boring a hole into me as he spoke. I looked away from them both, reaching up to brush my hair off my face as I fought the hopeful flickering of my heart.

"What an interesting charm," Alex remarked, catching the glint of my silver bracelet in the sunlight. "May I see it?"

I wasn't sure why, but my first instinct was to decline—to keep Javi's gift a protected secret from her. But I didn't know how to politely refuse the request, so I held my wrist out to her across the table. She inspected the delicate jewelry.

"Tiffany, isn't it?" she asked, still holding my palm. "How beautiful."

I wanted to snatch my hand back but resisted.

"It's a neuron. Javi gave it to me after I decided to specialize in neurology," I explained softly.

She let go of my hand, and I pulled it back quickly. My fingers subconsciously brushed over the charm.

"What a thoughtful gift," she finally added. I nodded but said nothing more on the subject.

The conversation gently shifted away, but the air at the table seemed to change. We excused ourselves from the table and drove away from the vineyard, this time in silence. We drove into town and wandered the quaint shops and boutiques as the afternoon faded into dusk. Blake and I looked around the shop we were in at one point, realizing that we hadn't seen Javi and Alex for several minutes. When they reappeared a little while later, something about them seemed off. Whatever had transpired in their short absence had obviously caused some tension between them. Blake looked at me with a curious arch of one eyebrow, as if to ask, *are you seeing what I'm seeing?*

Alex seemed quieter after that; her smiles more measured, her laughter a beat too late. Javi too, seemed different—more reserved, his usual casual grace and ease replaced by a careful and stiff neutrality. Though I was trying desperately to relax and enjoy my vacation, I found myself obsessively over-analyzing their expressions and body language.

We chose a popular indoor-outdoor bistro for dinner. We were seated in a courtyard with lattices of climbing vines with white and purple flowers overhead. The setting was incredibly warm and romantic, contrasting the cold chill that had settled over our group.

Our conversation over dinner was stilted. As dessert arrived—a decadent chocolate lava cake that melted under the assault of our spoons—Alex excused herself to take a phone call. Javi's face betrayed the faintest hint of concern as he watched her walk away. Blake's eyes darted between us, and she excused herself swiftly to use the restroom. I knew it was her way of giving us a moment alone.

"Everything okay?" I asked, my voice low. I leaned forward, resting a hand on his arm with concern. His eyes flickered down to where I touched him and lingered there. Though he didn't shake off my touch, he didn't look particularly pleased by the contact either.

He managed a half-smile, his gaze flickering away from my hand, back toward the direction in which Alex had left. "Yeah, she's handling some business stuff, you know?"

But that was clearly an excuse. I could feel it—the tension hanging heavily between us. I wanted to ask more, to explore the heart of his troubles, but I felt the lingering distance of the last six months between us like we were still on opposite ends of the country.

We settled into the Airbnb after dinner. It was a cozy little home close to town, with two bedrooms and one bathroom. The decor leaned heavily into wine country, with various art pieces, created by local artists I'd bet, out of discarded wine corks and bottles. We took turns in the bathroom before turning in for the night.

Blake rolled over to look at me in the queen bed we were sharing.

"What a first day, huh?" She smirked at me. I covered my face with my pillow and, very quietly, let out a muffled scream.

"I'm sorry I dragged you into this mess," I grumbled into the pillow.

"Are you kidding?" she asked. "I'm having a great time. I not only get to drink delicious wine, but I have free entertainment. It's like a soap opera."

I gave another muffled scream as my response, making Blake laugh.

"Do you want me to take her out?" Blake joked.

"No!" I insisted, shoving her arm. "I *want* Javi to be happy. Alex makes him happy, so she is a part of my life now. We have to make this thing work with her, or I'm afraid I'm going to lose him. And I'm not willing to do that."

"Okaaaay." Blake sighed. "But the offer stands if you change your mind."

I ignored her, turning off the bedside lamp and rolling over to go to sleep, determined that the following day, I would make the utmost effort to forge a relationship with Alex. I didn't want her to see me as a threat, even if some little part of me, tucked consciously away into the back of my mind, protested in a very threatening way.

The next day, we slept in, deciding once we had readied ourselves for the day to head into town for brunch before the next winery tour that afternoon. I did as I intended. I sought Alex out for every conversation. *Alex, isn't this restaurant so quaint? Alex, your French toast looks amazing.*

Alex, where do you get your dresses? Oh Alex, I wish I could pull off a hat like you, I don't have the face for it. And so on.

I could feel Javi watching me during these exchanges with a curious expression; not quite skepticism, but also not quite pleased at my obvious efforts to get to know his girlfriend. Alex seemed a little taken aback by my sudden enthusiasm, but she was willing to converse with me, nonetheless. As we drove from brunch to the vineyard, I asked enough questions to know basically her entire life story.

She was from Sacramento. She went to UCLA for undergrad and got her MBA at Berkeley. She had two younger brothers, one in college and one in his last year of law school, and she had a cat named Henry. I asked to see pictures of the fat orange kitty and the brothers, both just as attractive as their sister. I whistled low in appreciation at the image of her brother, the future lawyer.

"Is he single?" I asked with obvious appreciation. "Maybe you could set me up."

Alex laughed good-naturedly as if I were making a joke, but I could feel Javi and Blake shooting me equally dubious looks.

I looked down at my cell to see a text come through from Blake, even though she was sitting beside me.

> BN: Be cool. You sound like you're trying to get Alex to sleep with you instead of Javi.

I shoved my phone into my lap after reading the text, a blush heating my cheeks at her comment. I leaned back in my seat, realizing I had climbed all the way to the front of my seat to get closer to Alex as I interrogated her about her life. My phone *dinged* with another text, and I looked down, almost too afraid to read it.

> BN: I mean, she is pretty hot. Maybe they'll both be in love with you by the end of the weekend. Think they'll ask you to join in?

I wanted to throw my phone out the window. I glanced toward the front of the vehicle for a moment and saw Javi looking at me in the rearview mirror. My blush intensified when our eyes met, and I averted my gaze quickly, hoping he hadn't seen my reaction.

"Everything okay, Di?" Javi asked from the front seat, sounding half-concerned but also amused, as if he somehow knew what Blake had texted me.

"Oh yeah, everything's great," I replied, not meeting his eyes again. I heard the softest chuckle coming from Blake's seat, and I suddenly regretted inviting her on this trip.

We made it to the next vineyard a short while later. As we wandered through the fields with our guide, I linked arms with Alex, chatting with her animatedly, leaving Javi and Blake to follow behind us.

We explored the vineyard, as well as two others nearby, before we settled in for dinner in the final locale of the day. Dinner was a quiet affair, filled with the clinking of glasses and light banter of conversation. Later, we settled on the porch of our Airbnb around the fire pit, the night air crisp. It was during these moments, under the twinkling starlight, that I caught Javi's gaze lingering on mine, a silent conversation seeming to pass between us with each glance.

The third and final day dawned. We spent the day exploring a local farmer's market and a few more wineries. As the sun dipped below the horizon on our last evening together, the scenic backdrop was a bittersweet reminder of how fleeting these moments together always were for Javi and me.

Our conversation turned back to the wine, as we each tasted what was clearly the fan favorite of the weekend. Blake swirled the wine in her glass pensively. "You know, they say the best wines are the ones that have had time to mature, to really come into their own. It's kind of like relationships, in that way, huh? Those that have been nurtured for a long time, that have grown through shared experiences and challenges, those are the ones that truly stand the test of time."

She paused to let her words sink in, a small smile playing at her lips as she added, "It's the depth and the complexity that make them both more rewarding. Don't you think?"

"Well said," Javi muttered, looking a touch suspicious at Blake's declaration. I glared at her, though she simply smirked back at me.

That evening, the last night of our weekend together, we sat around the living room in our pajamas, enjoying the last few of the bottles we had selected from our vineyard tours. Blake, who had been exploring a cabinet in the corner, suddenly dropped a box onto the coffee table, startling everyone.

"Let's play!" Blake exclaimed, and I saw that she had dropped the box for *Code Names* on the table in front of us. Javi grinned—I had never once seen him turn down a board game—and immediately started setting up the cards. We split into teams, Javi and Alex vs. Blake and me.

Javi and Blake volunteered to give clues first, leaving Alex and I to guess which words related to their clues. It took a few rounds for each of us to understand the flow of our partner's clues and their thought process, but soon we were laughing and debating over each word and association.

Each time Javi gave a clue to Alex, and she in turn

spent time mulling over the words and his possible meaning, I fought the urge to answer in her stead. I *knew* Javi's mind. Sometimes, I thought, I knew it better than my own. And no matter how obscure the clue, his exact meaning almost always came to me immediately.

Blake and I were leading three rounds to one, and while he appeared to be enjoying himself, Javi was clearly irritated. He *hated* to lose. Few people could match his competitiveness. Blake sipped her wine, eyeing us across the coffee table.

"How about we switch partners for a couple rounds? Alex and me, Javi and Diana," Blake suggested. I didn't believe the innocent tone of her voice, not for one second.

Alex pursed her lips but did not argue. We rearranged the cards once more, and Blake and Javi set about thinking of clues for their words.

Blake and Alex only managed to guess one word with their first clue. Javi grinned at me smugly over the cards, and I knew instantly that he was not going to hold back just because his girlfriend was on the opposite team. He was going to win at all costs.

"For my clue: Orion." He eyed Blake and Alex, then looked back to me with cool confidence. "Times *five.*"

Blake guffawed. "Five words? There's no way."

I looked over the words between us, contemplating silently.

"Star. Belt. Space." I began, and Javi nodded with satisfaction as he plopped our blue cards on top of each word as I recited them. "Telescope. Soldier."

Javi placed our fourth and fifth blue cards, grinning in triumph. It took only one more round for Javi and me to clinch the victory.

Blake shook her head in mock exasperation as she

smirked at Alex. "Well, I surrender. I don't know why I bothered. It's like they have telepathy, right?"

"It is," Alex agreed quietly. Still glowing from our victory, Javi didn't seem to notice how Alex watched us, her brows furrowed with concern. I very purposefully grabbed my wine and a blanket and put some distance between Javi and me.

"I'm going to sit on the patio for a bit," I said to no one in particular.

"I should start packing up," Alex said, heading in the direction of the bedrooms.

Blake excused herself to shower. She teased, "Don't drink all the wine without me."

"I wouldn't dream of it," I told her as I opened the sliding glass door to the backyard. The night air was cool. The soft glow of hanging lanterns lit the wooden patio. I curled up on the little couch with my blanket around me, lifting my wine glass to my lips. My senses were pleasantly fuzzy with the effects of the several glasses of wine we had poured throughout the evening.

After a few minutes, the sliding glass door opened, and Javi emerged. He sat beside me on the couch, leaning back and looking up at the stars above as he quietly sipped his own glass of wine. We said nothing to each other for several minutes, but the air between us felt charged, heavy with unspoken sentiments that had built up steadily over the last six months, peaking this weekend with our proximity.

"Do you still think about those hours we'd spend on the roof of the library looking up at the stars?" he asked wistfully. I imagined the game had made him as nostalgic for those moments as it had made me. "We'd lay on that blanket we hid in the stairwell for hours. Even through all the fog and lights of the city, I'd find constellations to point out to you."

"Orion was always your favorite," I replied quietly, looking up at the stars with him, admiring our old friend in the sky, with his belt and bow made of starlight.

"Most nights, it was the only one you could see," he responded with a quiet chuckle.

The stars were so much brighter here than in Manhattan. For every star I recognized, there were another thousand that I felt I had never seen before.

"No matter how much I rambled on, you always seemed so fascinated by my stories. By my dreams," he mused. "You never once made me feel foolish or unreasonable. No matter how wild the dreams. I miss that sometimes."

I turned from the stars to meet his eyes, reflecting the flickering lantern light. There was an intense emotion blistering there. I tried not to delude myself into thinking that that emotion was anything akin to longing or need, the way it looked—the way I felt.

I swallowed against a hard lump in my throat. "I never got tired of hearing about your dreams. I still don't."

I could hear my heart pounding in my ears. I was keenly aware of how close we were in this moment, yet how far we had drifted apart.

I wanted to tell him. I wanted to tell him how much the last six months had killed me, feeling our connection to each other fade with each passing day. I wanted to tell him how I thought back to New Year's with equal parts longing and anger, knowing that what had transpired had strained what we had.

But instead of all that, I said, "Sometimes I wish we could go back to those moments. Before med school.

Before California. When it was you and me against the world."

He reached out and gently rested a hand on my knee. Even that small touch seemed to send a current of electricity rippling beneath my skin. "Me too."

The patio door slid open abruptly and Alex stepped outside, her presence slicing through the moment like a cold breeze. She stopped short when she saw us, an indiscernible expression crossing her face as she noted the proximity between us, Javi's hand on my knee. Javi lifted his hand and shifted away from me, as if changing his body language might somehow reset the atmosphere.

"Sorry, didn't mean to interrupt," she said, her tone neutral but her eyes sharp as she watched us. "I was coming to see if you wanted me to pack your bag as well."

"No, that's okay," he said, standing from the couch suddenly. "I'll go get that done now. Thanks though."

Javi walked inside quickly, leaving Alex and I alone on the patio. I silently cursed him for running away, leaving me alone with his clearly disgruntled girlfriend. I was tempted to make the same excuse and scurry away inside, but I knew that I would look incredibly guilty, even if she had walked out to see us in a relatively innocent scenario.

"Diana, can I be honest with you?" Alex asked, her voice steady, her eyes not meeting mine. She looked up at the stars, as Javi and I had been doing before. She studied them, seeming unimpressed, like she couldn't fathom what we saw in them.

"Of course," I replied, though I dreaded what I thought she might say.

"I see the way Javier looks at you," she began. "I saw the bracelet. I hear how he talks about you. It's clear you mean a lot to him—maybe more than just a friend should."

Her words struck a raw nerve. I recoiled slightly, my voice rising in protest, "Alex, you're misunderstanding things. Javi and I are just friends. Best friends. We've been through a lot together. But there's nothing more to it than that."

"It's not your fault," she told me calmly, musing on the subject like it was a mildly interesting thought experiment. "I think there are feelings there on both sides, that neither of you have really admitted to. Maybe you don't even see it. But I can't be with someone who has that connection with someone else. It wouldn't be fair to any of us."

I stood, shaking my head in protest. "No, Alex, please. You sound like you're going to break up with Javi over this, and I just couldn't bear it if I knew I was responsible for this not working. I just want Javi to be happy. I want you *both* to be happy."

She smiled a little sadly at me. "I know you do. And that's the problem. No one knows how to make Javier happier than you do. I can never compete with that."

Tears welled in my eyes. My voice was strained. "I'm sorry, Alex."

She shrugged. "I'm not. It's better to recognize these things now rather than later, right? I hope you two figure things out, Diana."

She turned toward the sliding door, and I panicked. "Alex, are you—"

"I'm going to go talk to him now," she said. "My friend is on her way to take me home. She'll be here soon."

After she had disappeared back inside the house, I sat back down on the couch and put my head down in my arms, feeling defeated. Her words echoed in my mind long after she left.

What were Javi and I doing? Were we denying a deeper connection, or were we merely holding each other back from making real connections with other people? What if Javi hadn't gone to California three years ago? What might have been? Would I have continued to deny this *thing* between us, merely to keep a vow I had made to myself years and years ago? Or would we have given up resisting this gravitational force long ago?

It was impossible to know what might have been. All I knew now was that this was my fault. Javi was inside, having his heart actively broken, and it was entirely my fault. I just couldn't bear knowing I had been responsible for someone hurting him.

When Javi emerged half an hour later, I wiped away tears and looked up at him expectantly. His eyes were red and puffy. He sniffled a little, his hands in the pockets of his black sweatpants.

"Alex broke up with me," he finally said.

"I know," I replied. "Javi, I'm so sorry."

"She told you." He posed it as a statement, not a question.

I nodded. "She did. She saw how we were together, how close we are. I'm so sorry, Javi, I tried to tell her we're just friends—"

"*Diana*—" He stopped suddenly, steeling himself, and I was shocked at the anger in his voice. I *never* wanted something like this to happen. I never thought Javi could be capable of being so upset or angry with me. I couldn't bear the thought of it.

"I've been thinking," I said, before he could continue; before he could find the words to express his anger with me. "Maybe we're too close."

The anger seemed to leech from his expression as quickly as it had appeared. His eyes searched mine, wide with an emotion I couldn't quite name. "Diana, what are you saying?"

"I'm saying maybe we need to take a step back," I explained miserably. "It's not fair to anyone we might date if they have to constantly wonder about us."

He stayed silent for a long time. Finally, he shrugged, conceding. "Maybe you're right. Maybe we need to give each other some space for a while."

I nodded, even though my heart ached. "I think it's for the best, Javi. We can't keep complicating each other's lives. We can't sabotage each other from finding happiness."

Javi turned back and went inside the house. I walked to the room I was sharing with Blake. When she saw me standing in the doorway of our room, she ran to me immediately, taking me into her arms. The second my head hit her shoulder, I burst into tears. I kept my sobs as quiet as possible, not wanting Javi to hear me in the adjacent room.

"They broke up?" Blake asked quietly.

"They broke up," I confirmed miserably.

"I heard some of the discussion," Blake admitted. "Di, I'm so sorry."

I shook my head, sputtering pitifully, "It's all my fault."

She looked at my face, wiping tears away that were only replaced by more. "It's not your fault. You two were just meant to—"

"We're going to give each other some space for a while," I told her.

"Some space?" Blake asked, looking shocked. "But Di, this is... you two..."

"It's for the best," I said finally. Blake looked skeptical but didn't argue with me. She patted my back soothingly as I cried myself to sleep.

The next morning, we got our things packed and prepared the Airbnb for checkout silently, orbiting each other without speaking. We made the long trip back to San

Francisco International; Blake and I with our headphones on, Javi listening to the radio. When we got to the airport, Javi got out and unloaded our suitcases.

He looked at me sadly. I fought the return of tears looking at him.

He pulled me in for a hug. "Diana? Regardless of what happened, you'll always be my best friend. That won't change."

I nodded against his shoulder. I repeated, "Still my best friend."

Blake and I walked away, my heart breaking little by little with each step that I took away from him.

Chapter 12

Medical School

Fourth Year

The blue light of my laptop cast an eerie glow in my dark room, the tab bar at the top of my browser open with about twenty different home pages for neurology residency programs. My notebook was open beside me in my bed, with pros and cons lists for each program. The Match, the online program that sorted medical students into residencies, was set to open in a few days. I had all my ducks in a row—the lists of extracurricular activities, references from my mentors, a personal statement—ready to upload when the program went live. My score from Step 2, the second of our licensing exams, had posted the week before, and I was pleased that I had done significantly better on the second exam than I had on the first. All I needed to do was finish my list of programs to which I'd be applying in the coming weeks.

Startling me out of my focus, my phone began to vibrate against my thigh. I couldn't imagine who would be calling me, considering it was nearing midnight. I saw Javi's and my picture on the screen, and my heart clenched painfully at the sight. It had been three months since that ill-fated trip to California that had ended in the dissolution of Javi's relationship. We hadn't spoken since, true to our word about giving each other space. I held my breath and answered the call.

"Javi?" My voice sounded concerned, afraid.

"Diana," his voice cracked, and I knew instantly from his tone that something was seriously wrong. "It's my dad. He had a heart attack. They... they don't know if he's going to make it."

The world seemed to stand still, the background hum of the city out my window fading to nothing. My heart raced as I pictured Javi's proud father—quiet, kind, an incredible chef and musician, a wonderful father and grandfather. The image clashed violently with the reality of Javi's revelation.

"I'm so sorry, Javi," I whispered. "Where are you? Are you heading to Texas?"

"I'm at the airport now," his voice shook. "Diana, what if he doesn't... what if I can't get there—"

"Don't think that way," I replied sternly. "Just focus on getting there, and we'll figure everything out from there."

"We?" he whispered, sounding desperately hopeful.

"Yes, I'm coming." My fingers were already flying across the keyboard of my laptop looking at flight information. "I'm getting on the next available flight. I'll be there as soon as I can, Javi."

"Diana, you don't have to—"

"I'm coming," I interrupted, decided. There was no question in my mind. Javi needed me.

"Thanks, Di," he said, relieved. "I'm going to head straight to Corpus Christi Medical Center when I get there. I'll keep you updated."

"Please do," I replied, and the other line went silent.

I emailed the medical student coordinator at school to

let her know that I had a family emergency and that I would be out for the week.

I purchased a ticket on the first flight out in the morning. I didn't have time to contemplate how I had carefully allotted the amount of money in my bank account for the exorbitant cost of residency applications, which typically ran at least several hundred, if not over a thousand dollars.

When I arrived the next day, the air was a mix of warm, humid breezes and jet fuel. I had only packed a small carry-on and my backpack, so I bypassed baggage claim and went straight to meet my Uber. I texted Javi that I was on my way.

When I made it to the hospital, Javi was waiting for me outside, his figure leaning heavily against the wall, the strain of the previous night's events etched deeply into his features. I threw myself from the car as soon as it pulled to a stop. Our eyes met, and a mix of relief and sorrow passed over his face.

He pushed himself from the wall, opening his arms to catch me as soon as I ran to him. We clung to each other so tight, as if we could hold together the breaking pieces of our crumbling world. He buried his face in my hair and breathed in deeply. I ran my hands along his back, relishing in his warmth. It put into sharp relief just how cold the last three months had felt without him. I hated that it had to be for *this* reason, but I was so grateful to be near him again.

"Thank you for coming," he murmured into my hair.

"Always," I breathed back, pulling away just enough to look at him. "How is he?"

"Alive," he said with a sigh. "But not out of the woods."

I turned to thank my Uber driver. Javi took my bags from me and walked us into the hospital, to the wing of the medical ICU. The smell of antiseptic and the sound of beeping monitors greeted us distantly, a familiar atmosphere that suddenly felt cold and hostile given the circumstances. We met his family in the waiting room. His mother, normally a bastion of strength and life, looked small and worn.

I hugged his mother and his eldest sister, Gaby. Manuela and Valeria were in the room with their father, as only two visitors were allowed at a time. Javi's brothers-in-law had the kids at the house.

When his sisters returned, Javi and I made our way down the hall together toward his father's hospital room. His hand found mine as we walked, squeezing it tightly as if to anchor himself in the storm. His father was still sedated after his emergency bypass surgery the evening before. Javi sat in the chair beside the hospital bed, holding his father's hand to his lips as he cried against it. I placed my hands on his quivering shoulders, trying to provide what little comfort I could.

The next few days in the hospital blurred together under the sterile lights, each one melting into the next with little change in Mr. Valenzuela's condition. I found myself slipping easily into the role of mediator between the doctors and Javi's family, translating medical jargon into terms they could understand.

Javi's mother often found herself overwhelmed by the clinical coldness of the updates. She would grip my hand, her eyes searching mine for something more hopeful than the last prognosis. Each time, I would squeeze her hand back and offer whatever reassurance in whatever measure I could. But I had to be careful not to give her false hope when he was still in such a precarious condition.

I tried in vain to turn off the part of my brain that had memorized the long list of potential complications one could incur after a heart attack: congestive heart failure, ventricular fibrillation, pericarditis, rupture of the ventricular free wall, and unfortunately so much more. I could see the list from my textbook on the back of my eyelids as I fell asleep each night. Those possible outcomes, once nothing more to me than words on the page when I studied them in the past, now felt like all my worst nightmares as I watched the Valenzuelas suffer.

Javi and I spent the days wandering in and out of the hospital. We made coffee and food runs for his mother, who refused to leave the hospital for even one second. His sisters packed her a bag of clothes. In our idle moments, he and his family and I would muse over memories of his father in healthier days—his amazing cooking, his love of music, his quiet but sharp sense of humor.

Finally, after three days, they were able to safely take him out of sedation. While he was still weak, he was able to hold his wife's hand and tell her and each of his children *te amo*. That same evening, there was a subtle but noticeable shift in the doctors' outlook on his condition. They had only given guarded and somber updates thus far, but suddenly shifted to talking about recovery and the 'long road ahead.' I knew this meant that he was past the worst of it, though the more insidious complications still lurked in the back of my mind. I didn't tell Javi or his family about those possibilities. I let them revel in the relief that came with the first positive update they had received.

Gaby finally convinced her mother to leave the hospital to shower and rest at home for a night. She promised to stay by her father's side and call her with any updates. Manuela and Valeria excused themselves to check on the children. Javi and I wandered out of the hospital. We sat in his father's truck, which Javi had been borrowing.

Javi sat behind the steering wheel, looking ahead

through the windshield, though he made no motion to put the keys into the ignition. His eyes squinted against the setting sun, his brows furrowed. His lips were pressed together, the corner quivering involuntarily into a frown, as if he fought against it.

For the last few days, at least in front of his family, he had been putting on such a brave face. He had stepped into the role of the calm, cool-headed leader of the family —the role his father usually occupied. I could see how much it was killing him. I could see the thin precipice upon which he seemed to walk in order to maintain his composure, and how easily he could fall into despair at any moment.

I reached over to place my hand on his, where it rested on the leather bench seat between us. But as soon as my skin touched his, his composure seemed to break. He tugged on my hand, pulling me across the seat to him. He pulled me into his arms so forcefully I nearly fell across his lap.

He squeezed me to his chest, where I could feel the heaving motion of his sobs and the pounding of his heart. One of his arms wrapped around my lower back, pulling me fully to sit on his lap. His other hand wove into my hair, cupping the back of my head as he cried into my neck. I ran my fingers into his hair, the other hand wrapping around his neck. I didn't even question how intimate the position felt, how more inches of my skin seemed to burn against his than we had ever allowed before.

"I don't know… what I would've done… if you hadn't come," he gasped between tears.

"Hey… *Hey*." I pulled his face away from my neck, holding his cheeks in my hands as I stared pointedly into his eyes. They glistened with tears.

"Nothing could have kept me away," I assured him,

brushing his hair back from his face as I spoke. "There is nowhere else I'd rather be."

I remembered back to a time when he had said the same words to me, when I was at my lowest low.

He searched my face desperately, flitting down to my lips, begging for permission. My eyes went wide at the silent request, realizing what he wanted—what he was asking for. I stopped breathing in that moment, not knowing how to respond. But without conscious thought, I felt myself nod almost imperceptibly, just the briefest dip of my chin downward and back, giving the approval he was looking for.

Not even a second passed before he crushed his lips to mine. Unlike New Year's Eve, there was nothing hesitant, nothing uncertain about this kiss. It was hard and desperate and wanting. His lips pressed firmly against mine, demanding them to move with his. His fingers gripped at my hair, stopping just short of causing pain. We turned in unison, testing the angles of the kiss. His tongue traced my bottom lip, and I groaned into his mouth at the sensation. He understandably took that as a sign of approval and began to explore my tongue with his.

His hand ducked beneath the hem of my shirt, grazing against my hip. His skin was so damn warm, it was like he set a trail ablaze on my skin.

My hands slid down his face and his neck, settling on his pectoral muscles. I splayed my fingers across them, relishing how they flexed and jumped beneath my touch with his movements. His hand crept upward, over my ribs, his thumb tracing the cup of my bra, locating and circling my hardened nipple. The wanting, the need was coiling in my belly, settling lower and lower until it became an almost unbearable ache between my thighs.

The feeling became more pronounced when I realized I could feel him, hard against my thigh.

Oh God, I thought.

Or at least, I thought I had kept the words inside my head, to myself.

But from the renewed energy with which he kissed and teased with his tongue and ran his hands along my skin, I realized I might have said them out loud.

His hand started to sink lower, moving from my bra over my navel to the button of my denim shorts.

"Oh God," I muttered against his lips, this time definitely out loud and for a slightly different reason. It felt better than I ever could have imagined, to finally be kissing and touching Javi after all these years of wondering and holding back. But the second he started to undo the buttons of my shorts, the second he threatened to *go there,* was the second that a cold sort of panic crept into my awareness, bringing my mind just a fraction back into focus.

What are we doing? That cold voice of reason said into the blank pit that had once held my rational thoughts.

Javi and I had always been tuned in to what the other needed, and some devilish part of my mind argued that this is what he needed—a reprieve from reality, a way to distract his tormented brain from the unfathomable situation happening to him. I could picture how easy it would be to give him that—to trace my hands down his chest, across the firm muscles of his abs, to wrap my hands around him. To give him a release, a distraction from reality.

But I didn't want to be just a distraction.

The world seemed to slow back into focus at the thought. The heat in my core cooled little by little. My lips slowed against his. I pulled away, hovering just an inch from his lips.

"Javi," I whispered. When he tried to lean back in, I cupped his cheek in my hand tenderly and held him away. "Javi, stop."

"Please," he whispered, leaning his forehead against mine. My heart lurched in pain at the desperation in his voice. His eyes opened but remained heavily lidded, smoldering into me. "Please, Diana. Don't tell me you don't want this too."

"It's not that," I said gently. I stroked his cheekbone with my thumb. "I just… I don't want it to happen like this."

Outside the hospital where his father almost died. In his father's truck. When he's feeling vulnerable, seeking any comfort he can find.

I loved this man. I *wanted* this man—the reaction of my body to his touch made that abundantly clear. But I didn't want this to happen for the wrong reasons, at the wrong moment.

The burning in his eyes faded. He leaned his head forward and rested it against my shoulder, sighing deeply.

"You're right," he said finally. "I'm so sorry."

I made soothing circles with my hands into his back as he leaned into me. When he finally started to loosen his grip on me, I attempted to slide off his lap. I moved a little clumsily, unsure how we had managed to move against each other so smoothly in such a small space only moments ago. In my efforts, I leaned back against the steering wheel and was startled half to death when I accidentally hit the horn.

I jolted violently at the noise, falling onto the leather bench seat. Javi looked down at me, sprawled across the seat next to him, and broke into a bout of uncontrollable laughter. I draped my arm across my eyes as I too was inundated with a fit of giggles. We laughed for several minutes without stopping, sounding almost like deranged hyenas by the end, gasping for breath. Tears sprang from our eyes. The stress that we had endured that week combined with the boundary we had just broken in our relationship had left us feeling delirious.

When we finally composed ourselves, I pulled myself up to a seated position and buckled myself into the passenger seat. Javi followed my lead, buckling himself in and finally putting the keys into the ignition. We made the drive back to his childhood home, our hands intertwined between us on the seat.

The next morning, Javi's father graduated from an ICU bed to a normal hospital room, where multiple visitors were allowed at once. We brought breakfast for his family, and we sat around Mr. Valenzuela's bed as we chatted and ate. He looked on at his family, serene but seemingly happy and not in pain. It lifted everyone's spirits significantly.

Javi kept glancing at me furtively, smiling to himself whenever we caught each other's eye for a moment. The energy between us was different—almost shy, for the first time in our entire relationship. My stomach did somersaults whenever I noticed him looking, but I hoped none of his family members noticed. His sisters, especially Gaby, were incredibly perceptive, and I didn't want them to think we had the wrong priorities.

After we left the hospital that afternoon, Javi drove us to the beach. We walked along the shore listening to the sound of the waves breaking gently against the sand. This beach felt like holy ground to us.

Javi reached over after we had been walking for a few minutes and laced his fingers through mine. I stopped walking when he did it, looking down at our intertwined hands and back up to his face, as if to ask, *do you think that's the best idea?*

He grinned down at me, his eyes filled with mischief. He asked, far too innocently, "I'm not allowed to hold your hand?"

I raised an eyebrow at him. "No, you can hold my hand… I just don't want you to get any *ideas*."

"You know me, Doc," he quipped. "My head is always *full of ideas*."

The little smirk of his lips and sudden darkening of his eyes made it clear what kind of ideas he was alluding to. My stomach dropped into my ankles at the unexpected comment, but I shook my head at his antics.

Suddenly, I broke my hand free of his and ran down the beach away from him. I heard him chasing after me immediately, and I giggled wildly as he tried to catch me. I marched into knee-deep water, leaning down to cup a handful of water to splash at him.

He paused briefly when the water hit his face, but I knew the second he blinked the saltwater away that I was in trouble. He began to splash me wildly in retaliation, until my hair and my blue dress were soaked through completely.

I wiped saltwater from my face, looking at him in mock exasperation.

"You win!" I declared. "Are you happy now?"

"Almost," he replied. A devilish smile lit his features. I turned to run from him, but I had sunk a bit into the loose sand, and I was slow to escape his assault. Before I had taken three steps, he scooped me up into his arms and started marching into deeper water with me.

My hands snaked around his neck. I laughed hysterically while trying to plead with him.

"Please," I begged between gasps. "Please… Javi, No…

I'm already all wet… No, don't… Please, Javi, I'll do anything…"

He laughed. "Anything?"

I gulped, my laughter choking off in my throat. What a dangerous question.

I backtracked. "Well, not anything—"

"Kiss me," he demanded. I looked up into his eyes, searching for a trace of that same emotion from the day before—the desperation, the unhealthy need for relief. But his eyes were playful, teasing. This expression didn't scare me the way it did the day before. I reached up, cupping his cheek in my hand, pulling his face down to mine slowly as I searched his eyes. When our lips were just barely separated, so close we were already sharing one breath, the corners of his eyes crinkled suddenly with a wicked smile.

And that's when he plummeted us both completely into the water.

I burst through the surface a moment later, gasping, wiping saltwater and hair out of my eyes. I started marching back to shore in outrage, done with our game. When I was in knee-high water, I turned back to glare at him. The second I did, though, I regretted it.

He whipped his hair back, drops of saltwater flying. He was wearing a white t-shirt, which of course was now completely see-through, clinging to muscular, tan skin beneath. I stopped where I was, staring unabashedly.

He held my stare as he approached me in the water, flashing a cocky grin as he passed me.

Jesus. When did that happen? When did he turn from my best friend into a Greek god?

I followed him out of the water and plopped down beside him onto the sand. We leaned backward onto our elbows, letting the late afternoon sun soak into our skin and clothes as we panted from the exertion.

"I missed you these last few months, Jav," I said into the companionable silence. "I saw the article: *Forbes' 30 Under 30.*"

He grinned a little sheepishly. "It felt wrong not to call you when I heard."

I nodded in agreement. It had felt wrong to see the article and have heard nothing about it.

"I saw the featurettes on the news and the segment on Good Morning America, too," I added. Valeria had texted them to me with excitement, not realizing that her brother and I hadn't spoken in months. I watched the interviews with pride, longing to be there with him, basking in his triumph.

"It's really taking off," he said wistfully.

"And it all started here," I mused.

"And it all started here," he repeated in wonder.

He turned to me suddenly. "Di, can I ask you an honest question?"

"Of course," I replied, my heart thrummed in anticipation.

"What you said in California about how we should give each other space. How we're holding each other back from being happy. Is that really what you wanted? Or what you want now?"

I shook my head, angry at myself in hindsight. "Of course it wasn't. It *isn't.*"

"I was working through a lot of big feelings with the breakup at the time, so what you said seemed like it made some sense," he replied, shaking his head as he looked out to the horizon. "But now it just seems so ridiculous. I don't want space from you. I don't want other people. Trying to convince myself I want anyone else is *exhausting*. I don't want to act like you mean any less to me than you do."

His words sent a thrill through me. Some part of me

that I had been suppressing all this time was cheering in victory. *Javi wants you. Javi wants to be with you.*

But just as I had stifled and quieted this part of myself in the past, I made myself do it once more. I took a deep, steadying breath.

"Javi," I said, in a reasonable tone that hurt to use. "I don't think it's the right time."

"When, Di?" he demanded. "When is the right time? When we've accomplished all our career goals? When we retire? Is that when we get to be happy?"

I shook my head, knowing he was being silly.

"When you haven't just been through personal tragedy," I retorted softly. "I don't want this to happen just because your dad almost—"

"So, what if I am?" he interrupted, and I frowned. Seeing my expression, he took my hand in his. "Not because I needed to feel better, but because I realized just how fragile life is. I realized that I don't want to waste time when life is so damn short."

My frown only deepened, unconvinced. He could see the skepticism in my expression.

He let out a frustrated groan. "How long do I have to wait before I can prove to you that I'm not doing this for the wrong reasons?"

I laughed. "I don't know, Javi. It's not as simple as that. I can't just give you an exact date."

He sighed at my noncommittal response. "Fine. I can wait, then. You tell me when it's been enough time, and I'll be there. Just say when."

I couldn't fight the small smile that tugged at my lips.

"But in the meantime," he continued, "the last few months fucking sucked. Can we please, at least, go back to being friends? Even if you and I both know it's more than that?"

I sighed at him but smiled. "We can."

"It's settled then?" he asked, hopefully. "For now, we can go back to the way things were. Texting and calling whenever we want. Visiting each other whenever we can? FaceTiming each other every Friday."

And telling me you love me whenever we hang up, I added in my mind. Aloud, I said, "Yes, I'd like that very much."

"Tell me how things are going at school," he said, obviously pleased to be settling back into our normal routine. "Last year of medical school, and I feel like I barely know what's going on with you."

"Residency applications opened this week," I said, my stomach doing a few uncomfortable flips as I remembered that I had left my application pretty much abandoned in light of everything that had happened this week. "Interview offers will roll out soon, and the interviews will be held between October and January."

"And your research?" he asked.

I grinned. "My clinical trial is going to be published in a big journal. And I've been accepted to present at the American Neurological Symposium next month."

His eyes went wide with delight. "Diana, that's amazing! That's a big deal!"

"The whole team is really excited," I said.

"I bet. That's a huge accomplishment." He paused for a minute, looking away from me, his eyes scanning the waves ahead of us. "And, uh, are you dating anyone?"

I laughed dubiously, thinking back to that kiss. "Now you ask? A little late for that, isn't it?"

He grinned. "Answer the question.

"No, not dating anyone," I relented. "You?"

"Nope," he answered, shaking his head. "So that means we're *both* not dating anyone."

I smirked. "Yes, that is what that means."

"Interesting," he replied. "Both single at the same time."

I laughed, finding his too casual tone hilarious, considering everything that had happened in the last twenty-four hours.

"Hey," I said after a long, loaded silence. "Are you going to come out for my Match Day in March?"

Thinking of that day, the day that all medical students learned if and where they would be accepted to residency, made me want to vomit. But the thought of Javi being there, at least, calmed my unease a bit.

He nodded emphatically. "Of course I'll be there."

"And my graduation ceremony in May?"

"Wouldn't miss it for the world," he said. I linked my arm through his and leaned my head against his shoulder.

"Unfortunately, in order to match and graduate in the spring, I have to head back to New York soon," I reminded him sadly.

"Do you already have a flight scheduled?" he asked. His voice was timid, his grip on my arm tightening ever so slightly as if he subconsciously was not planning to let me go.

"No. I dropped everything and bought a one-way ticket when you called me," I explained. "But I should really try to find my way back this weekend. I have a new rotation starting Monday."

"If you must," he sighed. We stayed on the beach leaning on each other until the sun had fully set beyond the horizon. We reluctantly pulled ourselves up from the sand and strolled back to the truck.

The following morning, we returned to the hospital with the family. Javi sat beside his father, speaking to him with a wide smile as his father nodded along happily. Mr. Valenzuela's doctors came by throughout the morning, and

I listened attentively as they discussed upcoming plans for discharge and follow-up. They thought he might indeed be able to go home the next day. Javi's mother cried and squeezed the doctors with delight when they told her.

I found a flight out for the following morning, dropping another $150 on the ticket. I thought distantly that money this month was going to be tight. I had choices to make— would I subside entirely on instant ramen for the month, apply to half as many residency programs as I had intended to, or swallow my pride and ask my parents for money? None of the options appealed to me. I could already imagine the smug retorts that would greet me if I went crawling to my father for help.

I knew that Javi had the money and would lend it to me in a heartbeat if I asked. But I would never ask. I would never ask him to pay my way here to help him and his family this week. I had done that completely out of love and didn't want the money to ruin that. I supposed the lesser evil would be groveling to my parents. It was worth it though, for the Valenzuelas.

Javi drove me to the airport the next morning. He walked around to open the door for me and held me tight in his arms for several minutes before he would let me consider walking inside.

"Thank you again, for everything," he whispered in my ear.

"Anytime," I whispered back. "I'll see you soon?"

"See you soon," he promised. He hesitated for just a moment before he added, "I love you, Diana. I didn't miss saying goodbye to you, but I did miss telling you that."

God, I had missed it too.

"I love you, Javi," I finally replied.

I reluctantly tore myself from his arms and grabbed my backpack and suitcase, heading for the doors.

"Hey, Di?" he called.

I turned back to him expectantly, halfway through the sliding glass doors.

"Just say when. I'll be waiting."

My breath hitched in my throat at the promise. I smiled at him before I turned to walk inside. I thought to myself as I walked away that, unlike the last time that we had said goodbye, when it felt like the end of something, this felt like the beginning of something new for us.

Chapter 13

Medical School

Fourth Year

I smiled down at my screen as I walked into the grand conference center in San Antonio. My research team members and a few of my classmates from medical school joined me as we approached the check-in desk. The woman at the desk handed me a badge with my credentials: *Diana Richards, Medical Student, Columbia University.*

Nothing sexier than *business casual,* I thought with quiet amusement as I replied to his text. In the last month since Javi and I had parted ways in Corpus Christi, despite his promises that we would "return to being friends," our communication had taken a decidedly flirtatious turn. His texts were filled with suggestive jokes and innuendo that made me flush and laugh in equal measure. I was certain he must be having some kind of competition with himself to see how many times he could get me to blush in one day.

He had begun to request to FaceTime more often than phone calls, and he usually—*coincidentally*—made these calls to me from his bed, typically shirtless. The first time it happened—the first time I was greeted not only with his smiling face, but also the jump scare of several inches of smooth, tan skin over the curve of trapezius and deltoid and pectoral muscles—I had to act like I wasn't incredibly flustered the entire call. But it had happened so many times now over the last month that I was finally starting to become desensitized to it. I don't know why my brain had initially decided to act like a schoolgirl who had never seen a shirtless man before, but I was starting to regain a bit of my dignity.

The change that was continuing to leave me flustered and a little bewildered was Javi's new salutation, the new way he now ended each of our conversations: *Just say when, Diana. I'll be waiting. Love you.*

My heart lurched a little in discomfort at the thought. I was so surprised the first time he said it, I hung up without even saying goodbye. Now I typically rolled my eyes at him and said, *'good night, Javi, love you too,'* but even then, it took a lot of effort to remain nonchalant.

I didn't know what my end point was—when to take the leap, to see what this was between us. With Mr. Valenzuela home and doing well, making good progress on his recovery, I was quickly running out of excuses not to acknowledge it. But the 3,000 miles that stretched between us still loomed large.

I read his next message.

JV: What's on the agenda today?

I picked up one of the programs from the check-in desk to see for myself what the day held. There was a welcome breakfast going on now to which my group would be heading shortly. There were lectures on ethics and leadership and various neurological disorders to choose from; a panel of neurology residents speaking on residency interviews; a networking lunch. I knew that I would be presenting my research the following day in the morning before attending a residency fair in the afternoon. I typed a reply.

> DR: Looks like a lot of good lectures to choose from.

I followed my group as they headed to one of the larger conference rooms to grab coffee and bagels as we mingled with doctors and students from all over the country. I knew I should put down my phone and join the throngs of people conversing, but my eyes kept darting back down to the screen.

> JV: I bet you'd be very interested in the two o'clock talk on Sunday

My brows furrowed as I stared down at my phone in confusion. When I finally put enough brain cells together to take the program back out of my pocket to inspect, I read ahead to the last day of the conference.

Sunday, 2:00 pm – Keynote Address: *The Power of Innovation in Shaping Neurological Care, by inventor and entrepreneur, Javier Valenzuela*

· · ·

My heart leapt as I read the words again, not believing what I saw directly before me.

"Javi?" I whispered to myself. I whirled around, searching the room frantically.

"What's up, Doc?" A voice I would recognize anywhere teased from behind me. I whirled on the spot, my heart leaping as I saw him standing there with his trademark grin, looking dashing in his crisp gray suit—no tie, the top button of his white shirt casually undone.

"Javi!" I cried, my professional demeanor completely forgotten as I rushed into his open arms. I squeezed him to me tight, his hands naturally settling on my lower back.

I pulled away from him, hitting him playfully in the chest. "Javier Valenzuela! *How* could you not tell me?"

He looked incredibly pleased with himself, grinning widely down at me. "They asked me to give the talk months ago. I was considering backing out after everything that happened last month with my dad, but then I found out you'd be presenting your research here and it felt like it was meant to be."

Meant to be, I agreed in my mind. It *did* feel like fate. After all this time apart, running toward our goals on opposite ends of the country, our worlds were colliding.

"I can't believe you're here," I said in wonder. My heart felt like it could burst at the sight of him.

His eyes crinkled with the force of his smile. "Glad I can still surprise you after all these years."

Javi looked over my shoulder, and I followed his attention distractedly. I realized with some horror that several members of my research team and my classmates were staring at us, clearly interested in the person I was embracing in the middle of a professional conference. I quickly extricated myself from Javi's arms and brought him over to my group to introduce them. They were delighted to meet not only my best friend, but the conference's guest of honor.

"Are you planning on going to most of the talks this weekend?" I asked Javi after my colleagues had gotten their fill of him.

"I wish I could go to half the talks this weekend," he replied regretfully. "My schedule is unfortunately packed. I didn't realize when I signed up for this how many people would insist on meeting me for lunch, dinner, coffee, etc. But don't worry, I wouldn't miss your poster presentation for the world."

I couldn't keep the disappointment from my expression. He sensed it immediately, adding, "But maybe we can sneak out for a bit? Explore the city?"

I nodded gratefully. "I already made dinner plans with my team tonight, but maybe—"

"Dessert?" he completed my sentence.

I grinned. "Milkshakes? The night before a big presentation counts, right?"

"Definitely counts," he agreed. "Meet me at the fountain, out by the riverwalk around eight pm."

I nodded happily. Even if I wouldn't get to spend all the time with him I might have hoped for, every second with him was one I hadn't expected to have this weekend. I was delighted at the prospect. After breakfast had concluded, he walked me to the room where the first lecture would be held before hugging me goodbye.

After the first lecture, I wish I could have told you what was so interesting about myelin oligodendrocyte glycoprotein antibody disorders, but I would have been far more able to expound upon things like the texture of Javi's dark hair or the tiny white scar abutting the curve of his upper lip, where he had hit the corner of a coffee table as a toddler, or the dimple in his left cheek, so deep it looked like I could lose my pinky nail in it.

I sighed at the thought.

The rest of the day's events and the dinner with my colleagues—the second-best Mexican food I had ever tasted, only inferior to Juan Valenzuela's cooking—passed in a distracted blur after that. I made excuses to my group after the dinner, telling the classmate I was rooming with not to wait up for me as I parted ways with them.

I found the fountain promptly at eight, but was too jittery to sit and wait. I paced slowly back and forth in front of the streaming water feature. The evening was balmy despite it being well into October. I shed my blazer, more comfortable in my pencil skirt and camisole.

"Who said you were allowed to start taking your clothes off without me?"

I whirled, choking on a surprised laugh. He sauntered up to me, holding a paper cup out as he approached. I took the offered cup as I shook my head at him, taking a long sip from it. *Pistachio.*

"Take a walk with me?" he asked, nodding in the direction that led away from the conference center to the main thoroughfare of the riverwalk. We settled into a relaxed stride along the river, conversation flowing easily between us as we caught up. We met the crowds milling in and out of the restaurants and bars, the bright lights and colorful umbrellas over outdoor tables reflecting off the dark rippling water.

Maybe it was the romantic atmosphere, or maybe it was the feeling that the universe was conspiring to bring us together this weekend, but I felt my reservations and fears start to melt away as I walked alongside him.

Say when. I'll be waiting.

He had said it dozens of times over the last month. He

had made it abundantly clear that he wanted more from this relationship than friendship. I had found a dozen reasons to hesitate, to question, to worry. A little voice in my head would always tell me we were going to ruin something good by wanting more.

But what if we were denying ourselves something *even better?*

I leaned over and laced my fingers through his. He didn't pause in the conversation or stop to acknowledge the subtle action. But he squeezed my hand gently back, his thumb brushing along my knuckle as we walked.

After we had walked nearly the entire length of the riverwalk, we finally turned to head back to the conference hotel. When we were in sight of the hotel in the distance, Javi let go of my hand without discussion. My palm felt cold in his absence, though the evening was warm. I tried to hide my frown. I wondered idly if he was worried about being seen by people we knew. We stayed quiet until we were back in the lobby of the hotel.

"I'll walk you back to your room," he suggested. Even though I knew it was a completely innocent offer—he knew I had a roommate asleep in my room—I still felt suddenly nervous, a thrill of anticipation fluttering in my belly. We rode the elevator together to the third floor, down the hallway, before I stopped in front of my door and turned back to him.

"This is my room," I told him, fiddling with the key card in my hand.

"Big day tomorrow," he said.

I had been so preoccupied with Javi that my research presentation had been pushed far into the back of my mind. Now that it was brought once more to the forefront, I was nervous for *two* different reasons.

He leaned forward ever so slightly, and I looked up into

his face expectantly. He had one hand in the pocket of his slacks, his other hand brushing absentmindedly against the scruff on his chin. I was momentarily distracted when his finger brushed against his lower lip. And then his lips were suddenly all I could think about—I couldn't steal my eyes away from them. His lips curved into a little smile, as if they liked having my undivided attention.

He stepped forward and closed the space between us. I thought he was going to kiss me—probably because I couldn't think of anything but kissing him. But he drew me in for a hug instead.

"Good night, Doc," he whispered. "You're going to kill it tomorrow."

He relinquished me and turned to go.

I stood at the door as he slowly backed away, waiting with anticipation for him to say it: *Say when. I'll be waiting.* His reminder that he was ready for us to be something more.

But it never came.

When I saw him finally disappear behind the turn for the elevators, I felt my lips pull into a frown.

I turned to enter my room, feeling disappointed, my head mulling over this turn of events. I quietly prepared for bed, trying not to wake my roommate. Once I was settled in my bed, my head still felt like it was reeling.

Why didn't he say it? I thought. *Has he waited long enough? Am I too late?*

Chapter 14

Medical School

Fourth Year

The next morning, I woke up with the distinct feeling that I had slept fitfully. I suffered a nightmare that I was presenting my research to the judges, only to find that they all had Alex's face. They approached me in all her blonde glory, nodding along as I stuttered painfully through my presentation, only for her to tell me that I was too late to be considered for any awards or scholarships.

The symbolism wasn't lost on me.

I stared at the ceiling, taking several deep breaths, trying to reassure myself that it was just a nightmare. The presentation was going to be fine. I was prepared.

I dressed in my cream-colored suit, did my hair and makeup, and gathered my poster and presentation materials. I walked with my roommate down to the lobby to meet the rest of our group for breakfast.

An hour later, I tacked the poster I had created on our clinical trial to my designated presentation space and waited for the conference attendees and judges to arrive.

When it was my turn, the judges, a panel of neurologists and researchers, approached and listened to my presentation intently, occasionally nodding or jotting down notes. My heart raced.

"Can you elaborate on the implications of your findings on current treatment paradigms?" one judge asked, peering over her glasses at me as she held her clipboard aloft.

I gathered my thoughts before I explained our suggested pathways for new therapeutic interventions. As I started to answer more of their questions, I settled into a steady confidence. I knew this study well—better than anyone. I had been there nearly from the start of the trial. I had managed the data analysis, put the results into tables, and written the paper that was now published under my name. I didn't need to be nervous about presenting it, when I felt like I could have recited it in my sleep.

The judges gave each other little knowing nods and smiles that made me feel like they liked what I had to say. When they walked away a few minutes later, I was beaming. No matter what happened, I knew I had done my best work, and I was proud of myself for that.

And most importantly, no one looked anything like Javi's ex.

A little while after the judges left my station, I was explaining my trial to a group of neurologists from Houston when I felt a soft little tingle up my spine—not an unpleasant sensation. I glanced over the shoulder of the doctor closest to me and saw Javi standing down the aisle twenty feet away, watching me. I paused for the briefest moment in my description of our statistical analysis, an involuntary smile playing on my lips. I could feel his eyes on me until the second they left my station, when he finally drifted forward to fill their space.

I breathed in deeply when I finally was able to get a

good look at him. He was wearing a coffee-colored suit and had decided again today to go without the tie. He crossed his arms as he looked at me, expectantly.

"Well?" he asked, grinning.

My brows furrowed in confusion, but the corner of my lips crept upward in the start of a smile. "Well, what?"

"Well, let me have it," he said, gesturing to the poster behind me. "I want the full show."

I shook my head at him, laughing. "No, you don't. I'm certain you couldn't care less about amyloid-binding monoclonal antibodies."

He shivered as if the words had sent a pleasant thrill through his body. "Say amyloid-binding monoclonal antibodies to me again."

He looked at me with a smoldering expression that made me squirm beneath the heat of it. I blushed furiously. My eyes darted around, relieved when it seemed like no one else within twenty feet of my station seemed to be interested at all in our discussion. I cleared my throat, trying to compose myself, before launching into my presentation from memory.

Javi watched the whole speech, from start to finish, never losing that burning look in his eyes. His eyes seeming to trail over every inch of me, and my skin seemed to tingle with the weight of his attention. He clapped quietly for me when I was done, still not taking his eyes off me. I shook my head at his little display.

Finally, Javi stole his eyes from me and watched another group of people as they approached my station.

"I can't hog the show all day, I guess," he said, winking at me as he started to turn to leave. "Will I see you later?"

"We were planning to go out for drinks later," I said quickly, wanting to make plans with him before we were interrupted. "Join us?"

He smiled. "I have a dinner scheduled, but I'll come join you after. Text me where you end up."

I left the poster presentation a little while later, feeling significantly lighter now that my responsibilities were over for the weekend. I found my classmates and enjoyed the afternoon with them, attending lectures and networking events. We got dinner on the riverwalk before we set out for our real destination—alcohol, and lots of it.

We started at an Irish pub but moved quickly onto another venue, one with enormous margaritas for next to nothing. I texted Javi updates each time we changed locations. At the beginning of the evening, my eyes were glued to my phone, waiting for him to confirm that he was on his way to meet up with us. But the farther into the evening we got, the less time I spent obsessing over when he would join us and the more time I spent enjoying myself. When I finally found him, I had already spent quite a bit of time enjoying myself, indeed.

"Javi! Javi!" I screamed across the river. Javi was talking to a group of people in business casual clothing, clearly attendees of the conference.

I didn't care who he was talking to at this moment, I wanted him *here*, next to me, enjoying the evening with me. I couldn't imagine anyone in this world who needed to be close to Javi like I needed to be.

Javi finally heard my calls and looked in my direction. His expression changed from confusion to amusement the moment he spotted me waving at him. He excused himself from his company and moved toward the stone bridge separating us. I hurried to the bridge, meeting him at the top of the arch of the stone structure. I threw my arms around him as soon as he was in reach. His stiff posture seemed to melt beneath my embrace, and his hands curled around my waist.

"Javi, you're here!" I exclaimed. "I thought you'd never escape those suits."

He laughed. "I did! Are you enjoying your evening, Doc?"

"*Very* much so," I agreed exuberantly. He leaned away to take in my appearance. And, I imagined, the smell of tequila.

"I can tell," he replied through laughter. "Have you had a couple drinks?"

"I *have*," I confirmed, a little guiltily. "Did you know they have *giant* margaritas here for almost *nothing*? They're like four dollars. Can you believe it? I couldn't get an *ice cube* for four dollars in a New York City bar."

"Welcome to Texas," he replied, the faintest trace of his accent slipping out with the phrase. "Everything's bigger here."

"Everything?" I asked, giggling at the implication.

He averted his eyes, smirking. "That's what they say anyway."

"*Javi?*" I asked.

"Yes?"

"Did you know there is a place here where the bartenders dance on the bar in cowboy boots?" I explained, very excited. I had heard a few of my classmates talking about going. "I think we should go there."

"Oh, do you now?" he asked, greatly amused.

"I *do*," I confirmed. "I would like to see if they would let me try dancing on the bar with them!"

"Oh, wow," he said, carefully considering the idea. "As much as I would absolutely *love* to see you try that, I think we should probably hold off for tonight. Maybe tomorrow though."

"Aw, okay," I pouted. "If you insist."

"I do insist," he assured me. "Can I walk you to some other destination? Maybe back to the hotel?"

I shook my head emphatically. "No, thank you. I would like to continue enjoying my evening. And I would very much like you to accompany me, good sir."

"Well, I would be delighted, ma'am. But I would love to be privy to the destination, if you don't mind," he replied, in his very best southern drawl that made me want to squeal in delight. I *loved* cowboy Javi.

"Dancing?" I asked. "Not on a bar, but on a dance floor?"

"Do you even know how to two-step?" he asked.

"No. Do you?" I asked with surprise and delight.

"I was born and raised here. Of course I know how to two-step," he replied, sounding offended I could have implied anything different. "I'll teach you some time."

One of the river taxis suddenly floated beneath us, distracting me, and I leaned over the edge to peer at it passing by. Javi's hands stayed on me as I moved, as if he was afraid that I would lean right over the edge.

"Let's go on a boat ride!" I enthused.

"I'm pretty sure the tours are closed for the evening," he responded. "But you should go tomorrow. It's a pretty good tour."

"Damn!" I cursed. "Well, what do we do then? I can't go on the boats or dance in cowboy boots. What else is there?"

He put his arm around my waist, starting to lead me down the stairs off the bridge and back onto the riverwalk. He let me lean into him as we walked, keeping me on the side of the walkway farthest from the water. I looked over at the dark, rippling water beside us.

"One of my friends told me it's a $500 fine if you fall into the river," I remarked curiously. "Is that true?"

"I'd rather we not test the theory," he warned. "But I think I've heard that as well."

I giggled. "So, you won't let me drink any more giant margaritas. You won't let me dance on bars in cowboy boots. You won't take me two-stepping. You won't let me go on boats. And now you won't let me go *swimming*? You were a lot more fun in college, Javier Valenzuela."

"I don't deny it," he relented with a chuckle.

I looked up suddenly, realizing he had steered us all the way back to the hotel while we talked.

I started to protest, "Hey, I don't—"

"You want to get some room service?" he cajoled. "They put me up in a very fancy suite for the event. All the food is on the hosts."

I smiled widely. My brain in its current state needed no further convincing. "Say less."

I took his hand, letting him lead me into the lobby. We got into the elevator, and he took a key out of his pocket to scan a sensor before pushing the button for the top floor. When Javi opened the double doors at the end of the long hallway on the top floor, my jaw dropped.

"*Javi*," I gushed. "This is *very* fancy."

"I told you." He took his suit jacket off, grinning at my reaction.

I ran through the room, spinning around with my arms wide.

"*Javi*," I gushed again. "You're so *fancy*."

"I promise, I'm not." He shook his head, laughing at me as he settled onto the couch, opening the room service menu to peruse the options. "No matter how many fancy hotels people put me up in, no matter where I go, I'll still always be that same kid bussing tables in his parents' restaurant."

I threw myself onto the couch beside him, making him

bounce slightly with the force of my impact. "What are we eating?"

"I say we stay true to our roots," he said, picking up the phone beside him to make the order. "French fries and milkshakes."

I nodded in agreement. After he placed the order, I stood from the couch, holding my hand out to him. "Javier Valenzuela!"

He took my offered hand. "*Yes*, Diana Richards?"

"You promised to teach me how to two-step!" I demanded.

He laughed and took his phone out of his pocket, searching his music app. He put on a slow tempo country song, with the twang of guitars and a very deep-voiced singer. He led me to the middle of the sitting room and twirled me by the hand once before grabbing my waist and drawing me into his chest. I put my free hand on his shoulder. He began to march a steady rhythm of two quick steps to the right followed by one slow step to the left, on and on with the beat of the music. I looked down at our feet, struggling to catch the rhythm.

"Stop looking at your feet and let me lead, silly," he teased.

I sighed but laid my head against his chest and let myself melt into his arms. Once I stopped focusing on what he was doing, it was an easy pattern to follow, even as dizzy as I felt with the effects of tequila. He turned us in the small space over and over like it was a tiny ballroom, two steps to the right and one step to the left.

"Javi?" I asked as the song ended and he spun me around once more.

"Yes?"

Another slow country song immediately followed the first, and he pulled me back into his arms to continue our dance. I leaned heavily against his shoulder, the room spinning a bit.

"Do you ever wonder—" The question I was about to ask suddenly escaped me as my stomach lurched.

"I think I'm going to—"

I pulled myself from his arms and ran to the adjacent bathroom, barely making it to the toilet in time to violently vomit. As the copious sour liquid fled my body, I felt him behind me, pulling my hair into his hands to keep it out of the line of fire. Most of my mind was occupied with the horrid act of vomiting, but a small part of it wished that he wasn't watching it happen.

When the waves of nausea finally ceased a little while later, I leaned against the toilet seat, feeling like the act had drained me of all energy. Javi moved about the bathroom, collecting a washcloth and soaking it in cool water. He handed it to me, and I pressed it into my face thankfully. The cool water was soothing on my hot skin. I wiped my mouth before setting it aside. Javi left the bathroom briefly before coming back with a stack of clothes in hand. He sat down on the tile beside me, rubbing my back.

"I'm sorry," I told him miserably.

"Don't be sorry," he reassured. "You have a lot to celebrate right now—med school's almost done, you did amazing on your research presentation. You just celebrated a little too hard this time."

"Too hard," I agreed. "Too many four-dollar margaritas."

He laughed, handing me the stack of his clothes. "Stay here tonight. I'll take care of you."

I shot him a feeble smile, taking the offered clothes. "Don't you know doctors make the ?"

"Well, then, I'll just have to take advantage of the last few months before it's official," he said.

After he left the bathroom, I took off my suit and pulled his t-shirt over my head. It fell to my mid-thigh, and though he had left me shorts as well, my brain in its current state decided that the shirt was more than enough. I splashed cool water on my face. My mind still felt fuzzy with alcohol, but at least the room had stopped spinning, and my stomach had stopped roiling every time I moved—at least, for now.

I took a bottle of mouthwash from the arrangement of hotel toiletries and rinsed my mouth twice, for good measure. I walked out of the bathroom. The food had arrived while I was in the bathroom, and I could smell the salty smell of French fries wafting throughout the room. But I was too scared to put anything on my stomach, out of fear that I would only lose it shortly after. When he saw me, his expression flashed from concern to amusement, then settled into a tense sort of exasperation.

"Diana," he said, sounding very serious. "You're not wearing pants."

"I am not," I agreed. I gestured to where his t-shirt fell on my thighs, covering all the necessary parts. "I did not find pants necessary. Thank you for the shirt, though."

He laughed. One of his hands slid down his face. "You're killing me, Di."

I sat next to him on the couch, pulling my legs up beneath me until my knee was brushing against his thigh. He averted his gaze, like he couldn't even look at me while I had so much leg exposed. My brain was admittedly sluggish, but it didn't seem to make any sense. Only a few hours ago, in a room filled with people, he had been undressing me with his eyes. Now that I was next to him, in private, it was like he could barely look at me.

I took a moment to analyze his body language. He looked... *uncomfortable* was the best word I could come up with. My brain slowly muddled through what I was seeing. A muscle in his jaw jumped as it clenched. His chest rose and fell against the buttons of his shirt in a faster rhythm than it should have, considering that he was relaxing on a couch. And when I looked down at his lap, the realization hit me quite suddenly.

Oh. He's aroused.

The sight of it made some little wicked part of my brain snap out of its last restraints. Before I could think of the logic or the consequences, I launched at him, straddling his lap in one motion.

His expression turned panicked. "Diana, what are you doing?"

"Saying when," I whispered into his ear. He had been teasing me for a month, waiting for me to be ready. I had left my inhibitions behind about three margaritas ago, so I suddenly felt incredibly *ready*.

My hands slid upward from his chest to his neck. His hands braced my hips, and while I was initially encouraged by the action, I noticed he carefully held me aloft, not letting me settle onto his lap.

"You don't want this?" I asked him, my voice sweet and innocent despite the devilish turn my thoughts had taken.

His Adam's apple bobbed as he swallowed. I could tell he was incredibly conflicted at the question. He didn't smile. His hands firmly held me aloft, keeping me from sinking down onto him like I longed to do. But his eyes burned hungrily, and I knew with everything I was that he *did* want this, just as much as I did.

His voice was gentle as he said, "It's not that, Di. I just really don't want it to happen like *this*. Not while you're drunk."

The statement took a long time to register in my mind, but a wave of disappointment washed over me when it did.

The heat of the moment was doused instantly, like water over a flame.

"Oh," I said sadly. I slid off his lap, back onto the couch beside him.

The crash of the exhaustion hit me. I tried not to feel jilted but couldn't help it. Javi had left a pillow and blanket on the couch at some point, and I leaned over to bury my face into it. Sleep began to swallow me within the first few seconds. Before I fully succumbed, I sensed Javi rising from the couch. I felt his arms tucking beneath my back and my knees as he lifted me to his chest, cradling me against him. He gently laid me down on the exquisitely soft bed.

His lips pressed against my temple. "Love you, Di."

"Love you," I whispered back, falling instantly into a deep sleep.

Chapter 15

Medical School

Fourth Year

When I woke in Javi's hotel suite, I felt as if I had emerged into a different universe. The sunlight streamed through the curtains, far too bright. I could barely open my eyes against the glare.

The evening came back to me in hazy detail, but the first feeling that I had was embarrassment. I knew instantly that I had made a fool of myself the night before. I shook my head as the memories flooded back—flashes of the lights over the riverwalk, dancing in the sitting room, straddling Javi's lap. I groaned at the memory. My head throbbed mercilessly, each pulse in my ears a reminder of the night's excesses.

I sat up, the room spinning with the movement. After a long time spent taking in my surroundings, I was finally able to piece together a few details. The first thing I registered was the smell of Javi. My brain recognized it as clearly as if he were sitting next to me, though he was nowhere in sight. I looked down at the large t-shirt I had used as pajamas. I lifted the collar to my nose and inhaled the scent—clean and crisp, like sea air and citrus and mint, mixed with something heavier that I couldn't quite name but was distinctly *him*. I had the distinct, sudden and overwhelming desire to steal the shirt and never give it back. That was probably happening.

I moved to the edge of the enormous, lush comforter on the California king bed. I sat on the edge for a while, letting my brain equilibrate before I dared to stand. The suite was even more beautiful than I remembered from the night before, my memory obscured both by my hangover and the partial darkness in which I had originally observed the room. The suite had an enormous, modern sitting room with an *actual* fireplace. It was bathed in natural light, with floor-to-ceiling windows leading out to a balcony overlooking the river. The decor was a tasteful mix of modern chic and traditional Texas charm, with sleek contemporary furniture mixed with more quaint, rustic artwork.

The couch—the one upon which I had humiliatingly thrown myself at Javi—was made into a bed, with a blanket and pillow. He had obviously slept there last night, even though the actual bed was plenty big enough for the two of us, even if he had wanted to put several feet of distance between us. Apparently, he had wanted to put far more distance between us.

There was an elegant dining area with a table for six. I moved slowly toward the table, seeing a tray set with several plates covered in silver cloches. I lifted each one, my stomach turning a bit at the sight of fruit, toast, eggs, waffles, and bacon. There was a carafe of coffee, with a mug and containers for cream and sugar. A single red rose sat at the corner of the tray in a crystal vase. Beside the vase, there was a big glass of ice water and a note, leaning against a bottle of ibuprofen.

I took the ibuprofen and swallowed three pills gratefully with the ice water. I continued to sip on the water as I plucked the note off the table. It was written on the hotel stationary in Javi's looping scrawl.

Good morning, Doc. Sorry to leave you so early. I had already made breakfast plans, otherwise I never would have left. See you at the keynote. Love, J

I settled at the table, nibbling on toast and sipping at coffee as I read and reread the note Javi left for me. When I had kept down some breakfast without the threat of it coming back to greet me, I moved to the bathroom. I took a long, soothing shower in the enormous glass rainfall shower, feeling like the heavy steam might purge my system of the previous night's toxins.

I reluctantly put my clothes back on from the previous day, though I carefully folded Javi's shirt to take back with me. When I made it back to my room, I was grateful that my roommate wasn't there. She probably was already at the conference for the first few sessions of the day. I readied myself, my stomach fluttering with butterflies as I dried my wet hair and did my makeup. I put on a black dress and a dark pink blazer.

Today was Javi's day—the keynote address. I felt even more terrible about my actions the night before, having Javi stay up to take care of me while I was drunk and vomiting, knowing he had to give a speech to hundreds today. The thought of facing him today after last night's near-miss sent my stomach in knots.

I just really don't want it to happen like this, he had said.

I winced at the memory. *Of course* he hadn't wanted it to happen that way. I felt so stupid, throwing myself at him, forcing him into a situation where he would have to decline my advances. Because *of course* he would decline when I was in that state. Chivalry came naturally to Javi—it always had. He would never let me make decisions like that while I was drunk.

When I walked down to the conference center, I found my classmates, all of them looking a little haggard after our night out. I attended the mid-morning events with them, my nervous energy steadily increasing as we neared the keynote address.

When it was finally time, I found a seat in the center of the crowded auditorium. The air was thick with anticipation, or perhaps it was my anxiety elevating the chatter in the room to something more. When the president of the American Neurological Society announced Javi's name, my heart lurched.

As he took to the stage, greeted by applause, several overwhelming feelings assaulted me. Looking at him, so confident, the very image of success in his sharp suit, commanding the attention of the entire room, I was so incredibly *proud*. I was so proud to know him, to call him my friend. I thought of that boy I met in the hallway seven years ago compared to the man standing before me today, and I couldn't believe how lucky I was to have been along for the journey. A few tears sprang to my eyes, and I hoped sincerely that none of my classmates would notice. It would be impossible to explain to anyone why I was crying. But they were completely captivated by him as he began to speak.

"Ladies and gentlemen, esteemed colleagues, and brilliant minds of tomorrow, it is an immense honor to stand before you today. Not only to speak to you about what I've done with my life but to celebrate the incredible potential that fills this room. Looking at all of you today, I feel *so* incredibly lucky. I couldn't quite believe it when the committee asked me to speak. Seven years ago, when I first came up with the idea for the Artemis, when I was just a college kid with a lot of big dreams, I never could have imagined this day. Back then, I had nothing but a sketchbook and a mind for inventing. Today, I stand before you as proof that dreams fueled by relentless passion can indeed sculpt reality.

Innovation—true innovation—is not only about creating new tools or technologies. It's not about creation for the sake of creation. It's about reimagining how our dreams can enhance human life, how our ideas can turn the tides of fates. It's about seeing a problem, however daunting, and daring to believe that *you* can be the one to solve it. It's about thinking of yourself as an entity capable of impacting the world.

My mom came to this country with her brother when she was barely fourteen years old. And it was her brother that inspired my device. The Artemis was conceived out of personal tragedy. When my family lost him to *status epilepticus*, an epileptic episode he never came out of, I devoted my life to making sure other families would never experience the pain my family went through. But the path from an idea to a tangible product that could change lives was not a straightforward one."

He took a small device from his pocket and pointed it at the large screen behind him. A slideshow of images started to play, and I smiled when I saw the first iteration of the Artemis appear on the screen, looking like nothing more than tangled wires and pieces of plastic. The picture faded to more and more versions of the device, mixed in with pictures of Javi and his mentors in the lab.

I laughed at pictures of Javi wearing the funny-looking cap covered in wires as he explained to the auditorium how he managed to turn the bulky diagnostic tool into a compact, wearable device. Because of Javi, not only could you now monitor high-risk patients for seizure activity during their daily lives, but you could easily diagnose patients without having to commit them to long, invasive tests. It was truly a remarkable invention, and I could tell, looking around the room, how impressed the crowd was.

"To paraphrase Edison, before I succeeded, I found about a thousand different ways to *not* make the Artemis. Throughout this journey, the hurdles were many. There were days I felt defeated, ready to give up. But what path in life is without obstacles? What path worth traveling presents itself as a straight line? What a boring journey that would be. Every innovator knows that challenges in life are not roadblocks—they are steppingstones, pushing us to leap further, to reach higher. They make you think in new, creative ways, to navigate the journey in ways you might not have considered."

The slideshow showed the device in its current form, the sleek, compact device in its stylish packaging. The next image showed Javi fitting a little girl with a pink device as she smiled from ear to ear. My heart seemed to swell.

"To the young visionaries in this room, my message is this: never let the fear of failure stop you from chasing your dreams. The world needs your ideas, your bravery, and your passion. You might feel that your dreams are too ambitious, too outlandish. I say, good. We need the ambitious, outlandish dreams to push humanity forward.

If I had quit dreaming when my dreams seemed unrealistic, my journey would have been finished before it even started. But I was one of the lucky ones, you see. No one in my life ever told me I was unrealistic or naive or crazy.

Of course, I couldn't have gone from that kid full of dreams to the man I am today, alone. Not even a little bit. I have the most supportive family, who not only inspired The Artemis, but encouraged me every step of the way. I had the most amazing mentors who helped me turn my dream into a real, physical, tangible thing, that's out in the world helping people today. And I…"

He paused, looking down, before he began to scan the room with purpose. I stopped breathing entirely when his eyes met mine.

"And I have someone very special in my life, who has always believed in me. From that very first moment. My muse. My greatest friend. Whose presence in my life has molded me into the man I am today. Who I would be completely lost without," he said before drawing in a deep breath.

"The Artemis wouldn't exist without you, Diana. You've been with me every step of this journey, not only believing in what I could do but showing me that we can dream bigger and accomplish more when someone stands with us."

It felt like he held my gaze for an eternity, so many unstated feelings passing between us across the auditorium.

He seemed to break from the spell suddenly, as if remembering he was giving a speech to hundreds of people.

"In conclusion, as we shoot for the stars, let us not forget to reach down and lift others up with us. Foster the dreams of the young, nurture their potential, and watch as they turn the impossible into the inevitable, because it's in them that the future lies. Thank you everyone."

The room erupted in applause, but all I could hear was the thunderous beating of my heart. I wiped the tears from my eyes before rushing to clap along with everyone else. His words echoed in my mind like the explosions of fireworks, my emotions weaving into a tangled mess in my heart. Javi left the stage. I wanted to rush to him, to tell him how proud I was, how moved I was, but my legs felt like they were made of lead.

I followed the crowd out of the auditorium in a daze. My classmates and the members of my research team kept looking over at me, some of them looking concerned, some in awe. But I was grateful that no one made me verbalize anything I was feeling. I wasn't sure I could if they asked.

There was a networking session in the atrium outside the auditorium immediately following Javi's address. The last thing I wanted to do was shake hands and schmooze. I *needed* to find Javi.

I wandered near the doors of the auditorium, not knowing where he might exit. Finally, he emerged from a door about a hundred feet away. Our eyes met, for the briefest second. And for a moment, it was just the two of us, the noise of the crowd going completely mute. I walked in his direction as if I was in slow motion. But before I could reach him, he was quickly swarmed by eager questioners and admirers. When his gaze broke from mine, the roar of the chatter flooded back into my mind.

I stopped in my tracks, feeling suddenly overwhelmed and out of place, dwarfed by his success and the attention it commanded. Javi was entirely obscured from my view by the bodies that surrounded him.

I took the opportunity to slip away. I needed space and time to process the flood of emotions that Javi's speech had unleashed.

Chapter 16

Medical School

Fourth Year

I knew the conference was over when crowds of attendees dispersed from the conference center, disappearing into the various restaurants and bars along the riverwalk. I had fled to the quiet sanctuary of the fountain outside, where I sat watching the water of the river dance in the fading light, lost in thought about the day's events and the tumult of emotions stirred in me by Javi's speech.

Javi had never been shy about telling me how much I meant to him. He had been telling me he loved me for years. So why did this feel so different? Perhaps because he had singled me out in front of a massive audience, who looked at us as if he was about to drop down on one knee and propose right then and there.

And why did the idea of that make my heart stutter? But I was being purposefully obtuse if I tried to pretend that I didn't know why.

I was in love with Javier Valenzuela. I wasn't sure when exactly had been the tipping point, the moment that had toppled my feelings for him from the realm of deepest friendship into love. All I knew was that I could never go back.

The sound of approaching footsteps broke through my reverie, and I somehow didn't need to look up to know it was him. I could feel him beside me before he had even said a word.

"Mind if I join you?" His voice was soft, hesitant.

I patted the stone next to me. "Of course not."

Javi sat down beside me, looking out at the water with me. His shoulder brushed against mine, sending a familiar thrill through me. The intensity of it almost made me angry. Just the brush of his shoulder was enough to send my stomach into flips. And I knew suddenly that my body had been reacting to him in this way for years. I had just ignored it.

"I've been looking everywhere for you," he said. "I wanted to talk to you after the speech, but I got swept up in the commotion. I feel like you deserve an explanation about what I said."

"You don't have to explain," I said. "I was moved by your speech. It was beautiful."

I turned to him; his eyes bored into mine.

"No, I need to say this. Diana, it's *more* than what I said up there on stage. You have been more than my muse. You are the reason I was able to take one of my many crazy ideas and turn it into something worthwhile. You are the reason I pushed so hard to make the Artemis a reality. And every late night, every setback—you were there. You got me through it. And it was all worth it, because I thought of how proud you would be if I succeeded. This is all because of you, Diana."

"Javi, that's ridiculous. I—"

"Just let me get through this, please," his voice caught on the final word. He took a deep breath before continuing. "But even with all the accolades and success the device has gotten these past few years, it all felt hollow without you *there* to share it with me. I don't want any of it if I can't have you by my side.

But I know that what happened last month scared you. I can see it in your eyes, any time I hold your hand or look at you too long or tease you. Your first instinct is to resist this *thing* between us. But I told you that this is what I wanted. I told you that I would wait for you, and I will. Just... just tell me I'm not waiting in vain. Please, tell me I'm not crazy. Tell me you want this too."

The corners of my eyes tingled with unshed tears. "Javi, I..."

"What is it, Di?" His eyes looked both desperately hopeful and concerned, likely wondering why his words had brought me nearly to tears.

"I made this vow, when we were in our first year at Columbia," I explained. "I told myself that your friendship meant too much to me. That I couldn't ruin what we had by letting my feelings get in the way. Because, I knew, even way back then, that a part of me did have feelings for you."

His eyes went a little wide at this admission, but he didn't interrupt.

"And I think, at the time, that that was true," I continued. "But since then, I've realized that I've been holding back for a different reason."

"And that reason is?" he asked, sounding almost afraid to know the answer.

"I've been struggling a lot these last four years." It was getting harder and harder to keep the emotion out of my voice, to keep the tears from falling. "I think there has always been a part of me that thought that if I gave into love, that if I let myself focus on *that part* of my life, that it would somehow undermine my abilities or my progress as a future doctor. Like I couldn't possibly have both. So I only let myself be in relationships that were doomed to fail with people who didn't threaten that goal, who had no chance of steering me from that path. I didn't feel strongly enough about them to lose focus."

The words seem to fall from my lips in a stream of consciousness. Only as I said them did I finally register that they were true.

"And then there was you." My voice broke with a little sob on the last word. "My best friend. The person who I've been completely in love with for the last seven years."

He shook his head, chuckling ruefully. He pulled at the lapel of his jacket as he said, "And to think... I've been trying for years to be *that guy*. To look like the guy you'd typically fall for."

It felt like there was a weight sinking into my gut at the thought. Of course, I had noticed the changes—the clothes, the grooming, the muscles, things he had never paid any attention to in college. But I had had no inclination that it had anything to do with me. The thought of him thinking he needed to do any of that for me to find him attractive nearly made me sick to my stomach.

"I'm so sorry, Javi. I never wanted you to think you had to change anything about yourself for me. Those men were distractions. You were the one who posed a real threat. You were the person who I *knew* could threaten everything I had worked for, if I let you."

His head shook from side to side, almost imperceptibly, a crease appearing between his eyebrows with concern, his lips pulling into a frown.

I continued before he could refute what I was saying. "Because I knew you were the one. I knew that there was no going back once I let myself admit that I was in love with you. I knew that, if I let myself really feel everything that I felt for you, I would fall completely, unequivocally in love with you. I would give up everything for you."

He took my face in his hands, his thumbs brushing the tears away as they fell. "Diana, I would never ask you to give anything up for me. You have worked so hard for this, and I am constantly astounded by you. By your intelligence, your kindness, your dedication to your patients. Why would I ever ask you to give that up? I don't *want* you to give that up."

I sniffled, wiping at my face. "I know you don't. But you live across the country, Javi. Something's gotta give, eventually. How can we ever make this work without making sacrifices?"

"Give us a chance, Di," he implored. He brushed my hair out of my face. "Give me a chance to prove that we can make this work."

I felt a wall I hadn't known I'd put up around my heart start to crumble down. I sniffled, then nodded.

"Okay," I finally said.

"Okay?" he asked, as if he didn't quite believe it.

I nodded again. "I'm saying when."

His eyes went wide, his disbelieving grin growing slowly into a brilliant smile as my words registered in his mind.

"Diana?" he asked.

I wiped the last of my tears from my eyes. "Yes?"

"What would you say if I told you I'm about to ruin our friendship?"

I laughed in surprise. "I'd say, bring it on."

Before the words had fully left my lips, he was kissing me. Though the kiss was gentle at first, exploratory, it quickly deepened, fueled by years of pent-up emotions and unacknowledged desires. The world could have been crashing down around us, and I don't think either of us would have noticed. It was like I had been swimming against a current for years and only now realized I could swim in the other direction. It was as easy as breathing. Kissing him felt more important than breathing, in fact.

My lungs did not agree with me, however, and we broke away from each other, breathless. He opened his eyes, and when our eyes locked, we burst into spontaneous giggles.

"We should go somewhere more private?" Javi asked, his voice husky.

"We should," I agreed.

Without saying anything, he rose from the fountain, pulling me with him by the hand. We made our way back into the lobby. In the elevator, we looked at each other, each grinning like we couldn't believe our luck.

As soon as we were safely in his room, Javi didn't hesitate. He pulled me to him, kissing me again, this time more assured than the first.

He broke away suddenly, taking the moment to look at me and softly brush my dark hair away from my face. "I can't even begin to tell you how long I've wanted this. How long I've wanted you."

I wrapped my hands behind his neck and swayed in his arms, like we were slow dancing.

"Javi, I have wanted you since you asked me to dance in your parents' backyard," I admitted. He drew me in for another kiss at the revelation.

"I have wanted you since the moment I found you outside your door in your towel," he countered.

I laughed at him, smacking him playfully in the chest. "No way! I don't believe you."

"You were the most beautiful woman I had ever seen," he explained. "Even crying in your pink towel with your hair soaking wet."

I shook my head at him in disbelief. "All this time?"

"All this time," he agreed, sealing the words with another kiss. "And to think, I was too scared to admit it because of some bullshit that happened in high school."

Seven years of wanting each other, never giving in to these feelings. But we wouldn't hold them back a minute more. I pulled off my blazer and threw it on the floor, before peeling Javi's jacket off, letting him know that I was ready to stop talking about what we wanted and start showing him. Our hands roamed each other's bodies, finally set free after years of being caged. I wanted to feel every inch of him that I had never allowed myself to even think about touching before.

His hands moved down my back to the zipper of my dress, and I turned in his arms to give him better access to the clasp. He slowly pulled the zipper down as he peppered kisses along my shoulder, the rough texture of his stubble along my sensitive skin sending goose bumps down my arms. When the zipper was down, he pushed the sleeves of my dress off my shoulders, and it fell in a pool of black fabric at my feet. He drank in the sight of me in my black lacy thong and bra, and a guttural sound escaped his throat.

"You are still the most beautiful woman I have ever seen. I have been dreaming about what you might look like for years, but nothing could have prepared me for the real thing." He sounded absolutely *agonized* by the sight of me.

I smirked at him, countering, "You've seen me in a bikini before."

"Not the same thing," he said, his hand wandering from my hip to my ribs, his thumb brushing along the underside of my bra. "You weren't looking at me then like you're looking at me now. And I wasn't contemplating tearing your bathing suit off you. Well, I might have been contemplating it, but I wasn't planning on following through with the idea."

"Well, since you've been so patient," I teased, reaching back to unclasp my bra and let it fall onto the floor on top of the pile of my discarded dress. His eyes smoldered with heat as he drank in the sight of my breasts. His right hand lifted as if it had its own mind, hovering just in front of me as if asking permission to touch. I took the half step forward until I was filling his palm. His thumb brushed over my nipple, and I whimpered at the sensation. His other hand lifted to cup my other breast, and he covered my mouth once more with his. He kneaded me gently as his tongue entwined with mine.

He grabbed onto me and lifted me up onto his hips. I wrapped my legs tightly around him, never breaking our kiss. My nipples brushed against his shirt, making me moan into his mouth.

He walked me across the suite and lay me down on the lush king bed where I had slept the night before. His hands traced a trail down my thighs, the backs of my knees, cupping my calves, until he grasped my shoes and pulled them off.

He stepped away from me and set to undressing himself. He took off his shoes and socks, but when he started to unbutton his shirt, I sat up. I grabbed onto the fine fabric and pulled him to me, wanting to take it off myself. When the buttons were undone, I splayed my hands against his chest and ran it down his stomach, relishing the firm contours.

"So, you did all this for me, huh?" I asked, leaning forward to kiss one of the swells of his abs. I moved down to the one below it and kissed that one too, and the next, like stair steps downward.

He groaned at the sensation of my lips on his skin.

"Every second I spent in the gym was worth it, just for this moment alone."

"Like I said," I whispered against his skin. "You never had to change a thing about yourself for me to love you… but I'm also not mad about it."

He laughed, and the motion made his muscles jump in very enticing ways. I ran my hands down them, down the thin line of hair trailing to the waistband of his pants. Another groan escaped him, and it emboldened me. I started to undo the belt buckle and button of his pants, feeling him hard and waiting for me beneath the zipper. I slowly pulled on the zipper and shoved the waist band and his black boxer briefs down until he sprang free of his confines. I made a sound almost like a purr and wrapped my hands around him.

"A little part of me has always wondered if I made you feel this way," I said, beginning to stroke him up and down slowly.

"*Fuck*," he said through gritted teeth. "More times than I can count: that first night we met. The night we first danced. Seeing you in your little bikini or in that red dress you wore to winter formal. Last night in my t-shirt. And about a hundred other times when you were just being you. I've been trying to hide erections from you for years."

I grinned, looking up at him beneath my lashes. He watched as I leaned forward to take him in my mouth. His head fell back, and he hissed with the sensation of my lips around him. His hands reached up and wove into my hair, gripping it at the roots.

I felt him hit the back of my throat as my tongue lapped at him, tasting him. He stayed so still, he was almost unnervingly statuesque, letting me dictate entirely how deep he would go. I played with the angles and depths, discovering what made him groan, what made his fingers pull ever so slightly at the roots of my hair. After a minute, his hips moved just a millimeter toward me and back, an almost involuntary little thrust.

He pulled me back, suddenly but gently, by the hair.

"Stop, Di," I wiped the corner of my mouth with the back of my hand, looking up at him curiously. "I want to look into your eyes the first time you make me come."

My whole body shuddered with pleasure. He let his pants and briefs fall to the floor. I moved slowly backward on the bed, letting him crawl toward me, his eyes hungry with need. He drew my face to his for another long, slow kiss, before ducking to leave a trail of kisses along my jaw and neck and collarbone. He nipped at my skin, drawing a grasp from my lips. His hand cupped my breast, kneading it, his thumb circling my hardened nipple.

His hand slid down my stomach, traveling downward until he dipped beneath the black lace. He found what he was looking for, wet and waiting for him, and started to make circular motions over my throbbing clit. His mouth moved to my breast and took my nipple between his lips. I gasped. He worked at both, until I started to see flashes of light against the back of my eyelids.

"Javi?" I said, breathily. He paid no attention to me whatsoever. "Javi, stop."

He stopped what he was doing, only pausing to nuzzle between my breasts before he looked at me.

"I want you inside me the first time you make me come," I told him.

He let out a feral sounding, very satisfied noise and yanked my underwear down. He threw them unceremoniously off the bed. He cupped my calf and hooked my thigh around his waist. He poised himself at the entrance and paused.

"Di, do we need a condom?" he asked, looking like it took every ounce of will power he possessed to bring it up.

"I have an IUD," I assured him quickly. "And I've been tested since the last time. It's fine, unless you're worried—"

"I'm not," he answered, pushing into me at the same time the words left his lips. The feeling of him filling me knocked the breath out of my lungs. My mouth fell open, and he covered it with his own, his tongue mimicking the motions of his hips as he thrust into me, slowly at first.

"Oh, God," I breathed.

No one had ever felt so perfectly made for me, like a puzzle piece I didn't know I was missing. No one had ever felt this good inside me.

His hips rocked against me, in different angles and paces that made me bite my lip to suppress the urge to cry out. Just when I was seconds from coming undone, he held onto me and rolled us over, never pulling out of me. He held me by the hips and settled me into position on top of him. I grinned and rolled my hips against him, appreciating the change in angle and the control I had over our rhythm. He watched me as I rocked against him, my breasts bouncing gently with the waves of our bodies.

"I could watch you ride me the whole night," he breathed. "*Forever*. But I don't think I can hold off—"

"*Don't*," I commanded.

I could feel his abdominal muscles tighten beneath my hands, and I knew he was close. He reached between us, putting pressure on my clit as he thrust upward several times in rapid succession. An explosion of pleasure suddenly wracked my body. We cried out each other's names as my walls tightened around him. I felt him pulse inside me in several quick bursts as he spilled into me.

The entire world seemed to stand still for a moment in the wake of our passion. The only sound was our rapid, unsteady breaths mixing together. I slowly lowered my head to his chest, not pulling my hips away from his. I didn't want to disconnect my body from his, not yet. His arms wrapped around me, holding me even tighter to him, as if he had the same thought.

"I would say it was worth the wait," he panted, sounding tired but very happy. "And it was, don't get me wrong. But I'd be lying if I didn't say that I think we should have been doing that the whole time."

We both laughed, enjoying the way the laughter felt in the places where our bodies were still connected.

"We'll just have to make up for lost time, I guess," I replied.

He drew my face to his for a kiss. I finally rolled off him and settled in under his arm, my hand resting on his chest.

"Have you ever felt anything like that before?" I asked him in wonder.

"Never," he answered without hesitation. "But that's not particularly impressive in my case, considering I only have two people to compare to. But I can't imagine it gets much better than that."

"*Two?*" I said, unable to shield the surprise in my voice before the question sprang from my lips.

"Two," he confirmed. And I knew, of course, that it had been Sofia and Alex.

Heat flooded my cheeks. I didn't want him to think less of me because I had been with more people than he had.

"And before you say anything," he said, reading my thoughts, "know that I don't care how many people you have been with, Diana."

"You don't?" I asked in surprise.

"I do not," he replied. "So don't stress about telling me. That's your business. I don't need to know. Nor do I want to hear about anyone else you've been with while you're lying naked on top of me."

"Oh," I said, unable to come up with anything more profound.

He chuckled. "But I would really love it if I could be *the last one*."

"The one to end them all." My tone was joking, but I knew in my heart that I meant every word, whether I was ready to admit it or not.

I felt a pressure in my chest, not like when I used to be crushed by my anxiety. It felt like my heart was ready to swell with joy until it burst out of my chest. This was the happiest I think I had ever felt, in Javi's arms, lying across his chest. I didn't want it to end.

But it was that moment when my stomach let out a very rude, grating noise that made Javi laugh.

"You hungry? I can order room service," he offered, looking out the windows where the sun had set since we arrived, as if surprised by the passage of time outside this room. I understood the feeling—it felt like we existed in a vacuum, separate from the rest of the world.

I nodded gratefully. Though I didn't want to let him out of my grasp, I was suddenly ravenous. He fetched us robes from the bathroom and ordered a long list of random items from the room service menu before joining me back in bed.

A little while later, we were perched across the bed from each other, with a makeshift picnic spread between us on a towel.

I grabbed a French fry and popped it in my mouth, inspecting him. He had tied his robe lazily around his waist, leaving a lot of his chest exposed where it gaped open. The sight of his smooth, golden skin made me want to reach out to touch him again. A part of me wanted to push him down and eat the food off of him.

A blush heated my face at the thought. *How does it happen?* I wondered. I had known this man for years. I had managed to conduct myself in an appropriate, friendly way with him for all this time. How did my brain shift so suddenly to wanting to do dirty, deplorable things to him?

He caught my blush and my intense gaze lingering on his chest, and he smiled knowingly.

"What are you thinking about?" he asked, like he was very much aware that he was dragging my brain from the deepest depths of the gutter.

I didn't tell him what I was actually thinking, but asked instead, "Did you ever worry that this wouldn't work? Us, I mean."

"Did I worry you would never realize that you were madly in love with me?" he asked, flashing me a grin.

"No, that's not what I mean," I replied with a laugh. I wasn't explaining it right. "I was never really worried about the emotional stuff being there for us. You know me better than anyone. I mean *physically*. Were you ever worried that it might be awkward, because we've been friends for so long?"

He thought about the question for a moment, chewing pensively. "No, not really."

"Never?" I insisted.

He shook his head. "I can't picture anything about us not being compatible. Can't imagine anything more perfect than being with the person who knows me best. "

I suppressed a groan at how perfect he was, how certain and confident he sounded in *us*. It made me feel more certain and confident too, chasing away the fear and the doubts from my mind.

After we cleaned up our picnic, he turned to me.

"What would you say to a bath? This suite has a very nice jacuzzi tub. I think it would be a waste not to take advantage."

I grinned and headed to the bathroom. I started the water and poured bubble bath into it that the hotel had provided. When it was full and steaming, we sank into the water together. He leaned against the side of the tub and drew me into him, my back to his chest. He started the jets, which shot out from both the sides and the bottom of the tub. The bubbles curled up between our bodies in a very pleasant way.

"Can I confess something?" Javi said, his breath brushing against my ear, the vibrations of his voice rumbling against my back.

"Hmm?"

"You know when we snuck up to the roof on graduation day?" he asked.

"Of course."

"I had a big plan that day," he admitted. He squeezed me a little tighter into his chest. "I was going to bring you up there and tell you that I was in love with you. But then with the news about California, I chickened out."

I ran my hands across his arms where they were wrapped around my stomach.

"I had no idea," I replied. "I mean you seemed upset, but I didn't realize that was the reason."

"Yeah," he said absently. "I was still kind of scarred from high school and didn't want to start our relationship long distance."

A long, loaded silence stretched between us after this declaration. If he didn't want to start things long distance last time, what did that mean now? Was it any different today, not knowing where I would spend the next four years of my life? These were questions I didn't really want to ask, especially when we were naked and wrapped in each other's arms, but they hung between us, nonetheless, wanting to be asked.

"And now?" I asked timidly. "Is this not us starting a relationship long distance?"

"It is," he murmured, "but it's different. You'll be going to residency in less than a year. You're coming out for your California interviews in a couple of weeks, right?"

I nodded, not saying anything. The interview offers had rolled out the previous week- I had received a dozen total—Columbia, of course; four programs in California, three around New England; and four other programs around the country. I had scheduled my California interviews so that I could complete them all in one two-week period, during which I'd be staying with Javi. The idea of those two weeks together was far more appealing with this recent turn of events, but the pressure to succeed at those interviews felt heavier now. Before, I had just been vaguely hoping we could be near each other. Now, it felt like it was up to me to wow those programs for this relationship to succeed.

I could feel my anxiety slowly creeping its way into my mind at the thought.

"Hey," Javi whispered into my ear, pulling me tighter into his chest. "I can practically see those gears turning in your brain. It's going to be okay."

I started to say, "But if I don't match in California—"

"No use stressing about that now," he whispered against my neck. "We have time to figure things out."

He kissed my neck, clearly trying to distract me from the topic entirely. Though my brain felt initially reluctant to acquiesce to his distractions, it didn't resist for long. One of his hands cupped my breast, kneading it, as the other drifted down between my legs. I leaned my head back against his shoulder as his hands continued to explore me, my breath becoming ragged.

When I couldn't stand another second without having him inside me, I broke free of his arms and bent forward over the edge of the tub, wanting to feel him from this new angle. I felt his hands splay wide across the soft curve of my cheeks, spreading them. I expected the sensation, the relief, of having him inside me once more, but was surprised when I instead felt his hot breath against my skin.

His tongue darted out to taste me, and the feeling was so simultaneously incredible and unexpected that I nearly came right then and there. I gripped the edge of the porcelain tub, flashes of light dancing across my eyelids as his tongue dipped into me. He painted a trail downward to my clit, circling and toying with it. All I wanted was for this amazing feeling to last, but I could feel my climax approaching with almost frightening speed. I couldn't resist any longer when he sucked me into his mouth, his teeth grazing against the incredibly sensitive nerves. The climax exploded out of me with a gasp, my muscles clenching and spasming.

Before the feeling had completely dissipated, he grabbed onto my hips and entered me, dragging me back to meet his hips as he plunged in. My body, never having fully recovered, immediately coiled once again toward another orgasm. He moved inside me, agonizingly slow at first. His fingers gripped onto my hips as he thrust into me so deep it drove the air out of my lungs.

His body tensed at the same time as mine, and only his hands holding me against his body kept me from collapsing against the side of the bathtub. My whole body felt agreeably wobbly and tingly, made only more so by the rippling bath water against our thighs.

He let go of my hips long enough for me to turn back

toward him. He drew my body back to his as he kissed me. When we pulled away, I spent a long second looking at his face, marveling at the expression of profound love with which he was looking at me. I shook my head as a few tears escaped my eyes. He brushed them with his thumbs.

"Hey," he said with concern. "What's wrong?"

I shook my head again, smiling. "I'm so happy. I don't think I've ever been so happy."

He returned my smile. "Me neither. You have made me so happy, Diana."

We left the bath, Javi lending a hand to help me out on my shaky legs. We dried ourselves with big fluffy towels and fell into bed beside each other. As soon as the cool sheets surrounded us, the exhaustion hit me. It had been such a monumental day, and the weight of it all suddenly began to settle in over my body and my mind.

My thumb brushed his cheek as he smiled into my palm. Staring into the depths of his warm brown eyes, I felt a strange duality in my heart. Here was the man I had known for so long, whose eyes had seen my highest highs and darkest lows, eyes that had held countless shared memories with mine. A part of me felt like I had known those eyes my entire life. Yet, it was like I was discovering him anew. It was like I was coming home, yet setting off on a new adventure, all at the same time.

"I love you, Diana," he whispered across the pillow. And though he had said it hundreds of times before, he had never said it quite in this way.

"I love you, Javi."

He pulled me into his chest, where I fell asleep, surrounded by his warmth.

Chapter 17

Medical School

Fourth Year

As the sunlight crept through the white gossamer curtains, I woke to find myself entwined with Javi. Though I woke in the same place that I had the morning before, the experience could not have been more profoundly different. The day before, I had felt not only physically in pain from the hangover, but anxious and shameful and alone. Today I felt like I had entered an alternate universe where feelings of anxiety or shame or loneliness were distant, foreign concepts.

I was in Javi's arms.

I studied the soft whisper of his breathing, slow and steady, a soothing rhythm in the quiet of the morning. I traced his features with my eyes, his face soft with sleep. Around other people, up on that stage the day before, he cut such an impressive figure. He was all easy charm and grace, knowing smiles and cool confidence. But in his sleep, his expression was softer, revealing traces of the boy I knew and loved from John Jay. The boy who would bring me snacks in the library and tell me about his dreams on the rooftop and dance with me in his parents' backyard.

But even though it seemed like a stark contrast from that kid I had met and the man he was now—the young businessman, boy genius, entrepreneur—I knew in my heart that they were the same. And it wasn't one part of the equation that I had fallen in love with, but the whole picture—the boy who made me feel at home and the man who made me feel wanted. It was as if allowing myself to stop resisting these feelings had painted a picture in my mind of who he was in perfect clarity. Everything that made Javi who he was, now woven into a grand tapestry that was finally on display for my eyes alone. And I felt so lucky to get a glimpse of it.

Likewise, I felt that I had woken up better able to understand who I was. I saw myself and what I was meant to do with my life more clearly than I ever had before. Being a successful physician and being the woman who was in love with Javier Valenzuela were not two entities in battle with one another. They could not be in battle, because they were one and the same. I was going to be the doctor I was meant to be because of my love for Javi, and I was in love with Javi because of who I was as a future physician. Not *or* but *and*. All the logistics would work themselves out, I was certain. We would work them out, together.

Javi's eyelids fluttered open. I watched consciousness settle over him as he took in my expression, glowing with relief as he realized, as I had, that it hadn't been a dream. A radiant smile lit his face.

"Good morning," he whispered, his hand gently grazing over my hip.

"Good morning," I replied.

"Last night was..."

"*Everything*," I supplied reverently.

"Everything," he echoed.

We spent a long time looking into each other's eyes in wonder, idly running our hands over the other's skin.

"What do we do now?" I asked in a timid whisper.

He grinned wickedly. "I can think of a few things we could do."

He pulled my hips against him until I could feel him hard against my thigh. My whole body instantly began to tingle in anticipation. His thumb brushed against my bottom lip before he kissed me.

When he pulled away from me, he asked, "What time is it, anyway?"

I pushed myself up until I could see the alarm clock.

"Almost nine," I said. "Can't believe we slept so late."

His eyes went wide. He asked, panicked, "Nine?"

"Yeah, why?" I asked, concerned when he started to untangle himself from the sheets enveloping us. I propped myself up on one elbow to watch his retreat.

"My flight back to California leaves in less than two hours," he said as he climbed out of bed. He walked to his suitcase to hurriedly put on a pair of clean boxers, joggers, and a t-shirt.

I got out of bed quickly. I collected my discarded clothing and put them on. I envied his access to comfortable clothes. I would again be leaving his hotel room in the same uncomfortable business attire in which I arrived. I scrambled around the room, throwing his things into his suitcase as he did the same. When he had all his belongings haphazardly arranged in his bag, he smiled at me ruefully.

"This is not how I wanted this morning to go," he pulled me by my waist until our bodies were pressed together.

"I know," I agreed, regretting that our bliss had to be interrupted by reality.

"Maybe I'll skip the flight," he mused. "Find another one later."

"I would agree with you," I said, pulling him down to my height by the collar of his t-shirt, "except I'm going to be at the airport just a few hours after you. And I would bet you have important business waiting for you."

He kissed me, longer than we probably had time for.

"Maybe. But nothing is as important as this," he breathed against my lips.

"Even so. We have places to be," I whispered back with a sigh. "Besides, I'll be in California in a few weeks for my interviews."

"Right," he agreed. "Just a few weeks."

He reluctantly pulled away from me, grabbing his suitcase and backpack. I grabbed my phone and my blazer and followed him out the door. As we waited for the elevator, I glanced back at the door to Javi's hotel room, silently thanking the universe for bringing us together in this beautiful place.

As his Uber drove up the elegant driveway of the hotel, Javi turned to me, his eyes flashing with concern.

"I love you," he said hurriedly, as if he was worried that he had somehow forgotten to tell me. As if we hadn't said it to each other dozens of times in these last twenty-four hours, both literally, out loud, and in so many other ways.

"I love you, too," I replied, trying to make my tone reassuring. "Go catch your flight. I'll see you in a few weeks."

He kissed me, reluctantly pulling away after a few moments to load his bags into the car. I watched his Uber drive off into the distance, my heart aching at the thought of not seeing him for weeks, after everything that had transpired this weekend.

I slowly turned back into the hotel. By the time I got back to my room, my roommate was done packing her things and was ready to meet the rest of the group to head to the airport. I would have to scramble to do the same. She scrutinized my clothing closely as I started to assemble my things into my suitcase. Clearly, I was in the same outfit as the day before.

"Hey, everything okay?" she asked. "Everyone was trying to get a hold of you yesterday."

I took my phone out of my pocket and looked down at the screen. It was completely dead. I hadn't thought to put it on the charger last night.

"Oh?" I asked absent-mindedly. "What about?"

"Your poster presentation," she said. "It won the top prize."

I paused what I was doing, turning quickly to look at her.

"It did not!" I said, in shock.

She grinned, a little sheepishly. "It did. Dr. Karam and the rest of your team accepted the prize for you. I think it was pretty good money too, like $3000 or something."

I blinked, dumbly. I had completely missed the closing ceremony. I hadn't even paid it a thought. I couldn't even remember the last time I had looked at my phone. My research had won an award, and I had completely missed it.

I had been entirely distracted by Javi.

I finished packing my things, my mind reeling in response to this news. I went down to meet the others to head to the airport. My research team cheered when they saw me, hugging me and giving me the envelope with my certificate and the check, which was indeed for $3000. Thankfully no one interrogated me on my whereabouts.

Maybe, after the clearly emotionally-charged keynote address the day before, they had guessed where I might be. I was a little humiliated at the thought of my colleagues assuming as much.

The second we landed at JFK that evening, I texted Blake. I knew this was a topic that she would want to hear about in person, in precise and excruciating detail. And I desperately wanted to have someone who knew what I knew. Having this exist only between Javi and me somehow made it feel less real, more fleeting, like I could still wake up at any moment and find out it never really happened at all.

> DR: Hey. Just got back. I could really use a girls' night.

> BN: Girls' night out or girls' night in?

> DR: Definitely a girls' night in.

> BN: Be there in an hour. Bringing Indian food.

I made it back to my apartment a few minutes before Blake came through the door, holding a large paper bag smelling of garlic and curry. I felt like the news was ready to burst out of me. As soon as she had put the food down, I pulled her to me for a hug. Once I released her, she held me at arms' length, inspecting me from head to toe with an expectant look in her eyes.

"Did something happen at the conference?" she asked, one eyebrow raised in suspicion. I nodded vigorously; my lips tight from the effort of trying to hold back a wild grin.

"Javi was there," I voiced, my tone breathy and excited.

Her eyes went wide. "He was there?"

"He was the keynote speaker," I told her. "It was a complete surprise."

"And you two...?" her voice trailed off at the end, suggestively. I couldn't fight the smile anymore. I nodded in confirmation, finally allowing myself to unleash the joy that I had been feeling since Javi's speech.

When the truth finally hit her, she started squealing and hugging me and jumping up and down in my little kitchen. It felt *so* good to tell her, to not feel like I was keeping it a secret in my heart. What I really wanted to do was shout it from the rooftops—*Javi and I are together, and I have never felt so happy*—but telling Blake was almost as good. It took her a full five minutes to stop the cycle of squealing in delight and hugging me.

"So how was it?" she demanded.

I shook my head in wonder, my cheeks flushing. "It was incredible. I've never experienced anything like it before."

Blake squealed again. "I need to know *everything.* Start from the *beginning.*"

We finally settled long enough to unpack our dinner, and when we were seated and tearing at our garlic naan, I told her everything, from the moment I laid eyes on Javi at the conference until we parted ways this morning. When I finished the story, she shook her head, a knowing smile on her face.

"I knew it," she said smugly. "You two were meant for each other."

Though some long held instinct to deny it resurfaced for the briefest moment, I didn't say anything to contradict her.

"But now, I don't know what's going to happen." I didn't hide the worry from my tone. "He's still in California. You know how the Match works—it's a complete crap-shoot. Even though I have a couple interviews near him, I could just as easily end up in New York for four more years or Massachusetts or North Carolina or Texas. There's no knowing."

"Don't count yourself out before the interviews have even started," she admonished. "I'm sure you'll get your top choice residency. But even if you don't, if anyone can make the distance work, it's you two."

"Maybe," I conceded, but the thought did nothing to settle my concerns.

"Look, I know you guys haven't talked through all the scenarios yet," Blake said. "But Javi is not the type to sleep with you just to sleep with you. He clearly is planning to make this work, or he never would have made a move to begin with. I think you are overthinking it."

"Me? Overthink things?" I asked sarcastically. "That doesn't sound like me at all."

Blake laughed. "I am so happy for you two."

"I'm happy for us too," I whispered.

Blake and I talked for several hours, long past dinner. When she finally bid me goodnight, I was suddenly keenly aware of how Blake's and my time together was coming to an end soon. We would be traveling for interviews for the next few months. Then there was Match Day and gradua-tion, and then we'd be parting ways to start the next adventure.

I was going to miss her so much.

She had been such a good friend to me over these years, and no matter how much we worked to stay close while in residency, I knew it could never possibly be the same. While I was celebrating this new start, between the beginning of my career and this new adventure with Javi, I also felt a little grief at the thought of what I was losing too. While I would *never* want to repeat medical school again, and I was very ready for the experience to be over, there was still space in my heart for some sadness at the thought of saying goodbye to this era of my life.

Chapter 18

Medical School

Fourth Year

W hen I stepped out of San Francisco International Airport for the second time in my life, the sense of déjà vu was nearly over-whelming. So overwhelming, in fact, that when I saw Javi leaning against his car in wait for me, I checked carefully behind him to make sure there were no blondes leaning on the hood. The unnerving feeling was quickly driven away the second I reached him, though.

I left my suitcase rolling after me as his hand curled around my waist, drawing my body into his as he kissed me. In just these few weeks of separation, I had somehow forgotten how soft his lips were, how good they felt against mine. He had kissed me only *twice* before the night we finally spent together, and it didn't feel like nearly enough. It didn't feel like it would ever be enough.

He smiled against my lips before pulling away. My lower lip jutted out in an involuntary pout at his absence.

"Hey," he said. "You made it."

He drew back and pulled a bouquet of peonies from behind his back. I touched the soft petals of the full, pink buds in delight. At the same time, I wracked my brain, trying to think of a scenario in all these years when I might have told him my favorite flower.

I took the bouquet, shaking my head at him. "How did you know?"

"I have watched far too many guys bring you roses and lilies and daisies over the years not to know what you like. I know you better than anyone, Diana." He winked, smiling in that self-satisfied, charmingly smug way.

I rolled my eyes, almost annoyed that he could remember such minute details all these years later.

He took my bags from me and loaded them into the car, opening the door for me after. He drove us to his apartment, our hands clasped between us on the center console the whole way.

When we made it to his apartment a short while later, I realized suddenly that I had somehow managed never to see it in the two years that he lived here. He had long outgrown the apartment given to him by his investor as a broke college student. This apartment was one that he had found for himself, that he owned.

When I finally stepped foot inside his home, it was both shocking and everything I would have expected of Javi. The first thing that was so surprising was the sheer breadth of the space. I probably could have fit my entire apartment into his kitchen. The size was even more exaggerated by the floor-to-ceiling windows revealing the mountains in the distance and the endless expanse of cloudless blue sky.

It was open concept, the space encompassing the kitchen, dining area, and living room. His furniture was neutral tones of white and gray. It was immaculately clean, like it belonged on a magazine cover, which I would not have expected of Javi. His dorm in college had always been more like organized chaos. He had a huge flat screen

TV in his living room, surrounded by bookshelves crammed with books and knick-knacks. The walls were decorated with framed patents and travel souvenirs.

"*Javi*," I gushed.

He grinned. "You like it?"

"I love it," I replied, wandering forward into the space. I ran my hands over his white and gray quartz counter tops, stopping to admire his collection of golden whiskeys and tequilas in decorative bottles.

He fetched me a vase and filled it with water for me. I arranged the bouquet of peonies in it, as he leaned against the counter beside me.

"Go over the full agenda for the week with me again," he said. When I was done arranging the flowers, he pulled me by the hips to settle me between his legs.

"Four interviews," I explained. We had gone over it a few times on the phone these last few weeks as we had solidified the details. "The interviews should each take a full day, with tours and several individual interview sessions. My interviews at Stanford and UCSF are this week, Wednesday and Friday. Then we'll head to Sacramento at the beginning of next week for my interviews there and in Stockton on Monday and Wednesday."

He nodded, clearly hearing no surprises. "I've pretty much cleared my schedule for you. Call me your chauffeur for the next two weeks."

I smiled, leaning into him. "And of course this week we'll be celebrating a *very* special day."

"Oh really?" he asked in mock confusion. "What day might that be?"

"November 11th," I said, my hands running down his chest. "The day my favorite person in the world was born."

"Ah, yes," he said, knowingly. "My nephew Theo is also one of my favorite people in the world."

I laughed, smacking him in the chest. "Not who I meant."

"Oh, of course," he amended with a smile. "I forgot Theo and I share a birthday."

"I don't think we've spent your birthday together since college," I mused.

"We haven't," he agreed, kissing me sweetly. "I'm looking forward to it."

"It's a little bit lame," I admitted. "I have a surprise planned, but you're going to have to drive us there, which ruins a lot of the surprise. It's really difficult to surprise someone for their birthday when you can't drive."

"You didn't have to—*wait*. What do you mean you can't drive?" he asked incredulously.

I shot him a withering look. "Technically, I have a driver's license, but I consider it mostly a theoretical one."

He laughed dubiously. "And what exactly is a *theoretical* driver's license?"

"I mean, I took driver's ed before we moved to the city, and my parent's made me go to Brooklyn to take the driving test when I turned sixteen, but that is where the story ends. I have not driven a day since then," I explained.

He looked at me dumbstruck. "You *really* can't drive?"

"I thought you knew me better than anyone. How did you not know this already?" I teased.

"You are *twenty-five-years-old*," he pointed out.

I glared at him playfully.

"And I have lived in the public transportation capital of this country for the last ten years. You drive us around every time we go to Texas," I countered.

He shrugged. "I thought it was because I knew my way around and you didn't. Not because you straight up didn't know how—"

"I know how. *Theoretically*. Like I said."

"You are very likely going to be living somewhere next year where driving is a *requirement.* Have you seen this place? You can't get anywhere without going on a highway," he insisted, unnecessarily. I knew this was true, of course. This particular source of stress was a topic I had chosen to mentally avoid.

"I know that. I was planning to figure it out after the Match," I said lamely.

"Oh, you are *so* driving while you're here," he replied with a wry grin.

My eyes went wide. "No, Javi—"

"It's decided."

"I *can't*," I protested.

"You *can*," he refuted. "You *have to*. Consider it a birthday present to me."

I groaned. "Fine, I'm taking your real birthday present back."

He laughed but grabbed his keys off the bar without comment. My eyes went wide.

"Right now?" I squeaked.

"Right now," he replied firmly.

"I just got here!" I whined.

"If we start now, you can practice for the next two weeks!" he argued, taking my hand in his as he made for the door.

I groaned again. "I don't see why you want to watch me wreck your Tesla for your birthday."

"I won't let you hurt Nikola," he assured me, holding the door open to his apartment.

I rolled my eyes at him. "*Of course* you named your car Nikola. How unoriginal."

He cackled.

Ten minutes later, he found a suitably empty parking

lot, put the car in park, and forced me to switch seats with him.

He patiently showed me how to adjust the seat and how to maneuver the gear shift—subtle mechanisms and buttons hidden behind the steering wheel and displayed on the massive digital control panel.

"It's honestly unfair of me to teach you how to drive on a Tesla," he explained, not sounding the least bit sorry about it. "These aren't the typical controls."

"I wouldn't call any of this fair," I retorted, pouting in the driver's seat.

He smirked. "I should go rent a stick and force you to learn on that instead. Have some *real* fun for my birthday."

"I didn't know you had a sadism kink," I replied dryly.

He sputtered out a surprised laugh. I glanced in his direction to see, with some satisfaction, that he was blushing.

"This is torture," I complained again.

"You'll survive."

"That is yet to be determined," I countered. "We haven't even put it into drive yet."

"Sounds like a great place to start."

I breathed in and out once, twice, then gripped the steering wheel with a white-knuckle grip. I followed his instructions on how to put it into drive. I was pressing down so hard on the break with my foot that I was starting to feel a pins-and-needles sensation in my toes like they were falling asleep. I took another deep breath in, but I felt Javi's warm hand rest on the top of my leg and curl slowly toward my inner thigh, and the breath abruptly caught in my throat.

"Hey," he said calmly, his thumb brushing my knee. "*Relax.*"

I let my breath out in a whoosh. "Having your hand between my legs is *not* helping me focus right now."

He smirked but took his hand away. "Drive. Give me two laps, and I'll put more than my hand between your legs."

A warm, tingling feeling spread from my center out into my fingers and toes, and I felt my grip on the steering wheel relax ever so slightly and my toes unclench. Very carefully, I released the break, waiting for something to happen. When the car stayed exactly where it was, I looked at him expectantly. He looked like he was carefully fighting a laugh.

"It's electric," he explained patiently. "It won't idle. You have to actually push the pedal."

I sighed in exasperation but moved my foot slowly over to the accelerator pedal and pressed with the weight of one toe. Javi gently directed me as we made a wide loop around the empty parking lot, going painstakingly slow.

"Great job," he said once the loop was done. "Now try it again faster than ten miles per hour."

I glared at him, but did as I was told, increasing the pressure on the pedal until the speedometer showed a whopping twenty-five miles per hour. When I finished the second lap, I parked the car resolutely, took my hands from the steering wheel, and scowled at him.

"There," I insisted. "Two laps."

He put his hands behind his head and leaned back into the seat, settling in. "Great. There's a good Chinese restaurant two minutes from here, why don't you take us to get some dinner."

"*Javi*," I objected. "You promised—"

"You need to practice," he scolded. "And don't worry —I'll keep my promises."

He shot me a lecherous grin, but the implication did little to distract me. I frowned at him.

When I made no move to put my hands back on the steering wheel, he whipped out his phone and started scrolling through it. "I can wait here all day. This car is going nowhere unless you make it."

I let out a very beleaguered sigh and put the car back into drive. Javi put his phone down in the cupholder with a satisfied grin and began to direct me toward the restaurant. They were small roads, the speed limit no greater than forty-five miles per hour, but that was thirty-five miles per hour greater than I was comfortable driving.

But I did it, slowly but surely, inching my way down the roads going well under the speed limit, people honking at me as they went around. By the time he finally directed me to turn into the parking lot for the restaurant, I felt like I had been holding my breath for five minutes straight, and it was making me a little light-headed. I parked well away from any other cars and looked at Javi with a miserable expression.

He laughed. "Alright! Enough torture for one night. Stop looking at me with those big, blue puppy-dog eyes. Let's go get some food. I'll drive us home."

I grinned in triumph, following him into the restaurant.

A little while later, we were sprawled on his couch as we watched TV. Javi ran one hand over my calf where my legs were draped over his lap. I was pleased by how easy and natural this felt, this little glimpse of domestic life.

I was lost in my thoughts, imagining how good it would be to once again spend all my free time with Javi after all these years apart, when he suddenly moved off the couch. He sank down to his knees on the floor in front of me, pulling my legs with him so that I was forced to turn to face him.

I looked at him wide-eyed, expectant, unsure exactly what he was doing until he gently spread my knees apart. He hooked his hands around my calves and pulled me to the edge of the couch.

"I made promises," he ducked to kiss the inside of my thigh, just above my knee, "that I intend to keep."

The brush of his lips against my sensitive skin sent a thrill through me. A giddy laugh escaped me at the feeling, and I realized I sounded nervous. Why did he always make me feel like I was experiencing these things for the first time? Was it because every experience with him felt brand new, like nothing I had ever felt before?

"I won't hold you to that," I whispered, my voice a bit shaky. He kissed an inch farther up my leg, his hands running slowly up my thighs. A heavy pressure was already building between my legs at his touch.

"You kept your end of the bargain and then some," he said. His hands dipped beneath the hem of my dress.

"Seriously, Javi, it's *your* birthday week."

"It is," he agreed, his lips moving another few inches up my thigh. His fingers hooked into my underwear.

"We should do what you want to do," I argued.

"I am doing what I want to do," he murmured against my thigh. He pulled my panties down and slipped them off before lifting my thighs onto his shoulders. Cold air hit my exposed center, and I shuddered with the sensation.

"I've been waiting my entire adult life for the opportunity to taste you whenever I want," he insisted. He kissed the crease of my thigh, his tongue brushing against my skin, as if to emphasize his point.

"*Jesus*," I breathed.

He shot me a truly devilish smirk from between my legs.

"It's Javier, actually," he corrected, and my shocked

laughter at his joke turned quickly into a moan as he suddenly buried himself in me.

His nose separated my labia, his tongue dipping inside me before stroking me upward. My back arched involuntarily, and I gripped the back of the couch to steady myself. He circled my clit, and the sounds that escaped me were not human. They were soft but entirely feral whimpers. I buried my fingers in his hair.

When he sank one finger inside me, I pulled his hair involuntarily by the roots. He slipped a second finger inside, and no part of me belonged to my conscious mind anymore. I rocked my hips against him instinctually as he sucked on me. He moved his fingers slowly out and back in, and my walls clenched around him, grateful for the friction he provided.

Some tiny voice in the back of my mind begged myself to hold on—to wait for him, to have him inside me. But that tiny voice was engulfed by the roar of this animal that he seemed to wake inside me. I arched completely off the couch with my climax, gripping onto his hair with both hands. My thighs clenched around his head, but it somehow didn't stop him from working me through to the very end, the motions of his tongue sending little aftershocks through me. I finally felt my body going lax, all my muscles turning to pools of warm liquid, but he never let me fall back onto the couch. He ducked beneath one of my legs, immediately scooping me up into his chest in a fireman hold.

He kissed me as he walked us to his bedroom, his tongue moving against mine, reminding me instantly of what magic it had just performed on me. I felt my body coiling again immediately in anticipation. He kicked open his bedroom door and broke our kiss to lay me down gently on his silky gray comforter. We discarded our clothes quickly before I pulled him down onto the bed with me.

Our hands explored each other's bodies, relearning all the lines and contours that we had forgotten over the last few weeks of separation—not forgotten, I should say. I could no sooner forget what his body felt like as I could forget my own. It was burned into my mind. Getting to touch him again felt like reconnecting with the other half of myself that I had been missing. And when he was finally inside me, I felt *whole* again.

That week felt how I imagined one must feel on their honeymoon—a constant, desperate longing for each other that let up for only short periods of time. Though we did have certain real-world distractions to think about—Javi's job, my upcoming interviews—we spent every other second together either lazily tangled in each other's embrace or in the frenzied process of learning each other's bodies.

We had spent all these years knowing each other's minds so perfectly, becoming nearly telepathic in our understanding and awareness of each other. This was the physical equivalent. While we had cultivated our mental and emotional connection over years, our bodies seemed determined to get to that same level with our physical connection in a matter of weeks.

When the weekend ended and Javi had to go to his office, I spent my days milling about his apartment—reading books off his shelves, watching his TV, absent-mindedly preparing for my interviews, trying in vain to distract my brain from the constant wanting of him. But it was futile.

The second he walked in the door each evening, I was ready for him. Before he even closed the front door, I was on him, kissing him and trying to tear his clothes off. And his body answered my need immediately and with equal intensity.

We ordered takeout for dinner most nights, as we could not be bothered to go grocery shopping or leave his apartment long enough to sit in public for a meal. Javi, however, adamantly refused to use a delivery service, instead making me drive to pick up our food each time, "for practice." After he was done torturing me with driving lessons, we ate from takeout containers, standing at his kitchen counter, usually in some interesting combination of undress—me, wearing his button-down work shirt and nothing else; him, in boxers or a pair of sweats.

But eventually, my interviews broke us somewhat out of our blissful reverie.

I had my interview with Stanford first, and I walked out after feeling like I was in a daze, hardly able to remember what I had said or done for the last eight hours.

"How'd it go?" Javi asked as I approached his car. When I reached him, he kissed me, then immediately held open the driver's side door for me. I grimaced at the waiting steering wheel.

"Please, no. I'm exhausted," I begged.

He grinned. "It's five minutes."

I sighed but was too tired to argue.

"So?" he asked when we were on the road. "Tell me about it."

"In case you were wondering what the equivalent of a marathon is for an introvert, it's trying to smile and make people like you for eight hours straight," I grumbled.

He laughed. He surely could not relate—this man could smile and talk for a week straight if you let him. "But did you like the program? Could you see yourself there?"

I scoffed. Stanford was *the dream*—an amazing program, only five minutes away from the person I loved. I couldn't delude myself into thinking I had a chance. The heartbreak might just kill me if I didn't match there, so it was better not to allow my heart to even consider it as a realistic possibility.

"It's not a matter of whether one *likes Stanford*," I explained. "It's whether Stanford likes you. This is a decidedly one-sided love affair. I'm way out of my league."

"I know the feeling," he replied, and I immediately laughed at the absurdity of the statement. When I didn't hear his laughter join mine, I glanced furtively over at him in the passenger seat, only willing to look away from the road for the briefest second. But when I did meet his eyes, he was staring at me with such serious and fervent affection that I realized he wasn't joking. My throat grew thick, my chest growing tight, in a pleasant way.

"You're ridiculous," I chastised him quietly.

"But you love me?" he asked.

"But I love you," I agreed, emphatically. I reached across the center console and squeezed his hand.

I realized a few minutes later, with some delight, that it was the first time I had ever felt comfortable driving with anything less than a firm, ten-and-two grip on the steering wheel. From Javi's self-satisfied grin when we parked, he must have realized it too.

My interview at UCSF that Friday did not give me nearly the same giddy feeling that my interview at Stanford had. The interviews went fine, but the program director seemed intense, the conversation with the faculty and residents didn't seem to flow the way it had at some of my other interviews. It was geographically the second most ideal location, but in my heart, I knew that I wouldn't be as happy there. As I walked out to Javi's car afterward, I was distracted by the thought of having to choose—did I rank the program with myself or my relationship in mind?

The thought left me with an uncomfortable feeling in my gut.

When Javi got out of the car, though, I knew that thought would have to wait. I pushed it consciously out of my mind and slapped a huge smile on my face.

"Hey, birthday boy," I said, pulling him in for a kiss. "You ready for our date?"

"Born ready," he joked. For the first time, I very willingly took the driver's seat, putting our destination into the GPS on my phone. I had researched ahead of time for the best places to see the stars in the area.

When we arrived at the destination a little while later and Javi saw the full spread set at the very top of the hill complete with candles and wine and a loaded picnic basket, he looked at me with surprise and delight.

"How did you manage this while you were in an interview all day?" he asked.

I shrugged, pleased by his reaction. "Found a service online."

It was not a cheap service, by any means. It was an expense that I couldn't really afford, but my recent $3000 prize for my research had at least made it a little more bearable. And it was worth it, for Javi. We settled in, pouring wine and helping ourselves to a charcuterie board from the basket.

I looked out at the brilliant orange and pink sky of sunset and raised my glass to his.

"To the two luckiest people in the whole world," I said wistfully.

He clinked his glass against mine. "This is a pretty amazing birthday."

"Oh, just you wait for the main course."

While the appetizer had been somewhat sophisticated, I knew that deep down, Javi was a simple guy. And he looked absolutely delighted at the In'N'Out cheeseburgers and French fries.

He took a bite of the greasy burger and hummed appreciatively. "The very *best* part of living in California is In'N'Out. Best burgers in the world."

"I won't argue with you, because it's your birthday," I replied, "but you know my devotion to Shake Shack runs deep."

He laughed. "That's fair."

We ate and talked, eventually sprawling out on the blanket to look up at the stars above. I curled into Javi's side, laying my head on his chest as he pointed constellations out to me.

I made sure we left our starlit picnic in time to be back at his apartment before eleven o'clock. I pulled a small cake from the fridge that I had ordered the day before and put a single gold candle in the center. Javi didn't question me when I didn't immediately light it, instead looking at my watch patiently until it struck 11:10. His family had started this tradition, after all—I had only upheld it whenever I could, with every birthday I spent with him. I lit the candle when there were thirty seconds to go, quietly singing the birthday song to him.

"November 11th, at 11:11," I said. *The boy who was born lucky.* "Make a wish."

His eyes reflected the flickering candlelight, the corners of his eyes crinkling with a brilliant smile as he blew out the candle. The second the light was extinguished, he pushed the cake aside and lifted me onto the kitchen counter.

"Oh look," he said playfully. "I got my wish."

He smothered my laughter with a kiss. When he pulled away, I leaned over, scooping a handful of frosting off the cake, which I promptly smeared into his face. He laughed, immediately pulling me back in for a very messy, very sugary kiss.

He pulled a dollop off my nose with his index finger. I grabbed his hand and leaned forward to lick it off—very slowly and very purposefully, holding his stare the entire time. A little moan escaped him at the sight. I flicked my tongue against the pad of his finger.

He promptly pulled me off the counter. He grabbed the cake box and my hand and led me to his bedroom.

A little while later, when we were tangled in each other in his bed, tired and a little out of breath, he said, "I have newfound respect for birthday frosting. It might be my new favorite food."

I laughed. "Oh! I nearly forgot your birthday present."

I went to my suitcase and pulled out the wrapped present, handing it to him before settling back into bed beside him.

When he had unwrapped the thin piece of clear acrylic, I flipped a switch on the underside of the stand, and an array of golden stars appeared on the surface. The golden light illuminated his face as he looked at it with appreciation.

"That's so cool," he said.

I explained, "It's the exact stars that were over New York City the night we first went to the roof of Butler. Or at least, it's how they would have looked, if we had been able to see them this well."

His eyes went wide with delight. He reverently placed it on his nightstand before turning back to me, pulling me in for a kiss.

We extended his birthday celebrations through the weekend. We met his coworkers the following day for dinner and drinks, where he introduced me to them as his *girlfriend*. Of course, we knew what we meant to each other, but I realized in the moment that this was the first time he had ever officially called me that.

The title made me feel giddy, but also sent a wave of fear and caution through me. Was now the right time to tell people that we were together? We hadn't even told Javi's family yet. Should we wait until after Match Day? Why get everyone we loved invested in a relationship that had such a precarious future? But I forced myself to staunch these fears so we could enjoy our time together.

The following week, we left Palo Alto to head to Sacramento for my remaining interviews. We spent the three days in Sacramento at a hotel while I interviewed for the programs there and in Stockton. By the time Javi picked me up from the fourth and final interview, I felt drained—mentally and emotionally exhausted. And I still had several interviews left: University of Arizona, Baylor, Duke, and Wash U.

We spent our last day together before my impending departure lounging lazily around his apartment. There was a distinct undercurrent to our actions all day long that put us both in a quiet, sad mood, realizing our two weeks of bliss were ending—our last meal together, the last sunset we'd watch together, the last time we'd lounge on the couch together until our eyes started to grow sleepy. Though it felt almost like a waste of precious time together, we didn't have sex—just fell asleep holding each other.

Javi brought me to the airport the next morning, where I'd be flying to Phoenix for the next interview. I looked ahead at the doors to the airport and felt suddenly paralyzed. Not a single muscle fiber in my legs seemed inspired to obey my commands. I took several shallow breaths.

Javi left my suitcase on the curb and walked to me

suddenly. He took my face in both his hands, staring intently into my eyes.

"Hey," he said, his voice falling into that soothing tone it always assumed the instant he realized my panic was taking over. "Take a deep breath. *Good. In and out.*"

I inhaled and exhaled on his command.

"What's going through your mind?" he asked.

I shook my head, angry at myself for letting my anxiety get the best of me, after years of having it under better control.

"These two weeks have been so perfect," I explained.

He smiled and pecked me on the lips. "They have been."

"But what if this is it? What if this is all we get?" I asked, my voice quivering.

His brows knit together in concern. "Why would you say that?"

"The Match. We don't know where I'll end up—"

"Only control what we can control right?" he reminded me. "Right now, we can't control the Match. All we can do is let ourselves be happy. I don't know about you, Di, but I've never been so happy."

His obvious joy was enough to, at least temporarily, staunch some of my panic.

"Neither have I," I agreed. I finally was able to move toward my suitcase and grasp the handle. He followed me to the door, pulling me to him for a long goodbye kiss.

"See you in a few weeks for Thanksgiving," he said. We'd both be going to Texas. Shortly after that, we'd spend Christmas in New York. And Javi had promised he would come out for my birthday in January. It wasn't the end, I had to remind myself.

I smiled up at him, but felt it stop short of reaching my

eyes. An agitating, demanding part of my brain still quietly warned: *Don't get used to this.*

Chapter 19

Medical School

Fourth Year

The tension and excitement in the air was palpable as I stood among my classmates, each of us clutching a sealed envelope that held our futures. The chatter around me felt distant as I gripped my own envelope, my name starkly printed across the front. The rapid drumbeat of my heart pounded in my chest from dread and anticipation. My parents and Javi sat at the table beside me.

As the dean began the countdown and the crowd joined in, my hands trembled uncontrollably.

"Three, two, one..." An eerie silence fell over the crowd as roughly 140 envelopes were frantically opened and their contents unfolded. There were screams of excitement rippling around me as my classmates realized where they would be spending the next three to seven years of residency, depending on the specialty to which they were matching on this day.

I was frozen, not able for several moments to open my own envelope and reveal my fate. I looked up and met Javi's eyes. He nodded and smiled encouragingly. I took a deep breath and tore open my envelope, unfolding the letter inside.

My eyes skimmed the words frantically. When I finally found it, my heart lurched and then sank.

Baylor College of Medicine in Houston.

I fought to breathe. It was an excellent program. I connected with the residents and the program director during my interview. I probably would have ranked it even higher, based on fit alone. But it wasn't in California. It wasn't close to Javi.

My top programs had all been within a few hours of Palo Alto, yet here was a binding contract telling me I would spend another four years halfway across the country from him. The room began to spin as the disappointment settled over me, heavy and suffocating.

I felt a hand on my shoulder and looked up to see Javi's concerned face.

"How'd it go?" he asked, giving my shoulder a reassuring squeeze.

Shaking my head, I felt the sting of hot tears in my eyes.

"Not the one I wanted," I managed to say, my voice barely a whisper.

I couldn't meet my parents' eyes. I couldn't look at my father and face his disappointment when I was already drowning under my own.

Without a word, Javi took my hand and led me outside, away from the noisy celebration and into the quiet of the university courtyard. The cool air hit my face, a small relief from the rush of emotions. My vision went in and out of focus. My chest ached, and it became more and more difficult to breathe with each passing second. My body felt distant and numb, as if it didn't quite belong to me. I couldn't feel my hands as they clutched the piece of paper that had sealed my fate.

I both recognized the feelings and didn't. My panic attacks had evaded me for so long now that the experience felt almost foreign, but not quite distant enough to forget.

"Talk to me, Di," Javi urged gently. He held my trembling shoulders in his hands.

I looked up at him, tears now freely streaming down my face. "Baylor. In Houston."

He looked shocked for just a moment, before mustering some enthusiasm to say, "Hey! Baylor's an amazing school. And you'll be in Texas! You'll be in the heart of Valenzuela country!"

I shook my head. "But I couldn't do it. After everything I worked for, I couldn't match in California. I couldn't bring us together."

I was quickly losing my composure, the sobs starting to wrack my body as I trembled. He looked conflicted; obviously concerned for me, but I wondered too if there was a trace of disappointment in his features, like he too worried about our chances of surviving another four years of separation. He pulled me into his arms, stroking my hair.

"Hey, hey," he soothed. "It's going to be okay. We can make this work—"

I choked on another sob. "Why is it always like this for us? Why do we always have to make concessions to be happy? Why can't things go our way for once?"

He squeezed me even tighter. He sighed against the top of my head. "I don't know."

He held me for several minutes as I cried. He finally pulled away, brushing the tears from my eyes. "I know this isn't exactly what we planned. I know you're disappointed with how things turned out, but I want you to know how proud I am of you. And how much I love you."

I hiccuped and tried to stop the shaking of my voice. "I love you too. And I'm so sorry, Javi. I tried."

"Hey, none of that," he scolded gently. "Don't apologize. I want you to be proud of yourself. We will figure everything out."

But there was nothing to figure out. Our fate was sealed. He would be in California, and I would be in Texas. And while I knew we would try to visit often, I saw the life we could have had together flash before my eyes—coming home to each other at the end of the day, someday getting married and having children. These were things I hadn't realized I wanted until this moment but that seemed inconceivable if we couldn't even manage to be in the same *state*.

But it was Javi, I told myself. I would take whatever I could get. A piece of him would have to be enough. I sniffled before taking a deep, steadying breath. "Shall we go back inside and join the party?"

He looked at me with concern. "Are you sure? We can stay out here as long as you need. Hell, let's leave the party all together—"

"No, no, it's fine. We should really get back inside," I insisted.

I wiped under my eyes to make sure my makeup wasn't smeared. He didn't look particularly enthusiastic about the idea, but he obediently led me back inside to the celebration. I found my parents and accepted their hugs when I was finally able to share my match results. My mom spoke animatedly about flying down to Houston to go apartment hunting and furniture shopping. My father spoke about the merits of the program and the contacts he knew there. I nodded and smiled along feebly, grateful for their enthusiasm, but unable to provide much of my own.

And I wanted to kick myself for not being more excited

and prouder of myself. Baylor was a *great* program. I really thought I would be happy there after my interview. And I had always considered myself a person who wouldn't upturn her entire life to be near a man, but here I was, grieving what could have been. And that grief seemed to swallow up all the good feelings, the entire sense of accomplishment and excitement in my achievements I might have had otherwise. It made me feel small and silly and childish.

I milled about the room with Javi and my parents, seeing my classmates excitedly write their match results on signs provided by the school. *I matched: Pediatrics at Children's Hospital of Philadelphia. I matched: Ob/Gyn at Brigham and Women's Hospital. I matched: Dermatology at Johns Hopkins.* I was in awe of the accomplishments of my peers. I found myself once again reminded that I was surrounded by some of the most brilliant minds in the country, maybe the world. I was in a room with people who would find cures for illnesses thought incurable, create new surgical techniques and make the world a better place. And I was right there with them, as I had been for the last four years. I had taken all the same classes, passed all the same exams. I had finished the same clinical rotations.

So why did I still feel like I somehow didn't belong? Like my accomplishment was somehow lesser than, just because I didn't match my top choice program?

I vaguely registered the figure of Michael feet ahead of me, taking a picture with his parents in front of a navy step-and-repeat decorated with Columbia-blue crowns. His sign read, *I matched: Orthopedic Surgery at the University of Miami.* Our eyes met for the briefest moment. He smiled, and I smiled feebly back. Javi wrapped on arm around my shoulders, and I watched Michael's eyes turn decidedly away from us, back to his family and friends. If I had been in the laughing mood, the sight would have inspired a laugh.

I heard the steady approach of high-pitched squealing before I felt Blake's arms wrap around me in a tight hug.

"Diana!" she exclaimed. "I've been looking everywhere for you!"

She pulled back, searching me for a sign or a paper, anything to tell her where I might have matched. I had left my sign on my seat, not yet filled in for the pictures I didn't have the heart to take. She lifted her sign for me to inspect. *I matched: Anesthesiology at USC!*

"Los Angeles!" I said, forcing every bit of excitement for my friend that I possibly could into my voice. My heart thudded a little at the thought. *Blake* is going to California. Not me. Both of them would be there, without me. I understood, of course, that California was massive, and USC and Palo Alto were not close, but it still hurt to know that Blake had made it to my desired destination when I couldn't.

A hint of concern broke through Blake's excitement. "Did you—"

"Baylor," I cut her off quickly, "in Houston."

"Oh!" She said, and I saw her eyes flit from me to Javi and back, as if in question. As if she wasn't sure what to say next, not knowing what the future had in store for us. I didn't know either. "Baylor's a great program!"

"It is!" I said, forcing some enthusiasm into the response.

Blake pulled me in for another hug, squeezing me tight. She whispered into my ear, so quiet not even Javi or my parents could hear, "I'm sorry, Di."

I patted her back reassuringly. "Don't be. We'll be fine."

I pulled away from the hug and looked at both her and Javi. "Now I have two reasons to visit California!"

Neither of them seemed to believe my feigned enthusiasm. Javi hugged and congratulated Blake on her match. She gave me another squeeze for good measure before she turned to rejoin her family.

I tried to rally some excitement after seeing Blake, but mostly I felt exhausted. The huge buildup that had led to this day, combined with the five stages of grief I had cycled through in the last half-hour, had left me feeling drained.

But I knew in my heart that if I didn't at least go through the motions of the celebration, I was going to regret it. This was a once-in-a-lifetime moment, no matter the result. So, I filled out my sign. I took the pictures with Javi and my parents and Blake. I found Dr. Karam, who was absolutely thrilled for me, and took a picture with her as well. And through the act of pretending, my feelings on the match started to change ever so slightly.

My parents had booked us a celebratory dinner that evening at one of the nicest restaurants in town. Even though I had grown up in their home, I felt out of place. I had been scraping by on loans for years, living like a college student. The idea of spending my entire month's grocery budget on caviar made my stomach turn.

As I watched Javi make light conversation with my parents, it struck me once more how different it felt to be around Javi's family compared to mine. The contrast between the stuffy, formal atmosphere with my parents compared to his family's typical colorful, loud home was never as stark in my mind as it was now. Wearing my tight formal dress, pushing a tiny pretentious portion of food around my plate, I knew in my heart which of the two environments felt more like home to me now.

Maybe the match in Houston was the universe trying to tell me that? I smiled to myself at the idea, the first genuine smile that I had felt all day.

"You're being very quiet, dear," my mom said with concern.

"Sorry," I replied. "I was thinking about the move to Houston. Starting to get excited about it, actually."

Javi analyzed my expression with an approving smile.

"Where was Houston on your rank list again?" My father asked, sipping a whiskey old fashioned.

I looked down. "Number five."

My father shrugged. "Probably for the best then that you didn't decide to go with surgery. If you only matched your number five in neuro, might not have matched at all in surgery."

"*Hunt,*" my mother exclaimed reproachfully.

I felt Javi stiffen beside me at the comment. His hand found mine beneath the table and squeezed it gently, a silent promise of solidarity.

"What?" my father said, his tone too-innocent. "I'm saying it's a field that not just anyone can enter. It requires a certain *caliber.*"

I remained silent, even as his cruel words hung between us. It stung more than I expected, even though I had long come to terms with the fact that I had no interest in surgery. I had matched into a specialty that I loved. I had thought my father, after our discussion during my third year, understood that. And after everything I had been through that day, the disappointment and sadness, the insult was just too much. My vision blurred momentarily with my anger, focusing back just in time to catch the flicker of indignation in Javi's eyes.

"I think what Diana accomplished is extraordinary," Javi interjected, his voice calm but firm. No one who didn't know him like I did would know that there was anger there, simmering just beneath the calm surface.

I stood suddenly, my chair skidding backward, making a rude noise that drew the eyes of several nearby tables.

"You know what, Dad?" I seethed, my tone dangerous and challenging. All reason and logic fled my body, leaving behind it only rage. "*Fuck you.* I have been doing nothing but trying to win your approval since my earliest memories. I went to fucking *medical school* trying to make you happy. And there were multiple times that I questioned my choices, wondering if I should have considered doing liter-ally *anything* else. But God damn it if I didn't fall in love with medicine anyway. But at least I have this one thing to set me apart from you. I love neurology. I am proud of myself for what I have accomplished. I know it may not be good enough for you, but I'm just now realizing that *nothing* will ever be good enough for you."

His eyes grew wider and wider at my speech, the rage bristling behind his mask of shock. My mother's eyes darted between the two of us, looking completely distraught. I briefly felt sorry for upsetting her, but not enough to apologize. I wouldn't apologize for finally standing up to my father, after all these years.

I extended my hand to Javi, saying resolutely, "Come on, Javi. Let's get out of this place. It's pretentious, and the food isn't even that good."

He took my hand with a wry grin, throwing his napkin down onto his plate and his untouched foie gras. He saluted my parents as we walked away. "Lovely as ever to see you, Dr. and Mrs. Richards."

An hour later, we sat on the steps of Low Library, at the foot of *Alma Mater*, eating burgers and French fries from Shake Shack as we looked out at the campus where we had met.

Javi cleared his throat. "I know you might not want to talk about it—"

"Not really," I interrupted.

"But," he added, amused, "let the record show that watching you stand up for yourself was hot as hell."

I grinned at him. His suit jacket was long abandoned— he had put it on the stone step for me to sit on. He had loosened his tie and run his fingers through his hair, sending it into a sexy disarray. I reached for his tie, pulling him to me by it. I pressed my lips to his.

"Why don't we go home so you can tell me more about it?" I whispered, and he grinned at the idea.

Even though there was a lot of uncertainty and doubt that still lingered in the back of my mind about the future, we had excellent ways of distracting ourselves from those feelings.

Chapter 20

Medical School

Fourth Year

I was once again a drop of blue in an ocean. Only this time, I felt like a drop that carried some weight to it, like a drop that could make a vast ripple in the world, even when falling into a pool as large as this one. I found myself once again in the row of bleachers assembled on the steps of Low Library.

I was a very different person than the woman I had been when I sat here four years ago. The graduates of Columbia College sat to my left, and I could almost picture a younger version of myself sitting there today. That girl was riddled with anxiety, desperate to outgrow the weight of her father's shadow. That girl was about to discover that her best friend was moving across the country.

Now, that woman was in love with that same best friend.

I was trying not to let the obsessive thoughts of Javi and how we were going to make long-distance work distract me from this momentous day. *I was graduating from medical school*, I had to remind myself. My graduation gown was the same Columbia blue as my undergraduate gown, but it had wide bands of black velvet down the front and sleeves. It was made of thicker material, and my neck was adorned with the green doctoral hood. The hexagonal velvet cap with its gold tassel sat atop my thick brown hair, in curls to my shoulders.

The commencement speeches were made. The dean of the medical school led my class in the recitation of the Hippocratic Oath, pledging to do good for the world and for our patients. After today I was to be known as Diana Richards, M.D.

But throughout the speeches, my brain kept wandering back to him. Somewhere behind me on the lawns, Javi was there, watching me achieve my dreams. John Jay, where we had met nearly eight years ago, looked down on us from the corner of the courtyard like an old friend.

As the speeches ended and the caps were tossed, my heart thudded in anticipation, knowing I was finally free to find him. Blake found me in the crowd and squeezed me tight, already crying.

"I'm going to miss you so much, Di!" she exclaimed.

"I'm going to miss you!" I told her, meaning it fervently. She had been such a fierce friend to me. She was going to have the best time in LA, and I had already promised her I would visit as much as I could.

"Got to go find my family," she said. "Give Javi my love, will you?"

"Of course I will."

I hugged her again tightly before we said our goodbyes. I weaved through the clusters of blue-gowned bodies as I made my way back toward the lawns filled with waiting family members.

I found Javi waiting for me in front of John Jay. I threw my arms around him immediately.

When I drew back from him, he said, "I've got a surprise for you. Well, a couple of surprises, actually—"

Before he could finish, I was bombarded with the weight of six pairs of tiny arms in a massive hug. I pulled myself from his arms, looking down and around to see his nieces and nephews, all but the newest baby. My heart leapt with delight, and I looked around wildly until I saw them—*all of them.* All the Valenzuelas had come for my graduation.

Tears immediately filled my eyes at the sight. I ran to them, crying and hugging each one of them. Javi's father looked good—strong and getting stronger. I lost it the second his mother held me in her arms. Gaby, Manuela, and Valeria each embraced me, kissing me enthusiastically on the cheeks and leaving red lipstick stains all over my face. I didn't mind one bit.

I looked at them all, overwhelmed by the love they had shown me by traveling all this way for me.

"I can't believe you're all here," I blubbered, wiping at my tears. Javi moved to my side, wrapping an arm around my waist.

Gaby looked over my shoulder and cleared her throat. "Diana, I think that couple is waiting for you."

I turned, seeing my parents standing twenty feet away, looking expectant.

I looked at the Valenzuelas and then to Javi. "I'll be right back, okay?"

He looked over my shoulder at my father with concern in his eyes. "You want me to come with you?"

"No," I declined immediately. "I got this. Be back in a minute."

I approached my parents resolutely, crossing my arms in front of my chest when I made it to them. They looked as uncomfortable as I should probably feel after our less-than-cordial goodbye two months ago, but I couldn't feel any shame over how I had acted that day. My mom and I had texted a few times since then, but I had adamantly refused to acknowledge my father's existence. My life had been all the better for it.

When my mom started to get teary, some of my resolve broke. I hugged her to me.

"We're so proud of you, Diana," she murmured into my ear. "Please, hear your father out."

I let go of her slowly, glancing at my father. His face was impassive, betraying no emotion at all. My mom walked away, settling on a bench down the pathway, watching us nervously. I looked at my father expectantly. His stoic resolve cracked suddenly, and he rubbed a hand down his face, looking tired and older than I remembered. My brows furrowed, my frown deepening at the sight.

"Diana," he began, finding it difficult to look directly at me. He peered up at Butler Library beside us instead. "I'm not good at this kind of thing."

I pursed my lips in annoyance. He didn't have to tell *me*. I had twenty-six years of proof. I started to turn to leave.

"Wait, please," he begged, and when I turned back to him, he finally met my eyes. "As I said, I'm not good at this, but I'm pretty sure if I don't try your mother will divorce me."

I narrowed my eyes.

"Sorry, bad joke," he said miserably. "Look, Diana, I know this may be hard to believe. But however badly you think I've treated you, however horrible I have been at communicating or showing you affection, know that your grandfather was worse."

I raised an eyebrow. I had never heard him talk about my grandparents before, only to say that they had died when I was very young.

"It's not an excuse," he continued quickly. "I just want to explain that my dad left me with a terrible example of how a father should be, but I know that it's my fault that I never tried to be any better. My job was so demanding that it was easy to let your mother raise you, for me to only connect with you on the most superficial level. And now you're grown, and you don't need me for anything. You've made it on your own. You wouldn't even let me pay for medical school. I realize now that if I want you in my life at all, I have to work to be better."

I sighed. "It honestly feels a little too late, don't you think?"

"You're right," he agreed. "It is. But I'd still love it if you'd give me the chance. I can see how easy it would be for you to cut me out of your life entirely, and I don't want that, Diana. You're my child."

My eyes narrowed, my fist clenching at my sides. "Just tell me one thing. And please don't lie to me."

"Anything," he replied, his eyes searching my face hopefully.

"Did you pay Columbia to accept me to the medical school?" I stared at him resolutely as I asked the question, looking for any sign, any flicker in his eyes to tell me the truth.

He swallowed hard, looking guilty. "I won't lie. I considered it. Attempted it, actually. When you didn't get any other interview offers besides Columbia, I was concerned. I wanted you to get in because I thought that's what *you* wanted. But when I called my friend on the admissions committee, she said you had wowed them at your interview. You had already been unanimously accepted by the committee. I can't guarantee my role at the medical school had *nothing* to do with it, but I made no donations to get you in, if that's what you want to know."

I was mildly peeved, though not surprised, at his admission. But more than that, I felt a sense of triumph. All these years, a part of me had always been certain that he had paid for my acceptance. The degree I had earned today had always felt like it was built on a lie. But I had *wowed* them. I grinned.

"Thank you for your honesty," I told him. "Dad, all I ever really wanted from you was your approval, but I don't really need it anymore. It would be nice if you could just be my *dad*. Just support me and the path that I've chosen for myself."

He nodded. "I do. I *will*. I know I haven't been good at showing you, Diana, but I am *so* proud of you."

A small, hopeful smile pulled at my lips, and I tipped my head toward him in acknowledgement as I began to walk away. When I turned, I saw Javi watching me in the distance. I turned back to my father once more.

"Oh, and Javi and I are together now," I told him, as an afterthought. "If you want to be in my life, get used to him being there too."

He blinked in surprise but chuckled. "You two weren't together this whole time? I'm pretty sure I heard your mom calling the Plaza last week to book the wedding."

I rolled my eyes, laughing. That sounded about right for my mother. I waved and headed back toward Javi.

When I made it to his side, I looked around in confusion. His family had disappeared.

"How did that go?" Javi asked

"Pretty well, actually. Where did everyone go?"

"They went to get set up. They're throwing you a full fiesta back at the Airbnb." He beamed at me, and my heart swelled at the prospect. "But in the meantime, Dr. Richards, you and I have important plans."

My stomach fluttered with the sensation of butterfly wings.

"We do?" I asked, excited.

"We certainly do," he replied. He took my hand and led me to the familiar gray door on the side of Butler Library. His eyes darted around to make sure no one was watching us before he led us inside.

"Guess who still works here?" Javi asked.

"Loretta?" I asked, already knowing the answer.

"Loretta," he confirmed, and we made our way up the stairs, running like we were kids racing each other, laughing the whole way. A gentle breeze greeted us as we emerged onto the roof. We moved to the edge, where we could see our old view sprawling out before us, comforting and familiar and so special to us. When we had had a moment to revel in being up here once more, we looked at each other.

There was a single moment of hesitation before we launched at each other. We kissed each other with all the intense desperation that our weeks of separation and wondering and longing had left in us, until we were gasping for breath. Only after we were temporarily sated did we pull away.

"I missed you," he whispered, resting his forehead against mine.

"I missed you," I replied, but the phrase was not enough to express just how true the sentiment was. Nothing in my life at the moment was enough to distract myself from the longing for him—not the preparations for residency, the prospect of moving, the final days of medical school. Nothing could overcome the incredible emptiness in my life without him there. The absence of him was a physical ache, one that had grown so much stronger and more painful since the conference. One that I hadn't yet learned how to manage. One that I knew I would *have* to learn how to manage, if I wanted to be with him.

And my God, did I want to be with him.

He pulled away from me to fetch a bag that I hadn't seen before, that had been waiting for us up here on the roof. He pulled out a bottle of champagne and two champagne flutes and poured us two glasses of the golden, bubbling liquid.

"To the two luckiest people in the whole world," he said, holding his glass up to mine.

I echoed his sentiment and clinked my glass against his, but before I could drink, he added, "And to the incredible, brilliant, beautiful, caring *doctor* who I am completely in love with. My best friend."

Warmth flooded my cheeks. I didn't know what to say to such lavish compliments, so I simply drank from my glass.

I thought about the last time we were up here together, almost exactly four years before, when Javi had planned to tell me he loved me. I could picture it—the alternate universe in which we had admitted our feelings for each other three years sooner. In that version of our story, would Javi's invention ever have made it out of the lab? Would I have ever learned how to go through my life without my anxiety governing my every thought and action?

I looked at Javi, resolved. "I'm glad you didn't tell me you were in love with me on our graduation day."

He lowered his champagne glass, his eyes going wide. "You are?"

I nodded. "Back then, I was using you like a crutch to

manage my anxiety. It wasn't fair to you. And I think if we had started our relationship then, I never would have learned how to do it on my own."

"I never minded helping you," he replied. "Not once."

I reached over and squeezed his hand. "I know. But I had to learn how to love you without *needing* you. I wasn't ready to love you four years ago."

"And now?" he asked.

I reached up to touch his face. "Now, I am *so* ready to love you, Javier Valenzuela. And I know you're afraid of how things will work long distance, but—"

"I'm not afraid," he said softly.

I clamored on, "I know we can make this work. What we have is worth it. I know my schedule is going to be tough, but I'm sure we can find ways to see each other—"

"We'll be seeing a *lot* of each other," he insisted.

"We'll FaceTime every night," I agreed.

"It'll be odd to FaceTime each other from the same room," he replied, his tone curious.

I paused abruptly in my rant. "What?"

"I sold the Artemis. Everything. The whole company." The words fell from his lips so abruptly that I almost didn't believe he had said them at all.

"You did what?" I asked, my jaw going slack. "Javi, don't lie to me."

"I'm not lying," he said, sounding hurt by the idea of it. "I would never lie to you."

"What do you mean, you sold it?" The words were sharp on my tongue, accusing. "We've been talking about this for years. You would never sell the Artemis."

"I already did. I signed the final contract three weeks ago," he said, and for once, he wasn't smiling. His face was completely calm, completely serious. It was unnerving to see him without a trace of mirth in his expression.

I shook my head frantically, like I was an animal trying to rid my ears of flies, trying to shake the words from my brain like they were nothing more than annoying pests.

"Javi, that doesn't make any sense," I insisted, sounding like I was trying to bargain with him, like he hadn't already done the unthinkable. "A company like that isn't going to take care of the Artemis like you will."

"No, they won't," he agreed, nodding a little sadly.

"Then why, Javi?" I demanded. "The Artemis is your baby, your legacy. It's your uncle's legacy."

"Nothing they can do can take that legacy away," he said, as if trying to console me. As if it shouldn't be me consoling him—like he hadn't signed away everything he had ever worked for. "I'm not quitting. I'm taking a step back. Taking more of a peripheral role in the company. I'll still be involved, just not responsible for everything. I won't have to fly around the world to advance the product."

I felt tears spring to my eyes, still unable to wrap my head around what he was saying. "But why, Javi? Why would you give it to them? The Artemis is everything to you."

"The Artemis is not everything to me," he disagreed.

"Yes, it—"

"*You* are everything to me, Diana," he said, with a finality that left me silent and dumbstruck. I stood still, convinced I could not have heard him correctly. He took my stunned silence as an opportunity to keep going.

"It has always been you, Di. Why do you think I named the device what I did? I named it after *you*." His tone was firm, begging me to believe him.

"What?" I shook my head, more confused than ever. "You named it after that statue and after your Uncle Arturo—"

"I made it *for* my Uncle Arturo, so families wouldn't

have to go through what mine went through when he died," he agreed. "But I *named* the device after my very favorite person on this earth, my best friend in the whole world. I named it after you. Didn't you ever make the connection? *The Artemis?*"

I shook my head again, unable to wrap my brain around anything he was saying.

"The idea did come to me that night at the winter formal," he explained, but that did nothing to help me either.

He sighed. He took both of my shaking hands in his. His hands were so warm, touching his skin chased away all the cool terror that had crept its way into my veins since his confession.

"Artemis was the Greek goddess of the hunt," he said slowly. "But the Romans knew her by a different name."

I blinked at him, disbelieving.

"Diana," I supplied, the final piece finally snapping into place. My heart felt like it might burst out of my chest.

"*Diana,*" he confirmed, and my name on his lips felt like a declaration. Like everything he was saying could be explained by the way he said my name alone. Like he held every second of our history and our future together within that breath.

I shook my head as tears started to stream down my face. He took my face in his hands and kissed the tears away before kissing me full on the mouth. The kiss tasted salty sweet.

"I can't believe you did this," I whispered. While I had wanted to sound stern with him for giving up his company, I instead sounded amazed, dumbstruck at this gesture.

"I'm all in, Di," he explained reverently. "We have spent the last eight years loving each other but too afraid to stop and admit it because our dreams came first, and I did it. I got my dream. But it wasn't when I made the Artemis. It was when I fell in love with you. You are what I want. I will do whatever I have to do to make this work."

"You're moving to Houston?" I asked, my voice thick and shaking with emotion.

"I'm moving to Houston," he confirmed, sealing the promise with another kiss. "And if you go to fellowship, I'll go there too. I'll follow you wherever you go and for however long you will let me."

I kissed him with profound desperation—like I was drowning, and he was my last source of air. He lifted me off the ground, and I wrapped my legs around his hips. He leaned me up against the inclined wall that acted as a ramp leading up to the highest part of the roof. I pulled away from him momentarily, running my hands down his chest until they reached his belt buckle. I started to undo it slowly, and his eyes darted in surprise from my hands back up to my eyes.

He let out a startled laugh. "Up here?"

I flashed him a wicked grin, nodding. "Up here."

He groaned when my hands found him, starting to stroke him. His lips found mine again, and he unzipped my graduation gown. He grasped my thighs where they clenched around his hips, moving upward beneath the fabric of my dress, until his thumbs brushed against the creases of my thighs. His hand dipped beneath the fabric of my panties, teasing me. I gasped against his lips.

He pulled my panties down, letting me stand long enough to let them fall to the ground between us, before he lifted me back up onto the wall once more. I shoved his pants and boxers down past his hips and positioned him at my entrance. I shuddered when he finally filled me. We froze for just a moment, completely immobile, appreciating the feeling of being joined again after so long apart;

reveling in the knowledge that we would not have to learn to live without each other any more. He was mine. And I was his. And we would be *together*.

He kissed me, breaking the temporary spell we had fallen under. I reached up to curl my fingers in his hair as he thrust into me. He kissed down my neck, burying his face between my breasts as they heaved over the neckline of my dress.

He increased the pace and power of his thrusts, and I knew he was close. I gripped his hair tighter as I approached my own climax. He made one final, deep thrust into me, his hands gripping onto my ass as we both tensed and gasped with the explosion of our pleasure. He held me aloft long after we had finished, and I leaned back against the wall, still gasping for breath.

I laughed, and he looked at me curiously, as if he couldn't imagine anything less funny than what had just transpired. "What are you laughing at?"

He finally released me, and I slid down his body until my feet met the concrete roof beneath us once more.

"I was thinking about the girl I was when you first met me; how scandalized first-year-of-college Diana would be if she knew future Diana would not only regularly trespass onto the roof of the library, but also have sex on it." I laughed again at the thought, as I straightened out my dress and graduation gown.

Javi laughed, buttoning his pants. "I can tell you right now that first-year-of-college Javi would be absolutely thrilled by this unexpected turn of events."

The thought brought the image of that boy into my mind, with those kind brown eyes and infectious smile. The boy who had wrenched an anxious introvert out of her shell and showed her how marvelous life could be when you really *lived* it. I was so grateful to that boy. And so wildly in love with the man he had become.

I leaned up to kiss him. We collected our discarded champagne flutes and the bottle and turned back to the exit. When we made our way through the door, I stopped. Javi looked at me expectantly, watching as I turned and plucked the very battered copy of *The Iliad* from the door. Without the thick book propping it open, the heavy door slammed shut. I tested the handle, confirming that the exit was now locked.

It was a definitive move, but it felt right. Some part of my heart and my mind knew that this would be the last time that we would ever come up here to the roof—the place that had been so pivotal in the development of our friendship and our love. Nothing could ever top what happened here today. Now, we couldn't go back.

I put the book in the bag Javi carried, next to the champagne. He raised an eyebrow at my actions.

"A souvenir," I explained. "Something to remember this day."

He grinned as he took my hand and led me back down the stairs.

Javi and I made our way to his family's Airbnb very slowly, taking the long way. We went to Riverside Park and strolled along the pathways hand-in-hand, chatting about what life would be like together in Houston, with me starting residency and Javi starting his new role as "consultant" for the Artemis. It was a salaried position—a generous one at that. And with his payout from selling his company, he had all the time and resources he could ever desire to plan his next venture.

As he spoke with enthusiasm about this new start, I was pleased to see that old spark in his eyes, a reminder of that kid who spoke about inventions and ideas with such passion. I hadn't realized how much the years dedicated to the business and manufacturing side of his invention had dulled that spark until now. But seeing it in that moment, seeing him so excited to be free to move onto new ideas after so many years dedicated to one, finally put me at ease that this was the right path for us both.

Epilogue

Residency, Third Year

Javi placed a cheese omelet in front of me, as well as a hot cup of coffee in my favorite mug—it said, "You know what gets on my nerves? Myelin." A classic neurology pun. He had given it to me on my birthday earlier this year.

"How are we feeling about today?" he asked, sitting beside me at our kitchen table with his own cup of coffee and breakfast. He was still wearing his flannel pajama bottoms and a t-shirt.

"Good," I replied, my voice coming out as a bit of a squeak. "Great, even. Really great. So great."

He laughed. "Say great one more time, and I might believe you."

I shot him a reproachful look over my mug.

"Are you sure you don't want to spend the day here? Call in sick?" he asked in a cajoling voice. "That way, I'm here with you when you get the news."

I shook my head fervently. "No, really. Staying busy is the best thing to do. If I sit at home, I'll be stressing about it all morning."

He leaned over, squeezing my hand as he planted a kiss on my lips. "What if I distract you until then?"

I smiled but pulled away. "Tempting. But I really should go to work. I'll be fine."

"Okay," he said, sounding disappointed. "But promise me you'll call when you find out? Before your mom?"

I laughed but promised him I would.

"What's on your agenda for today?" I asked, hoping to distract myself from my own plans.

"Got a virtual meeting with the Palo Alto office this morning," he said. "Planned on spending most of my time this afternoon at the lab, at least until you get off work."

Javi had been working with the lab at Rice University over the last year on a new device, an implantable neurostimulator targeted at chronic neuropathic pain. The patent was still pending, but Javi's investors were already salivating waiting to see how far they could take it. Seeing Javi dream and invent again made me so happy I felt like I could nearly burst with pride.

He had already promised that he would do things a little differently this time, if this new device launched as well as the Artemis had. This time, he was taking on the role of "consultant" early in the process—basically as soon as the device was functional. He would leave the business and the jet-setting to the "bright-eyed young bucks," which is what he called the engineering students whom he had brought onto the project. I always teased him when he said things like this, telling him he was a twenty-nine-year-old with the soul of a seventy-year-old man.

When I finished my breakfast, he took my dishes from me. I stood, gathering my white coat and my bag, before turning for the door of our apartment. On my way out, I lovingly tapped the copy of *The Iliad*, where it sat in a protective display case on a table in our living room, hoping it would give me good luck today. He met me at the door, leaning against the frame as he hovered over me. He kissed me slowly and sweetly.

"I love you," he said.

I grinned up at him. "I love you too."

For a second, I considered it—calling in sick and spending the day in his arms. But I knew it would be better to stay busy. I reluctantly pulled away from him and started walking down the hall, but his voice stopped me.

"Hey, Di?" he said.

I turned, seeing him still standing there in the doorway, watching my retreat.

"Yes?" I asked.

"You're gonna kill it today," he said.

I flashed him a brilliant smile. "Thanks, Javi."

I made it to the hospital a little while later for rounds. I was a couple weeks away from starting my fourth and final year of residency. A few weeks before, I learned that I had been named Chief Resident, and I was excited but nervous about the immense responsibility of leading the program the following year. I was still working out how I was going to balance the increased workload of being chief with my passion project: the Hearts and Minds clinic.

I had worked with some of my attendings and co-residents during my intern year to bring my vision to life: a free clinic focused both on general healthcare, as well as a particular focus on free screening and early diagnosis of neurological disorders. We had been fortunate enough to receive a grant for funding, allowing us to provide substantially subsidized medications. Not to mention, we had received *quite* the donation of Artemis devices to help diagnose and manage patients with epilepsy in the community.

After rounds, I met one of the residents from the year below me, Camila Escobedo, for coffee, where we discussed the logistics of running the clinic. I had been gradually preparing her to assume my leadership position at the clinic, so that it would continue long after my graduation the following year. We spoke animatedly about the project, and I knew from the way she spoke about it that Camila cherished the clinic as much as I did and would take good care of it in my absence.

"Oh, I'm so sorry, Camila," I said, cutting her off suddenly as I looked down at my watch. "But I have to run. Same time next week?"

She bid me farewell, and we left the hospital cafe. It was 10:55 A.M. Only five minutes to go. I hurried out of the front entrance of the hospital. I found an isolated bench off to the side and sat with my phone clenched in my hands. My heart pounded furiously. I almost had a heart attack when my phone chimed suddenly and loudly with a text from Javi.

> JV: Whatever happens, we're in this together. You got this. Love you.

I smiled shakily at the message, taking a deep, steadying breath. I held my phone to my chest, closing my eyes as I waited for the final minute to pass, the beating of my heart like a ticking clock counting down the final seconds.

Eleven A.M. arrived. My hands shook as I refreshed my screen, thinking I might black out when the email immediately popped up from the Match.

Subject: Fellowship Match Results

Congratulations! You have matched!
Sub-Specialty: Epilepsy

Program Name: Harvard University, Brigham and
    Women's Hospital

I didn't move for nearly a minute, paralyzed completely as I scanned the words on my phone screen at least a hundred times. Then it took me nearly a full minute of screaming and dancing wildly in front of the hospital before I was able to compose myself enough to call Javi. He answered within milliseconds of the first ring.

"Well?" he asked expectantly.

"Harvard," I told him, the word sounding distant and unreal coming from my voice.

"Harvard?" he repeated in awe.

"Harvard," I confirmed. My cheeks hurt from smiling so hard.

"We're moving to Boston," he murmured in wonder. "This is amazing, Diana. *You're* amazing. I'm so proud of you."

I started to ask him, "You're not worried about your work—"

"Don't you even *start* to worry about me," he admonished me quickly. "My work goes where I go, and I'm *going* with you. Besides, I have some buddies at MIT who I'm sure will help me get into a lab there."

I shook my head, grateful, as I always was, that Javi seemed to either have friends or make friends everywhere that we went. I was confident that Javi would thrive in Boston. Besides, we had a full year left in Houston for him to settle things with the project at Rice before he would have to part ways with his team.

I called my parents next. My mom was thrilled for me, of course, especially since I would be closer to home. And even though I had long abandoned the need to please my father, I was at least a *little* gratified that he had never sounded quite so impressed with me as he did when I told him I got into Harvard. And that's when my dad admitted something to me that I don't think he had ever told anyone before.

"Wow, kid, that's really something. Not even I was able to get into Harvard."

I didn't think I was going to be able to stop smiling for the rest of the day after that.

The rest of the workday passed in a blur. My attendings and co-residents stopped me as soon as they saw me to ask about my match results, and I got to relive the celebration each time. I congratulated my classmates who also matched into fellowships—two of them in Child Neurology, one in Neuro-Oncology, and one in Neuro Critical Care.

The second I stepped through the door of our apartment after work, Javi swept me up into his arms, swinging me around as I laughed in delight.

"There she is!" Javi exclaimed. "My amazing future Harvard fellow!"

He kissed me and held my face in his hands as he looked into my eyes.

"We're going out tonight to celebrate!" he declared.

"Where?" I asked.

"The nicest restaurant in town," he proclaimed decidedly. "Dress accordingly."

I laughed. "How are we supposed to get reservations for *the nicest restaurant in town* at the last minute?"

"I take your tone to mean you doubt my abilities," he challenged.

I shook my head, laughing. "I wouldn't dream of it."

He made no more explanations, nor did I overhear him making calls to any restaurants while I readied myself for dinner. I almost didn't believe it when I watched him change into one of his best suits, thinking we might genuinely be going to the nicest restaurant in town, but still unsure how he might have pulled off such a feat. I didn't question him, just obediently dressed in one of my favorite dresses: a pale blue, tea-length brocade with a pattern of ivory flowers that I knew Javi liked because it complemented my eyes. I curled my hair and pinned the curls into a twist at the back of my head. I wore my favorite earrings —dangling silver and diamond neuron pendants that Javi had had custom made to match my bracelet.

Javi looked very pleased with my choices, giving me an approving whistle when I emerged from the bathroom. We got into his car, but I was surprised when we didn't immediately head for downtown. In fact, we headed the exact opposite direction, directly away from the lights of the city. When we had driven for over thirty minutes without stopping, seemingly putting more and more distance between us and civilization, I looked over at him, worried.

"Do you know where you're going?" I asked with concern.

He smirked. "I do. It's a bit off the beaten path."

"*A bit*," I remarked, "is an understatement. Can it be the nicest restaurant in town if it isn't *in* town?

"It's a big town," Javi supplied but made no further explanations.

Finally, after twenty more minutes of driving, Javi slowed the car, pulling off onto a long drive. We hadn't seen a house, a gas station, or even another car for miles.

When we parked, we were in a large green field surrounded by a thick border of trees. On a grassy hill ahead, there were three dome-shaped buildings atop a cement platform. Javi stopped the car and walked around to open the door for me. I took his offered hand but looked up at him with some trepidation.

"Where are we?" I asked nervously. There was not another soul in sight. The sun had set on our drive here, and it was nearly pitch black out. "This looks more like a place to hide a body than have dinner."

He laughed at my concern. "George Observatory. Part of the Houston Museum of Natural Science."

"And the nicest restaurant in town?" I asked skeptically.

"Tonight it is," he explained, his grin wide and mischievous. I shook my head at his antics but let him lead me toward the dome-shaped building in the distance.

Javi held the door open for me, but I stopped short as soon as I stepped foot inside the circular room. The domed ceiling was open down the center, giving way to millions of stars above us. The largest telescope I had ever seen was pointed upward through the gap. The perimeter of the room was covered in dim candlelight. At the base of the telescope was a table set for two, with a black tablecloth, a candelabra at the center, and two silver cloches.

"How did you…?" I asked in wonder. He grinned, exceedingly proud of himself.

"I've had this planned for weeks," he explained. He walked over to the table and pulled out one of the chairs for me.

"You only asked me if I wanted to go out to celebrate a few hours ago," I said with an incredulous laugh. "What would you have done if I hadn't matched?"

He looked at me with so much love and admiration that I thought I might just melt into a puddle at his feet. "You're a star, Diana. I never doubted you for even a second. I *knew* we would be celebrating tonight."

I pulled his face to mine for a long kiss, unable to quite believe that someone as perfect as Javier Valenzuela existed and that he was mine. When I finally let him go, I took the offered chair. I jumped in surprise when a waiter appeared, seemingly out of nowhere, bringing us a bottle of wine and pouring it into two glasses. He uncovered our salads and disappeared almost as quickly and quietly as he had appeared. He emerged later with the entree and the dessert course, ducking in every now and then to refill our water or wine. While we enjoyed the delicious meal, Javi and I enthusiastically discussed what life might look like for us in Boston in a year.

As I was finishing the last bites of the incredible crème brûlée, I looked around for our very stealthy waiter.

"So," I asked Javi conspiratorially, "are we actually allowed to look into the telescope or is that strictly forbidden?"

Javi laughed. "No, we're allowed—encouraged, even. In fact, I asked if they wouldn't mind finding a particular star for me ahead of time. Go look."

I grinned, rising from the table and moving quickly to the telescope. I leaned forward over the eyepiece, seeing the brightest, most brilliant blue star centered into view.

"It's Rigel," Javi explained from behind me. "One of the brightest stars in the night sky. And it just so happens to be part of our old friend, Orion the Hunter."

I smiled, backing away from the eyepiece after a long moment of admiring the star. I turned to face Javi, but my breath caught suddenly short when I saw him.

He was kneeling in front of me.

"Javi?" I asked, disbelieving and breathless.

He smiled dazzlingly up at me, his eyes sparkling with the reflection of starlight.

"Surprised?" he asked, the corners of his eyes crinkling with his smile.

I nodded but knew if I said anything at all, I would start crying. He reached out to take my hand, and I gave it to him.

"Diana Richards," he began. "I have spent the last decade loving you, from the day I found you outside your dorm room; from the nights we would spend on the roof of Butler looking up at the stars together, to this very moment. You have been there with me through every triumph, every setback, every important moment of my adult life. You were there, believing in me when I doubted myself, your faith in me unwavering, always encouraging me to chase my wildest dreams. I have watched you over these years become the most incredible, brilliant doctor. I have watched you undertake this journey with such resilience and poise. I am in constant awe of you. You are my rock when things get tough. You are the person with whom I want to weather every storm. You are the love of my life."

He took a bright, Tiffany-blue box out from the pocket of his suit jacket and opened it toward me, the brilliant emerald-cut diamond sparkling, reflecting a mix of candle-light and starlight.

"Diana, would you do me the honor of marrying me?"

"Yes!" I cried, throwing myself at him the moment he stopped speaking, nearly knocking him over in the process as we both laughed and cried with joy. After a minute of alternating back and forth between kissing him and wiping the tears from my eyes, he finally got me to settle down long enough to put the ring on my finger.

He held my hand as he led me out of the room, and I marveled at the feeling of the ring between our intertwined fingers. It was going to take some getting used to.

Just when I thought he couldn't surprise me anymore than he already had, a chorus of "Surprise!" rang out as soon as we stepped foot outside. Somehow, in only the hour and a half since we had disappeared into the tele-scope room for dinner, the observation deck had been completely transformed into an engagement party. I looked around in shock at everyone I loved. *Literally* everyone—my mom and dad, my mom's sister and her husband, my co-residents and all my friends from work, the entire Valenzuela family, and best of all, Blake.

I screamed when I saw her and ran immediately into her arms. She looked amazing in a mini dress in stripes of bright yellow and pink and blue. I squeezed her so tight.

"You're getting married!" she squealed into my ear.

An idea came to me immediately, and I pulled away so I could look into her eyes as I asked, "You'll be my maid of honor, right?"

She screamed and hugged me again, which I took as a yes.

I hugged my parents and my aunt and uncle, greeted my co-workers, finally ending with the Valenzuelas. The second I met Alba Valenzuela's eyes, so warm and welcoming as she looked at me, I broke down again in tears. I had been crying so much, I probably looked like a complete mess. Javi's family moved forward to wrap me in a group hug, before claiming me for individual hugs.

"Welcome to the family," Gaby whispered in my ear when she held me. "Officially, I mean."

This is going to be my family, I realized in wonder. Of course, it was merely a formality, at this point. I already spent basically every holiday with them. We made frequent visits down to Corpus, and Valeria and I got lunch together almost weekly. They had always treated me as if I belonged to them. Even so, I had been dreaming of officially being a Valenzuela for so long, and now it would be true.

When everyone had finally had their chance to hug us and congratulate us, the sneaky waiter from our dinner was joined by a crew of other waiters, who brought out cake and champagne for everyone.

Javi brought me to the side, away from the crowd for a moment once everyone was distracted by the food. He grabbed two glasses of champagne from a waiter and held his glass up to mine. I clinked my glass against his.

"To the two luckiest people in the whole world, the future Mr. and Dr. Valenzuela," he said, "and a future as limitless as the stars."

Letter from the Author

The premise of *Stargazing with You* came to me in its entirety on a five-hour drive home after a job interview. I was just about to start my final year of residency, and I basically hadn't written anything other than admissions essays and patient notes in eight years. Writing had once brought me such joy, and I hadn't given a second thought to losing that part of myself in the long trek to becoming a doctor.

Then one day, inspiration strikes, and I go from an idea to an 88,000 word novel in *three months*. Even when I was writing for my degree, I had never done anything like this.

It's not like I suddenly "had extra time to write." No resident "has extra time" (except my friends in dermatology). The number one thing people in my life say when they find out I wrote a book is, "I don't know how you found the time!" In addition to being a resident, I have twin toddlers, so time is a precious resource in my life. This book was written almost entirely in the hours between eight P.M. when my toddlers went to bed until whatever time I could no longer convince myself to keep my eyes open.

Regardless of what comes of this book, I am so happy and grateful that I did this for myself. I have long felt that doctors *need* creative outlets to keep us centered, to give us a way to balance how grueling our lives can be. And it doesn't have to be a personal essay detailing the gritty, raw side of medicine. Honestly, living and reliving the gritty, raw stuff is exhausting. That is why I wanted to create something light and happy and romantic, something that made me feel good to write and hopefully will make someone else feel good to read.

When it came to writing my very first book, I followed the old adage, "write what you know." So I wrote about the halls that I walked at John Jay and all the anxiety and imposter syndrome that I felt while going through medical school.

I will stress that while the book was based on my experiences, it was not based on my life. Though I did have a best-friends-to-lovers romance with a handsome engineer, this story otherwise has nothing to do with our story. But in writing Javi, I wanted to show the world just how remarkable a human has to be to agree to be a medical school / residency spouse. The emotional, physical, mental, and financial investment you have to put into someone to get them through this process is unmatched (no pun intended).

This book is very deservedly dedicated to my husband, who not only fully supported me through my day job, but has also completely thrown himself (again, both emotionally and financially) into helping me get this book out into the world. But beyond that, this book is dedicated to all the partners who have stood beside their doctors on this harrowing journey: proudly watching us receive our white coats, holding our hands and bringing us sustenance while we study for exams, anxiously standing beside us on Match Day, and every moment in between.

This one's for you.

Acknowledgments

1. To my mom, the woman who introduced me to the romance genre, who encouraged me to "get the M.D. as a backup to my writing career," who got me through medical school, who was my personal interior decorator for all my dorms, apartments, and homes, who still requires I call her every day to tell her about my day on the way home from work. Who, ironically, has not been able to read this book, because there is sex in it. Love you more than all the cracks in the world.

2. On that note, let me thank my dad and clarify that Diana's dad is in no way based on my dad. My dad is my biggest cheerleader (but is also not allowed to read this book). I love you 3000.

2. To my editor, Hilari Cohen. I can't thank you enough for helping me get this book to print and for having the patience to work with a first-time author. When I found out you had three doctors in the family and a personal shopper at Saks, I knew it was meant to be (and I was also incredibly intimidated).

3. To my cover designer, Mary Anne Smith. Thank you for your beautiful work.

4. To my beta readers, both formal and informal: Sonya, Alison, Sarah, Hunter, Sean, Cat, Ana, Paige, Jess, Stephanie, Kate, Jennell, and Juliette.

5. To Michael Dang, the medical student who heard I was writing a medical school romance novel and asked to be written into the story as the "toxic med school boyfriend

character." Hope it met all your expectations. Good luck in ortho.

6. To the various artists whose music inspired me while writing this book. Here is the official "Stargazing with You" Playlist:

Stargazing – Myles Smith (the inspiration for the title)
Down Bad – Taylor Swift
Dress – Taylor Swift
Dancing with Our Hands Tied – Taylor Swift
I Like Me Better – Lauv
Rather Be – Clean Bandit feat. Jess Glynne
That Way – Tate McRae
Stupid in Love – Max
I Miss You – Julia Michaels
Birds of a Feather – Billie Eilish
We can't be friends – Ariana Grande
All in My Head – Tori Kelly
Like I Can – Sam Smith
The Other Side – Jason Derulo
Chronically Cautious – Braden Bales
Rewrite the Stars – Zendaya and Zac Efron, from *The Greatest Showman*
My Green Light – Jeremy Jordan, Eva Noblezada, cast of *The Great Gatsby* Musical
Ocean Away – Barlow & Bear, from *the Unofficial Bridgerton Musical*
Bloom – Stephanie Torns, Joey Contreras, Antonio Cipriano, from *In Pieces* the Musical
My Days – Joy Woods, from *The Notebook* Musical
Take it Like a Man – Christian Borle & Laura Bell Bundy, from *Legally Blonde* the Musical

About the Author

Jacquelynn Harbell received her undergraduate degree in creative writing from Columbia University before attending medical school. Though she maintains her day job as a doctor, she never lost hope of seeing her name on the cover of a great romance novel. When she isn't practicing medicine or writing, she spends her time with her engineer husband, her twin daughters, and her two dogs.

Want to read a sneak peek of Jacquelynn Harbell's second novel? Turn the page…

instagram.com/jacqueharbell_writes
tiktok.com/@jacque_harbell

The Sweetest Scheme
Chapter 1

Palmer

In and out. He doesn't need to see you. Nobody needs to know.

This will be the quickest setup I have ever done (without compromising the work, obviously).

I take a deep breath to steady myself, a difficult task while holding the bulky white box against my chest. I brace the heavy load against my body and ring the doorbell of the Barlow mansion. I'm not sure if the word *mansion* is adequate to describe the sprawling, white stone complex of buildings. The Barlow Estate, maybe? The Barlow *Kingdom*?

That feels right. The Barlows are as close as we get to royalty in Charleston.

An older woman answers the door and aside from not having a British accent, she looks like something straight out of Downton Abbey. She sees me holding the heavy box and brings me to the part of the house where they are holding the party. I can't tell if they have a dedicated ballroom—do people have those in real life?—or if they have simply cleared furniture from a large enough space in the house to make room for rows of wooden tables ornately decorated in white roses and greenery. Either way, most of the dedicated wedding venues I have seen look far less regal. The room is dripping in white roses from every visible corner.

The woman shows me to my table, where I set down

the heavy box and start to unpack the tote bag with my supplies. At the center of the table, they have a large silver cake drum with a halo behind it made of more white roses. They have set the stage perfectly. I couldn't have asked for a more beautiful display for my work. And this is just the engagement party. *Just close friends and family*, they had said. This would be but a small taste of what was in store for the main event.

The thought of what the actual wedding will be like—the wedding of the century, it is being called—makes me simultaneously giddy and nauseous. How can it be that *I* am the baker the bride chose, out of all the bakeries Charleston has to offer? And let's be honest, the Barlows could afford to go far outside of South Carolina, if they had desired. They could fly some Michelin-starred chef from France if they chose. And yet, they chose me.

Now, I just have to make sure I don't screw it all up by running into the groom, or letting the bride know we used to sleep together.

I carefully slide the two-tiered cake out of the box and set to work. For a moment, the anxiety of being here and knowing *he* is here flees my body, and I lose myself in the process, as I always do. The base tier is tall—six layers of lemon chiffon with blueberry coulis and vanilla buttercream. The top tier contains layers of chocolate with espresso mousse and chocolate buttercream. Both layers are wrapped in pure white fondant that I meticulously painted with white flowers over a delicate lattice of green leaves. I center it carefully on the drum and inspect it for any flaws that might have appeared in transport. I carefully smooth a bubble out from the fondant with my icing spatula. I fix a smudge in the edible green paint with a clean paint brush and some water.

I take the silver cake topper from the packaging and

carefully stick the prongs into the top layer. It says, "Bennett & Grant" in pretty, silver cursive letters. My stomach gives an uneasy jolt as I make sure it is placed perfectly, to honor *the happy couple.*

I step back to admire my work. It looks perfect. Everything the client envisioned. Beautiful. Understated. Elegant. Just like the bride.

It makes me feel sick to my stomach.

I hear a soft *click.*

The unexpected sound pulls me violently from my focus. I turn to meet the source of the sound: a camera. And behind it, a man. He lowers the camera a little, revealing his face. He flashes a sheepish smile.

And *my God.* He is gorgeous.

My whole body had felt coiled with tension since the moment I arrived, dreading the possibility of running into Grant. Knowing that if I did run into him, I would likely lose the best thing that had ever happened for my small business: the Barlow wedding.

But that all fades somewhere distantly into the back of my mind at the sight of the man behind the camera. He has a crop of dark brown curls atop his head, with the sides shaven close. He peers at me with warm brown eyes—exquisitely sensitive eyes, turned downward at the outer corners. He wears a black button down with the cuffs rolled to the elbows, with brown suspenders over his broad shoulders. I wonder to myself how he manages to pull them off so well, without looking like an eighty-year-old man or a German yodeler. I have never seen anyone make suspenders look hot before. I can see the edge of a black tattoo etched into his light brown skin, just peaking out below the cuff of his shirt.

He holds the large, expensive-looking camera in both hands, and I watch him look at the preview for the picture he just took. He smiles down at it, clearly approving.

The photographer for the party. I clear my throat and start hurriedly cleaning my supplies off the table.

"I'm so sorry," I say. "You want to take pictures of the cake. Let me move my things—"

"I wasn't taking a picture of the cake," he corrects me, his voice deep and warm. He looks from his camera to my face, his smile growing slowly wider. "Here, take a look."

My brows furrow in confusion. I drop my tote bag to the ground and approach him. He holds the camera out for me to see.

It's a picture of me. But it looks somehow unlike any other picture or reflection of myself I have ever seen. I look *stunning*.

No one has ever just pointed a camera at me and captured me in such a raw and beautiful state before. I'm not smiling or posing. I'm just inspecting my cake, as I have done thousands of times before, the faintest hint of a focused crease between my brows. My lips are just barely parted. The light from the windows reflects off my cheek-bones and brings out the gold in my honey-blonde hair that I have pulled back into a claw clip. My eyes look impossibly green. I have always considered my eye color to be more of a dull, mossy green, not the bright and clear emerald, as in this photo. And this is just the raw photo— he has not even edited yet.

I look up into his face, searching it. I shake my head in disbelief.

I begin to ask, "Why would you—?"

He grins. "I love capturing artists and their work. It seems silly, making art out of art. But I just love creative people."

I shake my head, a blush warming my cheeks. "I'm not an artist."

I would know. My mom is an actual artist. Sculptures and paintings and drawings. She could make something beautiful out of any materials.

He gestures to the cake. "I would beg to differ."

I laugh. I'm not trying to be falsely modest. I know I can decorate a cake, otherwise I would not have started my business. But I wouldn't call myself an *artist*. Not like my mom is. And not like this man, who can pull the beauty out of someone with just the click of a camera.

"Silas Howell," he says, offering his hand. I reach my hand out and rest it in his.

"Palmer," I reply. "Palmer Sullivan. Sweet P Bakery."

His eyes grow wide with delight. "Sweet P is your shop? I've tasted your cakes before. They are amazing! Weddings suck significantly less when there's a Sweet P cake there."

I sputter out a dubious laugh. "Wow. I should have you write our next advertisement."

He grins. "It's true, though. Your cakes are fantastic. And wedding cakes usually suck. So dry. Never your cakes though."

I shrug, bashfully. "Well, I've only seen one photo so far, but I can see why they chose you as the photographer. Your work is amazing. Do you have a website or a social media page I can follow? So I can see more?"

He smirks. "You can see as much as you'd like. Do you want the wedding stuff or the real stuff?"

"The wedding stuff isn't real?" I ask.

He shrugs. "Pays the bills."

I know instantly and deeply what he means. Being in the wedding business can be a thankless task—dealing with people on one of the most important days of their lives, when expectations and anxieties are at their highest. But people will pay good money for quality when it comes to one of the most important days of their life. So, while it may be thankless and stressful at times, it is the most lucrative part of my job. I may have more fun making a four-year-old's whimsical Elsa-themed birthday cake, but my living is made on the dreams of brides.

"Well, I'd love to see the real stuff then," I reply.

And it is true—I would love to see more of his work. But there's an implication behind the words that sends a thrill through me. In just our short conversation, we've started drifting toward each other like there is a magnetic force drawing our bodies together. I realize I miss feeling like this—feeling that initial frisson of attraction shivering down my spine. He looks at me with such earnest appreciation that it draws an instantaneous, irresistible response from my body. My heart begins to race, my mouth goes a bit dry. This is what it feels like to feel *wanted* again.

And if he likes me now, just wait until he sees me put some effort in. I know I can do better. I'm wearing black jeans and a black long-sleeve shirt with clouds of smudged powdered sugar all over them. I had put minimal effort into my hair or makeup this morning; I was not expecting to meet anyone of significance today. In fact, it had been my intention to be seen by as few people as possible.

I hand him my phone, with my Instagram profile left open. "Find me your handle?"

He smiles and takes the phone from me, adding himself as a friend on my account. I look down briefly at the screen, seeing the thumbnails with beautiful, vivid pictures lined in a grid pattern. I look back up at him, delighted.

"I can't wait to see more," I tell him.

"Me neither," he responds, and I don't think for a single second that he is talking about my cakes.

I force myself to draw away from him, to pull my body away from the magnetic force that has brought me within inches of him. To pack up my things and leave. An unhelpful part of my brain tries to remind me that this was supposed to be a quick setup, and I have just spent the last ten minutes flirting with the photographer.

But *damn*. Who wouldn't want to spend ten minutes flirting with him?

And a part of me is relieved to feel like this again. A part of me had wondered if I would ever feel like this again. Maybe time does heal all wounds?

I grab my bag and shoot Silas a dazzling smile over my shoulder before turning to leave.

Which is precisely when I run directly into him.

Grant Foster. *My ex.*

I stumble backward, nearly tripping over my feet in the process. I look up into his blue eyes that have gone wide, as if he has seen a ghost.

Oh shit. Oh shit, oh shit, oh shit, oh shit.

"Grant," I whisper. My whole body freezes in pure, undiluted panic. God, he looks good. Painfully good. His light brown hair is neat and styled. He has always been well-dressed, but I wonder if being around the Barlows has forced him to up his game. He wears an immaculately tailored gray jacket over light slacks and shirt.

"Palmer?" he asks. He sounds dazed, as if he might be dreaming. Or having a nightmare, I guess. "What are you doing here?"

"I, um," I falter, looking over to my cake where it stands proudly on display, "I made the cake."

I fixate on my cake, trying to look anywhere but directly into Grant's eyes.

"You made the cake?" he asks, incredulously. "For my *engagement party*?"

And hopefully your wedding, I think to myself, though I do not offer that information in this moment. I scramble for something, anything helpful to say in this moment. But there is nothing to say. I was an idiot for taking this job. I only brought this on myself.

A squealing noise slices through the tension between us. And we are joined by none other than Bennett Barlow herself, the heiress to the Barlow empire. The princess to this unfathomable kingdom.

She looks unsurprisingly stunning. She's wearing a fitted white knee-length dress with off-the-shoulder sleeves covered in white ruffles. The dress hugs her curves like second skin, and I know there's no amount of Spanx that would ever make my body look like that in a dress. Her hair, so dark it is nearly black, is impossibly glossy and in perfect waves to her shoulders.

And you simply cannot look at Bennett Barlow without noticing the enormous—and I do mean *truly* gigantic—rock adorning her left ring finger. How can you miss it? I am certain they must be able to see it from the International Space Station. Does the woman not have carpal tunnel? How can she even lift that hand at all?

But Bennett Barlow looks like the kind of woman who works out. And not normal people workouts like running, but something cool and sexy like pilates or hot yoga. I am certain she has been preparing her entire life to wear a diamond ring like that.

I breathe in sharply and hold it.

"Sweet P!" she squeals, grasping me by the shoulders and shaking me from side to side with the force of her excitement. My brain rattles a little in my skull at the intensity of her greeting. "I'm so glad I caught you—*Oh. My. God.* Look at that *cake!* It's perfect! It's everything I imagined it would be. You have outdone yourself. Grant, isn't it just perfect?"

"Just *perfect*," he echoes, though he could not have said the words more sardonically.

She looks at him curiously, raising an eyebrow. She shakes her head, staring at him pointedly as if to say, *Sweetheart, you're being rude.*

"Grant, Honey?" she asks, hesitantly. "The cake is perfect, *right*?"

"Perfect," he confirms again, still sounding bitter. "Palmer's cakes are always perfect, though."

She looks at him in shock, as if she cannot believe how rude he is being. But then it hits her. The way he is looking at me. The way he knows my name without being formally introduced.

She looks nervously to me and back to her fiancé. "You two know each other?"

"She's my ex-girlfriend," he says, and the title hits me like a punch to the gut. As much as I don't want it to hurt, it still does, even a year later.

"Your ex-girlfriend is Sweet P?" she asks, sounding heartbroken by the idea.

He presses his lips into a thin line. He takes a deep breath through his nose like he's trying to gather every ounce of his patience as he says, "You know that's not her legal name, right?"

She rolls her eyes, as if this is a dumb question. I'm still marveling over the fact that I got through the entire consultation with Bennett weeks ago without her asking for my *real* name, happy just to call me "Sweet P," but I wasn't one to look a gift horse in the mouth.

"Of course I *know* that," she insists. "I just thought it was a stage name. Like Lady Gaga."

I press my lips firmly together to keep myself from

laughing at the absurdity of the comment. Nothing about this is funny. But comparing me to Lady Gaga might just be ridiculous enough to break the last shred of my sanity.

Grant chooses to move past this comment, and turns to me, fixing an accusing stare on me. I balk beneath it.

"Palmer, why would you agree to this?" he asks sternly. His tone is so patronizing it coils up some small, petulant animal inside me.

I shrug, though I feel anything but nonchalant about this exchange. "It was too good an opportunity to pass up."

He frowns deeply. "An opportunity to do what exactly?"

"To get close to Grant again?" Bennett asks, as if this is the most logical conclusion. But she doesn't say it meanly or accusing. She says it with her blue eyes wide and genuinely concerned, as if worried that I'm plotting to steal her fiancé. The thought of Bennett Barlow being threatened by me is so ridiculous it's laughable.

And I do laugh, though it doesn't seem to mollify either of them.

"No, no!" I insist, raising my hands in protest. "I'm not trying to get closer to Grant—"

"What else do you have to gain from this?" Grant asks, spoken like a true child of wealth. Not only had Grant grown up with money, but he makes fabulous money as an investment banker. And now he is marrying into money beyond my wildest dreams.

This wedding is one of the highest paying individual jobs I have ever received. How could I pass up a gig this momentous? How could I decline the *exposure*? This wedding was going to have 300 people there, celebrities included. This could potentially open doors to more high-paying jobs for my business.

But Grant is looking at me so coldly, so skeptically, and

Bennett is looking at me with so much hurt and fear. I can see the mistrust kindling in their eyes. How do I tell them that this isn't personal? How do I prove to them that I don't want him back? Even though the latter might not be entirely true, if I was being honest with myself.

"I'm seeing someone!" The words burst out of me, loud and desperate, before I can think better of them. There is no logic left in me, only panic. I need this job. I can't lose it for such a stupid reason.

I continue, "Please, you don't need to worry about me. I'm happy, and I want you two to be happy. I promise, I'm not plotting anything. I'm not trying to get closer to you. I didn't want to run into you today. I only intended to bring my cake and leave."

Grant's eyes narrow. "You're seeing someone?"

I swallow hard, averting my eyes. "Yes, I am. You don't need to worry about me."

"What's his name?" I look up into his stern expression, and my brows furrow together. What right did he have to question me? Even if I was lying through my teeth.

"His name is—" I hesitate. And it's a terrible, awkward length of hesitation. It's so long a second that I might as well have stamped "LIAR" across my forehead.

A name, I think. *What is a name? Why can I suddenly not think of any name in this world for a man?*

I try again, as if a name will magically come to me, despite there suddenly being an endless blank pit between my ears where my brain used to reside. "His name is—"

I feel an arm slide over my shoulders, and I tense at the contact.

"Silas Howell."

There is a feeling like a wave of cool water washing over me at his voice, washing away the panic. He coolly offers a hand to Grant to shake, bobbing it up and down with a firm grip as he squeezes me comfortably into his side. I look up from their joined hands into Silas's face, marveling at the warm smile there as he introduces himself to Grant.

"The photographer," he offers, "*and* Palmer's boyfriend."

The look on Grant's face at this revelation is something I wish I could have bottled and kept on my shelf for the next time I'm having a bad day. He looks so stricken. So disbelieving. So *jealous*. His whole body tenses, and his shoulders square as if some primal instinct arises in him to fight for me. And while I know it is petty and silly and entirely unhealthy of me; the look delights me. I know part of me still wants Grant to fight for me, even if I know the battle is long lost.

He's getting married, I try to remind myself. *I need to move on.*

But even if I haven't been able to move on in the last year, in contrast to his rapid and highly successful ability to do so, at least I will have this moment to hold onto. At least I know, from the immediate and visceral reaction he has to seeing me with someone, that a part of him still loves me. A part of him still doesn't want me to be with anyone else.

"You're the—" Grant says, pausing to inhale sharply, then starts again, "You're the photographer? And you two are—?"

"Dating," Silas confirms with a wide, genuine smile. Grant looks him up and down, from his dark curls to his shiny leather boots. His eyes linger on the tattoo for a long moment.

"*How long?*" Grant asks. His voice is clearly meant to sound chill and mildly curious but instead comes out through slightly gritted teeth. I grin a little in triumph. I snake my arm around Silas's waist, my brain finally catching up to the situation enough to play along.

"About a month?" I say, looking up into Silas's toffee-brown eyes as he looks down at me, as if we are asking each other, *isn't that right, darling?*

"A month?" Bennett asks with some excitement, clapping her hands together. Apparently, all the fear she felt a moment ago regarding my plot to steal her fiancé has disappeared, leaving only her bubbly personality behind. "That's about when I hired you both! Did you meet because of *our* wedding? Wouldn't that just be so—"

"No," Silas corrects her quickly but not unkindly. "We met a while back on the wedding circuit. We got together after my little sister went in for a cake consultation. She is getting married this October."

The whole story comes to him so easily and naturally, I wonder if part of it is true. *Is his sister getting married in October? Am I making her a cake?* I wrack my brain trying to remember if I met a bride with the last name Howell who would be getting married in October. Nothing comes to mind.

"Oh, how cute!" Bennett gushes. "You two are like a wedding power couple! This is amazing. Isn't this amazing, Grant?"

Grant says nothing. His eyes are entirely fixed on Silas's face, where there is a coy, slightly smug smile pulling at the corner of his lips.

"*Oh my God*, I have a completely brilliant idea," Bennett says, squeezing Grant's arm, though he does not drop his gaze to acknowledge her. "We should *double-date*."

These words seem to break Grant of whatever spell Silas has put him under, and he looks at Bennett with a dubious expression. "No, Benny, this is not—"

"It's settled!" she cuts him off with an eager squeak. "How 'bout next Friday? You guys down?"

I am about to say, *absolutely not*, when I hear Silas say, "That sounds great!"

I shoot him a glare. I met this man ten minutes ago. Why is he trying to ruin my life?

Grant seems like he is about to open his mouth once more to protest, when Bennett says, "It's settled!"

Grant clears his throat. "Benny, I—"

Bennett suddenly drops the enthusiasm from her face and her voice, as quickly as flipping a light switch. She looks pointedly and seriously into Grant's face, challenging him. "What's the matter? What's a little double-date between friends? You two have both moved on, *right*?"

Grant's rebuttal is cut off abruptly in his throat at her tone. He presses his lips together as if to keep the words tucked away.

I realize, with the drop in her facade, that the peppy princess persona is an act. She is testing us. She wants us to prove that there isn't anything still between us. And I need to prove it, if I'm going to keep this job.

I squeeze Silas a little closer, wrapping my other arm around his waist in a hug. Somewhere in the back of my mind I register just how *sturdy* he feels in my arms.

"Of course," I say, with all the enthusiasm I can muster. "We would love to."

Bennett's alter ego is back as quickly as it had disappeared. She drags her eyes from Grant's face to shoot me a dazzling smile. "Wonderful! I'll get us reservations at Chez Claire. Eight o'clock?"

I smile feebly, nodding. "Sounds great."

"Well," Silas says with some finality to his tone, "you have to get back to the bakery, don't you, babe?"

I blink a little in surprise at how easily the term of

endearment rolls of his tongue, but I nod gratefully. I unwrap my arms from around him and straighten my tote bag on my shoulder. "Right. I do. Still have that wedding cake for tomorrow."

"Of course," he says, as if this is a detail he has known for weeks; as if we didn't just meet for the first time ten minutes ago. "I'll catch up with you later, then?"

I turn to leave, but he leans in before I can move. He cradles my face gently in one hand, and the action makes my entire body freeze, paralyzed in anticipation of what he is about to do. His thumb brushes my cheekbone before he plants a gentle kiss on my forehead. His lips are incredibly soft against my skin, and though he only maintains contact for a second, the spot on my forehead seems to tingle in his absence.

I look up into his smiling face, a little dumbstruck. I make no motion to move.

"*See you later?*" he urges gently, and the tone is firmer, as if to remind me that I should be getting the hell out of this house while I still have the chance.

I reclaim the ability to move my legs suddenly and turn, walking quickly and with purpose away from Grant, Bennett, and Silas without turning to look back. I can feel their eyes on me as I retreat.

When I make my way out the front door, I don't stop, not pausing to consider what just occurred. But my mind is reeling.

How are we going to pull this off?